Abby's Story:
Betrayed by Love
(A Second Chance at Love Novel)

Karen Anderson

PublishAmerica
Baltimore

© 2007 by Karen Anderson.
All rights reserved. No part of this book may be reproduced, stored in a retrieval system or transmitted in any form or by any means without the prior written permission of the publishers, except by a reviewer who may quote brief passages in a review to be printed in a newspaper, magazine or journal.

First printing

All characters appearing in this work are fictitious. Any resemblance to real persons, living or dead, is purely coincidental.

At the specific preference of the author, PublishAmerica allowed this work to remain exactly as the author intended, verbatim, without editorial input.

ISBN: 1-4241-8069-4
ED BY PUBLISHAMERICA, LLLP
www.publishamerica.com
Baltimore

ed in the United States of America

This book is for my husband, Jim, who always believed.

It is also dedicated to our two children: James and Caralyn, and their families, with all my love.

Thank you to my sisters: Sherry Shaw, Charlene Marker, Debbie Kerr, and my sister-in-law, Robin Craig, for putting up with all my endless writing 'talk' throughout the years. Your love and support means everything to me. A special thank you to Charlene and Robin for reading the final version of this book. Their suggestions and input were invaluable.

I am also deeply grateful to my writing sisters: Jacklyn Craft and Jane Sargent Nodwell for keeping me going in those moments when I was ready to give up. We call ourselves the W-3 (three wild, wacky women writers) and we truly are.

Chapter One

Prologue

Though nearly ten at night, it was muggy and warm in Howard's Bay, a small town on the southeastern shore of Lake Nipissing in Northern Ontario.

As Abby Fulton locked the door of 'The Scrap Bag,' a light breeze lifted her long brown hair and cooled her hot cheeks, but she barely noticed. After working non-stop in the fabric shop since eight that morning, she might have noticed a category five hurricane. Then again, perhaps not. She was beat. Dog tired.

Rolling tight, aching shoulders she searched in her over-sized leather shoulder bag for car keys. Time to go home. Long past time.

A shaft of moonlight glinting off something metallic to her left stilled her search. Abby took a step forward and confirmed what her brain already knew. Cameron's truck. Parked in front of the new flower shop next door. *Must be working late on the renovations.* She paused in the shadows of the covered wooden verandah, her exhaustion dropping away like a discarded winter coat.

Abby was a woman ruled by her head, not her heart. She'd learned the hard way after a nasty divorce. Right now common sense and self-preservation were telling her to get the hell out of there and go straight home. Though every cell in her brain screamed, *mistake! mistake! mistake!* she turned and headed for the darkened shop next to her own.

She still might have been all right if the door had been locked. But it wasn't. The door opened easily so she slipped inside and paused, her hand resting on the knob. Even at that point, the choice was still hers to make. She could have turned away and carried on with the life she'd laid out for herself. And been happy. Well, reasonably so. But then she heard an awful sound and her life changed forever.

Somewhere in the shadows a man was crying. If you could call the gut-wrenching sobs echoing through the darkness crying. Hot tears scorched Abby's eyes, but she swept them away. Cameron Wallace didn't need or want her grief. He had enough of his own.

Hesitantly, she closed the door, then leaned back against it as she glanced around the dim room. A naked bulb suspended from the ceiling radiated a small field of light around a long wooden work table, but left the rest of the room dark.

As her eyes adjusted, she saw Cameron sitting on the table, his head bowed, his arms dangling loose between his open legs. His muscular shoulders lifted and dropped in rhythm to the deep sobs that racked him.

Abby was shocked, torn by indecision. Part of her, the part that had always been drawn to this man, wanted to rush over, pull him into her arms, and shush away his tears. But propriety and self-protection held her back. She had no right to comfort him, no right to hold him close. Only Leah, his wife, had that right. But Leah wasn't here. Abby took a step forward, her arms rising with a will of their own.

With one last deep shudder, Cameron eased off the table, wiped his eyes with the heels of his hands, then began to curse—one cold, vicious expletive after another. Cameron swearing! That stopped Abby in her tracks. Cameron didn't swear. He had a strict 'no swearing on site' rule for the employees of his construction company and led by example. So the foul words coming out of him were all the more startling.

Abby smiled grimly as the swearing continued. For a man who didn't swear, he sure knew a lot of cuss words. She started to make a wisecrack, but he shuddered and turned slightly, and she saw the anguish on his face. Something was wrong, terribly wrong.

Mindful of her new celery-green linen pants, Abby stepped gingerly over a pile of lumber near the table, then cleared her throat.

Caught off guard, Cameron turned his head and stared at her, his face haggard and drawn. He looked lost, defeated, overwhelmed by life.

Abby had seen that haunted expression before—in a magazine, on the face of a UN soldier standing in a burned-out village in Somalia.

Cameron still hadn't spoken, but neither had she. She couldn't. He looked like a stranger in the shadowy room. Not the Cameron she knew. Not the Cameron she…

The eyes were the same striking emerald green, fringed by long, sooty lashes. The jaw was just as square, chin just as firm. But his usually ruddy skin was grey and drawn and his cheeks looked hollow. Though only in his mid-thirties, he looked much older. He seemed drained of energy, as if all the life had been sucked out of him. He was still tall, still muscular. But no light shone behind his eyes. No smile curved that beautiful mouth.

"Cameron," Abby whispered, stepping toward him as she spoke.

His hand shot out, warning her back. He grimaced, then swiped at his eyes, glaring at her as if all his misery were somehow her fault.

"What are you doing here, Abby?" he growled. "For God's sake, it must be after ten. You should have been home hours ago." His hands-on-hips stance and glittering eyes warned her off as much as his words.

"I was working late. Getting my sales tax forms in order," she told him. "I saw your truck outside and wanted to pass on a message."

"What is it?" He was brusque, so unlike the man she knew.

"Libby called this afternoon from Toronto. She's been trying to get in touch with you for days. To get an update on the renovation."

Cameron snorted. With a sweep of an arm that encompassed the room, he added, "As you can see, it's not done. I've been a little…distracted lately." A bleakness filled his eyes that was painful to see.

Abby swallowed hard. She was so afraid she knew what was coming.

Cameron exhaled deeply, then looked around the half-finished flower shop. "I'll call Libby first thing in the morning and give her a full report."

His eyes slid sideways and connected with Abby's for a moment. Then he added abruptly, "Thanks for passing on the message, but you'd better head home. It's late and I still have a few more things to do here."

His tone left no room for argument so Abby headed for the door. Once there, she faltered and turned back. She just couldn't leave without knowing. "I heard you crying, Cameron. What's wrong? Is it…Leah?"

"I don't want to talk about it!"

Abby took a step back toward him but his anguished stare held her off.

"We're friends, Cameron," she told him. "Sometimes it helps to talk things out." Her voice was soft and soothing, her eyes gentle in the harsh glow of the bulb.

"What a goddamned asinine thing to say!" he roared.

The sudden rage on Cameron's face was so frightening, Abby flinched as if physically struck.

Cameron saw her reaction and groaned. "Abby...I'm sorry. You caught me at a very bad time. I didn't mean to shout at you."

Abby stepped gingerly toward him. "Talk to me, Cam. Tell me what's wrong. Frankly you're scaring the hell out of me." She smiled to take some of the tart from her words and, reaching his side, gently placed one hand on his arm.

He jerked as if touched by an electric wire, then crossed his arms against his chest. "I can't...talk about it. I don't want to say the words out loud. It'll make this nightmare all too real." His eyes were puffy and red-rimmed, his full mouth taut with grief.

Abby nodded slowly trying to ignore the alarm she felt. Tentatively, she raised a hand toward his chest, then halted in mid-air when he jerked away.

"Don't!" he said sharply. "Don't touch me, Abby. My...uh...clothes are full of sawdust."

Surprised by his reaction, Abby glanced down. Sure, there were bits of sawdust here and there on his green work pants and shirt, but nothing to cause such a reaction. Abby cringed inwardly. She got it. Her mother didn't raise any fools. Cameron didn't want her to touch him, not even in friendship. That hurt more than she cared to admit.

She stepped back, her eyes wary and aloof.

"Oh, for God's sake, Abby, don't look at me like that! I've got enough on my plate without worrying about you, too." His jaw clenched. "It's bad enough that you heard me blubbering like a baby."

When snapped at, it was Abby's nature to retaliate in kind, but instead she bit her tongue and turned to go. But, when Cameron swore again under his breath, she let loose. "For a man who doesn't swear, you're sure doing a lot of it tonight," she snarled over her shoulder.

A sound that might have been a half-hearted chuckle followed her words, then Cameron said, "Ah shoot, Abby, wait! Don't leave like this. We're friends...and I'm acting like an idiot."

Reluctantly, Abby faced him, her eyes seeking his like beacons in the dark. "Are you going to tell me what's wrong?"

Cameron slowly shook his head. "I don't know if I can. I feel so helpless, Abby. It all hit me tonight. First time I've cried since eighth grade. The night my mother died."

Abby's throat tightened at the painful confession. He stood like Atlas, bent by the weight of the world, his arms tight across his chest. His eyes were glittering again with unshed tears.

Gingerly, Abby closed the space between them. "Tell me," she demanded huskily. "Get it out."

Cameron sighed, his eyes bleak. "You're like a dog with a bone, Abby." He paused for long seconds then said, "You're right. It's…Leah." His throat worked furiously for a moment before he continued. "When they took her breast, we were so sure she'd be fine. She'd beat it. She's young, strong. We were both so optimistic. But yesterday the doctors said she's not responding as well as they'd hoped. They found several new tumours in the lymph nodes and they think the cancer may have spread to both lungs. On top of everything else, the chemo makes her really sick, weak as a baby. After all these treatments, we'd hoped she'd be better. But she's not.

"When I talked to her tonight, for the first time since this nightmare began, she sounded defeated. She didn't eat at all today and barely drinks. And, with her in Toronto—and me here—I feel so damned guilty I can't think straight! But I had to come back home. Leah knows I had no choice," he added, his voice gruff. "Four of my crew are off sick and we're way behind in all of our major contracts. She told me to come home, but it breaks my heart to leave her there all alone. Especially now." His eyes, naked with anguish, welled up again.

"It wouldn't be so bad if I were with her every day. If I could stay right there, rub her back, comfort her when she's down. But I can't. I have men depending on me, crews that need direction, jobs that need to be finished. So, I only spend weekends with her. And each time I walk into that hospital room, she seems worse than the week before."

He twisted away and his voice dropped so low that Abby instinctively moved closer, straining to hear his words.

"If it was a lung she needed, I'd give her mine. But this cancer is so insidious, it's eating away at her piece by piece. Tonight, when I talked to her, she didn't even sound like my Leah. She said…she said she could feel the life draining from her day by day." His face wild with grief, Cameron said, "What in hell do you say to a comment like that, Abby?" His eyes beseeched her to understand.

Without thinking, Abby stepped closer and one slim hand reached up and gently began to stroke Cameron's arm, soothing him as she would a wounded animal. If he noticed, he never let on.

"You *know* Leah, Abby. You know what she's like," he said. "She's always so up, so bubbly, so full of energy. When we first met, she radiated a joy of life that was so intoxicating I felt almost punch-drunk whenever I was with her." A muscle flexed in his jaw. "She has no energy now, Abby; it's all she can do to sit up."

Abby was hard-pressed to hold back tears. The love in Cameron's eyes and the pain in his voice was ripping her apart. She leaned closer, her hand riding up his arm.

Frowning slightly, Cameron edged back a pace, breaking contact. "Don't get me wrong," he muttered, "she's still my beautiful Leah. But she's lost so much weight, it's like carrying a small child when I hold her on my lap." He glanced away, then added quietly, "It broke her heart when they cut her long hair. She doesn't have a vain bone in her body, but she sure was proud of her hair. Now, it's short, and so thin, I can see her scalp through the wisps of blond. She refuses to look at herself in a mirror." Cameron sighed, then recrossed his arms over his chest. "She says she doesn't look like herself any more. I keep telling her she'll always be the most beautiful girl in the world to me, but she won't listen."

"Give her time to get used to all these changes, Cameron."

An ugly laugh punctured the gloom. "That's the problem," he growled. "We're out of time. And we both know it." Raking both hands through his hair, he said, "knowing time is short, I should be with her. But…it's like she's pushing me away. Lately, she doesn't want me to hold her, or kiss her, or even touch her hand. I'm losing her. I know I am! I keep urging her to fight, but she won't. It seems like she's given up hope and is just waiting to die. It's killing me, Abby. It's just killing me and I'm so afraid!"

Like a dam breaking during spring flood, Cameron's grief took him. Loud sobs filled the darkness and he dropped to his knees on the floor.

Mindless of the dirt, Abby knelt beside him. She pulled his heaving shoulders against her and rocked him, cradling him as she would a frightened child. When he rooted against her and wrapped his arms around her slim waist in a viselike grip, Abby was stunned, overwhelmed by feelings of forbidden pleasure. She knew she was on the edge of a slippery slope, but couldn't help herself.

For long eons out of time, she relished the pleasure of this man in her arms.

ABBY'S STORY: BETRAYED BY LOVE

She stroked his dark hair, pressed him close to her body, soothed his shaking frame. Later she would not be able to say just how it happened, but somehow, she was on her back on the hard floor and Cameron was on top of her, his body heavy and urgent. His head was buried in her neck, his mouth was open against her throat, but he didn't move, as if waiting for a signal to continue.

Knowing she had no right, Abby did the unthinkable. She touched him, stroked his strong back, fingered his spine as he hunched over her body. When did her movements stop being an offer of comfort and turn into a caress? Did he move first...or did she? Who knew...or cared?

Abby's touch ignited the passion fueled by Cameron's pain and they were both lost. His hands were everywhere, ripping buttons in his haste, his touch as feverish as her skin. Cameron took her mouth, demanding entrance. She opened for him, her tongue eagerly snaking with his.

Abby was shaking from head to foot, her whole being *starved* for this man. She'd ached for him forever and now at last she could touch him at will. It was almost too much to bear. As he groaned and ground against her in an insistent imitation of what he needed, Abby pressed against him, her body already wet and wanting.

"Let me," he muttered. "For God's sake, don't stop me now. It's been so long." His hand was shaking as it burrowed between their straining bodies, his open mouth and wet tongue burning the tender skin by her ear. When his tongue trailed a path upward, then across her cheek, she shivered helplessly.

"Yes," she whispered as she ran her hands up his straining arms. *She wanted him inside her now!*

Undoing the zipper on the side of her linen slacks, Cameron's hands shook as he pulled the slacks down her long legs.

Impatient to get on with it, Abby kicked her puddled slacks off. When his work-roughened hand touched her lace bikini briefs, her breath caught in her throat and she almost came. But instead of removing her panties, he shuddered powerfully, then dropped his head between her breasts.

"This is *so* wrong," he said harshly. "But I can't seem to help myself. I've wanted you for so long, Abby. Wanted you...and hated myself. If I were any kind of a man, I'd get the hell out of here right now. Get out of here before I destroy what little self-respect I have left." He swore viciously under his breath, then reached for her. "But I can't, God help me. I can't let you go!" He pulled down her lacy briefs and tore them from her body.

Abby moaned aloud at his frantic touch. *If I were the kind of woman I should be, I wouldn't touch another woman's man. But I can't let this chance pass. I've wanted you for so long. Needed you forever.*

The sound of his zipper opening was loud and abrasive in the darkness. Unwanted tears filled Abby's eyes. She felt him lean up to pull down his own pants and she didn't stop him. That time was long gone. She should have pushed him away. That would have been the right thing to do. But the burning need throbbing through her body superceded all else. With tears dripping silently down her cheeks, Abby lay there, naked from the waist down, her legs spread wide, waiting for his possession. When his fingers grazed her opening she flinched—not from the shame she should have felt—but from hunger.

"God, you're wet," he growled, his breath fanning her ear. His sex prodded at her entrance, moving slowly, insistently, into her heat. "Are you sure?" he muttered, as he leaned up, poised to thrust.

Get on with it! Do it! Abby moaned in anguish. She couldn't take any more questions. Couldn't wait any longer. Wrapping her legs around his muscular thighs, she grabbed his firm buttocks, and raised up to meet him.

Cameron reared at the contact and thrust hard, embedding himself fully in her fiery sheath. After that, there was no holding back. Both were too far gone; both were out of control.

Leaning over her heaving body, Cameron pounded into her, his thrusts hard, hot, almost brutal. He wasn't a gentle, tender lover. He was relentless, lost in a world gone mad with lust. His arms strained. Sweat poured off his body. His nostrils flared as the musky smell of her arousal hardened him to a point where pain and pleasure overlapped. He was beyond reason, beyond caring. Like a male lion pleasuring his mate, he growled deep in his throat and thrust harder, her matching groans of pleasure spurring him on.

As he shifted his arms for more leverage, a sliver of moonlight flickered through the window and highlighted her face. Her eyes were half-lidded, her nostrils flared, her curved, swan-like neck thrown back in pleasure. The look on her face filled him with awe. There was no doubt her passion equalled his. Never before had he seen a woman so absorbed by lust. Then Leah's gentle face swam before him, a look of reproach in her lovely blue eyes.

He pulled out abruptly. "I can't…"

Abby almost screamed in frustration. *She was so close! Surely he wouldn't leave her like this!*

He didn't. With rough impatience, Cameron turned her on her stomach, raised her bottom slightly, then plunged into her sheath from behind.

Gasping in pain at the unfamiliar position, Abby moaned but soon matched his rhythm. With her long hair sweeping the floor and her lean body bucking back against his, she was female to his male, consumed by pleasure. She was moaning repeatedly in time to his thrusts. She had never felt this way before, never felt so hot, so wet, so wild for more. Never felt more alive. With every hammer stroke he pushed her higher, his hands on her waist moulding her to him. As if from afar, she heard him groan and curse, puncturing the darkness with sounds that didn't seem quite human.

He drove deeper, his every thrust a flame of fire scorching Abby's core. She throbbed and burned but couldn't stop. A rhythmic, slapping sound, the music of their mating, filled the air. Then she came, soaring over the edge, her body convulsing helplessly. Her spasms triggered Cameron's climax and he drove into her hard, his hot juices spilling his seed into her welcoming flesh.

As his heat flooded her body, Abby peaked again, waves of hot pleasure pulsing to every nerve ending. Long moments later, as the spasms finally receded, she eased her burning face onto the cool floor, her body languid and replete. When she felt him begin to withdraw, she clenched her inner muscles in a faint attempt to keep him inside.

But Cameron pushed her away, his hands almost brutal.

In that instant her stupor fled and Abby closed her eyes in resignation. Time to face the music. Pushing hair out of her face, she twisted her head, watching silently as he stood and pulled up his pants. His harsh breathing echoed through the silent room.

Abby stayed on the floor, too drained, too mentally unhinged to say a word. *What on earth had she done?*

The rasp of his zipper was like the sound of a whip. Abby cringed, her head dropping back into the dirt.

"Get dressed, Abby." The words were cold, his voice trembling with a loathing that was almost palpable.

When she made no move, he swore, crudely.

Hot tears filled Abby's eyes as she slowly turned over and met his flint-like stare. She flinched at the disgust that hardened his face. At the condemnation that filled his eyes. In that moment, Abby knew a shame that equalled physical pain. She wanted to look away, but couldn't.

"Get dressed...now!" he snapped. "The sight of you makes me sick."

Shocked beyond comprehension, Abby's eyes widened, pain knifing her gut. "There's no need to be so vicious," she snapped back. "What we did was wrong. But there were two people on this floor—not one."

"Do you think I don't know that! I took you like a dog takes a bitch in heat! While my wife is fighting for her life in the hospital, I'm rutting in the dirt with you! Have you any idea how low I feel...how my skin crawls when I realize what we just did!" Cameron groaned, then turned away, his hands on his hips, his head bent low in anguish.

What else could be said? Abby sat up, searching for a way to cover herself. She winced when she spotted her ripped panties. It was pointless to put them on. Instead, she eased stiff, aching legs into her slacks and stuffed her panties into a pocket. Then, like an old arthritic woman, she got carefully to her feet. With shaking fingers she zipped her pants, then smoothed back her long, baby-fine hair.

Her self-respect as tattered as her panties, she stiffened her backbone, reined in her misery and said, "If it's any consolation, I never meant for this to happen."

Cameron spun around, his face grim in the faint light from the far window. "It should *never* have happened!" he snarled, his eyes bitter with loathing. "And it wouldn't have happened if you hadn't showed up here tonight...with your soft hands and hot eyes."

Abby jerked as if he'd struck her.

"You sanctimonious prig! That was uncalled for!" Her voice shaking with fury, she took a step toward him, itching to smack him down. "Don't play the innocent with me, Cameron Wallace! Do you think I haven't noticed the way you look at me—even when Leah's around? I see the need in your eyes...the way you stare at my mouth...and my crotch! You've been hot to trot for a long time!"

Cameron sucked in a harsh breath. His eyes narrowed, his hands balled into fists at his side. "Oh, I noticed you all right. What man wouldn't! Tight jeans to show off your ass and endless legs. No bra half the time so your nipples show through those silk blouses you always wear. Oh, yah...like half the men in town, I noticed. Noticed...wanted...and finally gave you what you wanted. Am I proud of myself? No goddamned way! It wasn't you I really wanted, it was Leah, my wife—the woman I love with all my heart. Tonight, you were just a substitute, and a poor one at that. The wrong woman...in the wrong place...at the wrong time!"

He shook his head and glared at her. "As God is my witness, Abby, I would never have touched you, never have broken my vows to Leah, if you'd left me alone. I love my wife—do you hear me! Love her with all my heart! She's pure and fine and the best wife a man could want. It's not her fault we haven't....we couldn't..."

His voice broke then and he jerked away. When he spoke again his tone was as ugly as his words. "I may have had sex with you, Abby, but make no mistake, that's all it was. I was horny and you were here. I will regret this night for the rest of my life."

"You wanted me," she faltered.

Cameron swore again. "You just don't get it—do you! I wanted sex…a warm, willing body. And to me, that's all you were. With Leah, it's making love. With you, it was just sex. Raw animal sex." Cameron glared defiantly. He knew he was hurting her but couldn't seem to stop. For both their sakes, he had to nail his point home. "This can never happen again," he told her grimly. "Get out of here, Abby, and stay away from me. Don't call me. Don't seek me out. Don't even look at me sideways. Or, so help me God, I'll make your life a living hell!" With one last look of disgust, Cameron turned away and walked toward his work table.

Quivering with rage and pain, Abby bit back the retaliation on the edge of her tongue. If she said one word, she'd never stop. Better just to get out with what little dignity she had left. Stumbling backward, she almost fell over a piece of timber but caught herself just in time. She straightened, stiffened her spine, and opened the door. Though tempted to smash it shut, she closed it quietly, never once looking back.

After the door closed, Cameron pounded the table with his fists. *He'd been so vicious, so cruel! How could he have treated Abby that way? She didn't deserve what he'd just done. She'd always been a good friend to him and Leah. It was his fault. He was responsible. He never should have touched her. But Lord, how he'd wanted her.*

From the moment they'd met two years ago, he'd wanted her. He loved Leah and was content with their life together, so he'd fought his feelings for Abby. Until tonight when lust had overrun his common sense.

He'd betrayed Leah! That thought had him gritting his teeth in despair. Leah, his childhood sweetheart, the love of his life, his best friend, his gentle love. Leah…sunshine and light…rainbows and wild flowers growing in a field…fresh air after a rainstorm…picnics at the beach. Loving her was easy. Always had been. Being loved in return had been the core of his well-being. And now, he'd jeopardized all that—for a few moments between Abby's legs.

Abby. Cameron groaned as he remembered her rising up to meet his last thrust. Abby was so different from any other woman he'd ever met—Leah included. Abby was moonlight…wild and deep and alluring. Her scent drove him wild. She was intoxicating, erotic, sensual—so far and away beyond what he was used to. He wasn't an experienced man. He'd married young. Had never strayed from Leah's side. Had never felt the need. But, from the moment Abby's wide blue eyes met his, some primeval part of him recognized her, connected with her in a way that jolted him like an electric shock. And scared the hell out of him.

Abby called him, like the sirens called the mythical men of ancient Greece. Her azure eyes, honeyed lips, and willowy body haunted his dreams. He'd heard she'd been a model in Toronto for a while and he could see it in the way she walked. She carried herself with a cat-like grace that was almost hypnotic. Yet it wasn't just her body that drew him. Her deep, husky laugh often caught him off guard. She was witty and smart and had a tart sense of humour. He liked her; she intrigued him. That much, at least, he was willing to admit.

Though he'd found unimaginable pleasure in her arms, he had to forget Abby. Had to forget what had just happened. He belonged to Leah—always had, always would. After ten years of marriage, he'd betrayed his vows to his sweet wife, something he'd never imagined himself capable of doing.

Cameron closed his eyes in remorse. He'd have to forget Abby…forget her wild responsiveness…forget the joy of burying himself in her fiery heat…forget the most incredible sex he'd ever had in his life. As his brain flooded with memories of Abby, his body hardened and Cameron groaned in self-loathing. *What kind of a man was he! The best sex…who was he kidding! It just felt that way because he'd been celibate so long. He'd been horny for months. Sex with any woman would have been just as great.*

Cameron sighed. He might be a bastard but he wasn't a fool. It was pointless to lie to himself. It was Abby he'd wanted; Abby who'd made the sex so incredible. He'd wanted her forever, his body hard every time she was near. And tonight, he'd taken her, taken what he'd wanted—with no thought for Leah. Or his vows.

Cameron groaned, shaking his head from side to side, like a wounded beast. He'd betrayed Leah when she needed him the most; he'd hurt Abby and treated her like dirt. He felt like the scum of the earth, didn't like what he'd become that night. But, even knowing it was wrong, if Abby came running back through that door, his hands would be all over her in seconds. God! What a mess he'd made of his life.

Then he thought of Leah. Leah, his sweet love who needed his strength and devotion. A muscle jumped in his jaw as he realized what had to be. This night *did not* happen! He had to close the door, lock away the memories, focus on getting his wife through the coming months. Even if it killed him in the process. As for Abby—he'd avoid her at all costs. Never be alone with her again, stay out of her range. Maybe then he could be the man Leah deserved, the husband she'd married, the man she'd trusted with her love.

His decision made, Cameron straightened his spine, but his eyes were bleak. He knew what he had to do. Knew it was the only way to redeem the terrible mistake he'd made this night. But forgetting Abby wouldn't be easy.

But he would do it. Even if it killed him. Perhaps then, he could look in the mirror, and not be disgusted by the man he'd become.

Chapter Two

Mentally driving on automatic pilot, Abby steered her Saturn home, her mind torn by grief and disbelief. As she turned down one street, then manoeuvered into another, she was wracked by knives of shame. Not only had she betrayed Leah and Cameron, she'd betrayed herself. She'd always had a mental line in the sand, a line that said, *don't go there*. Others might, but Abby Fulton—never. Tonight, that line had been crossed. Tonight, she'd changed from the woman she'd always thought she was into someone she barely knew. Someone she didn't like.

She should not have gone into the flower shop. That was mistake number one. She'd known he was vulnerable. She'd seen it in the lines of worry that scored his face. She'd also known how much he loved Leah—loved her dearly. How could she not know? Each time Leah walked into a room, his face lit with joy, his hands reached for her as she walked by.

Abby sighed, her throat tight. Oh, she'd known how he felt about his wife. Known—and chose to ignore that fact. That was mistake number two. Cameron lived for Leah and she for him. Yet tonight, Abby had repressed that knowledge. Let common sense be overrun by an overwhelming hunger for the man who held her heart. Mistake number three.

But he had been hungry too. For a woman's touch? For warmth? Or, for something more fundamentally basic? God, it hurt to think that any woman could have satisfied him tonight. Any warm body willing to sate his physical needs. Abby groaned as she turned a sharp corner. Had he been thinking of Leah when he took *her*? Was it Leah's face he saw when he came?

Abby shuddered as a sudden thought hit home. My God! They hadn't used any protection! With Cameron, AIDS wasn't a concern. But pregnancy sure was. Cameron wasn't promiscuous but he was a very potent male. Could they have made a child? Probably not. With her fertility problems, the chances were almost nil. But, for an instant, a vision of Cameron's child against her breast filled her mind and choked off her breath. She held that thought, then pushed it away abruptly. Wishful thinking and nothing more. She didn't need, or want, that kind of complication in her life. And neither did he.

Would he *want* her baby? Foolishly, like a bleeding hangnail, the thought persisted, inflicting another small wound on her soul. Of course not! If he were to have a child, he'd want Leah's baby, not hers. She bit her lip, her mind turning as much as the steering wheel. Cameron and Leah had been married over ten years, yet had no children. Was that by choice?

Not her worry. Abby flipped the turn signal, then eased into the driveway that led to Maggy Blake's house and the small cottage behind that Abby rented from her friend and partner. A light was on in Maggy's living room. But Abby didn't stop. No way could she face Maggy right now.

Abby pulled into the small parking spot in front of her home, her mind still focused on babies. Why was she worried? The chances of her conceiving were slim to none. The doctors she'd gone to while married to Nick had made that fact very plain. But still, though she'd never admit it in the light of day, a small part of her craved his child. Wanted Cameron's child in her belly.

Abby turned off the ignition, then got out of the car, her body sore and bruised. She barely noticed the warm, fragrant air redolent of the blossoms from Maggy's garden. Didn't appreciate the pleasant summer night, or the faint stars twinkling overhead, or the moon bathing the path in a silvery light as she walked to her door. She was too immersed in pain. Too weary to feel. Too overpowered by shame and remorse.

Unlocking the door, she stepped inside, then kicked off her shoes. With a heavy hand, she closed the door behind her, then, with growing haste, began to strip. She wanted a shower, needed to feel clean again. By the time she made it to the small bathroom off the kitchen, Abby was naked, fat tears streaming down her face. The water was brutally hot as she stepped inside the tub enclosure. She gritted her teeth and endured the punishing pain, her soul far more tortured than her flesh. She wanted to howl, and curse, and pound the walls. Instead she cried. Like a baby, hurt and alone.

When she could stand the scalding heat no longer, she stepped out and dried off, her long, lean body trembling with fatigue. At the sink, she automatically lifted her toothbrush, then paused and wiped the steam from the mirror. Did she look any different now? Shouldn't a huge red 'W' for whore be burned into her forehead? Though no letter marked her reddened skin she felt branded by shame none the less. She stared at the mirror and saw someone she barely recognized. The angular face was the same, the jaw still too strong, the eyebrows still finely arched, the nose too haughty for classical beauty. A striking face many said. But the face of a woman she didn't know—or like.

Abby sighed wearily. Yes, she did look different. She looked defeated, subdued, definitely older than her thirty-four years. Tonight had marked her. Her wide blue eyes, always her best feature, were cloudy and dull, as if the flame of life that lit them had dimmed. Her wide mouth, with its too-full bottom lip, wobbled as fresh tears overflowed. Quickly, Abby wiped them away, refusing to let them fall. She stared at the woman in the mirror and despised what she saw. "You still love him, don't you—you damned fool! When will you smarten up!"

Abby's shoulders drooped and she turned away, unable to face what she'd become. "Tonight," she murmured in the darkness as she padded into her bedroom. "You can mourn him tonight. And then it's done." Naked, she dropped onto her bed, and sobbed, hour after hour. Cried until spent. For lost hope…lost love…lost self-respect.

Hours later, when she finally drifted off, she slept fitfully, tossing and turning through the night, her dreams haunted by images of Cameron pounding into her—and Leah's accusing stare. Around five, she woke, startled and wide-eyed. With a category three headache dulling her vision, she muttered, "To hell with it," and got up.

Dragging on a turquoise silk robe, she belted it tightly and headed for the kitchen. She needed coffee—and lots of it. Thankfully her Tim Horton's coffee maker brewed mercifully quick. She made a full pot knowing she would need all the caffeine she could get just to face the day. Minutes later, after downing the first cup of strong black coffee and pouring a second, she headed for the couch. She lay there unmoving, her eyes unfocused, her brain shut down. For the first time in years she craved—no would kill—for a cigarette.

ABBY'S STORY: BETRAYED BY LOVE

Abby was a creature of habit. Habits gave her life form and substance. Gave her the boundaries that made her feel safe. She'd always taken great pleasure in the morning rituals that defined her way of life. No morning rush for this lady. Each morning, she got up slow. Made a pot of coffee. Grabbed a piece of toast made from freshly sliced bread and a bowl of fresh fruit that included a banana, then allowed herself thirty to forty minutes to watch the news or read. Nothing earth-shattering about her routine. But morning was her special time. She needed the solitude of her mornings, like a runner needs the challenge of a marathon. It calmed her and rejuvenated her spirit.

But this morning, she couldn't eat, couldn't watch TV. Couldn't read. And the smell of coffee was making her slightly nauseous.

You're a fool, Abby Fulton. A damn fool! The tears came again, unbidden, streaming down her face, making splotches on her robe. *Enough! This pity wallowing has to end!* Abby put her coffee down, then walked on shaky legs to the front door and opened it. For once, the rising sun gave her no pleasure. She took several deep breaths of the crisp, sharp air, then closed the door again. Nothing helped. Her head ached and her eyes burned, so Abby headed back to the bedroom and dropped onto her bed. A vision of Leah flashed before her eyes. Abby groaned, clutched her belly, and howled.

"Abby, shush...stop. You're going to make yourself sick. Hush now. Stop!" Maggy eased onto the bed and pulled her weeping friend into her arms.

Abby started to hiccup. She laid her head back against Maggy's shoulder and cried all the more.

Bewildered, Maggy rocked Abby as she would one of her children until the tears finally started to subside. "Do you want to talk?"

"I can't."

"I think you have to. I've never seen you like this, Abby."

Abby slowly sat up, then reached for some tissue from the night table. "This isn't something I want to share with anyone."

"Ah...I see. So, it's about Cameron."

Abby's long neck stiffened. She turned her head and locked eyes with Maggy. "You know?"

"I think I know. Now, tell me what happened."

Abby shuddered as her mind whipped back to the night before. "God Maggy," she said, her face haggard in the early morning light, "I am such a fool."

"Join the club. Maybe it's not as bad as you think. What happened?"

With a shaking hand, Abby pulled her robe tighter and leaned back against her pillow. "I screwed up—big time." She groaned and shook her head. Then, in a low, flat voice said, "After I closed up shop last night, I stayed to get my quarterly tax slips in order. But that was just an excuse. I could have done the work at home. I stayed because I knew that Cameron was next door building shelves in Libby's new flower shop."

Maggy closed her eyes and bit her lip, but said nothing.

Abby looked away. She couldn't bear to see Maggy's face. In a halting voice she added, "After I finished up my paperwork, I went to see him. I told myself I was just going to ask how Leah was doing. But that was a lie. I wanted to see *him*." A sob cracked the stillness.

At the pain on Abby's face Maggy wanted to cry herself. Instead, in the firm tone she used with her children she said, "What did you do?"

Abby's eyes filled with fresh tears. "He was crying," she whispered brokenly. "When I went into the shop, he was crying. And…I couldn't walk away. Somehow…we were in each other's arms…and…we…Oh God! Maggy…I never meant for it to happen. I swear I didn't!" Abby collapsed against Maggy's shoulder and sobbed all the harder.

Maggy closed her eyes as the enormity of the situation washed over her. Carefully, in a voice devoid of emotion, she asked, "And Cameron…?"

Abby eased away again, then wiped at her face. "He hates me and hates himself. Though maybe not in that order." Abby pulled at her robe, her eyes downcast. "Afterwards…he pushed me away as if the sight of me made him sick. He said he never wanted to see me again. Said it was all a mistake…a terrible mistake. He said he loves his wife and always will."

"He *does* love her, Abby. You know that."

Abby turned, her eyes wild with grief. "I know that! And that's what's killing me. I can't believe I did something so despicable, so low. And to poor Leah." Her head dropped against her heaving chest. "I know better. Yet I did it anyway."

Ignoring the anguish in Abby's voice, Maggy said briskly, "The woman's fighting for her life, Abby. She has to come first. How are you going to handle this?"

"Forget Cameron Wallace exists," Abby snapped. "What else can I do? The man loves his wife. And hates me. He made that very clear. And so he should. God," she shuddered, her voice tight with self-loathing, "how low is it to have sex with a man who's wife is battling cancer!" In a frenzy of pain, Abby raked her hands through her long hair. "I have to forget that last night ever happened. It's the only way I can keep what little dignity I have left." She glanced sideways at Maggy. "Do you hate me too?"

Maggy sighed, her eyes somber. "Of course not, Abby. But don't expect any pats on the back from me. What you did was wrong."

Abby flinched as if struck.

Deliberately, Maggy softened her tone. "Look, Abby. We all make mistakes. Some mistakes are just harder to deal with than others."

Abby sat up, every bone in her body aching. "I know. I'll deal with this. It'll never happen again." She turned on the bedside light and glanced at the clock. "God, it's already six." She rubbed her red-rimmed eyes, then frowned. "Maggy...it's six o'clock in the morning. What on earth made you come over here so early? Is something wrong?"

Maggy turned green, then deadly white. She gagged, grabbed her mouth, then took off for the bathroom.

Instantly, her own problems forgotten, Abby raced after her. At the sound of violent retching, Abby pulled to a stop and grimaced. Then took a deep breath and went inside.

A few minutes later, Maggy flushed the toilet, closed the lid, and managed to sit down.

Grabbing a cloth from the rack, Abby wet it with cold water and began to bathe Maggy's trembling face.

"So..." Abby began cautiously, "does this mean...?"

"It means I'm pregnant all right." Maggy smiled wryly at the startled expression on Abby's face. Slowly, her legs still shaking, she hobbled over to the sink and poured a glass of water. She drained the glass and then another.

"But...how?" Abby sputtered.

"The usual way."

"No...I mean...I thought Ross was sterile."

"Funny...so did I. That husband of mine has some explaining to do when he gets back from Toronto." Maggy smiled slightly, then wiped her face some more.

"So...you're pleased then? About the baby, I mean."

"As pleased as any middle-aged woman is who finds out she's unexpectedly pregnant." Maggy sighed, absently folding the face cloth. "Trust me, Abby. This is going to take some getting used to."

"Thirty-five is not middle-aged."

"Tell that to my kids. Kyle and Kyra think I'm ancient. They're going to be horrified when they hear about the baby. Kyle will be for sure." Maggy flipped back long auburn curls and stared at Abby in the mirror. "Aren't we a pair?" she muttered. Grinning weakly she turned and gently stroked Abby's tear-streaked face.

Abby slowly nodded. Easing away, she said, "I can't believe I'm saying this, but I think we both could use a cup of tea. I'll ask forgiveness at Tim Horton's on the way to work. But first, promise me two things."

"What?"

"One…don't throw up any more when I'm around. I have a very weak stomach."

Maggy lifted one fine brow. "I'll try to keep that in mind," she grinned dryly. "And…?"

"I get to be your baby's godmother."

Like a river overflowing in Spring, Maggy's emotions burst free and tears streamed down her face. This time Abby offered comfort as Maggy sobbed.

After two pots of tea, they were both all cried out.

"Oh Lord, it's nearly seven," Maggy muttered as she glanced at the clock on Abby's stove. "I've got to get back home and get ready for work. There was a problem with the steamer yesterday. I need to get to the tea room early to see if the night crew got the strawberry jam made last night."

With her feet up on a round-backed wooden chair in the middle of her kitchen, Abby slurped the last dregs of her tea. And shuddered. "God Maggy, I can't believe people actually drink this stuff every day."

At the other end of the honey-pine pedestal table, Maggy said, "You either love it or hate it. Thankfully for my business, many people love their tea." She yawned but made no move to get up. "Damn. I'd better move my ass. Ardith'll be at the house any moment." Maggy stood up and stretched, then dragged floppy slippers back onto her feet.

"She has a key, doesn't she?"

"Sure. But I try to have the coffee ready when she gets in. She's not exactly a morning person."

Abby chuckled. "I know the feeling. Mind you, you're sure lucky to have her. She could teach Martha Stewart a few things about keeping house."

"You got that right." Maggy stifled another yawn. "She grumbles a lot when the kids mess up, but she's really an old sweetie. After Jarrod died, and I started the bakeshop, she was the glue that kept us all together. Many times when I was working double shifts, the kids would have starved if not for her."

"I forget…did she ever marry?"

Maggy frowned and crossed her arms as if cold. "Twice actually. She said her first husband, John, was a good man. He was killed in a mining accident in Sudbury. Ardith was just a kid herself, working as a waitress in K-Mart when he died. She was so lonely she screwed up and married an older man, Larry Dawes. A jealous, mean-spirited old fart from what I gather."

"What happened to him? Ardith's been a widow as long as I've known her."

"Oh, after beating her silly one night in a drunken rage, he took off walking down to the corner hotel."

"And...?"

"Never made it."

Abby's eyes widened and her brows rose. "What happened?"

A hint of a smile lifted one side of Maggy's mouth. "They found him the next morning in a ditch."

Abby frowned. "Heart attack?"

"No, just a bit of northern justice. Ardith said that night was one of the coldest ever recorded in Sudbury."

"Didn't she go out looking for him?"

Maggy snorted. "The man had just beaten her to a pulp. For the umpteen time. Would you go looking?"

A soft breath left Abby's mouth. "Oh, my," she said quietly. "Who else knows about it?"

Maggy's eyes narrowed. "Not many people and Ardith wants it kept that way. She's a very private person. Kind of prickly at times."

Abby slowly nodded. "Don't worry, I won't let on I know. But how does she feel about your remarriage. Does she like Ross?"

Maggy laughed, a rich, throaty laugh that floated through the room. "She said he reminded her of her first husband, John. If she were twenty years younger, I think she'd have gone after him herself."

"Get out! Ardith?"

Maggy grinned. "Yes, Ardith. She's the one who pushed me to marry Ross. She said a woman needs a good man in her bed. And she figured Ross was a good man in and out of bed."

"Good lord!" Abby choked. "Who knew Ardith even thought that way."

Maggy grinned wryly. "Most women do——they just don't admit it. Sometimes, when she starts reminiscing, it gets pretty hot and heavy in my kitchen."

"Especially when Ross is home?" Abby teased.

Maggy grinned, happiness softening her eyes.

"I still can't believe you married our accountant."

"Believe it. I'm more happy than I ever thought possible. Mind you," Maggy said, with a worried glance at Abby, "this baby might change things in more ways than one. It's a good thing we're adding on to the back of the house. Ross is already complaining about how cramped the place is."

"How do you think he'll take the news?"

Maggy shrugged. "I honestly don't know. I suspect he's going to be as shocked as I am. I mean...he told me he was sterile. That's why he and Adriana, his first wife, never had any kids. I just hope he'll be pleased—once he gets over the shock. He's great with my two kids, but it's going to mean a lot of adjusting for everyone." Though she tried to hide it, it was clear Maggy was worried.

Abby stood, walked over, and wrapped her arm around Maggy's shoulders. "Hang in there, chum. We've been through a lot in the last few years and we'll handle this new baby just fine." In an attempt to lighten Maggy's spirits, Abby added, "Remember when we met at that auction...the night we bought our building? When we decided to pool our money instead of bidding against each other? You were a widow, I was divorced, and we both swore we'd forget about men and concentrate on opening our own businesses."

"Which we did," Maggy said, smiling softly. "We turned that old Victorian monstrosity into one of the busiest places in town."

"That's right. We sure did." Abby felt like a cheerleader rallying the team, but she could feel Maggy's spirits lifting, so she kept it up. "You have the best bakeshop and tea room in the area and I have my fabric shop and gift den. And soon, when Libby Cornell opens up her flower shop in September, our 'Quilters' Corner' will be full. Just like we planned."

"Sometimes things don't always go as planned," Maggy said, a hand absently caressing her stomach. "I hope Libby can handle it—her own business, I mean. She's awfully young."

Abby bit back the exasperation she felt. They'd had this talk so many times before. "She's twenty-five, Maggy, not a baby. So stop worrying about her. She probably has more experience running a business than you and I combined. She cut her teeth working for her father in Cornell Industries. Anyone who trained under that shark—and survived—can surely run a small flower shop."

"I know you're right, Abby. Don't mind me. I think my hormones are all out of whack. I seem to be worried about every little thing lately. It's just that Libby's so petite and pretty. It's hard to remember she's got a sharp brain under all those blond curls."

Abby grinned ruefully. "I know. I feel like the Jolly Green Giant when I'm standing beside her."

"You and me both. Before I forget, did I tell you what happened the other day when Libby was in Ross's office?"

"I knew she was coming to town to set up her banking and accounting."

"Yes, Libby was meeting with Ross and his partner, Tom Powers. But, all hell broke loose when Tom's brother, Rayce, showed up and tried to make a move on Libby."

"Rayce Powers, the new bank manager?"

"That's the one," Maggy confirmed. "And, from what I hear, a real hunk."

"Interesting. So...how did our little Miss Toronto handle the backwoods hunk?"

Maggy laughed as she tossed tangled hair over her shoulder. "Ross says he won't have to use the air conditioner for a week after the way Libby put Rayce in his place. She took an instant dislike to the man and didn't bother to hide it. Ross says she can chew a man out without batting an eyelash."

"Our Libby? Little Miss Pocket Venus?" Abby's fine eyebrows arched incredulously.

"Our Libby."

A wolfish smile spread over Abby's face. "And you were worried about the kid. I think she's going to fit in just fine."

"I hope you're right," Maggy said as she glanced at a clock by the door. "Damn! Look at the time. I've got to go." She hesitated, then asked, "Are you going to be all right?"

"I should be asking you that," Abby sighed. A hint of pain darkened her eyes. "Aren't we a pair. Go get ready for work, Maggy, and don't worry about me. I'll be fine."

When Maggy still hesitated, Abby pushed her toward the door. "Go! I mean it. I can't stand weepy, sentimental women, so get out of here. I'm late as it is. I'll see you later at the shop."

Grinning, Maggy shook her head and left, not fooled in the least by Abby's gruff tone.

Abby shut the door and leaned against it, her eyes gritty. She meant what she said. There'd be no more tears. In the last few hours, she'd cried enough to last forever. Something she seldom did. Unlike her drama queen of a mother, Abby didn't cry. In fact, she hated weepy women, cringed around them. But she hated it even more when *she* acted that way. Only one other time in her life had she given in to grief and cried her heart out. That time had been over a man too.

Her husband. Her handsome, witty, charming, couldn't-keep-his-zipper-zipped bastard of a husband. She'd cried one night for him too. One night. And then no more.

And all because of the flu. She, who never got sick, caught the flu. She'd been in Montreal on a modelling shoot for a Sears catalogue. But after two days of hacking and coughing, the director had sent her back home to Toronto. Reeling with a raging temperature, she'd barely put the key in the door when she heard them. Probably the whole building heard them. Her husband and her best friend. In her bed, thank you very much!

God, what a cliche, Abby thought, as she remembered that night. Remembered how her shock had given way to a white-hot rage that fuelled the storm she'd unleashed. Now she could gloat about how she'd picked up Nick's prized Chinese vase and heaved it at him, knocking him off Celine in the process. A slight grin twitched her mouth but didn't reach her eyes. She'd howled like a dervish that night as she'd raced through the apartment breaking every piece of Nick's cherished porcelain collection. What kind of a man collected porcelain anyway!

Oh, she could smile now. But not then. Not that night. After fleeing to a hotel, she'd cried all night long. Cried until she made herself sick. When her tears had finally dried up, any feelings she'd had for her husband were buried deep, along with her fairy-tale dreams of happily ever after. She'd filed for a divorce immediately and never looked back.

Oh, Nick had tried to sweet-talk her into trying again—once his lawyer let him know how much Abby's lawyer was demanding. But by then, she loathed him and wanted out.

She'd walked away from their marriage with a hefty bank account, tattered remnants of her self-esteem, and little else. The money had helped to sooth her wounded spirit, but most of it was her own anyway. Both she and Nick had earned good money modelling, but it was his world—not hers. Once she'd found out that Nick's affair with Celine was one of many, she'd known it was time to move on, and move away.

So, she'd found a little studio apartment in downtown Toronto, invested her money, and worked for several years with a fabric wholesaler she'd met at a party. It wasn't the most fascinating job in the world, but she'd learned a lot. And, in time, she made her move.

She'd always wanted to live in a small town. Run her own business. So she'd pull out a map, picked a spot, and, for absolutely no reason at all, decided to move north to North Bay. Eventually, she'd settled nearby in Howard's Bay. And started a new life. Made new friends.

Was it accident or fate that she'd run into Maggy Howard at the auction? Who knew. They'd both planned to bid on the old Victorian building but had ended up pooling their money and buying the building together. In the ensuing months, each had renovated a third of the building and opened a business. Maggy opened her bakeshop/tea room and Abby started a fabric shop she'd named 'The Scrap Bag.' In those early days, with her bruised ego finally on the mend, Abby had thought life couldn't get any better. But it had.

On a whim, she'd offered an unused backroom behind her shop to a group of older ladies who needed a place to meet and quilt. That one spontaneous act of generosity had resulted in the expansion of her business to include a gift den. Now, Abby sold the unique hand-made quilts, purses, vests, and runners that the quilters made with such exquisite detail. The quilters and their friends were good for business and, when Maggy suggested they name their building 'Quilters' Corner' after the group, it seemed just right.

Abby had been living in Howard's Bay for about a year when Leah Wallace had walked into her shop. A fragile blond, with a smile so gentle it made Abby want to wrap her in cotton and tuck her away, Leah had explained that her husband, Cameron, had decided to leave the family construction business he ran with his two brothers in the Ottawa Valley and start his own firm in Northern Ontario. And they'd chosen Howard's Bay.

In a shy, hesitant voice Leah had asked about the quilting group. Said she'd quilted all her life—as did all the women in her family—and missed it. Abby had taken an instant liking to Leah. And, when the quilters saw what a truly gifted quilter Leah was, they'd welcomed her with open arms. Within weeks, it was as if Leah had been a member all her life. Everyone liked her, felt drawn to her.

Especially Abby. Usually it took Abby a long time to ease into a friendship. And even then, friends were always kept at arm's-length. Yet, since moving to Howard's Bay, she had a new best friend, Maggy, and a growing circle of friends she liked and trusted. A circle that now included Leah.

Then the fragile contentment that permeated her life dissolved, disappeared in an instant, the afternoon Cameron Wallace showed up to pick up his wife, Leah.

Abby closed her eyes and winced. Even now, years later, it still hurt to remember what an impact he'd made.

She walked to the kitchen table, picked up the cups, and headed for the sink. She dumped the remnants from her teacup into the sink and refilled her cup with cold water. She hated tea. Seldom drank the vile stuff. Yet somehow, this morning, she'd craved it. *A cup of tea soothes all ills.* Had her grandmother said that? Not her mother—that's for sure.

Cup in hand, Abby sat down at the table and heaved a deep sigh. As she sipped the cool water, his face swarm before her eyes. *Of all men to choose from, why had she fallen for him. Cameron. Leah's Cameron.*

She even loved his name. It suited him. Strong, upright, dependable, honest. Everything Nick wasn't. After meeting Cameron, she'd finally accepted that she'd never loved Nick. Not like this. Not with a hunger that seared her gut with longing. A hunger that never went away.

He'd come into the shop one afternoon. And, in that second, Abby had stopped breathing and just stared. While modelling, Abby had met many good-looking men. Nick was handsome. Brad Pitt handsome. But this man...he was drop-dead gorgeous! A vibrant, giant of a man with laugh lines radiating from large emerald eyes fringed with black, spiky lashes, he was tall and muscular, with a body that belonged in an underwear ad. His wavy hair, a rich mahogany colour, was short at the back, but long on top. A few curls dropped onto his broad forehead.

As he pushed his hair off his face his hands caught Abby's eye. Large hands. Work-calloused hands. Hands that made her squirm inside. Then he smiled and a large dimple creased his right cheek. In that moment, Abby knew he was trouble. And she'd been right.

As if it were yesterday, she could still feel the impact of that smile when he'd grinned, offered his hand, and asked for Leah, his wife. In horror, Abby had realized that the dreamy man was taken, belonged to lovely Leah, her new friend. Another piece of Abby's heart broke in that moment, and it was all she could do to gesture toward the backroom where Leah was quilting.

She'd pasted a smile on her face as they walked past her arm in arm, his large body bent protectively around his beaming wife. Even a blind person could see the love they shared, the love that excluded everyone else. Shattered, drained of all feeling, Abby had watched them leave, her eyes filled with longing.

ABBY'S STORY: BETRAYED BY LOVE

In the last few years, she'd tried to be his friend…and Leah's too. And suffered every time she saw him with Leah. Time after time, she berated herself for being a fool. Tried…and failed to deny her feelings and find someone else. Since meeting Cameron, she hadn't dated. Not once. What was the point? None of the men appealed to her. They weren't *him*.

Knowing he adored his wife, she'd hidden her pain. She thought she'd been so smart. So clever. Such a silent martyr to love.

Until last night. For a few brief moments she'd had him. All to herself. Now he hated her. As she hated herself.

Abby groaned as she remembered his words from last night. She hadn't fooled him one bit. He'd seen her…knew she watched his every move. He'd said she devoured him with her eyes. And sadly, it was true. When her chance came, she'd taken it…and him…with no thought for the consequences——or for Leah.

Well, no tears could undo the damage she'd done. Crying wouldn't help. Never did.

Life would go on. She'd open up the shop each morning, close it each night. Her days would be the same, even though she was changed forever. She'd lost his friendship. Something she'd always treasured. A sob bubbled in her throat, but she held it down. She didn't deserve the luxury of tears. Never again would she enjoy his laughter. Or share his pain. That was over. And she had nobody to blame but herself.

She'd been selfish…and a fool. Now, she'd have to deal with the loss of Cameron in her life as she'd dealt with Nick's treachery. One day at a time. Smiling on the outside. Hiding her hurt from the world. She could do it. She'd done it before. But, this time…the pain was deeper, sharper…more visceral. Abby bit down hard on her lip, drawing blood. She turned and padded to her room to get dressed. Time to get on with her day.

Chapter Three

Two years later…

On Monday morning, Abby opened the door to Maggy's tea room and walked inside, the heavenly smell of freshly baked bread reminding her that she hadn't eaten much this morning. She walked across the crowded room, smiled at several people she knew, then stepped into the office at the back.

"You're late. We started without you." Maggy bit into her muffin without the slightest bit of repentance in her eyes.

"I know, I know," Abby sighed, rolling her eyes with dramatic flare. "It's five after eight. So sue me. Since we started these weekly meetings last year, Libby's been late five times and you, Maggy, have been late too many times to count."

"I was only late when Sasha had the chicken pox last spring and when Rayce hauled me back to bed once or twice," Libby teased. "So, that doesn't count."

Maggy wiped her hands on a napkin. "I'd like to see you manage to be here by eight while breast-feeding twins and dealing with a teenager overdosing on hormones. Not to mention a clingy eight-year old and a growly bear of a man who loses a sock every morning."

Don't I wish! Abby hid behind a careless smile. Her wide mouth curved sardonically, her azure eyes smiled with good humour but, inside, she felt raw and lonely.

"Why don't we start while Abby gets her coffee and muffin," Libby suggested, her light blue eyes already on the agenda in front of her.

"You know, Libby, it's scary how organized you are. You're wasting your time running a flower shop in a little backwater like Howard's Bay," Abby told the tiny blonde. "You should be running Cornell Industries instead of your father."

Libby's mouth thinned to a tight line. "Don't remind me. He's still bugging me to come back to work for him."

"Boy, that man has gall," Maggy muttered. "I mean, after fighting you and Rayce for custody of Sasha—and losing—you'd think he'd give up and get on with his life."

"Not Dad," Libby said grimly. "After Mom divorced him and married Raphael Lafortunata, he pestered her for months to come back home. Raphael finally had to have a word with him."

"Oh, dear, that must have been some word." Maggy chuckled. "Raphael is not a man to cross. He's a dead ringer for Donald Trump in more ways than one. He has so much money, it's almost obscene."

"He also has sexy bedroom eyes," Abby said, arching her brows.

Libby giggled. "I don't know what he has, but Mom is lapping it up like a cat with cream. She positively purrs whenever he's near. I must say it's a little hard to get used to—the thought of Mom and Raphael—in bed. Mom always seemed so cool and remote."

"Not any longer." Maggy's eyes twinkled as she said, "I caught them in my kitchen last Christmas when they came to our party. It was kind of cute."

"Dad's furious," Libby said. She grinned and added, "He told me she's acting like a randy teenager."

"Did you tell your mother?" Abby asked.

"No. But the next day, I hauled Mom off to a lingerie store and made her spend a fortune. We had a ball."

"Serves your father right," Abby said. "If he had paid half the attention to your mother that he did to all his *secretaries* over the years, they'd still be married."

"But then I wouldn't have Sasha," Libby said softly, referring to her seven-year old half-sister. "When Kristi died and made me Sasha's guardian, it changed my life for the better. If not for Sasha, I wouldn't have quit working for Dad and wouldn't have moved here. I wouldn't have opened my flower shop." She looked at her two friends and smiled. "I wouldn't have you two for partners, and I wouldn't be married to Rayce. So really, it's all Dad's fault."

"True," Maggy said, her light green eyes glittering for a moment.

"Maggy! Don't you dare go all weepy on us! Oh dear God," Abby muttered, "you're not pregnant again—are you?"

"Bite your tongue," Maggy laughed.

Abby drained her cup and poured herself another coffee. "Let's get this meeting started. I've got a killer of a day ahead."

For the next forty-five minutes, they discussed their building tax account, the possibility of repaving the parking lot, the need to upgrade their air conditioning system—all the myriad of details involved in the joint ownership of the old Victorian building that housed their shops.

Abby listened with one ear, but this morning, her mind wandered. She was so lucky to have these two for friends. If not for them, she would have cracked several times in the last two years…when Leah died….when Cameron left for Saudi Arabia.

When Libby started to discuss their tax situation, Abby tuned back in. The woman was a whizz with numbers. Although, to look at her it didn't seem likely. Petite, but lushly curved, with a wide-eyed innocence in her blue eyes that denied the razor-sharp brain beneath her curly blond head, Libby was a woman no one took for granted. At least, not twice. She was raising Sasha, the child of one of her father's many mistresses, with Rayce, her tall, handsome banker with a killer smile. Libby and Rayce had had a rough time of it before they finally married, but now were ecstatically happy.

Maggy lifted the coffee pot and raised her brows at Abby to see if she wanted more.

Abby shook her head. She'd had too much caffeine already this morning, even for her. She watched as Maggy absently tucked a long auburn strand behind her ear and retied the pale lilac ribbon holding back her curly hair.

What I wouldn't give for just a bit of Maggy's curl in my own straight mop, Abby mused for the umpteenth time. Maggy's hair was long and curly, a fiery red with gold highlights. Her face was creamy smooth with pale auburn brows, a straight nose, and a strong jaw. She was tall and lush, reminiscent of Maureen O'Hara in her prime, her body curving and flowing even when she was still.

Her partners were strikingly different, yet both were vividly beautiful in their own way.

"Well, I think that's all," Libby said, as she placed her agenda into the file she kept of their meetings. Though the youngest of the three, Libby's cool head for business had made her the unspoken leader in their partnership.

"Did your father finally sign the papers for Sasha's trust fund?" Maggy asked as she tidied the cups onto a tray.

"Friday." Libby scowled. "But it took some arm-twisting before he picked up a pen. Damn—that man is something else."

"Well, it's done," Abby told her. "And Sasha's where she belongs, with you and Rayce. Where is that gorgeous husband of yours anyway? I thought he was starting his holidays today."

"Tomorrow. He had a last minute meeting to take care of first. Apparently, a film company is making a movie in North Bay and they want to open an account at Rayce's bank. The director, some guy named Nick Van-something-or-other insisted he'd only deal with the manager. You know the type."

Abby stilled. *Nick...her Nick? Couldn't be! Though, come to think of it, she'd read somewhere that he'd stopped modelling and was doing something in movies. But...a director? That sounded like way too much work for her ex-husband.*

"Would his name be Nick Vanopoulos?" Abby asked sharply, dreading the answer.

"That's it!" Libby said. "Do you know him?"

"Too well," Abby muttered. "He's my ex-husband."

Maggy and Libby stared in wide-eyed wonder. Abby had shared few details of her marriage or divorce, so both were beyond curious to know more.

Abby read the avid interest in their eyes and sighed. "Close your mouths ladies. You're catching flies."

Both women drilled her with knowing eyes, demanding that she give it all up.

Abby rolled her eyes, then said dryly, "So...here's the way it was. We were both models...I met him at a catalogue shoot—big surprise. He was drop-dead gorgeous with a body that wouldn't stop and a mouth to match. Before I knew it, we were married and in bed—in that order. I think if I'd slept with him first, we never would have gotten married." She sighed dramatically and Libby giggled.

"The first year it was hectic but good. Our careers took off, we bought a terrific apartment, had lots of money, jetted all over the world. But we were seldom together. Then he began to lose interest and so did I. Mind you, when I caught him in our bed with a model friend of mine, it hurt—a lot more than I expected. Stubborn pride I guess. I can be very possessive.

"Anyway, I screwed him one last time in the divorce court and I haven't seen him since. Though he still sends me white roses on my birthday."

"Maybe he'll call when he arrives here next week," Libby said. "He told Rayce he'll be here for awhile, till the middle of August."

"Maybe," Abby agreed, but her eyes were cool.

"Can we change the subject for a minute?" Maggy asked.

Something in Maggy's voice…a hesitation…caught Abby's attention. She knew that tone.

"Ross and I are having a small party next week at our house. A barbeque. We were planning to have one for our second anniversary last month, but the twins got that bad flu bug, so we never did get around to it. Will you both come?"

"Great!" Libby beamed. "We were going to take a week's holiday but we've put it off for few weeks. So, we'll be available."

"What about the shop?" Maggy asked. "And where are you going?"

"Delia's going to take over so we can take Sasha to Tom's cottage for a week."

A flush slowly crept up Maggy's smooth neck and she wet her mouth nervously before saying, "What about you, Abby? Can you come?"

Abby saw the flush and knew something was up. "I suppose," she answered, her eyes sharp.

"You'll never guess who's going to be at our party," Maggy said to Libby.

Dread burned in Abby's stomach, dread mixed with foolish hope.

"Who?" Libby asked as she stood and shook out the wrinkles in her sundress.

"Cameron Wallace." Maggy spoke quickly, her cheeks beet-red. "He's back from Saudi Arabia. He called Ross last night from Toronto to say he should be in North Bay this morning."

Abby froze. Her eyes…her hands…her breath. With Maggy and Libby watching so carefully, she didn't so much as blink. Not for a moment would she let anyone see what it cost her to keep from howling like a fool. *He was finally coming home. She didn't know whether to laugh or cry.*

Abby smiled cooly, the kind of smile that card sharks wear when they're on a roll. "Is he just here for a visit…or back to stay?" She cringed inside as soon as the words were out. She hadn't wanted to ask about him at all. But couldn't help herself.

Maggy smiled in relief at how calm Abby sounded. She knew just how close Abby had come to a total breakdown when Cameron left town after Leah's funeral and how hard she'd struggled to get on with her life. But, by the same token, Maggy also knew that Abby had never forgotten Cameron—nor he her.

"In his last letter he mentioned that the shopping mall he was building in Riyadh was nearly completed, but apparently the prince wants another one built in Jedda. Cameron said he wasn't sure if he wanted to stay there for another two years or come back home. I guess he made up his mind."

"I guess," Abby murmured. She stood and walked rigidly to the door. "See you later," she said quietly and left without her customary smile or cheery wave.

Libby sighed and frowned. "Do you think she still loves him?"

"Without a doubt," Maggy answered bluntly. "I probably shouldn't have told her that way, but I didn't want him to show up out of the blue without her knowing he was back."

"Do you think he'll come to see her?" Libby's blue eyes narrowed. "He was so vicious to her at Leah's funeral. I was so afraid he would throw her out of the funeral home."

"I was too," Maggy agreed with a shudder. "But Abby is a classy lady and handled it well. She was adamant she wanted to say 'good-bye' to Leah, so he really didn't have much choice."

"He avoided her like the plague though. Did you notice?"

"Yes. And so did she."

"You'd think that after all this time she'd forget about him and move on."

"Would you—forget Rayce, that is?" A hint of a smile curved Maggy's full lips.

When the younger woman smiled and shook her head, Maggy nodded. "Neither could I forget Ross. When he left me after I told him I was pregnant, I wanted to forget him—believe me. After I bashed him silly of course. But I couldn't do either. The heart has its reasons," she murmured softly.

"What did you say?"

Maggy grinned self-consciously. "It was something I read, that stuck with me when I was at my lowest. I was mad at myself because I couldn't get Ross out of my mind. Then I read a quote in a magazine that made a terrible kind of sense. Something like…'the heart has its reasons which only reason understands.'

"That's the way it is for Abby too, I'm afraid. She couldn't stop loving him when Leah was alive, I doubt if she can now." Maggy shook her head sadly.

"I hope Cameron has come to terms with all that happened between him and Abby. I don't think she can take much more."

Libby frowned. "She didn't act too upset."

"Don't you kid yourself," Maggy snorted. "That was all an act."

"Oh dear." Libby shook her head and added softly, "I have a feeling Abby's in for a rough time. I don't think Cameron feels the same way she does. Mind you, I don't know him that well, but I saw him at Leah's funeral. The man was nearly out of his mind with grief. He didn't seem like a man in love with someone else."

Maggy shook her head. "I'm not so sure of that. In the eighteen months that he's been away, he's written to Ross and I every second week. Regular as clockwork. He seemed desperate for news of home, so I got him a subscription for the local paper and I kept him up to date on everyone here. For the first few months, I didn't make any mention of Abby. Then he asked about her in one of his letters. Wanted to know if she was well, or something like that. After that, every letter had a question about Abby. Sometimes several."

"I think he was always attracted to her," Maggy mused. "I know he loved his wife. But, there was always *something* between him and Abby. Something dangerous. He'd watch her, stalk her with his eyes. I saw it many times. Yet he loved his wife, no doubt about it."

Maggy pushed a lock of hair out of her eyes. "If it's possibly to love two women at once, I think that man did. I think it tormented him terribly to feel that way about both of them. Leah was so sick and needed him, but his feelings for Abby were growing stronger. It must have been a living hell for him. God, what a mess!"

"And now he's coming home." Libby smiled grimly. "Should make for an interesting party."

Maggy groaned. "That's what I'm afraid of."

As if the world had not just shifted on its axis, Abby opened up her shop, prepared the cash register, set up a new display of quilts in her front window, and dealt with a steady stream of customers. All morning long, she pasted a frozen smile on her face and did what needed to be done. Not once did she think about Cameron. She didn't dare.

Around one she took her lunch break and closed herself in her office. She sat down in the creaky chair that matched her ancient rolled-topped desk and closed her weary eyes. And saw his face as he'd looked the last time she'd seen him...wild-eyed with grief, his cheeks hollow and pale, his jaw clenched with fury, adamant that she had no business being at his wife's funeral.

Abby nearly wept at the memory, but held the tears in check with a fierce will. Tears were a luxury she no longer allowed herself.

So, he was coming home. *Big goddamned deal!* she thought bitterly. Well, he was in for one hell of a shock. The Abby who had followed his every move with calf-like devotion was gone. There'd be no scenes of remorse or anguish, no abject apologies from her!

She'd made her peace with Leah——long ago——months before she died. At that thought, Abby winced. She didn't want to go *there*. Didn't want to remember the day Leah had come to Abby's shop. But she couldn't help it. That memory often haunted her at strange moments. Haunted her, and yet filled her with a strange kind of peace.

It had been bitterly cold——even for the end of January. Abby had just come in from checking on Maggy in the tea room. She'd been worried about Maggy that day. And for good reason——the twins were born that night.

Leah had come in alone, a pale, walking skeleton with pain-tinged eyes. Abby had been appalled to see her condition. And afraid to look her in the eye.

In a husky voice drenched with exhaustion, Leah had shook off Abby's attempts to get her a seat. Her nurse had dropped her off for a few minutes, she'd said. She wouldn't be long, but there was something she had to say to Abby.

Her heart filled with dread, Abby had led Cameron's wife into the privacy of her small office. Without a word being spoken, Abby had realized that Leah knew!

It was the worst ten minutes of Abby's life. In a halting, breathless voice Leah told Abby she was dying. No surprise to either.

'*Cameron refuses to face it. But we both know the end is near. It's tearing him apart...he won't eat...can't rest. He's constantly trying to find some way to help me—when there's nothing more he can do.*'

Leah paused then, her pain-dulled eyes worn and exhausted. '*There's something I want you to do for me, Abby.*'

Abby winced, *afraid of the words to come.*

'I want you to...look after him...when I'm gone. He'll be so lost...so alone. I don't want him to suffer, Abby. I love him so dearly. As do you—I suspect.'

Abby was overcome by shame at the sad knowledge in Leah's eyes.

'I don't blame you.' Leah smiled wistfully. *'Cameron's a wonderful man. In other circumstances...in another time, I would fight you like mad for him. But I won't—not now. He's been a wonderful husband to me. He'll be the same for the woman who comes after I'm gone. I hope it's you, Abby. He needs to be loved so desperately. Give him the children I couldn't—the children he wants with a passion. And love him—love him the way he deserves.'*

Leah's strength was waning, but she waved away Abby's concern and continued. *'Let him remember me, though. Let him enjoy his memories of our years together. Don't make him hide them away from you.'*

Abby finally found the courage to speak. *'It's you Cameron loves,'* she whispered brokenly. *'Only you. I don't mean anything to him.'*

'Abby please, don't.' Leah sighed wearily, a withering look in her eyes. *'I wish that were true—but it's not. And we both know it. Oh...I know he would never have left me—he's not that kind of man. But he longs for you in a place I can't reach. I've seen the desire in his eyes when he watches you. It hurts—more than I care to admit.'*

For the first time Leah's eyes filled with tears. *'Whenever we were at a party and he saw you, he always made love to me afterward with a desperate kind of need I couldn't satisfy—no matter how hard I tried.'*

Abby winced and looked away. Leah's pain was too raw, too real.

Leah sighed and stood on shaky legs. *'I know there's something between you, Abby. I may be dying, but I'm not a fool.'*

When Abby tried to interrupt, Leah held her off. *'Stop right there, Abby. No lies, please. I promised myself I wouldn't make a scene. And I won't.'* Her voice was breathy. Even speaking was taking its toll. *'Don't get me wrong. I'm no saint. If I weren't dying, we wouldn't be having this conversation.'* She faltered then, as if the words were too painful to speak. In a voice barely above a whisper she added, *'It's just...I love him more than I...envy you. So, remember what I asked, Abby, and look after him when I'm gone. You owe me that much at least.'*

The next time Abby saw Leah, she was in her coffin, free from pain at last. That was the last time she'd seen Cameron as well. He'd left for Saudi Arabia the next day.

ABBY'S STORY: BETRAYED BY LOVE

By four o'clock, Abby was exhausted. With the business day winding down, she sent her assistant, Delia, home early and handled the remaining customers herself. For the next hour, she cut fabric, wrote up an order for a quilted runner and matching place mats, and reluctantly sold a vest to a lady who would never be able to get into it. No matter how hard she tried. Then, following her usual routine, Abby spent twenty minutes moving from bin to bin straightening the various remnants that had been picked over that day.

When she'd first opened up shop, Abby hadn't bothered with display bins. She'd stacked all her fabrics horizontally on a solid display unit that ran the full length of the wall beside the entrance. But it hadn't taken her long to realize that her customers loved a bargain, real or imagined, so she'd had a local carpenter make four long rectangular bins that matched the wall unit, triangular cash station, and huge cutting table. The varnished pine he'd used to make her bins added a homey feeling that blended well with the various handmade fabric fans, toppers, swags, and swatches of fabric lengths that Abby displayed around the room.

At closing time, Abby headed to the front door to lock up. She had just closed the turquoise linen drapes that flanked one of the front windows when the overhead bell pealed and Nick Vanopoulos walked through the door, shooting her the lazy grin that had made him a fortune.

Abby's jaw dropped. After their bitter divorce, she'd never expected to see him again. Then she grinned. She couldn't help it. He might be a jerk, but Nick Vanopoulos had a lethal smile. Abby crossed her arms under her breasts and stared at him unwaveringly, a cool sardonic glint in her eyes to match her crooked smile. Without her knowing, her red lace bra peeked flirtatiously in the gap of her blouse.

But Nick noticed. His chocolate brown eyes narrowed with sudden interest. Abby had such *perky* breasts. Then he noticed the frost in her eyes and his ardour cooled.

"You're not going to…throw something at me?" he asked sheepishly. Just in case, he kept his distance.

Abby laughed, a throaty laugh, filled with genuine humour. "No, Nick, my throwing days are over." She grinned openly at him, eyeing him appreciatively. Nick was good-looking eye candy.

He was dressed for the balmy summer day in crisp tan shorts and a white and tan collarless shirt. Without being told, Abby knew the simple outfit cost a mint. Nick always did have expensive taste in clothes. He wore handmade leather sandals on his long, elegant feet and carried a pair of designer sunglasses in one hand. The epitome of the well-dressed man about town. Nothing new there.

"So, Nick...what brings you to Howard's Bay? Did you turn north on Yonge Street instead of south?"

Nick frowned. He'd expected ranting and raving...maybe the odd dish thrown. But he hadn't expected the smile on Abby's face or his reaction to her elegant beauty. Abby had been a knockout when they'd married, but now, with maturity giving her face a mysterious allure, she was positively breathtaking.

Nick cleared his throat, at a loss for words—a rare occurrence in his thirty-eight years. He cleared his throat again and said, "Actually, I'm making a movie in North Bay. One of those voyageur epics—you know. Trappers and Indians and conflict in the wild north. I'm here for the next month, so, I thought I'd look you up and say 'hello.' For old-times sake."

Nick's eyes narrowed as he watched the lack of expression in her startling blue eyes. He frowned, unsure of himself again. He didn't like that feeling. Where women were concerned, Nick liked to be in the driver's seat.

"You...a director?" Abby laughed softly. "Somehow, that just doesn't compute."

Nick bristled at the insolence in her eyes. Abby had changed over the years he realized. She was more centred...more controlled...almost aloof. He wasn't sure if he liked that or not—but Mr. Happy had been ready from the moment he saw her.

"I went to Monte Carlo—after the divorce," he said, his eyes raking hers for reaction. When he got none, he added brusquely, "A pal of mine, a director in Quebec, lost to me big time at the tables. We made a deal. Instead of paying me off, he took me on as assistant director of his new film and gave me a chance to break into the business. We worked together for a few years, and then I branched out on my own. This is my third feature film. Turns out I've got kind of a knack."

"What happened to the modelling?"

He laughed, a careful, self-deprecating laugh that was just a shade too practiced. "I got too old—too fast. Time to move on."

"And...Celine?" Abby had to ask, though her smile never faltered.

Nick flushed at her mocking tone. "Oh...I married her. After the divorce, I mean."

"And where is she now—while you're here talking to me?" Abby drawled insolently.

"At home in Toronto…with the kid." Nick's face was very flushed now, his full mouth tight.

"*You* have a child?" Abby laughed incredulously. "Oh that poor kid!"

"Ashley's the best thing that's ever happened to me," he snapped.

Abby's jeering smile slowly died. As strange as it seemed, Nick appeared to be telling the truth. His anger seemed genuine. "Do you have a picture?" she asked.

In seconds Nick Vanopoulos, the king of the bed hoppers, was whipping out a wallet filled with pictures of an adorable baby with chocolate eyes and ringlets of fine black hair.

"She's just turned fifteen months old," he gushed to Abby. "She walked at ten months and already talks a blue streak."

A pang she couldn't repress twisted Abby's heart. This could have been *her* child. "You must miss her. She's absolutely adorable, Nick." Abby smiled gently, her eyes searching Nick's face as he talked about his child. She almost didn't recognize this side of Nick.

"That's the worst part about this business. I miss her too damn much," Nick growled. "But I see her every weekend when I go home."

"And Celine…how is she?" Abby asked the question only out of courtesy. She didn't give a damn about the bitch.

"The same." Nick shrugged, a knowing glint in his eye. "We understand each other. Celine goes her way. I go my way. It works for us."

Abby's smile cooled. *If he thought his way was back in her bed—he could think again!* "How very lucky for you, Nick. You two deserve each other." There was no mistaking the contempt in her eyes or her voice.

"Now Abby," he smiled, switching on the deadly charm he'd used on so many. "Is that any way to talk to your husband?"

"Ex," she insisted tartly. "And that's the way it's going to stay."

Nick smiled, shaking his head. "You'll never change, Abby. One mistake and you never let a guy forget it. I was hoping that we could be friends again. We were very good friends, before we got married."

The man was a pig and wouldn't change. But perhaps it was time to forget the past and move on. After all, he was right. They had been friends once upon a time—before they'd messed things up by getting married. And, when he wasn't trying to get in her pants, he could be very amusing.

"One mistake, Nick? One? If you really want to be friends again, let's try a little honesty for a change."

Nick shrugged, pleased that she seemed less hostile. He didn't mistake it for anything but what it was...a chance to renew an old friendship. He grinned, then put an arm around her shoulder, "Well Abby, when you get right down to it, one or one hundred—does it really make a difference?"

His outrageous statement was stated with such charm, such confidence, Abby couldn't help it. She laughed uproariously for the first time in ages.

"Oh Nick," she muttered when she caught her breath at last, "you might be a bastard, but you're never boring."

Nick flashed the old grin she'd once found so captivating. "Speaking of changing, Ab, I have to admit this is the last place I expected to find Abby Fulton, catalogue queen." He glanced around the shop as he spoke, his raised eyebrows speaking volumes.

Abby smiled serenely, not in the least offended. "That's just the point, Nick. This is the new me, small-town business lady and proud of it. My interest in modelling is long gone. I got older and so did the whole glamour scene. I don't miss it in the least. I love having my own business, being my own boss."

"But...a shopkeeper. Come on, Abby. That's a long way from super model."

Abby bristled at the implied put-down, then slowly relaxed. "First of all, I was never a super model and we both know it. But I am a shopkeeper—complete with apron and broom. I'm home at six each night, I can walk to work each day if I choose, and a new wrinkle in the mirror isn't a big deal any more. Being twenty-five and trying to look seventeen is very tiring, Nick. I'm glad to be out of it."

Nick flushed at her steady, knowing gaze, then grinned lazily. "You really mean it, don't you, babe," he murmured softly. "So...how about the grand tour?"

Abby shook her head and laughed. "Sure, why not? It'll take all of two minutes." She grabbed Nick by the arm and added, with just a touch of theatrics, "Welcome to 'The Scrap Bag.' We offer a wide range of fabrics to suit the most ambitious of sewers and everything a quilter needs to create a work of art. I can sell you thread, needles, trim, lace—you name it. We aim to please."

Nick laughed out loud. "What kind of a name is 'The Scrap Bag?' Sounds kind of grungy."

Abby smiled reprovingly. "Most quilters keep a bag of interesting scraps, pieces of odd and ends, that are still choice pieces of material—hence the name," she explained. "The shop started out as a fabric centre but sort of evolved into what you see today. A group of quilters took over my backroom, then asked for a place to display their work. The ladies are truly gifted. They make wonderful handmade quilts, table runners, purses, vests—all kind of incredibly beautiful craft items. They make them; I sell them. In the summer, the tourists just eat up my stock."

Nick looked around and noticed, for the first time, a large display area on the far wall filled with colourful quilted items and shelves of handmade quilts. He nodded slowly. "This is good, Abby. Different from what I'd ever expected from you, but good."

"Oh, thank you—I think," Abby teased, just a hint of dryness in her voice.

"Ah…come on, Abby—let's be honest here. When we were married, you never even owned a quilt. When Sue Leblanc mentioned you'd opened a shop outside of North Bay, I just assumed it was a dress boutique of some sort. You were always a clothes horse."

"People change," Abby said, the laughter draining out of her eyes. "When I moved from Toronto I was ready to turn a corner in my life, and I did."

"Yah, one hundred and eighty degrees!" Nick snorted.

"I'm happy." Abby smiled quietly. "That's all that counts."

Nick stared at her intently for a long telling moment, then grinned and nodded his head. "You're right, babe. That's all that counts. So, how about having dinner with me—for old-times sake." His dark eyes watched hers, waiting her response. While he'd sought her out with a faint hope of a tumble or two, he realized now that wouldn't happen. She'd moved on. But Abby had always been good fun, always good for a few laughs. Strangely enough, that suited him just fine.

"Dinner? Sure…why not," Abby agreed slowly. "When?"

"Tomorrow night?"

Abby paused, then nodded. In minutes they'd agreed to meet at a quiet Italian restaurant Abby liked at the end of Main Street in North Bay.

Then, with a breezy brush of her lips, he was gone.

Abby locked up and headed outside to her car. She was smiling as she did so. And there was a skip in her step as she ambled down the steps. A dinner date! Who would have thought that her first night out in months would be with her ex? It would be fun, she knew. Good wine, good food, good company. Without the worry that he'd expect anything more.

And as for Cameron Wallace, well, he could go to hell!

Chapter Four

Cameron opened the door of his new home and stepped inside the cool foyer. When he'd called Ross from Saudi Arabia and mentioned he needed to find an apartment, Ross had offered the condo he owned in North Bay. The rent was expensive, but with the enormous salary he'd saved while in Riyadh, money was not Cameron's major concern. At least, not for a while.

Dropping his bags beside a suede couch in the living area, he stretched wearily and kicked off his shoes. God it was good to be home. After eighteen months of dry, sandy desert it was good to be back where he belonged.

He whistled softly as he glanced around the tasteful condo. Furnished in shades of grey and navy, it was spaciously modern, right down to the slate-trimmed fireplace. *Not bad,* he thought. *At least I'm getting my money's worth.*

He walked over to the patio door and opened it, a warm summer breeze from Lake Nipissing lifting his hair. He breathed deeply. Even the air smelt cleaner...fresher here at home. Riyadh was hectic and challenging, but it was hot, dusty, and dry. Dry in more ways than one. Finally he could have a cold beer wherever and whenever he wanted.

Picking up his luggage, he headed into the larger bedroom. At the entrance he stopped dead in his tracks. "God lord," he muttered, looking around in dismay. The room was elegant and fussy but definitely not to his taste. The dressers, four-poster bed, and matching side tables seemed to be genuine antiques. Perfect for some maiden aunt's bedroom. But not his. He tried to picture Ross sleeping in that short bed and shook his head.

At least the room had a large walk-in closet. After the small, monk-like room he'd lived in for so long, this room was quite luxurious. And, except for the bed, would do.

With the methodical precision that was second nature to him now, Cameron threw his bags on the bed and began to unpack. He'd learned over the long, gruelling months since Leah's death to take life one task at a time, one day at a time. He'd learned to eat—when he wasn't hungry, and sleep—when he wasn't tired. Over time he'd built a workable daily routine, and slogging through each day, he'd managed to hold off a mental breakdown. Something he'd very much feared might happen. He'd survived by working like a bull—long strenuous hours supervising his men—or working right beside them when his memories became too much.

At night, he'd read voraciously—anything he could find—or listened to music and wrote in his Journal. Early on, when his mind was refusing to function, he'd started his Journal as a way of recording details he was afraid he might forget. Gradually his writing had become a source of pleasure—the only one he allowed himself. In the privacy of his own mind he could pour out the emotions he had to keep hidden by day.

Just a few weeks prior to the end of his contract, the prince had offered an extension. And a terrific bonus. He'd been tempted to accept, but instead, he'd had asked for a few days to think it through. Should he stay or go home? He didn't know what he wanted.

While sitting at his desk later that night, he'd been glancing through his Journal when something caught his eye. Something that had him sitting up straight. Page after page, he'd written about Abby. *What was she doing? Was she seeing someone? Did she hate him for the way he had treated her? Would she ever forgive him?*

That's when it came to him. It was time to go home. Time to face Abby and deal with the past. Once that decision was made, he'd been impatient to leave.

From then on she'd haunted him by day and tormented him at night. Did he love her? He honestly didn't know. He was obsessed by her, he knew that much. He wanted her desperately. But was very much afraid it was too late.

In all the time he'd been gone, he'd never dated any of the few unattached women in the compound where he stayed. Never felt the slightest urge to hold one in his arms.

Not that he was a saint. Far from it. At first, he'd been too torn up by Leah's death. Too filled with remorse and shameful despair. In those first few months he'd barely allowed himself to think about Leah—let alone another woman.

But one night, about six months into his contract in Riyadh, Abby slipped unbidden into his dreams, tempting him with her sultry lips and knowing hands. He'd woken with a start, his body drenched with sweat and the sticky evidence of a violent release.

Appalled by the betrayal of his body, he'd cursed hotly in the darkened room. Called himself every scumbag name in the book. After all these months, nothing had changed! He was still hung up on *her*.

He'd tried, God how he'd tried! Like a runaway kid, he'd travelled halfway round the world to forget the past. And, in the process, worked himself into a state of near exhaustion. Each day in Riyadh, he worked, ate, and slept, driving himself like a demented robot. His men kept away from him, called him the slave-driver behind his back. But over time, they'd grudgingly acknowledged that he worked harder than any two of them. They weren't to know he worked like a madman to keep his nightmares at bay.

When the dreams of Abby became more frequent, they upset him more than he cared to admit. But, in a strange way, the dreams acted like a catalyst, waking his emotions, forcing him to feel again. After months of beating himself up with guilt, he finally allowed himself to think about Leah. Allowed himself to remember her gentle laughter. Slowly, he began to relive cherished moments with his wife and with each memory came a small measure of peace.

But when images of Abby drifted through his mind, he'd punish himself with long hours of physical work. Anything to forget her, forget what he'd done.

But nothing worked. Weeks later, after another heart-pounding erotic dream left him covered in his own juices, he took a good hard look in the mirror and didn't like what he saw. He looked old and haggard, haunted even.

That night was a turning point for Cameron. Facing that haunted man in the mirror, he'd realized it was time to let go of his grief, time to confront his mistakes.

After much soul-searching, he'd decided that changes were in order. Small changes maybe, but a start. First, no more swearing—not even when he was alone. Leah had detested that habit. He would do it for her—to honour her memory.

Second, like a judge reviewing a case, he forced himself to think about *that* night with Abby. Thought about it long and hard, relived it over and over until he could think about it clearly. Like the pieces of a long familiar puzzle he refit that night together moment by moment. And finally saw it for what it was. A mistake. A stupid mistake. Not Abby's fault, but his.

Over time, Cameron finally accepted Leah's death. Accepted the fact that he'd loved her and lost her, but would hold her in his heart forever. Eventually, his nightmares abated and he found a semblance of satisfaction in his work. And as weeks turned into months, he began to learn how to live with himself again. Though Abby haunted him still.

Throwing the empty suitcases on the floor, Cameron lay down on the bed. With his feet dangling over the edge, he grimaced and eased as far up the bed as possible. *Great!* he thought. *At least in Riyadh I fit into my old camp bed.* Though this bed was short and lumpy, it would have to do until he bought another. He turned on his side and looked at the phone. *Should he call her? Maybe just say hello? But what if she hung up on him? Then what would he do?*

He jumped up and walked out of the room. Better not take that chance. He'd see her soon enough at Maggy's party. That would be a safer place to meet for the first time. With so many people around, he wouldn't do something stupid. At least, he hoped not.

Picking up the phone, he decided instead to call Pete Reilly, his long-time foreman. Before Cameron left for Saudi Arabia, Pete had bought a half-interest in the business. During the last eighteen months, they'd talked often, so Cameron knew business was sluggish, but Pete had managed to keep it going without laying off any men.

"Cameron, you old dog. It's about goddamn time!"

Hearing his friend's voice hit Cameron hard. "I thought I'd let you know I'm finally home," he said, a wide smile splitting his face. They talked and joked for the next twenty minutes while Pete brought him up to date. When Cameron explained his tentative plans, Pete made it amply clear that he wanted Cameron to resume his position as head of the company. Cameron closed his eyes in relief and agreed without hesitation. He needed to be his own boss again.

"So, I'll see you in the office tomorrow," Cameron told him. "I'll even spring for dinner tomorrow night." Cameron hung up, grinning at Pete's avid acceptance. At six-four and two hundred and forty pounds, Pete never refused a meal.

Cameron was still smiling as he picked up his keys and headed out the door. Needed some fresh air, he told himself. Maybe pick up a bite of supper. But those were just excuses. Before long, he was out of the city, cruising down the highway toward Howard's Bay.

He hadn't made a conscious decision to go there, he just went. Twenty minutes later he pulled off the main road and headed for the small lakeside community named after the Howard family—Maggy Blake's first husband's family. As he drove along the familiar route, his heart started to beat faster. He was excited, like a kid coming home from summer camp. Not so surprising really. He'd lived in the small community for nearly three years. Shared a home with Leah in the small town. Built his new business there. Met Abby.

He turned onto the main street and drank in the familiar sights. The gazebo in the park was full of laughing teenagers, old men were sitting on a nearby bench enjoying the early evening breeze, and flowers bloomed in large pots everywhere. This was *home*, he realized. Not Canada, not Toronto, not North Bay, but *here*.

Though he told himself he was acting like a damned fool, he turned onto the street where Abby's shop was located and pulled over across from the 'Quilters' Corner' building. It stood alone on a small block with two vacant lots on its right. He turned off the rental and sat there, fixated on the old-fashioned brick building. Since it was after six, the covered wooden walkway that connected all three shops was empty. But it was full of memories for Cameron.

His eyes narrowed as he checked the walkway for wear. And found none. His company had built the covered walkway, built it to last. And he, himself, had done much of the renovations to Libby's flower shop. Working there had helped keep him sane in the weeks before Leah's death.

His eyes drifted toward the end shop and lingered. It had been there, in Libby's shop, that he'd made the worst mistake of his life. Cameron groaned as memories of that night flooded his thoughts. *Was it too late to rectify the past and start over?* He honestly didn't know. But one thing was clear. He had to see Abby again, or that night would haunt him for the rest of his life.

He started to open the car door, then stopped. *What if she wasn't at work? What if she'd already gone home?* It was late, the two end shops were closed, but there were still lights on in Abby's shop and two cars were parked out front.

Just then, the front door of Abby's shop opened, and a man came out. A tall, good-looking man with a smile on his face and a jaunty walk. Cameron frowned darkly. *What was that man doing in Abby's shop after closing? He wasn't a salesman—that's for sure. Not in those swanky clothes! Abby's boyfriend maybe?* That thought burned in his gut and Cameron bit back the curse on the edge of his tongue. For the first time in months he was tempted to swear.

His eyes bleak and hooded, Cameron watched the man drive away. Instantly, visions of Abby locked in the man's arms ripped through his brain and made him almost physically sick. He was jealous, he realized, jealous when he had no right. As his throat filled with a sour, acid taste his mouth tightened in disgust.

Then the lights in the shop went off.

His heart started to pound viciously in his chest. *She was coming out!* His mouth was dry and his hands were sweaty as Cameron waited impatiently for his first glimpse of Abby in eighteen months.

Dressed in a light green outfit, her tailored slacks and silk blouse suited her tall, lean frame. *She's lost weight,* he realized with a start. Her face, when she turned, was sharply angled, her cheekbones like carved alabaster in her narrow face. She seemed remotely aloof, with no smile on her full lips or in her blue eyes.

He wasn't sure what he wanted to do. Part of him wanted to get out of the car and run to her...pull her into his arms...beg her to forgive him for all the pain he'd caused. But uncertainty held him back. After eighteen months would she even talk to him? Or would she turn her back on him, as he had done to her?

Trapped by indecision, he watched as Abby stepped into her car and drove toward him. Frozen inside his rental, Cameron was sure she would spot him and look away. Instead, she drove past without a glance. Not sure if he was relieved or disappointed, Cameron sighed wearily and leaned his head back against the seat. He stayed that way for a very long time.

Abby walked into the small family restaurant and noticed Nick immediately. Seated in a secluded booth at the back, he was flirting with a young waitress. Abby grinned sardonically as she watched Nick in action. He would never change. Thank God she wasn't married to the man any longer!

As she waited for the owner to seat her, Abby smiled at a waitress she knew. Well-known for its excellent Italian dishes, smart decor, and friendly service, the restaurant was one of the busiest places around.

Abby straightened the halter neck of her dress. In a shade of blue that matched her azure eyes, the dress was one of her favourites. Though absurdly expensive, she had splurged on the flowing silk dress because it was a perfect match for a pair of earrings Maggy had given her. And, with its form-fitting bodice and full skirt, it enhanced her long, willow body and made her feel good. She wore the dress, her version of female armour, on those special occasions when she needed a touch of the *wow* factor. Like tonight. The white leather pumps on her slim feet and the matching clutch bag she held under her arm provided the perfect finishing touches. She felt cool and elegant. Just the look she wanted.

Abby crossed the crowded room behind the genial owner, then smiled with genuine pleasure as he pulled out her chair. Finally she looked at Nick, and almost purred in satisfaction.

The man was positively drooling. *Hot damn!* All the extra care she'd taken had just paid off in spades! Let the bastard see what he'd tossed away so carelessly. While she wouldn't take the snake back even if he'd just won the lottery, it did wonders for her ego to see the dog-in-the-manger look on his face.

"My good *God* Abby! You look fantastic!"

"You think?" she murmured slyly. "Now aren't you just a little bit sorry you treated me so bad?"

Nick's dark eyes sobered. "Yes, I am. You have no idea."

He looked like he really meant it! Abby snorted derisively. "Now don't start getting all maudlin on me, Nick. That's just not your style."

Nick grinned, then chuckled. Nodding in agreement he said, "You're right Abby. It's not. But you sure are a sight." His smile widened as his eyes wandered her face. "How about some wine before we order?" he suggested. "Then tell me all about life in Howard's Bay."

Much to Abby's surprise, the wine and conversation flowed non-stop. Over Chicken Cacciatore and tart Caesar salad, they caught up on each others' lives as if they were very old friends.

Cameron walked into the restaurant in front of Pete Reilly. He was laughing at a joke Pete had just told, so he didn't spot Abby at first. Then he heard a rich, throaty laugh and chills rode up his spine. He knew that laugh.

Would recognize it anywhere. He scanned the restaurant and sure enough, Abby was in a back booth looking way too cozy beside the dark-haired guy from the night before. As he took in the intimate scene, heat flooded his face and Cameron had difficulty swallowing. Abby was leaning forward, her long fingers playing with a half-empty wine glass. Because she was seated facing into the room, Cameron had a clear view of her animated face and teasing smile. The smile that had haunted his dreams for far too long. Her blue dress was cut low, exposing the gentle swell of creamy breasts, her date's nose halfway down her cleavage!

Instantly enraged, Cameron wanted to pulverize something. He'd been so lonely, thought of nothing but her for long, empty months. But obviously, she hadn't missed him one little bit.

Gritting his teeth to stop himself from doing something stupid, Cameron followed Pete and their waitress to a table. But his eyes never left Abby's face.

Perhaps some of the violent emotion he was feeling charged the room and caught her attention. Because she looked up then and stilled, her wine glass frozen in mid-air. Across the room her blue eyes looked enormous against her pale face.

"Excuse me for a moment," Cameron said brusquely to Pete. "I see an old friend. I'll just be a moment."

As he walked stiffly across the room, Cameron knew it was a mistake, but he couldn't seem to help himself. His obsession to see her, to hear her husky voice was more powerful than reason. The room was like an empty tunnel as he closed the gap between them. No one else existed. All he saw was her.

Like a deer trapped in a spotlight, she watched his approach, her eyes never wavering from his.

"Hello, Abby. It's been...a long time."

Just hearing his voice again, Abby shuddered visibly. It was almost too much to bear. Why had he come home? Why now—when she could finally sleep at night without crying out for him?

A burning anger bubbled in the pit of her stomach. So, he finally came home. Big goddamned deal! Staring at her like a sad-faced puppy! Big green eyes...his dimple peeking out from one cheek! Well, that hound-dog look may have fooled her once, but no longer.

"Hello, Cameron," she said cooly. "Well, well, well. The prodigal returns. Had enough of that desert sand, did you? Or are you just passing through?"

Cameron winced inwardly at the cold, dismissive tone. She wasn't going to make this easy.

"You're looking well." Forcing himself to be more civil than he felt, he glanced at Abby's companion and said, "I'm Cameron Wallace. Abby and I are old friends."

Noting the hard smile and angry glint in the man's eyes, Nick smiled lazily, then decided to have some fun. "I'm Nick. Abby's...husband," he said smoothly. "It's nice to meet an old friend of my wife's."

Cameron reared as if struck by lightening, his eyes glazing over as he rocked on his feet.

Nick's eyes widened. The guy looked like he was going to pass out! Glancing at Abby to gauge her reaction, Nick read the storm clouds in her eyes. Something was very wrong here. Abby should have been shooting thunderbolts at his use of the word 'husband.' Instead, she seemed coldly pleased that this Cameron guy looked sucker-punched.

"I'm sorry to disturb your meal," Cameron said, his voice tight. "I just wanted to say hello."

Abby longed to vent the anger she'd held in for so long. But now was not the time or the place. Her narrowed eyes were those of a feral animal scenting prey. She wanted to pounce, needed to rip and tear, but instead pasted a frozen smile on her face. "You said what you had to say. Perhaps now you'll let us finish our meal."

Cameron blinked, then turned and walked away.

"Abby...Abby...Abby," Nick chuckled, "I knew you could be cold, but that was downright frigid! What on earth did that guy do to you?"

"Nothing I'm willing to talk about with you—*husband*!" she snarled.

"Oh, you caught that, did you? Hmm. Then, how come you allowed me to get away with it? I thought for sure you'd hand me my head on a platter." Nick grinned cheekily, enjoying the sparkle of anger in her eyes. She'd always been so much fun to tease—especially when she was furious.

"Because it *suited* me, you louse." Suddenly drained, Abby felt sick to her stomach. She leaned back in her chair and closed her eyes, pain replacing the rage she felt.

Understanding lit Nick's eyes and the laughter died away. "This guy—he means something to you—doesn't he, Ab?"

Abby turned away, her profile aloof and sad. "Once," she answered softly, "but no more."

Nick frowned, unsure how to continue. This wasn't the Abby he knew. He'd never seen her look so desolate and lost. Not even on the night she'd caught him in bed with Celine. She cared for the jerk, he realized. Perhaps far more than she'd ever cared for him. That hurt.

Something unfurled inside Nick. Something new, untested. He felt almost...protective towards her. Strange, because he'd never felt that way when they'd been married. Perhaps it was the vulnerable shadows in her eyes, or the pain that tightened her lips.

Nick felt awkward, like an explorer in new territory. But for once, he didn't try his usual glib jokes or snarky comments. Instead, Nick the heel, did the right thing. He suggested they leave and go for a drive.

Her head splitting, Abby smiled gratefully, then stood and followed him out the door. Head high, she passed the table where Cameron quietly nursed a beer. Casually, she glanced down, but didn't speak. The man with Cameron looked vaguely familiar, but Abby couldn't place him.

As she walked by, Cameron smelled her perfume and saw her long, shapely legs, but never looked up to meet her eyes. He refused to give her another chance to shoot him down.

By eight o'clock on Saturday morning, Cameron had been sitting at the kitchen table for two hours trying to make sense out of the piles of papers and files before him. It had been a long, frustrating week during which he'd spent way too many hours meeting suppliers, checking out tenders, trying to drum up new business. It was going to be harder than he thought to pick up where he'd left off. Eighteen months was a long time to be out of the construction game.

When the doorbell rang, he frowned, then got up and walked across the living room to the foyer. Pete had said he might drop by. But why so early?

"You look like hell, Wallace," Ross Blake said cheerfully. "Mind if we come in?" Without waiting for an answer, Ross and Rayce Powers barged passed Cameron and plunked themselves down on the living room couch.

Cameron ran a hand along his whiskered cheek and grimaced. He wasn't exactly fit for company. In nothing but cut-off jeans, with hair all on end, and a beard up to his eyeballs, he could pass for Tom Hanks in 'The Castaway.' And he hadn't showered in two days. Which explained why he smelled kind of ripe. Too bad...their problem.

"You met Rayce Powers before you left—didn't you, Cameron?" Ross asked, gesturing toward the tall, athletic man at his side. Dressed in grey slacks and a navy cotton golf shirt, Rayce looked relaxed and cool. As if he'd just stepped off the pages of GQ. In navy walking shorts and a crisp, white T-shirt Ross looked equally urbane.

Feeling incredibly grubby by contrast, Cameron dropped into a chair opposite the men and stifled a yawn. Whatever it was they wanted, he wished they'd get on with it and leave. He had hours of work ahead of him laid out on the kitchen table. "I think we met at the hospital," he muttered. "Just before Leah died. You were with Libby Cornell."

"She's Libby Powers now," Rayce told him, his sherry-brown eyes smiling as he spoke. "She finally put me out of my misery and agreed to marry me."

Cameron managed a wry grin. "You look like you're holding up. When I renovated her shop, I found out pretty fast that she's one sharp lady who knows her own mind. I'm glad things worked out for you."

"Almost didn't." Rayce glanced at Ross for a moment, then crossed one long cotton-clad leg over the other. "Before we actually met, Libby overheard a very nasty scene between me and another woman, so I had a rough time convincing her I wasn't the sleezebag she thought."

At the startled look on Cameron's face Rayce added breezily, "That was her name for me—sleezebag. Though she had a few others."

Cameron's mouth gaped open. "I didn't think Libby was the type to hold a grudge."

"Well...the other woman *was* married to Raphael Lafortunata at the time," Ross explained dryly.

Cameron whistled. "That would do it."

Rayce laughed. "That's not the best part. Raphael divorced his wife, Carla, and ended up married to Libby's mother. Now he's my step-father-in-law! I feel like I should be playing the banjo every time we have a family get-together."

Cameron's green eyes widened. "Holidays around your house must be fun," he mumbled, as a wide yawn escaped. He stood up and took a step toward the kitchen, then asked, "Hey...you guys want a coffee or something?"

"Nope," Rayce told him. "We want you to get dressed and come down to the golf course with us. We're one man short."

Cameron frowned and started to shake his head in refusal.

"We're not going to take 'no' for an answer," Ross said firmly. "We promised our wives we'd get you out of here for a while. Besides, a golf course is a great place to drum up new business."

"It'll mean our heads if we don't do as we're told," Rayce grinned. "Libby can be a real hellion when she's crossed."

Cameron sighed. "Look guys, I appreciate the offer. But I'm really not in the mood for company right now."

"Sounds familiar—wouldn't you say, Ross?"

"Sure does, Rayce. Woman trouble—right?" Ross grinned good-naturedly, hiding the sympathy he felt. Cameron Wallace looked totally miserable.

Cameron glowered darkly, his mouth thinning to a fine line. "Hey! Don't push it! I know you mean well, but butt out!"

"Yep, I was right—woman trouble, for sure." Smiling knowingly, Ross shook his head as he stood. "Take it from one who's been there, it helps to talk it out."

"Talking's a waste of time! It won't change anything," Cameron snapped. He turned his back to them and leaned against the fireplace wall. In a raw, low voice he added, "You don't know what I've done. She'll never listen to me now, and I can't say I blame her."

Rayce stood and moved closer. "I take it you're referring to Abby?" he said, winking on the sly at Ross.

Cameron spun around and glared at the men. "Of course I'm talking about Abby. Who else—for Pete's sake!"

At the pain in his old friend's eyes, Ross cut the teasing tone. "Cameron, no one knows more than I the hell you're going through. After my first wife died, I was a basket case. I felt so guilty to be alive when she was dead I couldn't think straight. Even though our marriage was a mistake from start to finish."

Cameron hung his head, his eyes narrowed and intent. But he was listening.

Ross knew he was getting somewhere. "When I married Maggy, I had no intention of repeating the mistakes I made in my first marriage. So I played it cool—and blew it—big time. When Maggy got pregnant, I called her every name in the book and left." He sighed heavily. "I was a damn fool. I was so sure she'd cheated on me, because I thought I was sterile." He touched Cameron's arm to get his attention. "You see, Cam, I was hurting so bad, I didn't think, I just reacted. Rayce sat me down, tried to knock some sense into me. But I wouldn't listen. I was too busy wallowing in my misery. Well, when Maggy had the twins, I knew right away they were mine because twins run in my family. Talk about a screw-up!"

He grinned broadly. "Fortunately for me, Maggy is a very forgiving woman. Mind you, every once in a while she reminds me how lucky I am. That's the price I pay for being such a jackass."

Cameron sighed and slowly shook his head. "It's too late," he muttered wearily. "Eighteen months too late. If I'd apologized after the funeral for the way I treated her that day—and for other things—she might be willing to listen now. But I didn't.

"Anyway, it's pointless to even think about it," he said bitterly. "I've hurt her enough. She's happily married now and I don't want to cause a problem between her and her husband."

Ross's eyes widened. "What husband?"

Rayce glanced at Ross in bewilderment. "What in hell are you talking about, Cam? Abby's not married."

For the second time that week, Cameron reared back as if sucker-punched. "What are *you* talking about? I met her husband the other night at a restaurant. He was with Abby. Nick something-or-other—I think she called him. He introduced himself as her husband."

Rayce laughed and dropped back onto the couch. "I bet it was Nick Vanopoulos," he told the others. "Was he—tall and dark, too good-looking—in a slick Hollywood kind of way?"

"That's him!" Cameron growled, his hands balling into fists.

Seeing the fists, Rayce smothered a laugh. The tiger was already awake. Not a good time to twist his tail. "That's Abby's *ex-husband*," he said pointedly. "I think someone was pulling your leg. The guy's an ex-model turned film director—if you can believe that one. He just opened a business account at my bank."

Cameron sagged against the wall in relief. Then he frowned and said, "But...Abby never said a word. She let me think he *was* her husband. Why would she do that?"

"Oh, payback time," Rayce chuckled. "That's a very good sign."

Ross nodded in agreement. "He's right. That was her pride talking—or shutting her up—in this case. She wanted to make you suffer. I know...Maggy's done that to me once or twice."

"Libby's a master of the art," Rayce added ruefully.

"So...you think she wanted to hurt me because she might...care for me...a little? That sounds so twisted!" Cameron's voice was hoarse and raw, his eyes dark with feeling.

Ross took pity on the man. He walked over, then put a hand on Cameron's shoulder. His voice rang with sincerity when he spoke. "She cares, man. Believe it. Abby hasn't dated another man in years. She's a beautiful woman. She could have her pick of men. But she turns everyone down. You come home and she lets you think she's married. Doesn't that tell you something?"

Cameron closed his eyes and shook his head as if trying to make sense out of the muddle he was hearing. Seconds later, when he opened his eyes again, they didn't look quite so bleak. "Give me ten minutes to shower, guys," he told them. "I think I'll play a few rounds after all. I have a few more questions that need answers." Then he headed down the hall and closed a door behind him.

Rayce and Ross grinned and gave each other a high-five.

"I think our wives should be suitably grateful tonight," Rayce said smugly.

"Until they come up with another hairy idea." Ross grinned. "I wonder if Cameron has any idea what he's up against?"

"I'll say. That Abby's a formidable woman."

"Abby—hell! I was referring to our wives!"

Chapter Five

Abby had been pissed off for days and everybody around her was very aware of that fact. Just now she'd barked at Delia who'd finally snapped back, suggesting Abby take a break before she scared all the customers away.

Delia was right. And it was all Cameron's fault! Mistake number one had been when he'd come over to her table at the restaurant. If he'd ignored her as he did before he left, that would have made perfect sense. But no! The damn man had to walk over and say hello. Walked over with big, sad, puppy-dog eyes. Then, mistake number two, he didn't make a follow-up call! Though it defied all logic, a small part of her wanted him to at least call. But he hadn't. Hence her cranky behaviour. She was tempted to go home and get drunk, stupid, fall-down-on-your-ass drunk—but knew she wouldn't. Booze just made her sleepy or weepy. The mood she was in, she couldn't handle either.

When Maggy, then Libby, walked into her shop, Abby frowned. Damn! It couldn't be two o'clock already! But, when Maggy grinned and tapped her wristwatch, Abby knew she'd lost the whole morning thinking about that blasted man.

Every Saturday afternoon at two o'clock the three partners dropped everything for a bitchin'/gossip session with a group of older ladies who quilted in the backroom of Abby's fabric shop. In a bare, oblong room the quilters' group sewed for hours, sitting around a huge scarred table that almost filled the room. Over coffee, tea, and muffins, the women caught up on the latest happenings in Howard's Bay while they ripped apart fabric and sometimes reputations.

Muttering under her breath, Abby stepped forward to take a heavy coffee pot from the tray Maggy was carrying.

"We brought you something to eat, Abby," Maggy said, grinning sardonically. "From what I hear you've been taking a bite out of customers all morning."

Abby groaned. "Don't start. I just went three rounds with Delia—and lost."

"We were hoping that funnel cloud that's been following you for days might have finally lifted," Libby said as she balanced muffins with one hand and pushed blond curls off her forehead with the other.

Abby rolled her eyes. She wished she could go home and burrow under blankets for a week. Instead, she pasted a sick smile on her face and headed for the backroom.

"Well, there you are Abby! We haven't seen hide nor hair of you for days." Polly McMaster, a jovial, retired schoolteacher grinned at Abby as she threaded a needle. Never without a smile or a kind word, Polly was happily married for thirty-five years and the mother of two grown children. She was content with her life and it showed.

"Thought you were hiding out—or something." Edith Gavin, an elderly quilter, raised her frail head and grinned slyly for a moment before catching her older sister's frowning glare. Esther was older than her sister, Edith, but appeared younger, though the two gaunt spinsters looked very much alike. With gray wispy hair, skeletal limbs, and leathery cheeks, the sisters could have passed for twins.

"Ardith phoned a little while ago, Maggy. Said she won't be down this afternoon. Something about Jonathan teething again." Rebeccah Solomon, a retired librarian with flaming red hair, flashing blue eyes, and an expensive taste in clothes, passed on the message with a casual smile.

Maggy glanced up and nodded as she poured the tea. "He was fussy this morning, poor baby. He's just like his father when he gets sick—needs a lot of TLC. Jessica's cutting teeth too, but you'd hardly know it." Maggy grabbed several more cups from the tiny sink in the bathroom alcove, filled them, then handed out refreshments.

"It's a good thing Ardith has Kyra and Sasha to give her a hand," Libby said, trying to keep a straight face.

"Yes, I'm sure she's just thrilled!" Maggy snorted. "Did you hear what those two little hellions did last Saturday?"

Wendy Hughes smiled. "Probably nothing worse than you did at their age," she reminded calmly. As the mother of six grown sons, there wasn't much that got her upset any more.

"I *don't* think so!" Maggy said as she poured more tea. "Those little…witches! My dear daughter, Kyra, and Libby's angelic little sister, Sasha, decided to make themselves up like models. With *my* makeup and *my* new negligees. They had lipstick and eye shadow from one end of my bedroom to the other. Ross was rolling on the floor when Kyra came downstairs with my new black nightie trailing behind her. It's a wonder Ardith doesn't hand in her notice."

"She loves minding the kids," Libby said with a smile. "After the twins were born, I suggested taking Sasha to another sitter and she just about went ballistic."

"Ardith Dawes is the kindest soul alive," Wendy added. "She loves housekeeping for you Maggy—so never you mind. And Libby, if you take Sasha somewhere else, you'll break her heart." Wendy's no-nonsense tone said 'end of discussion.'

As she poured herself a second cup of coffee Abby finally started to relax. "How's that aqua Wedding Ring quilt coming?" she asked Esther.

"Oh…coming. Should be done in time to fill that order next week. But we won't be able to start the new one for Agnes Pearls until you find us some fabric with sunflowers on it. Agnes insists her daughter's mad for sunflowers—of all things."

"I'll call my supplier when I get back to the shop," Abby promised, reaching for a slip of paper to write herself a reminder.

The room was silent for a few moments as the women munched on muffins and drank their tea and coffee. Then Edith cleared her throat.

"So…I hear that Cameron Wallace is back in town."

"Edith!" Esther's frail voice cracked with fury. "I told you to mind your own business." Esther's rheumy blue eyes apologized silently to Abby.

Abby turned away, wishing she could drop to the floor and crawl out the door. Was there anything these old ladies *didn't* know?

"Cameron's a fine man," Wendy said quietly. "I'm glad he's back. We miss him."

"I miss Leah," Rebeccah murmured sadly. "She was such a beautiful girl—inside and out."

A saint, Abby thought bitterly. *How do you compete with a saint?*

"She was a very gifted quilter," Polly added, unaware of the pain her words were causing.

"Those two youngsters were very much in love. When cancer takes a loved one it's a terrible thing." Rebeccah's heart-felt sigh drifted through the room.

Maggy quickly glanced at Abby and almost groaned aloud. Abby was too still, and there was a glazed, vacant stare in her blue eyes. "Yes, it *is* sad," Maggy stated firmly, "but life does move on, and hopefully Cameron will too. He's too young to grieve forever. He deserves some happiness after what he's been through."

Libby realized what Maggy was trying to do and jumped right in. "I didn't know them well, but from what I hear, Cameron was a wonderful husband to Leah. I'm sure she'd want him to make a fresh start—now that she's gone."

Abby knew exactly what her friends were up to. They were so easy to read, and so sweet.

Hiding a swift smile, Wendy bent over her sewing. Maggy and Libby were right on the mark. No one doubted that Cameron had loved Leah, but it was time for a new start. Perhaps with Abby. Abby had pined for Cameron long enough. Maybe it was time for some gentle meddling.

"Maggy, what can we bring to your party next week?" Wendy asked.

"Nothing. I'm having it catered."

Everyone laughed. They all knew who the caterer would be.

"Why don't we make it a potluck?" Polly suggested. "That way you'll get to enjoy your own party."

Maggy hesitated…a moment too long.

"That's a great idea," Abby jumped in. "I could make my cabbage rolls." And in the next few minutes, the menu was arranged.

Wendy bided her time, then said, "I think you should invite Cameron, Maggy. A welcome home for the poor man."

Maggy winked conspiratorially at the older woman. "Great minds think alike. He's already been invited. Mind you, it wouldn't hurt to remind him." She turned and smiled sunnily at Abby. "I've got a lot on my plate just now. Would you make that call for me?"

Abby gritted her teeth. She glared at Maggy, words of outrage poised on her tongue.

"Now, that's a good idea," Polly said turning to Abby. "You and Cameron are such good friends. He'd probably love to hear from you."

Without meaning to, her friends were pouring salt on an open wound. "I don't think so," Abby muttered grimly. "It's your party, Maggy. You can make the call yourself."

From the mutinous look on Abby's face, Maggy knew she'd pushed too hard. "All right, but will you come over early to give me a hand?" Maggy wasn't taking any chances that Abby might skip out—to avoid Cameron.

"Sure, why not?" Abby said, her eyes livid in her pale face. Then a feral grin curled her lips. "As long as you don't mind me bringing an extra guest," she added.

"Who?" Maggy's face was blank.

"My ex-husband, Nick. You know—the film director." As expected, the quilters froze, their faces lighting with renewed interest.

Libby frowned. She knew damn well why Abby wanted to bring Nick!

"Of course you can bring him, if you want to," Maggy answered grudgingly. She stood and began to clear the tea clutter, her mind working furiously as she rethought her plan.

When Abby moved closer to place cups on the tray, Maggy whispered, "I hope you know what you're doing, Abby."

Abby nodded abruptly, then headed back to work.

In her office, she dropped into her chair and closed her tired eyes. She hadn't slept in days and felt too weary for words. It was very foolish to haul Nick to Maggy's party. But more foolish to go there alone.

The following Saturday afternoon precisely at one, Nick rang Abby's doorbell. He glanced around as he waited on her step, intrigued by Abby's home. A miniature of the large grey house up the drive, the small carriage house was Victorian in detail right down to the white fancy trim on the roof of the porch. A far cry from the expensive apartment they'd shared together in Toronto. Looking around, he noticed neatly tended flower beds and window boxes filled with healthy geranium blooms. His dark brows raised in astonishment. Who knew Abby had such a green thumb! In the past, the only flowers she'd appreciated were hot-house orchids and American Beauty roses—by the dozen. Abby had changed in more ways than one.

In fact, from what he'd seen so far, she'd changed drastically. When they'd been married, Abby had been a frenetic, restless butterfly, always ready for the next thrill, the next challenge. Money, clothes, and endless parties had been her priorities. From one day to the next, he'd never known what to expect from her. One night, he'd come home to find a note that read, 'gone to Cannes for a shoot' dropped on the kitchen counter. That time he hadn't seen her for three weeks. Another time, in the middle of a party, she made plans to go on a safari, then took off the next day for Nairobi. Neither time had she thought to check with him—to see how he felt—or if he wanted to go too.

Perhaps, if she had, they still might be married. Or, perhaps not. In hindsight, he'd been just as selfish, just as self-centred as Abby. Maybe that's what had drawn them together in the first place.

But Abby had changed...mellowed...in some indefinable way. Her smile was just as sardonic, her eyes still unfathomable, her laugh just as seductively wicked. But she listened more attentively now and seemed more comfortable with herself. The wild recklessness that had captivated him in the beginning was gone. But oddly enough, this new Abby was even more attractive. Too bad she'd made it so clear she wasn't interested in a little light flirtation; she'd always been great in bed. Until she lost interest in him, that is. They'd been finished long before the scene with Celine.

Abby opened the door and smiled in welcome. "Come on in," she told him. "I'm just about ready." She eyed his all white outfit with raised brows. "You look like you're dressed for a lunch in Cannes," she teased. "We're going to a backyard barbeque, Nick. Jeans might have been a smarter choice."

Frowning dubiously, Nick glanced down at his Ralph Lauren shirt and tailored walking shorts. Then he grinned cheekily. "Got to show the rednecks how it's done."

"Don't say I didn't warn you," Abby said dryly. "Grab a seat. I just have to finish my makeup." She stepped through a door on the left and shut it behind her.

Nick glanced around the tiny living room, his director's eye noting all the subtle details. He found it hard to believe that this was where Abby lived.

The main living space had an intimate feel. Perhaps because it was filled with colours that were easy on the eye. Or perhaps because each item of furniture fit the room like a piece of a jig-saw puzzle. He sensed that Abby had chosen everything in the room after much deliberation. And that surprised him.

When they were married, Abby had never bothered much with their apartment. She'd hired a decorator, then left the rest to him. She never cleaned or cooked, and never added the little touches that personalize a house and turn it into a home.

But she had done precisely that in this little cottage. The place screamed personality. The living area was dominated by a camel couch and armchair piled high with lush pillows in various shades of burgundy and pale green. Three small pine tables, covered with silver-framed pictures, candles and knick-knacks, were strategically placed around the room. On the cream walls, scattered groupings of watercolours and country settings caught the eye immediately. Golden oak floors, gleaming like mirrors, reflected the beauty of the room.

On a honey-pine dining table, fresh flowers from the garden spilled over a crystal bowl, filling the room with their tantalizing scent. Even more amazing, the tiny kitchen that backed off the living room actually looked used.

Nick moved closer to look at the pictures on the tables. Sadly, there was none of him. Several included a gorgeous redhead and two children. In others, the redhead was cuddled against a dark-haired, solemn-eyed man, the same kids, and two babies. Nick sighed as he looked at the happy family. He missed Ashley in that moment—and Celine too, in a way.

He moved over to another table and inspected four more pictures. The same three people were in all the shots: a stunning blond with enormous blue eyes, a sweet little girl with a mass of blond curls, and a tall, dark-haired guy who looked very pleased with himself. *Looks like the bank manager*, he thought.

Nick glanced at the table in the corner, and something caught his eye. He walked over and inspected a photo that stood alone. It was of a man and a woman. Nick froze. He knew that man! It was the guy that Abby had cut dead in the restaurant the other night. Nick leaned closer to study the picture with more care. He glanced at the woman. Pretty enough in a baby-doll kind of way. *The clingy type,* he decided. The woman was clutching the guy's arm as if her life depended on it. Nick hated that kind of dependency. But the guy in the picture didn't seem to mind. He was smiling down at the little blond with evident affection. Nick looked closer and noticed wedding rings on both their hands. His eyebrows raised in astonishment. Abby and a married man! Now that he found hard to believe. Abby was many things, but she was too much of a straight arrow to go after a married man.

He was still studying the picture closely when Abby entered the room.

He raised his head and watched her intently, not moving away from the picture. His eyes held hers, demanding an explanation.

Abby sighed. She rubbed her forehead as if it had just begun to ache. "So...what do you want to know?"

"The obvious." Nick's dry tone said it all.

"His name is Cameron Wallace. The woman is...was his wife, Leah. She died eighteen months ago." Abby's eyes were frosted and cool, daring him to ask more at his peril.

Never one to ignore a challenge, Nick arched a brow and said, "I got the impression the other night that you and this guy had...something going?" His voice questioned but his eyes didn't. They stated a fact.

Abby bristled at his knowing look. "You're mistaken," she said impatiently. "We're just old friends."

"If looks could kill, your *old friend* would be in a coffin by now." Nick's eyes laughed in delight as he watched Abby squirm.

"Damn you." She turned away and dropped into a camel-coloured armchair. With her long, jean-clad legs draped over one arm of the chair, she glared balefully at her ex-husband. "You really are a bastard, Nick. Now I remember why I divorced you."

Nick grinned all the more. He had her now and they both knew it. He hadn't had so much fun in years. "You might as well spill the beans," he told her. "I'll worm it out of you anyway."

Abby decided to get it over with. So, in a matter-of-fact voice she told him the bare essentials.

A few minutes later, Nick sat back and whistled, his eyes narrowed with concern. "Damn, Abby. You've got yourself in a real mess this time."

Abby stood up and moved restlessly around the room. "I don't see why," she muttered. "I have no intention of having anything more to do with Cameron. That part of my life is over."

"If you believe that crap, you're dreaming!" Nick's snort of derision made Abby wince. "From what I saw the other night, this Cameron guy is not going to walk away from what he wants. And I think he wants you, Abby."

"Oh, I can handle him." She smiled carelessly, her eyes grim.

Nick almost pitied her then. She was trying so hard to pretend she didn't care—when in fact, he'd never seen her so fragile. "Abby," he said softly, "you need to decide what it is you want. I suspect you care for this guy a lot more than you're letting on." When she started to protest, Nick cut her off.

"Don't try to pretend with me, Abby. It won't work." He paused, then eyed her intently. "Remember that night—when you caught me in bed with Celine?"

"How could I forget?" she said dryly.

Nick grinned. Then the grin faded away. "You were furious, Abby, but it was more hurt pride than anything else. If you had cared more, perhaps I wouldn't have been there in the first place."

Throwing him a look filled with scorn Abby crossed her arms over her chest. "You are so full of it," she snapped.

Nick walked over to her chair and leaned over her, forcing her to meet his eyes. "Admit it, Abby," he said softly. "Only your pride was injured that night. You weren't in love with me. I doubt if you ever were."

There was no condemnation, no accusation in his gentle voice, only truth.

Abby hung her head, ashamed that she had married this man without love. "Damn, when did you get so smart?"

"After you left me and I realized what I'd lost."

Abby's eyes flew to his. She frowned, then lifted one slim finger to gently stroke his cheek, her eyes dark with regret.

"I'm sorry, Nick," she whispered huskily. "Sorry for being such a lousy wife. I never should have married you; you never should have married me. But let's not compound that mistake with another. Contrary to the way it looks, I don't make a habit of chasing after married men. Cameron...was a madness I couldn't resist. I've grow up a lot since then."

Nick straightened, smiling wistfully for what might have been. Since seeing Abby again, he'd come full circle. In his own way, a part of him would always love this beautiful woman, though he knew she would never love him in return.

"For such a smartass, you're sure acting pretty dumb. Why aren't you going after this guy and nailing his butt to the nearest bed?"

"Because I don't want him!" Abby's eyes glinted stubbornly as she glared at Nick.

"Damn right you do. It's only pride or fear holding you back." His smile was razor-sharp when he added, "It's not like you to back away from a fight. If you really want this guy, it's time to let him know."

"I can't!" Her eyes burned with misery. "You don't know how he hurt me."

"Maybe he's hurting too. If you don't take a chance—you'll live to regret it."

Abby wanted to scream. It was all so unfair! Her tidy little world seemed to be coming unravelled at the seams. "Why are you pushing me this way, Nick? After all these years, what gives you the right to tell me what to do?"

Nick stared into Abby's stormy blue eyes, their brilliance enhanced by her pale face. "The right of an old friend...who cares about you."

When she scoffed and tilted her stubborn chin, he leaned down to take her face in his hand and gently made her eyes meet his. "Believe me, Abby. It's true. Maybe I washed out as your husband, but give me a chance to be your friend." He stepped away and waited. The choice was hers to make.

As if seeing a total stranger Abby stared at Nick, then something inside gave way and she eased back to really look at him. "Friends," she muttered. "That's something I thought we'd never be." She sat back in the chair, clearly thinking. Then a smile lifted her lips and a light danced in her eyes. "I value my friends, Nick. And...I guess I could use one more. But that's all I want from you. Is that clear?" She grinned to take the sting out of her blunt words, but they both knew she meant what she said.

With a mocking lift of one brow, Nick smiled broadly, but not before Abby caught a hint of sadness in his eyes. "So be it," he said. "Message received loud and clear." He pulled Abby to her feet and led her toward the door. "Time to get this show on the road."

Abby smiled as she closed the door behind her, hoping she wouldn't regret this new friendship. While strange to be sure, it seemed somehow right to have Nick in her life again.

Abby and Nick wandered across the lawn into Maggy's backyard. Gingerly holding a pan of steaming cabbage rolls, Abby picked her way carefully through the freshly-mowed grass.

Nick whistled softly, his director's eyes moving over the well-kept Victorian home. "Nice place if you like the type."

Abby bristled and she glared at Nick. "Remember what I told you! These are all great people so don't act like Mr. big-shot director with them."

Nick grinned. "What did I say? I was just talking about the house."

Abby's mouth thinned. She knew his tone, knew she was being played. But she was so nervous she actually felt sick. Maybe bringing Nick here wasn't the best idea, like bringing fire to a gunpowder room.

Nick saw how uptight she was and decided to ease up. "So...the house. Tell me about it."

Abby's eyes narrowed. "Do you really care?"

Grinning engagingly, he said, "Not really, but you never know...I might need a place like this down the road."

"Always hustling aren't you," Abby said dryly. "Well, for your information, this place was one of the first built in the area and belonged to Maggy's first husband, Jarrod. His great-great-grandfather Howard was one of the pioneers of the town. When Jarrod took over the family home, he did a total renovation, added new vinyl siding, new windows—the works. Maggy says he designed the closed gable front verandah from some old family photos."

"Sounds like quite a guy."

Abby nodded. "From what I hear he was. I never knew Jarrod. He died before I met Maggy; but, from the way her eyes light up whenever she says his name, he must have been very special."

Abby looked around for Maggy but couldn't find her anywhere. Though she saw many people she knew and a few new faces as well. "Let's get rid of this food," she told Nick, "then I'll introduce you to some of my friends."

Crossing the lawn, Abby smiled at Esther and Edith Gavin, who were covering long tables with blue-checkered cloth. She caught their bird-like stares and knew she was in for it.

Oblivious to the rapt interest he was causing, Nick craned his head and looked up, still focused on the house. "So…this back piece, it looks new."

"That's right," Abby replied distractedly, her eyes still on the Gavin sisters. "When Maggy married our accountant, Ross Blake, they built a new family room and office on the bottom floor and expanded their bedroom upstairs. Maggy did the decorating herself and it's really homey inside. Now that they have the twins, they really need the extra rooms."

"Abby, bring that pan over here."

A red-headed woman in a yellow wrap sundress was calling from the deck area, the smile on her face as sunny as her dress.

Nick knew he'd been spotted when the smile disappeared. *Ah-hah*, he thought, *must be Maggy, the partner. Looks like she's not too thrilled to see me with Abby!* To check his theory, he put his arm around Abby's waist and the redhead positively fumed. Nick grinned slyly and thought, *Might as well have some fun.*

"Nick!" Abby hissed. "Get your hands off me! What are you trying to pull?"

Nick raised both hands in the air and grinned engagingly, his eyes feigning innocence. "Just being friendly."

"Well quit it!" she snapped. "Don't make me regret bringing you here. Behave yourself—I mean it!"

Abby stormed up the steps and followed Maggy inside, leaving Nick to wander around on his own.

He spotted a keg of beer on a table and helped himself to a glass. He drained half, then glanced around. Off to the left under an oak tree he noticed several men talking and recognized a familiar face. It was the bank manager he'd met a few days before. The guy held a wiggly baby boy squirming like an octopus. The other man, grinning like a damn fool, was holding a baby girl with bright red hair. *Must be Maggy's husband,* Nick figured. The baby was the image of its mother. A young girl, with a riot of blond curls, leaned against the bank manager and nibbled on a carrot. Nick felt a pang. She reminded him of Ashley.

Deciding it was time to make his presence known, Nick strolled over and deliberately inserted himself into the conversation. "Nice to see you again," he said to the man holding the wiggling boy. "Rayce Powers—isn't it? We met the other day at your bank." Turning to the other dark-haired man, Nick said urbanely, "I'm assuming you're my host, Ross Blake—right? I'm Nick Vanopoulos. I'm here with Abby."

Ross and Rayce both stared at the interloper as if examining a bug under a microscope. Neither said a word.

Nick dropped the hand he'd extended and chuckled. "Now why do I feel like the temperature just dropped twenty degrees? And I'd heard so much about northern hospitality."

Ross frowned, then cleared his throat. "Sorry," he said, though he didn't sound it. "The beer's in the keg and supper's in an hour. Make yourself at home." Ross's voice was clipped and hard. No smile of welcome accompanied his words.

Nick had a hard time keeping a straight face. No doubt about it, Ross Blake was itching to toss him out on his ear.

"I wouldn't want to spoil your dinner, so I think we should clear the air." Nick gave them his best Hollywood smile. "It's obvious you're worried about Abby—and me. Well, don't be. I'm here to make a movie—not a move on my former wife. I'm married with a little girl of my own, and Abby and I are just friends." He paused for effect, then added smoothly, "Abby invited me here for a pleasant afternoon. If that's not possible, tell me now, and I'm out of here."

Ross eyed Nick for a long moment, his stare still decided chilly. "I can live with that. What about you, Rayce?"

A muscle jumped in Rayce's jaw; his eyes narrowed as he stared at Nick. "Abby's had a rough time of it in the last few years. We don't want to see her hurt."

"I have a feeling you're warning the wrong guy," Nick said ruefully. He nodded in the direction of another man stepping onto the grass. "I think *that's* the guy you should be worried about. Not me."

The other two men glanced over their shoulders and spotted Cameron

Wallace walking toward them, a deadly glint in his eye.

"Oh damn," Ross sighed. "Looks like Cameron's out for blood."

"Mine, I think," Nick said cheerfully. "He saw me with Abby the other night at a restaurant. He might have misinterpreted something I said."

Rayce grinned at Nick. "Is that a fact? Well now, this could get very interesting."

Cameron halted in front of the men. Dressed in jeans and a light-blue cotton shirt he looked hot, uncomfortable, and decidedly pissed off.

"Hello Ross…Rayce," he muttered. "Good to see you again." Cameron shook both mens' hands, then turned to Nick and deliberately shoved his fists into the pockets of his jeans. "I believe we met the other night," Cameron said coldly, his brilliant green eyes snapping with fury. "You told me you were Abby's husband."

"So I did," Nick agreed, his teeth flashing brilliantly in the sun. "Actually, I *was* her husband——a number of years ago."

"That's not the impression I got the other night!"

Nick grinned openly at the man's scowling face. "I was just trying to get Abby's goat. And you got in the way. No hard feelings I hope."

Cameron's anger had been building for days. He itched to punch out a few of those perfect teeth, but the man wouldn't give him an opening. He ached to pulverize the wiseass!

Then the gooing baby in Ross's arms grabbed his shirt sleeve and his anger melted. "Good lord," he laughed. "With that hair, this has got to be Maggy's daughter." He glanced up at Ross and said, "You're a lucky man."

"And don't I know it." Ross beamed proudly and held out his daughter.

Cameron hesitated. His hands seemed too big to hold such a tiny, fragile baby. But when Ross urged him on, Cameron lifted the baby gingerly into his arms, then settled her against his chest. Jessica blew bubbles and stared at him with her father's solemn eyes. Then she grinned, showing several small white teeth. Like a tire with a slow leak, the remnants of his anger seeped away and, for the first time in days, Cameron began to relax. He listened to the talk surrounding him and offered a comment or two while bouncing Jessica up and down.

But every now and then he studied Nick Vanopoulos, and several times caught the other man doing the same.

Is this what Abby wants in a man? Cameron wondered sourly. *A pretty boy in fancy clothes with a toothy smile?* Cameron's eyes glazed over and his mouth thinned. One thing he knew for certain. She sure didn't want *him*.

Chapter Six

"I put the relish trays on the coffee table in the family room, Abby," Maggy said as she returned to the kitchen.

Abby nodded. "This garden salad is just about ready."

"When it's done, put it beside the relish trays. We'll leave everything on the table until we're ready to take the food outside." As she wiped her hands on a tea towel, Maggy wondered whether or not to warn Abby.

"What the hell," she muttered, "she'll know soon enough." Maggy straightened and said, "Cameron's here, Abby. He's outside right now, talking to your ex."

Abby groaned, the knife in her hand dropping to the table. She wiped her sweaty hands on her jeans, then almost ran to the patio doors in the family room. Edging against the wall, she cautiously peeked out. Instantly her eyes locked on the two men and her face paled.

With what looked like murder in his eyes, Cameron was glaring at Nick. She couldn't hear what was being said, but from the grin on Nick's face, it wasn't good. Filled with dread, Abby waited, but nothing happened. After talking to Nick for what seemed like hours, but was in fact probably a minute, Cameron turned away and took baby Jessica from her father. As he stared tenderly down at the baby, Abby's heart flip-flopped in her chest. *If only he could look at her in that way.* Abby sighed, then drifted away from the window, her eyes shadowed by pain.

When Abby came back to the kitchen table, Maggy glanced up but kept silent. She carefully placed pieces of cheese on a platter and waited for Abby to speak.

"He's holding Jessica," Abby muttered.

"Good."

"He looks...tired."

"Probably still jet-lagged," Maggy said quietly.

"He looks the same—yet different somehow."

Maggy dried her hands with slow deliberation, then looked Abby firmly in the eye. "He's been through hell and back, Abby. That's bound to change anyone. The man made mistakes—but so did you. It's time to let go of the pain and move on." At the mutinous look on Abby's face, Maggy sighed in frustration. Sometimes talking to Abby was like talking to a brick wall!

"If you love him Abby—and I strongly suspect you do, then give him another chance. Give *yourself* a chance to be happy."

Abby frowned and opened her mouth to speak, but Maggy held up a hand in warning. "No, listen to me, Abby. It's about time you faced some home truths. You're your own worst enemy. You're so damned proud, you'll cut off your nose to spite your face—rather than admit you still want the man. It's time to stop being so damned foolish. Which is more important, your hurt pride or your feelings for Cameron?"

A muscle jumped in Abby's cheek. She wanted to lash out, but something held her back. Perhaps the fear that Maggy might be right.

Instead, she picked up a knife and hacked the tomatoes to pieces.

Maggy grinned. *Better those tomatoes than my head!*

Just then Libby walked into the kitchen, her hands loaded down with platters of cold cuts. "Where do you want these platters?" she asked. "Rebeccah and Polly brought them."

"Gosh, I don't know," Maggy muttered. "My fridge is full as it is. Let's have a look, Libby."

While Maggy and Libby rearranged the fridge, Abby went outside and circled the yard. She stopped for a while and chatted with Harley Hammond and his wife Bessie. Harley played Santa every year for good reason. With his white hair, beard, and rosy plump cheeks, he was perfect for the part. As chubby as Harley was, Bessie was thin. The old couple lived next door to Rayce and Libby and often babysat Sasha, Libby's little sister.

ABBY'S STORY: BETRAYED BY LOVE

When Abby noticed Cameron heading her way, she scurried along to talk to Ardith Dawes, Maggy's housekeeper, then sighed in relief when Cameron got cornered by Harley.

But all too soon, he turned in her direction again, his eyes meeting hers for the first time.

Abby panicked at the intensity in his dark stare. She felt flustered and nervous, and didn't like feeling that way. *Damn the man! Damn him for coming!* She glared at Cameron, then deliberately walked over to Nick, and stayed glued to his side until Maggy called everyone to dinner.

They all sat together, seated at several long tables, with Maggy and her family at one end and Libby and hers at the other. With nearly three dozen people at the tables, including two babies, dinner was a noisy affair.

Abby sat halfway down the table between Nick and Harley. Cameron sat opposite her, but three seats down. She tried not to look at him, but on several occasions couldn't help herself. Each time she glanced his way, he was watching *her*.

Abby barely tasted her food. She chatted with Harley, laughed at Nick's jokes, but couldn't have said what she put in her mouth. Time and again her eyes sought Cameron out. He looked so handsome, yet so alone. He'd lost some weight, but it didn't detract from his dark good looks. He smiled tentatively at her once, a dimple creasing his right cheek.

Abby almost groaned aloud. *Damn! That dimple did her in every time!* She forced herself to smile cooly, then turned away, missing the hint of anguish that dimmed Cameron's eyes.

But Nick didn't miss it. The guy was hurting all right. Whenever Abby brushed too close to Nick's arm the guy bristled like a pit bull. But she wasn't immune either. Not if the red flush staining her neck was anything to go by. It was time to play the good guy for a change, Nick decided. If Abby wanted this guy, perhaps he could help.

Nick stood, then banged his glass for attention. "Excuse me," he shouted, waiting for the clatter to die down.

While everyone stared politely at Nick, Abby cringed, dreading what he would say.

"For those of you who don't know me, my name is Nick Vanopoulos. I'm an old friend of Abby's. I had the good fortune to be married to her for a time and the stupidity to let her get away."

As expected, everyone laughed at Nick's performance—everyone except Abby and Cameron. Abby had a frozen smile pasted on her face and Cameron looked like he was made out of wood.

"I'm here to make a movie," Nick explained calmly, enjoying the rising excitement his news brought.

"I'll need some extras for a few crowd scenes and I thought some of you might like to try out."

As everyone started talking at once, Nick grinned down at Abby. She smiled tightly back but said nothing.

"As a matter of fact," Nick said loudly, "Abby would be perfect for the part of a dying Indian maiden. What do you say, Abby? Will you do it?"

Abby groaned and shook her head. *Play a dying maiden in his movie? Not if they pulled out every tooth in her mouth with rusty pliers!*

She was adamant in her refusal. But everyone else was equally adamant she should do it. Finally, when Nick explained she wouldn't have to say a word, she nodded grudgingly, agreeing to do the part.

One down...one to go. On a roll, Nick smiled slyly down the tables. "I also need someone to play the maiden's lover," he said with a mock leer. "A great part for the right guy." With a casual glance at Cameron he asked, "What about you? Could you play Abby's lover?"

Cameron's eyes narrowed. He knew a challenge when he heard one. "I'm no actor," he said cooly, "but I think I could manage the part." He stared at Abby, the ball in her court now.

Amid the hoots and teasing laughter Abby sat like a statue, absolutely stunned by the turn of events. She flushed hotly. *Why on earth had Cameron agreed?* She looked away. This was just too much! She couldn't take any more. With a hurried excuse to Nick, Abby fled the table and rushed into the house.

In the kitchen she gulped a glass of water, then leaned against the counter, and closed her eyes. Her heart was pounding erratically and she didn't know whether to laugh or cry.

"Are you all right?"

Abby's eyes flew open in shock. She moved to escape but Cameron blocked the exit.

"Abby, I asked if you were all right."

"Of course, I'm all right." Abby hated how breathless she sounded. "I...just wanted a drink of water."

"Funny," he mused softly as he moved a step closer, "I could have sworn you were upset when I agreed to play your lover."

Abby squirmed, her face flooding with embarrassment. "Well, if you want to know the truth, I expected you to refuse. You *should* have refused." Her eyes frosted over with a touch of defiance.

"Why would I turn down a chance to get you in my arms?"

Abby swayed on her feet. *What gall! What incredible gall!* She couldn't be hearing right! She glared at Cameron, ready to rip him a new one, then caught her breath at the look on his face. He was smiling at her…gently…tenderly…the kind of smile he gave her in her dreams.

Abby wanted to weep and stamp her feet in frustration. *It's too late,* she wanted to scream. *How dare he look at her that way now!* Though she wanted to pound his chest and wail her fury, she held back, afraid to even touch him.

"Why are you doing this to me?" she asked raggedly. "Haven't you punished me enough?"

Cameron winced at the pain in her wide blue eyes. "I'm sorry, Abby. More sorry than I can say. The way I treated you was inexcusable, but I won't ever hurt you again. I promise."

Abby wanted to believe him, wanted to with an overpowering desperation that had her shaking where she stood. But just looking at him brought back all the pain. Maybe he could forget the past. But she couldn't.

Abby shook her head in despair, then made to brush past him.

He stepped in front of her, blocking her way.

"Look at me, Abby," he insisted.

With a low growl, she turned and tried to move away, but his hands grabbed her and pulled her tight against his hard body.

Abby almost sagged at the contact. His body was so warm, so close. She could smell his clean scent that hinted of dark, quiet woods. She bit her lip and closed her eyes, praying she wouldn't moan out loud.

Cameron gently grasped her jaw and tilted her face until their eyes met fully at last.

He read the fear in hers and the dampened hunger.

She saw the desire in his and knew she was lost.

"It's not over between us, Abby," he told her huskily, his mouth moving toward her parted lips.

But, when she felt his breath on her lips, Abby panicked. She knew if he touched her even once, she'd lose it. And she couldn't allow that to happen. Not again.

Twisting out from under him Abby stepped away, her firm breasts heaving as she tried to force air into her lungs.

"How can you say that to me?" she gasped. "You've been gone for eighteen months without one single call or letter. And now you waltz in here like you're King Shit and expect me to drop at your feet. Well, that's not going to happen, mister! You hurt me, Cameron. There! I said it! Does that make you feel like a big man now? I was a basket case after you left. But I'm not any more. So back off, Cameron Wallace, and stay away from me!" Abby was in a full rage now, so angry she shook.

Cameron listened, trying to quell the slight smile on his lips. *If she didn't still care, would she be so mad?* He didn't think so. For the first time in days he felt a tiny spark of hope.

Abby saw the slight smile and exploded.

"You arrogant bastard!" she shouted. "Get out of my way before I knock you into tomorrow!"

Cameron stepped back and allowed her to pass by. When she slammed the door shut in his face, he grinned and leaned back against the counter. He'd let her have the last word—this time. He'd found out all he needed to know.

After waiting a few minutes, Cameron left the kitchen, then headed back to his seat at the table, but Abby refused to look at him. Instead, she focused her attention on Nick, her tone low and intimate.

Though he saw her tactic for what it was, Cameron felt a slow burn coiling in the pit of his stomach as he watched her lean against Nick's shoulder.

Watching from the sidelines, Rayce caught Cameron eyeing Abby and her ex. The man looked like a prowling panther ready to attack. Time to cool the guy down. "Hey Cameron, are you looking for any new business?"

Cameron blinked, then shifted his attention from Abby. "Always on the lookout for more," he answered, his green eyes lighting with interest. "What did you have in mind?"

"Libby and I just bought a piece of land on the lake. We're thinking of building a new house. We've picked out a plan, but that's about it. Any chance you can come by one night this week to have a look at our plans?"

"Sure can," Cameron said. Perhaps he might not have to lay off any of his crew after all. "Actually, I'm free tomorrow afternoon, if that suits you."

"Great!" Rayce raised his brows at Libby who nodded her agreement.

Just then Harley piped up, "So, Cameron...tell us about Saudi Arabia. What was it like?"

"Hot and dry," Cameron answered quickly. When everyone started to laugh, Cameron grinned wryly, then added, "It's a very different country from Canada, but beautiful none the less. I was working in Riyadh, the capital, which is more modern than I expected. We built a shopping mall on the edge of the city but it didn't look like a mall from the outside. It was uniquely Arabian in design.

"A few times I managed to get a weekend off, and went into the desert with Faisal, our site foreman. It was incredible, an ocean of empty sand at first glance, but teeming with life if you knew where to look. Faisal took me to his family's home and they cooked a goat in our honour. It was an experience I'll never forget."

Abby was fascinated but refused to showed any interest. She twiddled with her cold cup of coffee and stared at Maggy's dahlias.

"What about those Saudi women?" Wendy's son, the lawyer, grinned unabashedly when his mother poked him in the ribs.

Cameron smiled, but it didn't reach his eyes. "There were several young women in our office," he told the man, "but they came with their brothers and left that way too. The women there are very protected. It wasn't worth the effort—or risk—to get to know them better. Even if I had been interested. Which I wasn't."

At the flat, cold statement Abby sneaked a peek at Cameron. He was staring at her, his eyes glittering like green fire, his mouth a grim, tight line.

Abby was so startled by the intensity of his gaze she looked away. She felt raw, exposed, and terribly unsettled. Damn the man! It was all *his* fault!

Shortly after nine, several of the neighbourhood families started to pack up. Babies were getting whiny, children began to yawn. When Maggy went inside to bathe the twins and get them ready for bed, Abby tagged along to give her a hand.

Ross and Rayce carried wood to a large pit in the back corner of the yard and prepared a bonfire in the centre. In minutes they had a hot fire going. One by one the remaining families carried their lawn chairs close to the crackling blaze and settled down to enjoy the encroaching twilight.

Twenty minutes later, after helping Maggy get both twins in their cribs, Abby opened the patio door off the family room, and stepped onto the deck. The sun had just gone down and twinkling stars were lighting the velvet sky.

It was a quiet scene that greeted her, a relief after the noisy afternoon. The tables had been cleared and dismantled; the empty keg of beer replaced by a second; all the garbage and empty cans had been collected and bagged.

Groups of people sat around the edge of the rock-lined pit, a crackling fire lifting wisps of smoke into the night air. Here and there, soft, murmuring voices drifted around the yard interspersed by riffs of laughter. Off to one side, several mothers held blanket-covered youngsters in their arms, their madonna-like faces glowing in the light of the fire. Harley leaned against a high-backed lounger, snoozing peacefully, his hands folded across his ample belly. Sasha leaned on the arm of his chair, chin in hand, watching in total fascination as his mouth opened and closed like a fish while he snored. Kyle and Kyra sat cross-legged on a log, both armed with marshmallow-spiked sticks.

As Abby moved away from the patio door, Harry Hughes took out an old battered guitar and began to play a familiar love song, its haunting melody echoing through the still night air. Glancing around, Abby searched the crowd for Nick. She couldn't see him at first, then she heard his laugh and finally spotted him on the far side of the fire sitting between Polly McMaster and Rebeccah Solomon. He was in his element, talking expansively—with frequent smiles and elaborate hand gestures punctuating his words. Though old enough to be his mother, the two matrons leaned close to him, captivated, like teenagers with a rock star.

Abby grinned to herself. *Leave it to Nick. He collects women like I collect earrings.* Just then, Kyra lifted a long stick with a smoldering marshmallow on the end. She blew on the gooey mess to cool it down, then popped it into her mouth.

Abby was transported back in time. As if it were yesterday, she saw herself standing by a fire on a sandy beach, her father at her side, whittling a stick so she could toast a marshmallow. Her mother had been ill that summer, so she'd spent most of it indoors on the couch in Aunt Meg's cottage.

The summer when she was ten, the last time they'd truly been a happy family.

Most evenings her father had built a bonfire. It became their nightly ritual that summer to sit under the stars, just the two of them, and talk. Hour after hour he'd pointed out constellations and told her stories of Greek mythology. After her mother passed away the next winter, they never went back. Abby had forgotten that magical summer. It had been the only time she could recall when they'd played as a family and had fun. For the umpteenth time Abby regretted being the only child of elderly parents.

Her mother had been forty-nine when Abby was conceived, and often had seemed bewildered by her spirited child. Abby's childhood was a lonely one, filled with long hours in a quiet, tome-like house, always having to hush while her father worked or napped.

ABBY'S STORY: BETRAYED BY LOVE

Her parents had been hard-working people all their lives. Her mother, a meticulous homemaker—always scrubbing and cleaning. Her father, running his small garage almost single-handedly, was old before his time. He'd found it hard, Abby knew, to deal with a chattering child with too many questions. He preferred to hide out in his workshop.

In time, Abby learned to retreat into her own fantasy world, to move quietly throughout the house, to play alone with her dolls instead of other children. There were no brothers or sisters, or cousins for companions—her parents were the last of their lines—except for her mother's younger sister, Meghan. And of course, no pets.

Two months after her eighteenth birthday, Abby's father died too. And Aunt Meghan died shortly after Abby left Nick.

Abby shivered. She hadn't thought of her parents in a long time. But, tonight, seeing all the contented families, it brought home to her just how alone in the world she was.

Abby hugged herself and walked to the end of the deck, then stepped onto the grass. She inhaled deeply, smelling the sweet scent of Maggy's roses in the night air. Then small lights twinkling on the edge of the garden caught her eye. *Fireflies*, she realized in delight. Abby stood spellbound, fascinated by the blinking lights that mirrored the stars overhead.

"Come and join us, Abby," Libby shouted from the grass.

Abby nodded, then picked up a lawn chair and headed for the firepit. Libby and Rayce sat together, his arm cuddling her close. Abby pulled up a chair beside them but didn't say much, content to stare into the fire and let her mind drift. She knew Cameron sat under an oak tree off to the side. She'd caught a glimpse of him out of the corner of her eye as she walked across the lawn, but she'd kept her head down, in an attempt to block him out.

Cameron watched Abby sit down, her shiny brown hair dancing with golden highlights. Her head was drooped on her chest and she said little, he noticed. She seemed distant, almost morose, as she stared intently into the flames.

"Mind if I join you?" Ross asked Cameron before plopping down on the grass. Ross leaned back against the tree and sighed. "That fire was getting just a little too hot."

Absently Cameron continued to braid several grass blades. With his legs drawn up and his large hands dangling between his knees he looked relaxed, but wasn't.

"Why don't you go and sit beside Abby?" Ross suggested quietly.

"Brooding over here isn't going to do you any good."

"She called me an arrogant bastard a little while ago," Cameron muttered gruffly. "She's furious with me—not that I blame her."

Ross searched for the right approach, then decided to be direct. "What do you want from her, Cameron? She had a really rough time after you left."

Cameron sighed. "I guessed as much." He took a deep, ragged breath, then muttered, "I never meant to hurt Abby—or Leah for that matter. God, I made a real mess of things." He shook his head wearily. "You have to understand something, Ross. I loved my wife, loved her from the time we were teenagers. I love her still; I'll always cherish what we had. It was a good marriage—even though we couldn't have kids. While that really bothered Leah, it didn't matter to me. I just wanted her and we were very happy together.

"Then one day, I met Abby and my complaisant world shattered. I still loved Leah. Believe me, that never changed. I would *never* have left her. Never! But more and more, Abby filled my thoughts. And that ripped me up inside. Messed with my head. Each time I saw Abby, spoke to her, or just smelled her as she walked by, it got worse."

Cameron said hoarsely, "I felt like I was torn in two. I loved my wife—but wanted Abby. I kept hoping my feelings for Abby would go away. But they didn't. If anything, they intensified. It got to the point where I thought I should just take Leah and move away. Then Leah got sick, and the sicker she got, the more I felt God was punishing me for wanting Abby. I resented Abby but I was obsessed with her too. It was driving me crazy.

"One night, I was really low, and things got...out of hand...and Abby and I had sex." Cameron glanced at Ross then, to gauge his reaction.

Ross lifted his brows, but said nothing.

"That night haunts me still," Cameron muttered. He lowered his head, then rubbed his brow wearily. "It was the most incredible night of my life—and the worst. Leah and I hadn't made love in months, but that's no excuse for what I did. I wanted Abby. No excuses. I wanted her and I took her. Nothing else mattered that night. Not my wife, not my marriage, nothing."

"Was it worth it?"

"God, who knows?" he answered. "Don't get me wrong, the sex was...well...the best. But, that wasn't the problem. It was...after. I felt torn between elation and shame. I couldn't deal with my guilt, so I took it out on her...acted like a crazy fool.

"I called Abby terrible names, said it was only sex I wanted, blamed her for tempting me." Cameron snorted in self-disgust. "How pathetic can you get—right?"

He sighed, then said bitterly, "I'll never forget the look on her face...the horror...the shame. But I was so eaten up with guilt, I couldn't think about her. Only myself. God, I still can't believe I did that to her." Cameron's eyes glazed over with pain. "Now can you understand why I'm sitting here and not over there!"

"You still didn't answer my question, Cam. What do you want from her—now?"

Cameron rubbed his forehead again as if fighting a headache. "Ross, I wish I knew. A second chance—I think. I'm so tired of being alone. I want a wife...a family. I want to find some peace. But, after all that's happened between us, I'm not sure that's even possible.

"But I want her. I know that much. I ache each time I see her. There wasn't a night when I was away that I didn't think about her, dream about her. But my feelings for Abby are all tied up with my guilt over Leah. Before Abby, I was a good husband, Ross. I never strayed—never even thought about it. I think Leah knew about my feelings for Abby," he added brokenly. "God, I hope I'm wrong."

Ross didn't know what to say to ease Cameron's torment. "Why not take it slow," Ross suggested quietly. "Give her time to get used to you again. You were friends once. Maybe you can be again."

Just then, Abby stood up and walked over to Nick. She placed one arm around his shoulder, then leaned closer to whisper in his ear.

Cameron froze, his eyes blazing with banked fury. "How can I take it slow," he grated, "when just the sight of her touching that man rips my guts to shreds?"

Ross whistled silently in the dark, then grinned. He'd been there himself, knew all the signs. Whether or not he was ready to admit it, Cameron Wallace was in love. With Abby Fulton. Ross patted his friend's tense shoulder, then stood, and brushed the grass from his jeans.

"Looks like Abby...and Nick are going home," Ross said casually. He grinned in the dark when he heard Cameron's jaws snap shut.

Ross walked away with a light step, barely suppressing a laugh. He could see Maggy waiting for him by the fire, her eyes lit with avid curiosity. He had a feeling she would be very interested in all he had to say.

Nick walked Abby home, his arm on her elbow guiding her in the dark. As they passed by Cameron Wallace, Nick felt waves of cold fury emanating from the man. If Abby noticed, she didn't let on, didn't even bother to nod as they passed.

"That wasn't very kind, Abby," Nick teased as they stepped onto the path leading to her house.

Abby snorted, then climbed the steps and opened her front door.

"How about a nightcap?" Nick suggested.

Abby started to say 'no,' then changed her mind. It might be wise, she decided, to let Nick hang around for awhile. Just in case. She nodded briskly, then stepped inside. "Close the door quickly," she said. "Northern mosquitoes will eat you alive."

"Coffee or a beer?" she asked as she headed for the fridge. She stretched her neck, in an attempt to loosen badly-knotted muscles.

"A beer, I guess," Nick told her. "I only had one this evening."

Lifting one from her fridge door, Abby opened it, then walked over and handed Nick his drink. She winced and rolled her shoulders.

"Looks like your neck's all knotted again," he said frowning. "I could work it out for you, if you want."

For a moment Abby was tempted because Nick had magical hands. Then common sense prevailed. No point in giving Nick ideas. He had enough of his own. "I'll manage," she muttered as she padded across the living room. She turned a small table lamp on, then sat down in the armchair, leaving the couch for Nick.

His lips twitched as he sat down on the couch. Abby was keeping her distance and he couldn't blame her. She knew him too well.

"I have a bone to pick with you." Abby's eyes were flinty in the dim light.

Smiling wryly, Nick could guess where she was heading. "I take it you're not too thrilled about being in my movie. Is that it?"

"You got that right." Abby's mouth thinned as she crossed her arms over her chest and glared at her ex-husband. Then she winced again as pain radiated down both arms.

"Abby! This is crazy," Nick said. "Come over here and let me work those kinks out. If I don't, you'll never sleep tonight."

Abby knew he was right. She glared at him in warning and said, "I want my *neck* rubbed—and that's all! Clear?"

His eyes lighting with mischief, Nick patted the seat beside him. "Come to poppa, baby. I'll make you feel *so* good."

Abby groaned, then walked over and dropped on the couch by his side. "I need my head read," she muttered. "But my neck is killing me." She turned slightly away from him and held back her long, silky hair.

Nick placed his hands on either side of her neck, then using his thumbs, began to loosen the knots. In seconds, the tenseness left her shoulders. In minutes, she was purring like a kitten.

"Oh, that *is* so good," she rasped. "Do it harder. Yes…like that. Oh my God—you're good. Do it harder. Oh yes! Oh my God….that's *wonderful!*"

Just about to knock at her door, Cameron heard Abby moaning in pleasure and his heart slammed in his chest. He couldn't believe what he was hearing! Without thinking, he threw open the door and barged right in. "What's going on in here?" he roared as he spotted Abby slumped on the couch in front of her ex-husband.

Still caught up in the pleasure of Nick's massage, Abby slowly sat up, her mind in a stupor; she felt disoriented, unable to reason. Until she noticed the dark fury in Cameron's eyes. That woke her up like ice water in the face and the fog lifted immediately, replaced by a growing rage that equalled his.

She jumped up and marched toward him, her hands on her hips, her azure eyes brimming with cold fire. "Just what do you *think* is going on here, Cameron? As if I can't guess! You have a one-track mind where I'm concerned. So I can just *imagine* what's going on in that pea brain of yours. Where do you get off barging into my house, insulting me in front of my guest!"

"Who just happens to be married," Cameron snapped. "In case you forgot that little detail."

Abby paled as the shot hit home. Her anger deflated, as pain lanced her heart. "No," she said dully. "I didn't forget Nick is married. So kind of you to remind me." She glared at him, her eyes frigid with distaste. "Now, get out of my house, Cameron. Get out and don't come back!"

The minute the words were out of his mouth, Cameron knew he'd made a big mistake. Nick was frowning—not amused. Abby looked hurt—not guilty. Had he misread the whole situation?

Cameron swallowed hard, prepared to apologize profusely.

"I said—get out!" Abby snarled. She marched to the door, pulled it open, then stood in the entrance way with her arms crossed and her lips tight.

The mood she was in, it might be smarter to leave, Cameron thought. As he walked past her, he muttered softly, "I'll be back Abby. Count on it!"

Abby slammed the door at his heels.

Her throat raw with unshed tears, Abby knew she was ready to break and needed to be alone. "Go home, Nick," she begged. "Just leave me be."

Surprisingly, Nick didn't argue. He brushed her bent forehead with a butterfly kiss and said, "You might want to cut the guy some slack, Ab."

"Damn," Abby muttered. "Why do you guys always stick together?"

"Safety in numbers." Nick laughed softly, his eyes gentle for once. Then he headed out the door.

Abby closed the door behind him. She felt battered, scarred, her mind weeping even if her body couldn't. She wouldn't cry, she told herself as she prepared for bed. She wouldn't give that *bastard* the satisfaction. She slipped on a cool silk nightslip, then lay down in her quiet room. Her head throbbed and her eyes ached as she tossed and turned restlessly. She was still awake hours later when the doorbell rang.

Chapter Seven

As Abby stumbled to the door, her eyes gritty from lack of sleep, she glanced at the living room clock and swore. It was the goddamn middle of the night! Then her heart began to race. Something must be wrong with one of her friends!

She opened the door and stopped dead in her tracks, her jaw dropping in shock. "Cameron! What in hell are you doing here at three in the morning?" Abby glared furiously, unaware of the picture she made in her pink satin nightslip.

Like a man in the desert too long without water, Cameron's eyes drank in her high breasts and long, firm legs. To keep from grabbing her, he shoved his hands in his pockets, then glanced around. "Can I come in? If you're alone—that is?"

At his last comment, Abby almost sputtered with rage and moved to shove him out the door. His gall left her speechless, unable to string two words together.

"No, Abby—wait. I didn't mean to imply anything. Please—let me come in and talk to you. There's a few things I'd like to get off my chest."

Abby hesitated. Part of her wanted to punch his lights out; another part wanted to hear what he had to say. "All right," she muttered grudgingly. "You have five minutes. But if you start slinging accusations again—you're gone."

She turned abruptly, padded across the living room, and switched on a light. Only then did she realize her state of undress. Flushing in embarrassment, she glanced over her shoulder and caught Cameron's eyes stripping off what little she wore.

"Excuse me a moment," she said coldly, then stalked out of the room.

Cameron exhaled shakily and sat down on a chair. At least she hadn't slammed the door in his face. He glanced around Abby's home with avid interest. He'd never been here before, and was impressed by its casual elegance. He noticed photos on every table, then stilled when his eyes locked on one in the corner. He stood up, then moved quickly across the carpet. His eyes widened incredulously at the photo he picked up. In it, he was smiling at Leah, his arm around his wife. He could barely recall the day it was taken, it seemed so long ago—a lifetime ago. But what shocked him was that Abby had kept the picture all these years.

"She was my friend, Cameron—no matter what you believe. That's the only picture I have of Leah. I refuse to put it away." Abby's tone was defiant as he turned and faced her, her arms crossed tightly over her chest.

She'd slipped on a loose cotton sundress in a blue to match her eyes. From the look of it, she hadn't bothered with a bra. Instantly, his mouth went dry. Cameron slowly replaced the picture, then walked to a chair and sat down again. His eyes never left Abby as she followed and dropped onto the couch. She lifted her long legs and tucked them under her dress, exposing a long length of smooth thigh. When his body jumped in response he knew he was in trouble.

Clearing his throat, he said, "We have to talk, Abby. Long past time."

"At three o'clock in the morning?" She snorted derisively, then played with the skirt of her dress, picking at invisible lint. Anything to avoid looking in his eyes.

"I couldn't sleep," he said. He rubbed the side of his tired face and added softly, "Could you?"

An instant 'of course' jumped to the edge of her tongue, but she caught it just in time. She refused to add lying to her growing list of sins.

"Couldn't this have waited till tomorrow?" She sighed tiredly, finger-combing her silky hair as she spoke. She seemed unaware that her long neck arched provocatively exposing the delicate line of her throat.

Cameron almost growled. He'd been hard since she opened the door in that flimsy excuse for a nightgown. And now this. He wanted her so badly, he hurt.

"Abby," he grated, "you have every reason to hate me, but please, hear me out." He paused, as if struggling for words.

It was impossible to ignore the misery in his emerald eyes, or the tense set of his shoulders, or the way his hands flexed repeatedly. "All right," she said quietly. "I'll listen."

Cameron met her stare and the words finally came. "I wanted you, Abby," he whispered rawly. "Don't ever doubt that. I wanted you for a very long time—though I refused to admit it even to myself. I enjoyed your company, liked to hear you laugh, waited for your smile. But I was married...to a woman who'd loved me since we were kids. A woman I loved in return. No matter how much I wanted you, I didn't *want* to feel that way."

His voice dropped then, as did his eyes. "I respected the vows I said to Leah. Respected *her*. In all the years we were married, I never looked at another woman. Never even wanted to. Then you came along and everything I believed in turned to ashes. I couldn't eat...couldn't sleep...couldn't touch Leah without thinking about you. Even though I was technically faithful, I was living a lie.

"Then Leah got sick. And my life turned into a living hell...trying to take care of her...run my business...and forget about you. Do you understand what I'm saying?"

Abby nodded slowly, her eyes huge in her pale face. She was hearing words she didn't want to hear...facing a past she didn't want to relive.

"Then you came to see me that night."

"Don't, Cameron!" Abby protested rawly. "Don't go there."

"We have to," he insisted, his voice ragged with emotion. "I said terrible things to you...behaved inexcusably. It's time to set it right."

Exhausted in more ways than one, Abby leaned back against the couch and rubbed her forehead wearily. She wasn't sure it mattered any more. The past couldn't be undone.

Cameron saw the resignation on her face and frowned. "Don't turn me off, Abby. Let me explain——please."

Abby sighed, then stared at him again.

His mouth tightened. "The truth is...I lied to you that night, Abby. I said it was just sex, but it wasn't. I let you think that all I wanted that night was a woman—any woman. Well, that wasn't true either. It was you I wanted, Abby. Only you."

His eyes looked haunted. Abby wanted to believe him, but she was afraid to open that door.

"Why were you so cruel at Leah's funeral?" she said, her voice raw with suppressed emotion. "I need to know."

Cameron winced and glanced away again. Then his face hardened and he leaned toward her. "That day was a nightmare," he said grimly. "I was eating myself up with guilt. Leah had just died, and I didn't know how to deal with the pain or the remorse—so I blamed you. You see, through it all, I still wanted you and I despised myself for feeling that way. I couldn't deal with the guilt so I took it out on you. It was wrong. My behaviour was inexcusable. But I was out of my mind with grief. I *did* love Leah, you know," he added starkly. "You may not want to hear me say it—but I did."

Abby *didn't* want to hear him say it, but she knew it was true. Cameron loved Leah. Probably loved her still. That's what hurt so much. "What do you want from me, Cameron?" she whispered tiredly.

"A second chance, Abby. I want...a second chance with you. My wife is dead, but we're still alive. Is it so wrong to see if there's still something between us? There always was—right from the beginning. You can't deny that and neither can I.

"In the months I was away, I thought about Leah and finally accepted her death. But I never forgot about you, Abby. I thought of you constantly—night after night. It was because of you that I came back home." His eyes glittered with emotion as he waited for her to speak.

"So, what am I supposed to say?"

"How you feel."

"How I feel?" Her eyes snapped as she leaned toward him. "Well, I'll tell you how I feel," she said bitterly. "You're too late. Years too late." When his face paled she almost relented, but fear drove her on. "Maybe if you'd made just one call or written even one letter while you were away, I might feel differently. But you didn't, and I don't ever want to go through all that pain again. You were vicious that night, Cameron, a cold-hearted bastard who ripped me apart, and I don't know if I can ever forgive you. It's like a scar on my soul that just won't heal."

His eyes wild in his harsh-planed face, Cameron stood and pulled Abby to her feet, holding both her hands against his hard chest. "You can't mean it," he said hoarsely.

She swayed back, her eyes wide with fear, yet a part of her quivered at his touch.

"Are you happy, Abby?" he demanded. "Can you honestly say you are?"

She dropped her head, her long silky hair hiding her face. "Sometimes," she murmured softly. When she looked up again, her eyes glimmered with unshed tears.

"Are you involved with anyone else?"

"If you mean Nick—the answer's no." Abby's eyes narrowed and her spine stiffened in renewed anger.

"I didn't mean that, actually. But I'm relieved to hear it all the same." Cameron's smile was wry, but fleeting. His eyes were fixed on her mouth now, his body inching closer.

Abby was finding it difficulty to breathe. She felt tense and nervous with him so close.

"I left because of you, Abby."

When she raised her brows in surprise, he added, "I couldn't face you. Couldn't face seeing you each day and remembering that night. I knew if I stayed, I wouldn't be able to leave you alone. So I left. I needed to grieve for Leah—needed to grieve for the love we'd shared. I owed her that much."

When Abby tried to turn away, he caught her chin. "I won't lie to you about my feelings for Leah. It wouldn't be fair to her or her memory."

"If she were alive today, would you be here now?"

"Probably not."

Abby winced at his honesty. *'Let him remember me—when I'm gone.'* Leah's last request flashed into her mind, triggered by Cameron's words. Abby looked up, met his intent stare.

"Leah came to see me before she died," Abby told him bluntly, her eyes haunted as she searched his. "She knew."

Cameron flinched, then exhaled deeply. "I was afraid of that."

"She asked me...to look after you when she was gone." Abby hadn't planned to tell him that—it just came out.

"Leah loved me. She was the most unselfish person I knew."

The love in his voice hurt Abby more than she cared to admit. "Leah the saint," she muttered, her eyes dark with misery.

Cameron chuckled, then lifted Abby's chin. "She was no saint," he said, "just a wonderful, delightful human being."

"And you loved her."

Cameron nodded. "I did. But she's gone, and we're here. So, what happens next? It's up to you, Abby. And don't tell me it's too late. As long as we're both breathing, it'll never be too late."

Abby stood there, mired in a world of indecision, her body aching with need, her mind screaming *run, run, run.*

Sensing her indecision, Cameron tightened his grip, moulding her against his hard body.

He's so hard! Abby almost groaned aloud. *It wasn't fair! All he had to do was touch her and she melted.*

"You're driving me crazy—do you know that?" His mouth hovered over hers, his breath heated her lips.

Abby's mouth parted, anticipating his touch.

Cameron groaned and cupped her face in his hands. "It's been so long! I've got to touch you, Abby!" He took her mouth with an almost brutal force, his body straining against hers, his hands lifting her firm bottom against his hard, pulsing length.

All thought gone, Abby wrapped her arms around his neck and leaned in, needing to feel every inch of his body against hers. Her tongue darted inside his mouth and mated with his. Abby moaned, almost purring in delight. He tasted so dark and sweet, she trembled with need. She couldn't get enough of him!

Shoving one leg between Abby's thighs, Cameron gripped her bottom firmly, then rubbed insistently against her, showing her what he wanted. But it wasn't enough. Time and again his mouth devoured hers, his body moving relentless, mimicking the act they both needed. He wanted to bury himself inside Abby and put an end to this torment. He needed her desperately, now more than ever and hoped to God she felt the same. He lifted his mouth and stared at her, his eyes hot and narrow.

"I want to be inside you, Abby. I've dreamt of it night after night." Her eyes were half-shut, her face flushed, her mouth slightly parted. He'd seen that look before; it had haunted his dreams forever. His sanity shredded, Cameron pushed aside her flimsy dress and cupped one firm breast. With no bra to hold him back, he licked the turgid, rosy tip, then swallowed it with his mouth. And began to suckle. Hard.

Abby moaned rawly as the liquid heat in her core ignited. She thrust against his leg, her own arousal insistent and burning. Wet and aching, she arched against him, her hair dropping over his arm. When his mouth left her breast, she whimpered in disappointment till she felt fingers inching under her skirt. Then he was there—at last—under her panties, touching her swollen cleft. When one long finger penetrated her flesh, she sighed in relief and groaned long and loud, pushing against his hand.

Cameron was so hard, he was ready to burst his zipper. She was so incredibly wet, so hot, so responsive. Just as he'd remembered from that night long ago. He eased a second finger inside and heard her moan again. He was panting now, desperate to possess her completely. With fingers and thumb he pleasured her, primed her, watched her intently as she moved closer to release. God she was beautiful! So beautiful…so totally immersed in her own world of pleasure! In that moment, all he cared about was giving her what she needed.

When she came, it took them both by surprise. Abby's body convulsed around Cameron's fingers so violently, he had a hard time holding her upright. She trembled and jerked against his hand, writhing and moaning endlessly. His own passion barely held in check, he watched her face flush, heard her low moan and smiled tightly, pleased that he could give her such joy.

Then her body seemed to melt and her head dropped onto his shoulder. Her eyes were still closed and she was trembling, he noticed, as he reluctantly eased his fingers out of her body. Gently, carefully, he lowered her to the carpet, then lay down beside her, one arm under her head, the other holding her close. For the moment he was content just to have her in his arms.

Abby felt incredibly relaxed, almost weightless, at peace for the first time in too long. Rosy mists still clouded her vision, the bones in her body seemed to have liquefied, but Abby didn't care. She felt so good…so damn good!

Then soft, feathery lips touched her face and inched toward her mouth. It was Cameron… kissing her…nibbling at her neck. His body pressed insistently against her hip, making it clear he wanted more. *Oh dear God! What had she done?*

She opened her mouth to tell him to stop, but he captured her words with his lips.

After that, she was lost. Again. He eased over her, his hard shaft rubbing her mound relentlessly. Then his hand slipped inside the bodice of her dress and fingered her breast. When her nipples hardened, she barely heard his groan of satisfaction. Her breath came in pants as her fingers inched their way down his body. Finally she reached his zipper. In seconds he was free, startlingly erect in her hand. When she massaged his velvety length, he groaned against her lips, his tongue duelling with hers voraciously. She rimmed him with her fingers, and he reared up like a wounded lion. The time for play had ended.

Cameron braced himself. Then, like a man possessed, flipped up her skirt. When he saw her exposed lace panties, he buried his face between her thighs, his flicking tongue insistent and hot.

Abby moaned impatiently, that wasn't what she wanted—not now.

Then he pulled down her panties, and she lifted her hips eagerly, her thighs trembling and damp. With an impatience born of intolerable hunger, he spread her legs, lifted her knees, and positioned himself against her body. With one powerful thrust he was inside her and she gasped aloud in pain-tinged pleasure, his hard body lifting hers off the floor. Holding on for dear life, Abby met his thrusts with her own and gasped for more. He gave it to her, stroke after stroke, his body driving into hers with no finesse, no pause for tenderness.

But Abby didn't care. She was mindless with lust, her need for this man so overpowering, nothing mattered but him.

She wrapped her legs around his thighs, her arms around his back, and held on for the ride of her life. She was climbing again, her body steadily reaching for the pleasure she knew only he could give.

Cameron was out of control, lost in a world where only he and Abby existed. Again and again he ground into her velvety warmth, groans of pleasure erupting from his throat. It had been so long. So long since he'd been inside her. And she felt so incredibly good. So hot. So tight. He could feel his time coming, knew he couldn't hold on much longer.

Abby heard his pants, smelled his musky scent, and flew over the edge, her body soaring with the rapture she craved.

He felt her stiffen, heard her moan of completion and lost it. He threw back his head, arched his body and came…and came…and came. He jack-hammered inside her, spurting endlessly it seemed, then slowly relaxed, his body completely drained.

When he could breathe again, he dropped a slow, wet kiss onto her lips, then rolled to the side, taking Abby with him, his body still deeply embedded in hers. Holding her close, finally at peace, Cameron instantly fell asleep.

As morning light filtered through the windows, Abby woke with a start. She felt disoriented. Her muscles ached; her body felt stiff and cold. She looked around in bewilderment. Why was she on the living room floor? Then she heard Cameron breathing deeply at her side—and remembered.

My good God, I've done it again! she thought incredulously. She winced and tried to roll away, but Cameron's arm was heavy across her chest, and his leg held her prisoner. *At least he's not still inside me.* She sighed and closed her eyes wearily, details of the night flashing through her mind. *This has to stop,* she told herself. *It's madness to have anything more to do with the man.*

But she couldn't help snuggling closer for one minute more.

They were half on and half off the area rug that covered a portion of the hardwood floor. Abby's back was killing her and she felt cold and sticky. She wrinkled her nose as she smelled the stale sex in the air, knowing she needed a shower in the worst way. And she was going to have one, soon!

Taking a deep breath she pushed at Cameron's dead weight. Then pushed again. "Damn you, Cameron—wake up," she huffed as she struggled to get out from under his body. She saw his heavily-lashed lids flutter open, his green eyes still dull with sleep. Then he focused and smiled, giving her the sweetest smile Abby had ever seen in her life. She caught her breath and held it, suspending the moment in time.

"Good morning," he whispered huskily, as he pulled her against his hard length. He was aroused again she realized in alarm. That had her moving with incredible speed. In seconds she was on her feet and away, glaring at him from across the room. She tugged at her dress, then glanced around in agitation, searching for her panties.

As Cameron got to his feet, he spotted a piece of pink lace under him. He picked it up, stared at it blankly for a moment, then smiled again.

"Is this what you're looking for?" he asked, holding out her panties.

Abby's face flamed. "Well, at least you didn't tear them to shreds—this time," she muttered snidely, snatching them out of his hands.

What the hell! Cameron knew right then he was in big trouble. He stared at her, his mouth grim.

"What?" she demanded, nonplussed by the dark anger in his eyes.

"You tell me. We just made love—yet you're acting like you want me out of here."

"That's exactly what I want," Abby told him. "And just for the record—we had sex. Good sex—but that's all it was. Don't read more into it than that."

She was parroting his own words back at him. Cameron frowned, his eyes turning bleak at the thought. "Are we playing games here, Abby?" he demanded. "Is this payback time for you? Because if it is, it's a cheap shot."

Abby flushed, then looked away. She hadn't meant to be so blunt. The words just seemed to come from nowhere and trip off her tongue. "I think you should go, Cam," she sighed. "I just can't think right now."

Cameron knew she was exhausted and so was he. Perhaps now was not the best time to push any harder. He stepped closer and lifted her chin, forcing her to meet his eyes. She did so with genuine reluctance.

"I'll leave, Abby, because I know you need time to think things through.

But remember this. You're mine now. Just as you put your claim on me two years ago, I'm claiming you now. I won't let you run away from me, Abby—so don't even try."

He sighed and rested his head on her forehead. "Don't fight this, Abby. Give us a chance."

He brushed her lips with great tenderness, then turned to walk away. Then he stopped as if struck by lightning. "Oh f....fudge," he muttered, though it was evident he had another word in mind. His eyes were bleak, apologetic. "I didn't use any protection last night, Abby. I'm sorry."

"You didn't the first time either," she muttered, reproach in her tone. "Don't worry," she said wearily, "the chances of my getting pregnant are almost nil. That's why Nick and I didn't have kids."

"You mean...you can't conceive?"

Abby saw the deep concern in his eyes, and lifted her chin. "Probably not," she told him. "I have a better chance of winning a lottery."

Though she tried to downplay it, her blue eyes reflected a lingering pain. Cameron wanted to swear but didn't. It would only upset Abby more. Life didn't seem to give him many choices these days. He could have Abby—or kids—but not both.

He exhaled deeply then said, "I'll see you tonight and we'll talk." He kissed her gently and turned to go.

"Wait!" she shouted in panic. "If you want to come over tonight to talk—fine. But no more sex. I can't handle it. It clouds the issue too much."

The muscles in Cameron's jaw flexed, but he nodded slowly in agreement, his eyes dark and unreadable. Then he was gone.

Abby shuddered and sank into a chair, her panties still clutched in her hand.

Then the door slammed back on its hinges and Cameron marched across the room, his face grim. Without a word, he pulled her out of her chair and kissed her soundly. When he lifted his head and saw the bemused look on Abby's face, he grinned in satisfaction. "Just so you don't forget—you're mine now. See you tonight." He caressed her cheek tenderly, then walked out again, whistling softly as he closed the door behind him.

Abby couldn't move. She stared at the door in wide-eyed fascination. Then a slow smile curled her lips and gently edged up into her eyes. Her heart began to race with anticipation and her eyes began to shine. For the first time in years, she felt incredibly alive.

ABBY'S STORY: BETRAYED BY LOVE

Later that afternoon Abby slipped on a pair of cut-off shorts and a pink halter top and, in bare feet, picked her way across the grass.

"Anybody home?" she called as she opened the patio door to the family room and stepped inside. The plush grey carpet felt cool between her toes.

"I'm in the kitchen," Maggy answered back. "Coffee's on. I hope you don't mind if I finish this salad I'm making for supper tonight," she said as Abby stepped into the room.

"No problem." Abby padded across the cool kitchen and poured herself a cup of coffee. She took a sip of the strong, hot brew and sighed with deep appreciation. "Oh, this is good. The first cup of the day is always the best."

Maggy stared at her friend in amazement. Then her eyes narrowed. Abby's cheeks glowed, her eyes appeared tired, yet vibrantly alive, and her movements were languid and slow. All the signs, Maggy realized in dawning wonder, of a long night with the right man.

"It's two o'clock in the afternoon," Maggy said with a sly grin. "How come this is your first cup instead of your tenth?"

Abby flushed, caught in a trap of her own making. "I...uh...had a late night...so I slept in."

"You and Nick left the barbeque early enough," Maggy smiled. Then a thought hit and she frowned, her light green eyes filling with distress. "Oh Abby! Tell me you didn't!"

"Didn't what?" Abby stared at Maggy in true bewilderment, then awareness dawned. "No, I certainly did not sleep with Nick—if that's what you're implying," she said indignantly. "Nick left immediately, after he saw me home." Her blue eyes were haughty and cool, as she stared at Maggy over the rim of her cup.

"Sorry, Abby. I should have known better."

The green eyes were so beguiling, Abby had no choice but to back down. "It's all right," she replied as she dropped into a chair. As was her habit, she pulled another chair close and crossed her bare feet on the seat.

"So...why were such a sleepy head today?" Maggy teased.

Abby groaned. "Do you want the truth or a lie?"

The tone in Abby's voice warned Maggy to sit down. "I'd prefer the truth."

"Cameron came over. We talked. We had sex. He left. End of story."

Maggy's eyes rounded with shock. "Good grief, Abby. Do you think that was wise?"

"No, probably not." Abby sighed. "It was the second worst mistake of my life. But whenever I'm around Cameron, my common sense goes out the window."

"How was he—when he left? Did he yell and get mad again—after?"

"Hell no! Not this time. He was puffed up like a peacock, whistling when he left. Whistling like a kid after his first date." Abby shook her head in disbelief, then grinned wryly. "I know I'm a damned fool, Maggy, but I've been doing a lot of whistling myself this morning. Or trying, anyway. My lips are too damned sore to pucker."

Maggy chuckled. "There's nothing worse than a braggart, Abby."

"I know…I know. But I feel so good this morning, I couldn't resist." Abby sipped her coffee and grinned impishly at Maggy, her eyes twinkling with wry laughter.

In minutes the two women were roaring insanely, their laughter echoing through the empty house.

"So…how was it?" Maggy's eyes were sly and knowing.

"Too good for my own piece of mind." As she put her feelings into words, the truth of what she was saying hit home. Abby's laughter drained away and her eyes turned bleak and sad.

Maggy stretched out one hand and softly stroked her friend's shoulder. "What are you going to do?"

"Take it one day at a time—what else *can* I do?" Abby sighed deeply. "He says he wants me. Told me he wanted me from the moment we met. But he made it very clear he loved Leah and regrets breaking their vows. If she were still alive, he'd be with her. He admitted as much to me last night. I know I'm second best…and probably always will be. I just don't know if that's enough."

"Sometimes, a relationship starts out that way but ends up very differently," Maggy said quietly. Her eyes were sombre and brooding as she spoke.

"Is Ross…second best?"

Maggy gasped as if Abby had struck her. "Definitely not," she snapped. "I love him, with all my heart. It's just different than how it was with Jarrod."

"I'm sorry, Maggy. I didn't mean that the way it sounded." Abby grabbed Maggy's hand and held it tight, her eyes begging forgiveness.

"It's okay—really it is." Maggy leaned back in her chair and smiled, but her eyes still brooded. "I try very hard not to compare Jarrod and Ross," she admitted softly. "It seems disloyal to them both. But," she added, her voice breaking for a moment, "in my heart, I know the truth."

Abby leaned forward, her eyes rapt with attention.

"When I married Jarrod I was a young girl…overwhelmed by love and sex. Jarrod was a good man, wonderful in bed, a terrific husband and father. If he were alive, we'd still be married—both content with our marriage. But, Ross and I connect on so many levels that Jarrod and I didn't. We have the same taste in music…love the same books…can read each others' thoughts so easily—it's kind of eerie. I feel so disloyal saying this," Maggy mumbled, her eyes lowering with remorse, "but Ross fills something in me that Jarrod never knew existed.

"If Jarrod were still alive, I wouldn't have my business—he'd want me at home. I wouldn't have the twins—he thought two children were enough. I'd still be happy—but in a very different way." Maggy sighed, then stared intently at Abby. "Do you understand?"

"I…think so." Abby's eyes were shadowed, but less haunted. "And…in bed…is there a difference in bed?"

Maggy nodded slowly as a soft flush crept up her neck. "Jarrod was a wonderful lover. Very masterful, yet sweet. He satisfied me completely…made sure of it always. But, with Ross, I'm his equal. We know each other so well, match each other so completely, that it's…instant fusion when we touch."

"That's the way it is with Cameron and me," Abby whispered. "That's a perfect way to describe it—instant fusion." Her eyes were dreamy now, her voice soft and remote. "I never had that with Nick. Not even in the beginning. That's what worries me," she admitted. "What if I'm confusing desire with love."

Maggy's eyes were grave. "That's something only you can answer. I don't know," she mused, "maybe one leads to the other. Maybe you can't have love without desire first. Who knows? I wasn't attracted to Ross in the beginning. At least…I don't think I was. Then I looked at him…*really* looked at him. And I got a super bad case of the hornies!"

Abby giggled. "What a charming way to put it," she teased. "So…eloquent."

"It's hard to be eloquent when you haven't had sex in years," Maggy grinned dryly.

"Don't I know it!" Abby laughed.

"What do you know?" Ross said at he came into the kitchen dressed in low-slung shorts and nothing else.

Abby grinned at Maggy knowingly. "I know it's time I went home and gave you two some privacy."

"Oh…stick around," Ross said as he poured himself a cup of coffee.

"We're not doing anything this afternoon." He turned around, the cup halfway to his mouth, then caught an intent look in Maggy's eyes.

"Ah…that is…I think we might have…plans or something—after all," he muttered hoarsely.

"Could be," Maggy drawled as she ran her fingers through the curly mat on his bare chest.

Abby grinned and headed out the door. "Say no more," she teased. "I'm out of here." As she opened the patio door, Abby could hear two sets of footsteps racing up the stairs.

Chapter Eight

Once back home, Abby waited for Cameron to come over or call, but he did neither. She vacuumed the house, polished furniture, then tried to do some paperwork. When the phone finally rang at suppertime, she pounced on it with relief. Then sighed in frustration when she heard Maggy's voice inviting her for 'leftovers.' Abby wasn't really hungry, but she reluctantly agreed—just to get away from the phone. But before she left, she rewound the answering machine.

Maggy served up the remainder of the hot casseroles and salads outside, and, because she hadn't eaten much in the last twenty-four hours, Abby ate more than usual. Probably all the fresh air. She loved eating outside in Maggy's backyard, with the hot sun shining on her back and the air blowing through her hair.

When dinner was finished and they were sipping tea, Kyra asked, "Mom, can we get a dog?"

Maggy glanced at Ross and raised her brows. His face was bland and non-committal. "Oh, I don't know, Kyra," she answered slowly. "I'm not much of an animal person…and we're gone all day. It wouldn't be fair to the dog."

"Ardith said it would be all right, and she's here all day," the young girl insisted. "I asked her. She likes dogs." Kyra turned her big green eyes on

Ross. "Can we, Ross? I'll feed it and walk it and it can sleep with me at night."

"No it can not," Maggy snorted. "There'll be no fleas in our beds young lady."

"Actually, Maggy," Ross said, "there's this pill that dogs take once a month and, just like that, no flea problem."

"Just like that. Imagine." Maggy glared at the sparkling amusement in his deep blue eyes. *Thanks—a heap!* hers snapped.

You're welcome! his teased back.

Since no one jumped in to help her out, Maggy said grudgingly, "I suppose we could think about it." The words were barely spoken when Kyle and Kyra jumped for joy. "I just said we'd think about it!" she added. "The last thing we need is an animal underfoot."

"Aw, come on Mom! You know it'll be fun. Puppies are so cute," Kyle said, grinning at his mother's scowling face.

"Yes, but then they turn into big growling mutts."

"Tom's beagle had a litter several months ago." Ross said. "And there's one left." He winked at Kyra, then added, "We could take a run over now and have a look at it. They don't grow very big. And they make good house dogs."

Kyra yelled a loud 'Yes!' and was in the car before Maggy had a chance to say another word. She eyed her husband reprovingly. "Do I smell a set up?" she asked. She knew she was dead-on when he laughed heartily—then looked away.

"Dogs and kids go hand in hand," he grinned. "What's one more?"

"Well, you'll get up in the middle of the night with this one," she muttered. "I've already got my hands full."

Ross bent and dropped a kiss on her lips, then he and Kyle followed Kyra to the car.

"Can you believe that man?" Maggy sputtered as she glared at Abby, her eyes half-laughing, half-mad.

Abby grinned. "Who do you think really wants a dog—Kyra or Ross?"

"It's probably a toss up," Maggy said ruefully. "Oh well, what's one more inmate in the asylum?"

Just then Jonathan started to fuss. Maggy asked, "Will you stay and give me a hand bathing the twins?"

Abby nodded, "But if you're ever tempted to ask me to wash the dog—or dogsit, don't! That's where I draw the line."

ABBY'S STORY: BETRAYED BY LOVE

Several hours later, after the twins were in bed and Maggy's kitchen tidied, Abby wandered back to her own house. She checked her answering machine the instant she got in the door and, sure enough, the light was flashing.

"It's eight-forty five, Abby. Sorry I couldn't make it over, but I got tied up with Rayce and Libby. Call me when you get in—please!"

Abby heard a vein of excitement in his voice and wondered at the cause. She hesitated about phoning him, but most of her earlier resentment was gone. Besides, she was curious to know how the meeting with Libby went. So, she sat down and hit redial.

Cam picked up immediately. "Hi...is that you Abby?" His tone was low and intimate on the phone.

Abby shivered and gripped the handle tighter. The man was lethal—even from a distance!

"Yes, it's me."

"Where were you?"

"At Maggy's—for dinner. When you didn't show up this afternoon, I went out."

"Sorry about that," Cameron muttered. "I met with Libby and Rayce right after they got home from church. I only expected to be an hour or so, but we got so involved with the plans for their new house, the next time I looked up—it was five o'clock. Libby asked me to stay and have a bite with them. So I did. Got to keep the clients happy."

Abby gasped in excitement. "You got the contract to build their new house?" She knew his company really needed the work.

"You bet," he answered, a tinge of relief in his voice. "And they're planning quite a monster of a home."

"Tell me about it." Libby settled back, enjoying the happiness in his rich, deep voice.

"Well, they bought a property on Lake Nipissing just on the edge of Howard's Bay. They have the whole peninsula and want a house built off the road, under the bluff of a hill. They took me out to see the spot. It's overlooking the bay and has a spectacular view. It's an incredible spot for a home. They want to build a four bedroom tri-level. Their plans call for a cedar home with three stories of glass on the bayside and terraced decks leading down to the water. It's going to be a real showcase when we're done."

Abby smiled at the eagerness in his voice. "Sounds like it's going to be expensive."

"D…darn right. It's a good thing Rayce is a bank manager. It's going to cost a fortune—and that's just my fee," he laughed.

"So, are you coming over tonight?" *There! She'd said it!* with just the right shade of casual nonchalance.

"Afraid not," he told her, sounding tired for the first time. "Pete's on his way over here right now. Rayce wants the digging to start next week, so Pete and I have a lot of planning to do. Actually," he said, hesitation edging his voice, "I might not be able to get out to your place for a few days."

Abby frowned, then paled. *Was this—a polite brush-off?* "Fine," she managed abruptly. "I'll see you…around."

She was ready to hang up when he roared into the phone, "Like h…heck you will! Don't be like this, Abby! I'm not playing games with you. Don't play games with me. In the next few days, I have to hire more men—maybe even an office manager—if I can find one, find a place to live that could also double as an office, read up on the latest building codes, and take care of all the red tape needed to start this project. I'll be putting in twenty-hour days for awhile. The least you can do is be a little understanding."

Abby sighed and relented. "You're right," she murmured. "I'll see you when you've got some free time."

Cameron heard the bleakness in her tone and swore savagely in his mind. "No," he said firmly, "you'll see me on Thursday night—around nine. Is that all right with you?"

Abby hugged the phone and closed her burning eyes. "That'll be fine," she whispered. "I'll see you then."

Cameron slowly replaced the receiver, then slumped against the chair. His instincts told him to head right over to Abby's place and set things straight. But he knew what would follow. They'd make love for the rest of the night and he'd be a walking zombie tomorrow. He couldn't handle another day without sleep. Adrenaline had kept him going today, but tonight, his body was protesting—big time, demanding at least a few hours of sleep.

As it had all day, his mind drifted to the night before with Abby. It had been more than he'd hoped—and less. The lovemaking had been all that he'd remembered—and then some. But a part of Abby was closed to him now; he saw it in her eyes. A wall of aloofness surrounded her that wasn't there before. She didn't trust him—he was pretty sure that's what it was.

He sighed and closed his eyes. He couldn't really blame her. He'd hurt her so badly in the past. One day at a time...that's how he'd have to play it. He'd have to go slow with her. Let her see she could trust him again. He'd been so tempted last night to tell her how much she meant to him, but he'd held back. His feelings were so new, so raw, he knew he wasn't ready to share them yet. Just as Abby wasn't ready to hear the words—whatever they might be. Their time would come. He just hoped it would be soon.

When Cameron called the next night at ten-thirty. Abby answered on the second ring.

"I hope I didn't wake you," Cameron said.

"I just got into bed when the phone rang," Abby told him. "I didn't expect to hear from you so soon. I know how busy you must be." She paused, then added softly, "You sound tired."

"I'm bushed," Cameron admitted with a sigh. "I just got in the door."

"Did you eat?"

Cameron laughed huskily. "That's the first thing Leah always asked too."

Abby bit back a snappy retort and said nothing.

Cameron laughed again. "Cat got your tongue?"

"No," Abby said, then decided it was payback time. "I...was just taking off my nightie. It's too...hot in here."

Cameron groaned across the line. "Ouch! That's fighting dirty!"

"What do you mean?" Abby purred.

"Talking sexy to me when you know I'm too d....darned tired to get off this couch."

Abby grinned and decided to change the topic. "So...how did the day go? Did you get much accomplished?"

"More than I hoped," he answered tiredly. "Actually, Pete was a great help. He knew about this old place on the edge of Mill Street that's been vacant for a year. The Hutchinson place, he called it."

"I know it," Abby told him. "That's awfully big for an office, Cam. And it looks like it needs a lot of work too."

"It's structurally sound. When old man Hutchinson died eight years ago, the couple who bought it changed the wiring, updated the plumbing and heating, and replaced the roof and windows."

"Oh, that's good."

"No...that's bad. Now they're asking an arm and a leg for it."

"I see. So, what did you decide to do?"

"I got them to agree to a one-year lease with an option to buy."

"Well…that sounds better. But it's still a very big old place."

"I'm going to live on the top floor and use the bottom for office space."

Abby smiled in delight. "That means you'll be living in Howard's Bay again."

"As of next weekend," he told her. "The condo's great, but it's very inconvenient to live in the city when I have several big contracts in Howard's Bay. Pete snapped up the restoration of a tourist resort out on the edge of Callander. Eight cabins and the main lodge—a complete overhaul. We'll work on the outside until winter and do the inside when the snow hits."

"It sounds like you're going to have to hire more men than you thought."

"No…just a crew of three. Keep it lean. We decided it was more important to hire an office manager first."

Abby heard a hesitation in his voice. "Do you have anyone in mind?"

"Well, Pete's sister just moved back from Ottawa. She managed an office for a Member of Parliament down there, so she has quite a bit of experience. She's also a bookkeeper—that's a plus."

So…what's wrong with her? Abby was dying to ask. But didn't.

When the silence stretched just a shade too long, Cameron added heartily, "Actually, Abby, you and Lorraine should have a lot in common."

"Oh. And what might that be?" Abby asked dryly.

"Lorraine…uh…was a model too. She paid her way through college doing…uh…catalogue work."

"So…you've already talked to her?"

"Yah…Pete and I had lunch with her today—that's when she agreed to work for us."

"What kind of catalogue work did she do?" Abby asked cooly. "Perhaps we've met."

There was a short pause before he said, "I'm not really sure." Then he added quickly, "I'd better go. I'm beat. I miss you Abby and I'll see you on Thursday night—all right?"

Abby told him 'yes' then murmured 'good-bye.' She was not a jealous person by nature, but already she didn't like the sound of Lorraine Reilly. With so much to think about, it was a long time before she got to sleep that night.

The next morning Abby went to work an hour early, and headed straight for Maggy's tea room instead of her own shop. The tea room was full, as it usually was every morning. Abby grabbed a piping hot cup of coffee, a fresh carrot muffin, paid for them at the cash, then headed into the backroom where Maggy's tiny office was located.

As expected, Maggy was at her old desk preparing some sort of list. She glanced up in surprise when Abby walked through the door.

"Is it Monday again already? I thought we just had our weekly meeting yesterday." Maggy looked fresh and sunny in a yellow cotton top and matching skirt.

"I need to talk," Abby muttered briskly. "Am I interrupting something important?"

"No...not really. I have to phone in my order to the wholesalers, but I have a few minutes. What's up?"

"Do you know Lorraine Reilly?" Abby's eyes were as cool as her tone.

Maggy frowned. "Pete Reilly's sister? Not really," she mused. "I know of her—of course."

"So...give! What do you know?"

"I know she was a Victoria's Secret model for awhile. I found a picture of her under Kyle's mattress when I turned it last month." Maggy's eyes brimmed with amusement. "He's still trying to figure out where it went."

Abby groaned and slumped into her chair. "I bet she's gorgeous—right?"

"She's about five-eight, has black hair, dark eyes, and a voluptuous figure—what do you think?"

"I think I hate her already," Abby sighed.

"May I ask why?" Maggy tried hard to keep a smile off her face...and failed. Abby looked so comically tragic.

"Cameron just hired her as his new office manager. His voice was kind of strained when I asked him about her. He said she used to be a model but forgot to mention the Victoria's Secret part."

That wiped the smile off Maggy's face. "Lorraine Reilly working for Cam. Now...that's not good news," she said with a frown. "The woman's a certified man-eater. After she stopped modelling, she worked for an MP in Ottawa for a few years—until the guy's wife found out where her husband was spending his nights. Lorraine's been home for several months now. Looking for work apparently."

"Then you don't think I'm being paranoid," Abby asked.

"Well, let me put it this way. If I walked into Ross's office and she was working there, she'd be gone so fast, her dust wouldn't have time to settle."

"Oh God! That bad!"

"She's beautiful, but very cold...at least to women. With men...butter would melt in her mouth."

"So, what do I do?"

Maggy sighed, then patted her friend on the arm. "There's not much you can do—I'm afraid. Cameron hired the woman. If you say anything, you'll put him on the defensive for sure. Just pray she can't type or has terrible breath or something—and keep your eyes open."

Abby groaned. "I think I'll run away and join a nunnery. This being in love is for the birds."

"You in a nunnery? Won't work, Abby."

"Why not?"

"Two problems." Maggy's tone was serious but her eyes danced with mischief.

"I'm listening."

"One—you're not catholic. And two—you'd have to be celibate for the rest of your life. You'd never last."

"Spoilsport," Abby chuckled. She stood up and drained her coffee. "As you're no help at all, I'm going to work."

When Abby left the room, Maggy sat back and closed her eyes. *Lorraine Reilly. Why couldn't Cameron have hired some matronly grandmother? No...he had to go and hire a Victoria's Secret model! The man had no sense at all.* Maggy shook her head in disgust and got back to work herself.

Thursday afternoon, Abby was sorting a new shipment of printed cotton fabrics when Delia called her to the phone.

"Cameron! I'm glad you called," Abby said smiling. "I've missed talking to you. I'm really looking forward to seeing you tonight."

"That's why I called," he murmured regretfully. "I'm going to have to cancel. The new computer system for the office just came in today and Lorraine needs help to get it all set up. It's going to take hours to load all the programs in, so I'm afraid our date is off."

Abby leaned back in her chair and closed her eyes. He had no time for her, but lots of time for Lorraine. Why was she not surprised. "Sure Cameron...whatever," she said brusquely. "I've got to go."

"No Abby! Wait! Don't be like this." He sounded impatient and cool.

"No. You wait! You're the one that has no time for me, Cameron. It's been like that since day one. I'm tired of always being at the bottom of your list of things to do." Then she hung up and stalked out of the room in a deep, black funk.

Ten minutes later she was throwing cotton bolts left and right when Cameron slammed through the door and headed straight for her.

He didn't say a word—just grabbed her by the arm and hauled her into the backroom. He let go of her arm and glared at her, his hands on his hips, his back rigid.

"Why do you do this to me, Abby? Why do you always manage to push me too hard—at the wrong time?"

"Maybe it's the only way I can get your attention," she huffed. She crossed her arms over her chest and glared back. He didn't own a monopoly on fury.

Cameron stared her down, his eyes bleak in the dim room. "I'm trying to keep my company from going under," he said coldly. "I'm trying to get my life back in order and I don't need...." He seemed to catch himself then, because he snapped his mouth shut.

Abby sighed and nodded. "Let me finish that line for you. You don't need me messing up your life again. Fine. I'm out of here." She twisted away and headed back to the shop. She managed three steps before he stopped her forcefully and spun her around.

"Don't put words into my mouth," he growled. "That's not what I meant at all."

"I think you did," she said bleakly. She rubbed her forehead for a few seconds, then said, "This isn't going to work, Cameron. You and I are too different. I think maybe it's best if we just...go our own way."

Cameron's green eyes darkened with rage. "Is that what you really want?"

Abby nodded, and in that moment she was almost sure she meant it.

"And what about...this?" he demanded, pulling her close against his hard body.

"That's all there is," she said angrily. "And that's not enough, not for me. I'm sure you won't have to look very far to find someone to satisfy your needs."

Cameron pushed her away as if he couldn't bear to touch her any more. "Abby—you'd try the patience of a saint—and I'm no saint. I don't know what game you're playing, but I've had enough. You don't want to see me—you got it!" Then he turned on his heel and left, slamming the door behind him.

For the rest of the afternoon, Abby stayed in the backroom unloading boxes of new fabric—a job she hated and usually handed over to Delia. She was hiding—and she knew it, but she didn't care. Her eyes burned, her chest heaved, and her lungs felt raw and scarred. She was in no shape to deal with customers. She'd done the right thing by ending things with Cameron before they went too far, but why did it hurt so much?

At five o'clock, the shop was empty so Abby sent Delia home. She prepared the bank deposit, closed off the cash register, and was just filling in time dusting shelves when the door opened, and Cameron stepped quietly inside. He was still in his work clothes and his dark hair looked spiky from multiple finger rakes. His large hands were on his hips, the knuckles white.

"Can we talk?" he muttered, his eyes locked on hers.

Abby wanted to say 'no,' knew it was the most sensible thing to do, but somehow, a quiet 'yes' slipped from her lips instead.

"We could sit down in the backroom," she suggested. "I'll just lock up first." She eased past him, careful not to touch him in any way.

Cameron followed her into the back without a word.

Abby pulled out one of the chairs the quilters used, then sat down and waited while he took another close by.

He glanced at a frame leaning against the far wall with a half-finished green and pale yellow quilt on it. "Leah used to love coming here on Saturdays," he said quietly.

Abby sighed. The *last* thing she needed to hear right now was the name Leah. It was almost as bad as Lorraine. Abby crossed one leg over the other and stared at him. He looked tired and older than his years, she realized. Then she deliberately hardened her heart. She had to stop feeling this way about him. He was a lost cause.

"Why did you come back, Cameron? What's the point?"

He heard the impatience in her voice and saw the coldness in her eyes and wondered for a moment if it *was* worth the bother. Then he sighed and shook his head. "Abby, you're the only person I know who's as stubborn as I am. I knew d....darned well, if I didn't come back you wouldn't bother to call me. You're not the woman I thought you were, Abby. The woman I remember fought for what she wanted. She didn't give up as easily as you do."

Abby saw red. "How dare you!" she snapped. "I'm not the one who ran away. You're the one who treated me like dirt…who kicked me aside…who left for nearly two years. Then you waltz back home and tell me you want to try again, but won't make any time for me! I'm tired of being treated this way by you! I'm fed up. You tell me you want a second chance…to see if there's still something between us, but the only thing you seem to want from me is sex. That's what you wanted two years ago, and that's all you seem to want now. Well, that's not enough any more—not by a long shot." Abby's eyes raged with fury and her breasts heaved in her chest.

Cameron frowned, his eyes searching hers as if examining a strange species. "What's going on here, Abby? Aren't you overreacting a little—just because I cancelled our date?"

"Our *first* date," she corrected him coldly. "When we were finally going to sit down and discuss our relationship. That was very important to me," she told him. "We've had sex twice, but never even gone out for a cup of coffee. God, I don't need this aggravation." She sighed in deep frustration, running her hands through her long, silky hair.

"What do you need?"

Abby almost told him to 'go to hell.' His question was too little—too late. But something in his intent stare made her relent.

"Do you realize," she snapped, "you have never kissed me with any kind of gentleness, or tenderness. It's always been a violent struggle between us—harsh words and hard sex. Can you blame me for thinking that's all you want?"

Cameron stiffened as her words hit home. "You're right, Abby," he said soberly. "But when I'm with you, I feel...out of control." He frowned, then said, "I've wanted you for so long, that when I finally get to touch you, I lose it. I'm sorry if I've been too violent with you when we make love. I just can't seem to help myself."

She'd hurt him. She saw it in his eyes. *The man was so dense!* "Cameron! Listen to me. I'm not complaining about the sex. The sex is fantastic! I love the way you touch me, but I need some gentleness—once in a while. I need to spend time with you...talk with you...get to know you all over again. That's what I want. No sex, just talking and being together. But it's not going to happen, if you won't make time for me!" Abby's blue eyes weren't cold any longer.

"Did you mean it when you said you didn't want to see me any more?" Cameron stood, then crouched at her feet. He took her hands in his as he waited her answer.

Abby knew she should say 'yes,' but he was stroking her hand gently with his thumb and she couldn't think. She dropped her eyes, then managed a hesitant 'no.'

Cameron sighed, then pulled her beside him onto the floor.

"We always seem to end up on the floor when we're together," she said, grinning wryly.

When he saw Abby smile, relief lit his eyes and he grinned back, a dimple showing in his cheek. "I've been told I do my best work on floors," he teased. He leaned his forehead against Abby's and whispered, "So...are *we* all right now?"

She hesitated, then nodded.

He kissed her then, a long drugging kiss devoid of passion. "See," he chuckled, "I can do 'gentle.' At least for a little while."

Abby searched his eyes, then said, "If you really do want to be with me, Cameron, don't shut me out of your life. I had that with Nick. I won't live like that again."

"I'm putting in eighteen-to-twenty hour days, Abby. The only time I'll be free is in bed at night." He grinned and added, "Unless you've changed your mind about putting our sex life on hold?"

Abby almost relented. With a Victoria's Secret model around all day, she wondered how smart she was to insist that they wait before having sex again. But, if that's all Cameron wanted, it wasn't enough.

"I guess I'll see you when you have some free time," she whispered.

Cameron frowned at the look in her eyes. He thought for a minute then said, "Would you be willing to see me at really weird hours for awhile? I mean...just for a few months...until I can get Rayce's home built and my company reorganized."

Abby stared at him. "I...guess," she said slowly. "But what do you consider weird?"

"Maybe breakfast at five one day or supper at eleven another."

"I could live with that," she told him as she cupped his face. "Just don't shut me out any more."

Cameron kissed her then, a slow, sizzling kiss that quickly turned hot. They were both breathing heavily when he lifted his mouth.

"I really have to get back to work," he muttered. "I have to meet Pete at the tourist camp we're remodelling, then I have to be back at the office by eight to set up the new computer."

"Ah yes," Abby said cooly. "With Lorraine."

Cameron looked uncomfortable for a moment, then nodded abruptly. He stood up and pulled Abby after him, dusting her rear off with more care than was needed.

But Abby wasn't about to be sidetracked. "So tonight, you'll be alone in the office with Lorraine. The same Lorraine who modelled for Victoria's Secret—right?" Her arched brows matched her tone.

Cameron winced, then grinned. "I was afraid you'd react like that."
"Like how?"
"Like *that*!"
"If you're insinuating that I'm not overly thrilled that your new office manager used to work for Victoria's Secret, and is drop-dead gorgeous—you're right. I'm not. No woman in her right mind would be." Then she snapped, "And you can get that silly grin off your face right now!"
"Abby," he laughed, as he kissed her on the nose, "you're never boring. I'll give you that. Now, I really have to go. I'll call you later and we'll set up a time when we can talk."

He called at eleven-thirty that night and they talked for exactly three minutes. But he did promise to see her the next night around ten. That was enough to go on for now.

Chapter Nine

"You're not eating much," Libby said. "You've played with that lettuce for over five minutes."

"I'm just not hungry." Abby glanced absently around the tea room and wondered if she shouldn't relieve Delia early.

"I take it the date with Cameron didn't go well last night?" Maggy asked, with a lift of her auburn brows.

"Didn't happen at all."

Maggy and Libby exchanged knowing looks.

Abby caught on and sighed in exasperation. "Don't look like that. He's coming over tonight. He was busy last night. He had to set up his office computer."

"I hear he's hired quite the secretary," Libby said, then squealed when Maggy kicked her under the table. "Why did you do that? Abby should know about the competition."

"Speak of the devil." Maggy's eyes widened as the bell over the door chimed.

Abby glanced up and froze. *Dear God, please! Don't let that be Lorraine!*

A stunning woman in her early thirties, wearing three-inch spiked heels, was crossing to the counter, a confident smile on her full red lips. She wore a red, two-piece collarless suit with short sleeves. One gold brass button was all that held the low-cut top together. A curtain of silky sable hair swept her shoulders and accented her pale skin. Her eyes were slightly slanted, giving their black depth a mysterious quality. As she moved across the room she smiled slightly. She was the centre of attention, and didn't she just know it.

Abby hated her on sight.

"I'll have two chicken salad plates to go and two ice teas," she told the waitress. Her voice had a smoky quality that made Abby's skin crawl.

As she waited for her order, the woman glanced around, then seemed to notice the women at Maggy's table. She smiled cooly, then made her way to their corner.

"She's coming over here!" Libby gasped in mock horror.

"Cool it!" Abby growled.

Maggy pasted a calm smile on her face and waited for Lorraine to make her move.

"Hello, Maggy. Long time no see. I heard about Jarrod's death. Too bad. He was one hunk of man. I understand you married that accountant—what was his name? A strange one if I recall. Oh, right. Rossiter." She said the name with a slight sneer.

Abby and Libby gasped at the woman's rudeness.

Maggy merely smiled. "I see you haven't changed much, Lorraine. Still the same charming person you always were."

Lorraine smiled smoothly, but her eyes were coldly calculating. "I don't believe I know your friends," she added.

Maggy hesitated, then made the introductions.

Lorraine nodded to Libby, but her eyes narrowed when she heard Abby's name. "Ahhh," she drawled. "I believe I heard my boss mention your name. I work for Cameron Wallace, you know."

"I know." Abby's tone was clipped and abrupt. She'd met Lorraine's type before and knew the gloves were about to come off.

"I have to get back to the office," Lorraine added softly. "That poor man. He works so hard; he won't even take a break for lunch. Last night, he wouldn't have eaten at all if I hadn't brought him some of my homemade chicken."

Abby gritted her teeth and gripped the seat of her chair—anything to keep her hands off the woman's scrawny neck.

"Well, I'd better be going. I promised Cameron I'd bring him back some lunch. I can see my biggest job is going to be looking after that man." She nodded coolly, then turned and sashayed back to the counter.

Abby didn't breathe again till the door slammed shut behind her. "Is murder a capital offense in Canada?" she snapped.

Maggy sighed. "Don't let her get to you," she cautioned. "That's what she was after in the first place. And whatever you do, don't let Cameron see how she bothers you."

"How could he hire such a bimbo?" Libby said, disgust resonating in her voice.

"Her brother is Cameron's partner. They got her cheap—I guess." Abby grinned as a thought came to mind.

"Don't say it," Maggy giggled. "Let me. I think any man could get her cheaply."

"Oh—you two are terrible. It's no wonder Rayce says you're a bad influence on me." Libby grinned and stood up. "I've got a business to run. I'll see you later."

Abby drained her coffee. Then said in a matter-of-fact tone, "Lorraine's going to be a big problem—isn't she?"

"I'm afraid so." Maggy paused, then added quietly, "When Jarrod and I were engaged, she made a move on him at a dance—right under my nose. He thought it was funny, but it really *pissed* me off."

"Maggy!" Abby teased. "Such language!"

"You won't think it's so funny when she goes after Cameron. And you can bet your last cent she will!"

That sobered Abby and she bit her lip.

"Is Cameron worth the fight?" Maggy asked, with her customary directness.

"That's just what I was wondering." Wearily, Abby pushed back a strand of hair. "If I have to fight for him, do I want him anyway?"

Maggy bristled. "It's not like you to have such a defeatist's attitude, Abby. Why are you acting like this?"

Abby sighed, her eyes sad and tired. "I wouldn't compete with Leah—she was his wife. I had no business in his life when she was around. But now, I don't *want* to have to compete with Lorraine. If he doesn't want me for myself, then she can have him. I'm not going to chase that man any more. It's his turn to do a little chasing for a change."

Maggy's eyes widened at the stubborn tilt of Abby's chin. The mood Abby was in, there was no point in saying another word.

By ten-thirty, when Cameron still had not shown up, Abby slammed the door shut, locked it, and got ready for bed. She had just had a shower and was brushing her teeth when her doorbell rang. She knew it was Cameron and was ready to ignore it. But when he leaned on the bell persistently, she swore, slipped on a silk caftan, and marched to the door to let him in.

"I know you're mad," he grinned. He was holding a pizza box and looked very tired. "But I came as soon as I could."

"I'm in a filthy mood," she warned, as she stepped aside to let him in.

"And I'm starved," he told her, waving the steaming box under her nose.

"What! No homemade chicken tonight? You poor boy!" Abby's voice dripped with sarcasm.

Cameron froze, then started to chuckle. *Now how in h....heck did she know about that?*

"Not unless you made me some." He laughed out loud at the look of outrage on her face.

"I'll share my pizza," he offered softly as he sat on the couch and dropped the box on the coffee table. He looked at her expectantly, his dimple drawing her in.

Abby stared at him. She wanted to run her hands through his thick hair. She ached to taste his full bottom lip. She wanted to lick every inch of his hard muscular body. But she couldn't. Not yet. Not until she knew where she stood with him. She decided to settle for pizza instead.

Two hours later, the pizza was gone, several empty beers were on the table by Cameron's side, and she was curled up on the couch beside him, almost in his lap. They had laughed and talked for hours, about nothing—about everything. Abby hadn't enjoyed herself so much in a long time.

"You're funny," she teased, after he finished relating another hilarious mishap that had happened that day. "I never knew that about you. You always seemed so sober before."

Cameron sighed, pulled her across his lap, and settled her against his chest. "When I first knew you, we didn't have many opportunities to talk, did we?"

"Nope."

Cameron sighed again. "It's going to be hard, you know. We put the cart before the horse in our relationship. In some ways we're more intimate than many couples who've been married for years."

"But we still don't know much about each other."

"That's true," Cameron admitted. "But can you honestly see us being together night after night without touching at all?"

At the questioning glint in his eyes, Abby smiled, a mysteriously feminine smile that set his heart racing in his chest. "Oh, I didn't mean we weren't going to touch each other. I just think we should wait awhile before we sleep together."

At the disappointed look on his face, Abby made a sudden decision. "If you and I had just met…say three or four dates ago…and we really liked each other…"

"Yes?" Cameron read the arousal in her smoky blue eyes and hardened even more.

"Well…we'd probably be at the petting stage by now. Wouldn't you say?"

"Define *petting*!" he whispered seductively.

"I…touch you and…you…touch me. Gently…tenderly."

"That'll be a little…hard to take," Cameron muttered as he started to nuzzle her neck.

"Oh, I suspect it'll be a more than a *little* hard." She laughed suggestively as she began to unbutton his shirt.

When Abby began to play with his hard nipple, Cameron groaned, then nipped her ear. "You're driving me crazy woman—but you know that—don't you?"

"Don't you want to…play?" Abby's words were coy, but her eyes were deadly serious.

Was he willing to play along? Give them time to get to know each other better. That's what her eyes asked his. Cameron laughed shakily. "You can play with me all you like," he muttered hoarsely. "I'm at your mercy, but be gentle—please."

Abby laughed delightedly and so did he. But minutes later, their laughter turned to moans of pleasure.

Cameron kissed her deeply time after time, long tantalizing kisses that sent his blood pressure soaring. He forced himself to take it slow, to touch her gently as she'd asked.

Abby lay in his arms and floated on a cloud of pleasure. Her hands roamed his hairy chest, revelling in the silky feel of his thick, springy hair. His muscles were smooth and taut, his stomach lean where the arrow of hair headed south. She could feel his arousal against her bottom…pressing against her insistently. But, much to her delight, Cameron followed where she led and didn't take more than she offered.

Sweat beaded his brow as he fought to maintain control. Her hands and mouth were driving him crazy. She had nothing on under the silky thing she wore. He could feel her nipples grazing his chest and knew she wore no bra. Cameron skimmed one hand down her hip. *No panties either!*

He kissed her more passionately then, his tongue delving deeper into her mouth. She met him touch for touch and groaned into his throat with need.

He reared back his head and gulped for breath. "Do you think…if this was our four or fifth date, I'd be…pleasuring you with my hands…or my mouth?"

Abby heard the need in his voice and knew her own matched it. *Would it be so wrong to share that much?*

"I think we might be doing that much by then." She shuddered, then leaned up and suckled the underside of his chin. He tasted of dark woods and soft leather. Abby moaned and suckled harder.

He was breathing harsher now, his head thrown back against the couch. Then he hunched over her as if an invisible cord just snapped. His hand reached for her robe and drew it up her thigh, exposing the silky down between her legs. With barely restrained passion he took her mouth again, inching his long fingers up the inside of her thigh. In seconds he was at her cleft, then inside. Touching…stroking…pushing her higher all the while.

Then he lifted his mouth and gazed down at her, his eyes brilliant emeralds in the dim light. "I think I like…this playing," he whispered hoarsely. "Are you ready for a little more?"

He was asking—not taking—so Abby was willing to give.

With her shy nod, he moved aside and laid her down on the couch, placing a small pillow under her head. Then he kneeled beside her on the carpet.

"At least this time, you're not on the floor," he laughed shakily.

"So far," she teased, her eyes glowing with excitement.

He leaned up and turned off the lamp, the room dark now—except for the small light on the stove in the kitchen. "I think you'll enjoy this more with less light," he whispered as his breath moved down her thigh.

Abby tensed, knowing what was coming, aching for his touch. In seconds, she was spinning out of control, her hands moulding his dark head to her body as he suckled her most tender flesh.

Abby couldn't speak, it was all she could do to hold back the screams of pleasure exploding through her brain. His hot tongue and greedy mouth laved her unmercifully until she surrendered and climaxed against his full lips. Then she screamed softly. She couldn't help it.

He kissed her tenderly for a few seconds more as she came back down to reality. Then kissed her again, this time on the lips, her scent surrounding them both.

Abby's eyes were hot and heavy-lidded when he finally lifted his mouth.

"My turn," she whispered saucily. Then, pushing him backwards and onto the floor, she slipped onto the carpet at his side.

With shaking hands she unzipped his jeans and lowered them to his knees. After easing his briefs down his lightly-haired thighs, Abby sat back on her haunches and stared at him. Without knowing she did so, she licked her lips.

He groaned and reared up to take her in his arms.

"No!" she drawled insistently. "Lay back. Let me play with you—for awhile."

Cameron lay back, and grabbed a pillow for his head. "It may be a very *little* while," he laughed. Then he added softly, "Are you sure you want to do *this*? I know many women aren't comfortable with...ah...it."

"Don't *you* like it?" Abby purred, teasing him with her eyes. Then she leaned over and flicked him with her wet tongue.

"I don't know," he gasped, as if in unbelievable pain. "I've never...Leah wouldn't...oh God!"

Abby had heard enough. Too much if truth be told. She took him in her mouth and returned the pleasure he had given her. In seconds he was arching off the floor, his hips moving in time to her mouth, his legs rigid and straining. He was moaning constantly now, his hands bunched into the carpet by his thighs.

"Abby! I'm warning you! Stop soon or I can't..."

She didn't and he couldn't.

His shout of pleasure reverberated through the room as he reached a new pinnacle for the very first time. He groaned long and hard with each spasm, then called her name over and over again.

Abby smiled softly in triumph, laving him gently to bring him down, as he had her.

"Abby...my God! That was incredible," he whispered hoarsely when he could finally speak again. "You can play with me any time you want."

Abby smiled, then kissed him softly.

"I can taste myself on your lips," Cameron said, his eyes meeting hers for a long, telling moment.

The air sizzled between them and heated up again.

Cameron groaned and sat up. "If I don't go home right now, I'll be here all night. If I leave now, at least I'll get a few hours of sleep."

He stood up and quickly straightened his clothing, then yawned several times, weaving on his feet.

Abby frowned. He really was exhausted. "Maybe you shouldn't go home, Cameron. You could stay here if you want. I don't want you getting into an accident."

"I'll be fine, love," he murmured, then yawned again.

Abby stilled. *He'd called her 'love.' Did he know what he'd said?* Abby's eyes filled with hope.

"Be careful on the way home," she told him at the door. Then leaned up to kiss him a lingering 'good-bye.'

"Are you free this weekend?" he asked, his hand caressing her cheek.

She nodded, then waited with bated breath.

"How about coming over to my house on Sunday for lunch. I can only take a short break," he added apologetically. "I want to know if you think I should buy the place."

Abby's heart quivered with excitement.

"How about if I bring the lunch?"

"Great," he said, then added teasingly, "anything but chicken. It gives me indigestion."

Abby's infectious laughter followed him into the night.

Cameron turned off Pete's lawn mower, dropped down onto the front step, then wiped the beaded sweat off his brow. It felt good to be doing such a mundane task again. With Abby coming over for lunch, he wanted the yard to look a little more presentable. Now that the grass was cut front and back, and the biggest clumps of weeds pulled, the yard didn't look like a jungle any more. Cameron had even managed to trim the lilac trees and snowball bushes.

He stretched, then wandered around to the side porch, and went into the kitchen. The morning sun spilled through two large windows on the outside wall, but the room itself was very stark and plain, with white walls and appliances, and a grey slate floor. Cameron had been quite pleased by the floor when he'd first viewed the house. It felt cool under his feet and required little maintenance. In the middle of the room sat the old maple kitchen set he and Leah had spent one winter refinishing. Three days ago the movers had brought over his stored belongings, so Cameron had arranged what little furniture he had in the rooms he planned to use. Now the old house didn't look quite so bare.

The kitchen table was set for two, a bowl of snowballs filled the room with a hint of the outdoors, and all Cameron needed now was Abby.

He put a bottle of wine to chill in the fridge, then grabbed a coffee, and walked into a large room beside the kitchen. A small portable TV, a lazyboy chair, and a floral printed couch were the only furnishings in the room. But the room was cozy. It had a fairly new gas fireplace in one corner and French doors separated it from the large front room he'd turned into his office. With twelve-foot ceilings throughout and the original oak mouldings, floors, and staircase, the ninety-year old Victorian was a jewel that just needed a little polishing.

He'd fixed one of the five rooms upstairs as a bedroom, another as his own personal office, and left the other two empty for storage space. The fifth room was a revamped bathroom painted a garish shade of orange, but at least it was sufficient for his needs.

With a small two-piece bathroom in the hall beside the kitchen for office use, the house suited him perfectly. It was a bit rundown, but thirty gallons of paint would take care of that. If he decided to buy it.

Cameron glanced at his watch; it was only ten. He had plenty of time to shower and change before Abby showed up at noon. She'd offered to bring lunch, but he'd picked up bacon and eggs just in case. He was restless and no wonder. This was the first break he'd had in days. But he'd also got a lot accomplished. The excavation at the Powers' new home would start tomorrow, a crew had already begun work on two of the cabins at the tourist camp, and he'd put in three bids this week for several small inside renovation jobs that would be nice fillers for rainy days in the fall.

He sipped his hot coffee and let his eyes wander around the old house. It's tome-like quality didn't bother him; he found it oddly soothing. Leah would have loved this old house, he mused, his eyes softening as he remembered his wife. He could think of her now without pain, his memories of their happy life together overshadowing the tragic end.

There'd been no major highs in their marriage, but no terrible lows either. They'd dated in high school; married a few years after he finished trade school. They'd been the best of friends, content with each other and their life together. Their sex life had been sweet...fulfilling in a quiet way. Leah had been shy in bed, a virgin when they married. He hadn't had that much experience either. Though hesitant at first, she'd accepted his gentle loving with a touching joy. The only thing that had marred their happiness had been Leah's inability to conceive.

ABBY'S STORY: BETRAYED BY LOVE

Cameron thought of Abby and sighed. It wasn't fair to compare Leah and Abby—especially when it came to sex. But they were remarkably different. With Leah, sex had been gentle and loving. With Abby, it was uncontrollable passion.

Leah had been timid, reliant on him—accepting his love but never fully understanding his needs. Abby stood on her own two feet and met him as an equal. He found that a little disconcerting at times, but it also freed him. Abby didn't depend on him for her well-being or pleasure. She took care of herself. He admired her self-reliance, but sometimes he wished she needed him—just a little bit.

His wife had been a homebody, a wonderful cook—with a green thumb in the garden and a gift for making a comfortable home. Throughout their marriage, he'd looked forward to their evenings together, knowing full well she'd have a tasteful meal ready, his slippers by the door, and his paper on his chair.

Cameron sighed. Those days were long gone. Somehow he didn't think Abby was the slippers-by-the-door kind of woman. And he wasn't the same man either.

In Saudi Arabia, he'd found out a lot about himself. When he tired of the commissary food, he'd discovered he enjoyed cooking. So he had set up a little kitchen of his own and experimented with spices and strange combinations of foods. Some dishes, though, he only made once.

He'd also figured out how to mend his own clothes. Necessity had forced him to master that skill after he'd run out of safety pins. But more importantly, for the first time in his life, he'd come to terms with living alone.

But now, he was tired of coming home to an empty house. He was lonely, wanted a family of his own—with Abby.

Did he love her? He'd asked himself that question so often since he'd come home, it ran through his head like a mantra. He'd loved Leah—he knew that without a doubt. He'd loved her gentle kindness, her sunny personality, the way she always looked for the good in people. He'd loved her all his life, it seemed.

But...did he love Abby? Not in the way that he'd loved Leah. And that's what bothered him. Perhaps that overused word was too simple to define his feelings. He liked her, enjoyed her company, cared about her—just as he had cared for Leah. But with Abby—there was something more, something harder to define. He wanted Abby in a way that he'd never felt with Leah. He needed to see her, hear her voice, feel her touch. Needed her with a desperation that bordered on obsession. Since he'd come home, other women had tried—and failed—to get his attention. He just wasn't interested in them.

Not even the gorgeous, but obvious, Lorraine. Cameron grinned smugly. Abby was jealous of Lorraine—he'd seen it in her eyes. But she had nothing to worry about on that score. Lorraine had already made it amply clear that she was quite willing to provide any *extra* service her boss required. And Cameron had just as quickly declined. Normally he wouldn't have hired her. He didn't need that kind of hassle—but she was Pete's sister and very efficient at her job. Already she was well on her way to getting things organized in the office.

So, he'd kept her on, highly amused at times by her blatant flirting and sly innuendoes. Maybe having Lorraine around might nudge Abby into his arms. In the meantime, he was seldom in the office, so he could ignore Lorraine and get on with rebuilding his company.

Cameron noticed the time and stood up. He drained his cup of coffee, then headed upstairs to shower. He was whistling as he bounded up the stairs two at a time, his thoughts on Abby as usual. Perhaps she might want to *play* a little before he went back to work.

Abby knocked on the side door, her arms holding a heavy box. Cameron answered instantly and held the door open to let her pass. He was dressed in work clothes, with his sleeves rolled back to exposed muscular forearms, and looked more scrumptious than the food she carried.

"Hi," he smiled, his lips brushing hers. "Something smells good—and I don't mean the food. By the way, I like those skimpy shorts you're almost wearing."

"Down boy!" Abby quipped, a teasing smile curling her lips. She'd chosen the trim, light blue shorts and sleeveless top—tied at the midriff—for just that reaction. "I'm here for lunch and the grand tour, and nothing else."

His eyes danced. "I was hoping we might have a little…dessert later."

"I brought dessert," she teased. "Apple pie."

"That's not quite what I had in mind." He raised his brows in a mock leer and Abby laughed delightedly.

"I know exactly what you had in mind—but you're out of luck." She smiled as she placed the box on the table, but her tone was very adamant.

"So….no *playing* today?" he asked with a wink.

Abby groaned and flushed. "Don't remind me," she muttered. "That should *not* have happened. We spend all our time...*playing*...instead of getting to know each other better."

"Oh, I think we're coming along just fine. I know something about you now that I never knew before."

His voice was low and sensual, with a hypnotic quality that set Abby's pulse racing.

"And just what might that be?" she asked, her eyes sparkling with mischief.

He leaned toward her, then whispered softly in her ear, "I know you taste like wild strawberries and sunlight. I always imagined you'd taste more exotic...more musky. But you don't. You're a constant surprise." He nuzzled her gently for a moment where her neck met her shoulders, then moved away and gave her a lazy smile.

Abby shuddered, barely able to reason. "You're trying to seduce me again," she told him.

"You're right," he admitted with a grin. "But not right now. I have to meet Pete at one."

Abby shook her head in exasperation. "Let's eat—before I strangle you!"

Cameron chuckled, then helped her unload a container of turkey sandwiches made with homemade bread, a fresh garden salad, another container of large dill pickles, and an apple pie.

"You must have been at it all morning," Cameron said, his brows raised in surprise.

"Nope. I picked up the pie and bread at a bakery at the Lakeshore mall, and the rest at a deli on the way here. I'm no gourmet cook, Cameron. That's another thing you need to know about me." She stared at him intently, her eyes slightly shadowed.

Cameron cocked one brow then grinned, showing his dimple. "Is this my cue to say if you can't cook—we're finished?" Though he smiled, his eyes narrowed slightly.

"No...of course not," Abby muttered quickly. She dropped her gaze and started to load up her plate.

Cameron knew he was right on the mark. "I get the feeling I'm running an obstacle course with you, Abby. If I pass all the hurdles, are you my prize?"

Abby glanced up, a haunted expression in her startled gaze. "It's not like that. I just want you to know all of me...the good and the bad...before we get in too deep."

Cameron pulled her into his arms, ignoring her token resistance. "So, you think I'd drop you because you don't like to cook. Is that the kind of man you think I am?"

"Leah was a great cook—I know that," Abby said. "It's not that I can't cook—it's just not high on my list of priorities."

Cameron paused, choosing his words. "I don't...compare you to Leah, Abby...in any way." That wasn't totally true, but he had no intention of telling Abby that.

"You're lying," she grinned softly. "But I'll let you get away with it—this time." She kissed him gently, then pushed him away. "Let's eat. I'm starved."

They ate nearly all the sandwiches, salad, and pickles—or at least Cameron did, but left the pie alone. Abby was on her second glass of wine, feeling mellow and content, her long legs stretched out on Cameron's chair, when a knock sounded at the door.

Abby started to put her feet on the floor, but Cameron held them fast and yelled, "Come on in. It's open."

Lorraine Reilly walked in carrying a pizza box. Her eyes widened, then narrowed, when she took in the cozy scene. Dressed in ruby-red shorts and a matching halter top, Lorraine looked ready for action—not lunch.

"Well Cameron, I see you've finished lunch already," Lorraine said dryly. "And here I thought you might need some nourishment. My mistake."

Abby snorted and tensed. The woman was so obvious it was sickening!

"That was very thoughtful, Lorraine," Cameron drawled, a bland smile on his face, "but Abby brought lunch. Would you care to join us for a glass of wine?" The minute the words were out of his mouth, he felt anger radiate through Abby's body like electricity along a hydro line. Her feet dropped to the floor and she snapped to attention.

Cameron stifled a grin of sheer delight. He felt a little bad using Lorraine to make Abby jealous, but—tough. *She* was the one who had showed up uninvited.

"I'd love a glass of wine." Lorraine smiled warmly into Cameron's eyes, ignoring Abby completely. When he offered the glass, Lorraine's fingers touched his for a second too long before accepting it. She raised the wine to her lips and sipped provocatively, her eyes watching him all the while. Then she leaned forward again, her breasts grazing the table.

Abby was spitting mad. "Careful," she warned, "I'm sure you don't want those expensive babies to land in the mustard."

Lorraine swivelled her head toward Abby like a snake seeking its prey. "If you're implying what I think you are, you're out of line. Though...if you're interested, I'm sure I could recommend a good implant surgeon."

Cameron choked on the laughter bubbling up his throat at the outrage on Lorraine's face. Then he couldn't help glancing down at her breasts. *Hot damn,* he thought, *Abby's right. There's no way those boobs are real!* His eyes trailed up to Lorraine's face, then widened in shock. The look in her eyes as she stared at Abby was so malicious, it raised the hair on the back of his neck. "Lorraine," Cameron said abruptly, "sorry to cut this visit short, but I think you'd better leave. I have to go back to work in a few minutes." Cameron stood as he spoke and opened the door." I'll walk you to your car." His tone left no room for refusal.

Lorraine's sultry eyes narrowed, then she smiled, a wintry smile that barely curved her lips. "Whatever you say, Cameron. You're the boss." As she followed Cameron out, Lorraine tossed over her shoulder, "Bye, Abby. I'm sure we'll be seeing each other again."

Abby heard the icy threat in the other woman's voice and arched her brows disdainfully. When the door slammed shut Abby eased back into her chair. "Not if I see you first," she muttered, her tone as cold as Lorraine's eyes.

Cameron walked down the path beside Lorraine in silence, barely able to contain his fury. He opened her car door, and waited impatiently for her to leave. It was all he could do not to shove her inside and tell her to get the hell off his property.

She paused and stroked his arm with one long, red-tipped finger. In a low, husky voice she said, "You know, Cameron, I was hoping we might get to know each other better. Outside of the office that is. That's why I came over here today."

"I know exactly what you want, Lorraine," Cameron said bitingly, his eyes narrowed in warning. "But I thought I made it clear that you weren't going to get it from me."

"Cameron, I expected better of you. There's no need to be so unkind." She made a moue of protest with her full lips that looked contrived—rather than sexy.

Cameron had had enough. He stepped back and put both hands on his hips. "You have no right to expect anything at all from me, Lorraine. Now, if you can't accept that—I can have your termination papers ready first thing in the morning!"

Lorraine was a pragmatist. She knew how to play the game. She lowered her eyes to simulate remorse, then whispered quietly, "I apologize, Cameron. It won't happen again."

Cameron breathed deeply, then nodded in relief. She was an efficient office manager and he didn't want to have to look around for another. "Good," he said sharply. "I'll see you tomorrow." He turned and marched back into the house without a backward glance.

Lorraine watched the muscular sway of his buttocks and ground her teeth. She wanted the man and she'd have him yet. But first, she'd have to get rid of the competition. Lorraine sneered as she spun out of Cameron's driveway. Getting rid of Abby Fulton was going to be a pleasure.

"Would you mind explaining what that was all about?" Cameron asked wryly, as he stepped back into the kitchen. His look was quizzical, not accusing.

Abby looked at him over the rim of her glass. She was about to wave him off, then changed her mind. "I don't like Lorraine, Cameron. She brings to mind something else you should know about me," she told him abruptly. She paused, then smiled cooly, her bright blue eyes locked on his. "I don't share. I wouldn't even share my toys with the kids at school. Maybe it's because I'm an only child and never learned how, but I keep what's mine—or I throw it away—when I don't want it any more."

Cameron tensed, the teasing glint in his eyes gone. "Somehow, I don't think we're talking about toys now." He knew where Abby was going, and didn't like her tone.

"How astute," she mocked.

"Are you accusing me of something?"

"I don't have that right," Abby told him, her eyes direct and unwavering.

"And if you did?"

"If I did, I would expect you to be faithful to me. I'm not Leah. As I said before, I don't share."

Cameron winced and his mouth thinned. "That was uncalled for and you know it, Abby! I never ran around on Leah. That night with you was the only time I broke my vows. And I'm getting a little tired of defending myself to you."

Abby sighed. "Here we go again. You ask what I think, then get mad when I tell you. I'm going home. This is a total waste of time. When we're not having sex, all we do is fight. Maybe we should just call it quits right now. We don't belong together if all we do is make each other miserable."

Cameron bristled with anger but fought it down. "Who said I'm miserable? If you're miserable, you brought it on yourself. You're jealous of Lorraine—that's why you're acting this way! What we're dealing with here is lack of trust, Abby. Plain and simple. You don't trust me...and I admit...I don't trust you too much either. But—unlike you—I'm not ready to throw in the towel at the first hint of trouble. I'm not interested in Lorraine—there I've said it. I shouldn't have had to, but perhaps I'm partially to blame," he added evasively.

"And we don't fight all the time—so stop exaggerating. We have a lot of fun together. We just have some rough edges to smooth out." He sighed, then took her hands. "I think we can make this relationship work, if we both try Abby. Besides, you're more fun to *play* with than anyone I know. That counts for a lot—don't you think?"

Abby breathed deeply, then slowly nodded. "I guess it does at that. I...overreacted. I'm sorry, Cameron."

Cameron lifted his brows. It was clear she found it hard to apologize. His eyes roamed her face, noting the cloudy pain still lingering in her eyes. Then he said softly, "I'm not Nick, Abby. I won't run around on you."

Abby flinched, a chill running down her spine at his perception. "I know you're not Nick." She leaned into him, then caressed his cheek with the palm of her hand. "You're a good man, Cameron. That's something I've always known."

"I hate to leave you like this," Cameron muttered, "but I have to get back to work. Are we okay now?"

"You ask that each time we're together," Abby laughed. "Yes, we're okay. Why don't you go to work and I'll stay and tidy up."

Cameron hesitated, then stood and walked over to the counter. He picked up a key chain and took off a key.

"Here's a key to my house," he told her quietly. "Keep it. Come over whenever you want."

Abby stilled at the expectant look on his face. She took the key and pulled him close, kissing him fervently. They both knew he was offering more than just a key.

"*Now* you want to play!" Cameron kissed her lightly then added, "I'll call you later."

When the door closed, Abby collapsed into her chair. She was exhausted—woozy from the wine and slightly nauseated from the argument with Cameron. She was ashamed of her behaviour at lunch. She had been a real bitch. It was a wonder Cameron hadn't kicked her out.

"Sleep," she muttered. "I need a little sleep." She stood on wobbly legs and wandered down the hall, peeking through every door she saw, like Cinderella in the bears' house. She climbed the long flight of stairs in the front hall to the second floor, then glanced in several vacant rooms, a large gaudy bathroom, and a sparse office. Then found Cameron's bedroom at last. It was plainer than she'd expected, with an antique double bed, a tallboy dresser, a night table, and one flowery chair for furniture. No rug warmed the hardwood floor, no curtains graced the blind-covered window. But, what surprised her the most, was the lack of pictures anywhere. She'd expected at least one—of Leah. Abby dropped onto Cameron's tidy bed, smelled his scent on the pillows, and fell instantly asleep.

She woke around four feeling much better. After tidying the kitchen, she left.

Chapter Ten

Abby could hear the laughter before she rounded the corner into Maggy's backyard. Kyra and Kyle were chasing a small beagle puppy through the grass. The pup was constantly tripping over its long floppy ears as it tried to catch the ball of yarn trailing after Kyra.

Maggy was reclining on a lounger, dressed in a flaming-orange bathing suit, the twins cooing between her outstretched legs. She had a mellow smile on her face as she played with the tiny feet waving in the breeze.

They hadn't seen Abby yet and she hung back at the edge of the house feeling almost like an interloper.

At that moment, Ross came out of the house carrying a tray of lemonade in his hands. The puppy chose that moment to run through his legs and Ross overbalanced, the tray swaying alarmingly for a moment. Then he caught it, and himself, and grinned ruefully at Maggy's peal of laughter.

"Looks like the puppy's a hit," Abby said as she walked toward Maggy.

Maggy glanced up and shook her head wryly. "She's driving us insane. It's like having another child to look after," she groused.

Just then Kyra plopped down on the grass by Abby's feet. "We call her Toffee because Mom says her ears are the same colour as toffee candy. Don't you think that's a neat name?" Kyra asked, as she gasped for breath.

"That's a terrific name," Abby agreed. She watched the little girl jump up and chase after the pup again and laughed. "I wish I had half her energy."

Maggy nodded absently, her eyes softening as she watched Kyra lift the puppy tenderly against her face. "The kids love the little pup already. They really enjoy her."

"The kids!" Ross snorted as he sipped his lemonade. "She slept on *your* lap for an hour after lunch. And you were the one who insisted we buy the pillows and toys for the dog. I was just going to put her in an old laundry hamper." Ross bent down and kissed his wife. "You don't fool me one bit."

Maggy glowed with happiness.

She has it all, Abby thought wistfully.

"Where were you this afternoon?" Maggy asked as Ross ambled off to play with the pup and the kids.

Abby sat on the grass, then muttered, "At Cameron's—for lunch."

"How did it go?"

Abby sighed. "It was great—until Lorraine showed up and I threw a hissy fit."

"You didn't!"

"A doozy."

Maggy raised her brows then demanded, "Give me all the gory details."

Abby pulled a long strand of hair behind her ear. "That woman's after Cameron, Maggy. Like a shark after blood. She showed up in skimpy, tight shorts with her boobs hanging out, holding a box of pizza. Can you believe the nerve?"

When Maggy chuckled, Abby snapped, "It's not funny! Lorraine works with him all day. I've seen grown men drool when she walks by. Why would Cameron refuse what's right under his nose?"

"Because he wants you—not her," Maggy said calmly. "Abby, I've seen the way he looks at you. He's not going to bother with a cheap hustler like Lorraine, so relax. Have some lemonade. It might help you to cool down."

Abby grimaced, but poured herself a glass.

"Did you and Cameron fight about Lorraine?" Maggy asked. She saw the frown that pleated Abby's forehead and sighed. "Abby...tell me you didn't!"

"A little," Abby admitted shortly. As she read the exasperation on Maggy's face, she held up a hand in warning. "Don't say it! I already read myself the riot act on the way home. Besides, everything's all right now. We worked it out."

Abby drank some lemonade and frowned at the bitter taste. She swirled the glass, then said broodingly, "Sometimes I think I'm making a mistake by seeing Cameron. I don't know if I'm the right woman for him. I'm not like Leah. I'm jealous and cranky in the morning and I get mad too easily."

Maggy laughed, "Oh you're a bitch all right."

As expected, Abby grinned. "You don't understand. Cameron and Leah got along so well...were so happy together. They never used to fight at all. They were the perfect couple. Everybody said so." Abby frowned unhappily, her eyes bleak as she picked at a blade of grass. "Why would he want me—when he's had her?"

Maggy wanted to laugh at the wistful look on Abby's face, but wisely didn't. Abby was so fragile, so needy.

"Do you love him, Abby?"

Abby flushed, then glanced away. "Of course I do," she said. "I always have. I just don't know if that's enough."

"I think he loves you too. Give yourself a chance to find out. Don't run away from love."

Abby snorted. "You've been reading too many romance novels, Maggy Blake."

Maggy wagged her finger and said, "Just for that, I'm not going to invite you to dinner after all."

"I couldn't eat a bite anyway," Abby said. "I'm still full from lunch." Abby dropped a kiss on Maggy's forehead. "Thanks for listening to my nonsensical babbling," she said quietly, then walked home.

Abby spend the rest of the evening with a book and a dish of chopped fruit. She didn't even bother turning on the TV or radio, but wallowed in the peaceful bliss of being alone. Until nine o'clock when the doorbell rang.

Abby dashed for the door, hoping it was Cameron. All of a sudden, she was in a *playful* mood. But, when she opened the door and saw Nick on the other side, her face fell.

"Damn it Abby! It's hard on a man's ego when you do that." He smiled testily, thrust a bottle of wine into her hand, and walked past her into the house.

"Make yourself at home," Abby said snidely as she closed the door. She looked at the bottle in her hand, then grimaced. "I think I'll pass on the wine," she told Nick as she followed him into her living room.

He was settled on the couch, dressed in olive-green casual slacks and collarless shirt, with a bulky sweater tied loosely around his shoulders. With one leg resting on the other knee and sunglasses perched on the top of his glossy black hair, he looked calmly relaxed and amused.

"That doesn't sound like you," he laughed. "It's a bottle of your favourite Riesling. Are you sure you won't have one glass with me."

"Cameron and I killed a bottle at lunch. I've had my fill, thanks." Abby's eyes were cool and direct as she headed for the kitchen. "I'll get a corkscrew and a glass for you."

"Don't bother. Keep it for another time," Nick told her.

Abby paused, then set the bottle on the end table and sat down opposite Nick.

"So, how's the movie coming?"

"Good actually. My assistant director's been here for weeks now, so a lot of the prep work is already done. He hired about one hundred extras from Nipissing First Nation to play in the big fight scene that we'll be shooting here and they're using their own traditional costumes, so that's one big headache taken care of."

"You never did explain the plot," Abby told him as she settled back against the chair.

Nick frowned, then added hesitantly, "I didn't want to bore you."

Abby smiled. "Nick, if I didn't know you better, I'd say you were holding out on me for some reason. Now, what's the plot about?"

Nick grinned self-consciously. "Well, if you must know, I helped to write the script. I've bored Celine to tears going through all the rewrites. I didn't want to bore you too."

Abby was intrigued. Nick…a director…and now a writer. She found it almost impossible to believe. "Tell me about it. You've got me really curious now."

"Well, it's a fictionalized account of Samuel de Champlain's explorations of this region in the early sixteen hundreds. You and whatshisname will play young natives of the Nipissing tribe that lived in this area. In the scene you're in, Champlain, his men, and a group of young native guides return to the village just after an attack by Iroquois. The village is in ruins and one of the guides jumps out of his canoe to find the woman he loves. That's you. You live long enough to die in your lover's arms."

"I don't know if I can die convincingly." Abby frowned at the thought.

"Don't worry, that's my job. I'll walk you through it."

"This attack—did it really happen?"

"I'm the director, so I say it did." Nick grinned. "Actually, most of the film is based on documented facts," he told her. "I had researchers reading copies of Champlain's reports so we know what he wore and ate as well as where he travelled. Then another of my researchers studied this area. The tribe that lived here was called the Nipissing—hence the name of the lake. They hunted, fished, and traded extensively. They acted as middlemen trading between tribes and lived in this region hundreds of years before Champlain showed up. My set director visited the site last spring, then built the props we needed in Toronto. He's been at it for months," Nick said. "The wigwams—that's the birchbark homes the Nipissings lived in—were made in a shop outside Ottawa with the help of several native craftsmen. My crew has been setting up the village in Champlain Park for the last week and it looks pretty damn real. Too bad we have to burn it for the homecoming scene; it would be a real tourist attraction for North Bay.

"Our biggest problem was the birchbark canoes. Those suckers are up to forty feet long. Luckily enough, a canoe company in Southern Ontario made us excellent replicas—and under budget for a change."

Abby stared at Nick. "This is no fly-by-night production—from the sounds of it."

"No way! My budget is fifteen big ones, and I'll need every penny by the time I'm finished."

Abby gasped, her eyes rounding. "And you want *me* in this thing? Are you out of your mind?"

Nick laughed gently. "Sure…why not. You and whatshisname will have a ball."

"I hope you know what you're doing," Abby sighed.

"Wait till you see your costume. Laurie, my wardrobe mistress, said it's made from deerskin with authentic porcupine quill decorations. Mind you, it won't look so gorgeous once we put all the fake blood on it."

Abby shook her head. "I need my head read," she muttered. "How long will it take you to shoot the whole movie?"

"About four more months. We started shooting last January. And we've got most of the inside scenes already finished. We've been working at a sound stage in Toronto. Last month we got some footage in Quebec City in the old part of town, but we had to film at night—and that's a pain. My cameraman prefers natural light. Rene was a bitch the whole time we were in Quebec.

"We're only filming a few scenes at Champlain Park in North Bay, then one or two on Georgian Bay, then we head back to the studio. So it's all coming together. The sound and lighting equipment arrived today and the cast should arrive for rehearsals on Friday. So, the next few days will be packed. That's why I'm here. I wanted to let you know I'll need you and whatshisname a week from next Saturday."

"Oh Nick, maybe you should get someone else."

"You promised, Abby." Nick frowned at his ex-wife; he'd expected this reaction.

"I know…but Cameron just got a big contract and I don't know if he can get away."

"He's working on a Saturday?"

"He's a contractor. It's summer. That's what they do."

"Fine. I'll shoot your take first, then you can be on your way. Unless you want to stay and watch some more. Anyway, you have to be in makeup by six. Oh…and by the way…you'll have to wear contacts."

When Abby started to protest, Nick held her off. "It'll be fun Abby. I promise. You and whatshisname will have a great time."

"His name is Cameron," Abby said dryly. "I'm not even sure if he still wants to do it."

When the phone rang, Nick drawled, "If that's him, pass on my message."

Abby sighed and picked up the phone. Sure enough it was Cameron.

"Hi," he said warmly. "I just got back from the job site and thought I might come over. So we can talk."

Abby smiled at the tone in his voice, then said, "Actually, I have company right now. Nick's here." A long telling silence followed her announcement.

"I…see."

Those two words spoke volumes. "I think you have a hint of how I felt this afternoon," she reminded him tartly.

"Don't push it Abby!" he growled. "What does *he* want?"

"He's filling me in on what we have to do for that scene in his movie—if you're still interested, that is."

"When?"

"He said he'd shoot our little part first, so we have to be at the Champlain Park site at six o'clock on Saturday—not this weekend, but next."

"All right," Cameron said quietly. "That gives me enough time to get organized. I'll be there."

"I'll tell him," Abby promised.

"Is he staying long?" Cameron's voice had a hollow sound to it.

"No," Abby promised. "He's just leaving." She hesitated, then asked,

"Will you call me tomorrow?" When Cameron agreed, she hung up the phone.

She looked at Nick and wanted to wipe the smug expression off his face. *What had she ever seen in the man?*

"He'll do it," she sighed. "Now—go home, Nick—please. I'm bushed."

Nick grinned but stood to comply. "There was a time, Abby my love, when you wouldn't have been so quick to see me gone."

"When I was young and foolish," Abby drawled. "I know better now." She grinned at him and walked to the door, then held it open.

Nick smiled sardonically and followed her. "You're one hard cookie now, Abby. But I like you anyway." He patted her on the fanny with a sly wink.

Abby gritted her teeth. "Do that again, and I'll knock you into tomorrow."

"Can't blame a guy for trying," Nick teased. He bounded down the stairs and jumped into his car.

Abby sighed, glad to see him gone.

The next week passed in a blur. Delia got the flu, so Abby was rushed off her feet keeping on top of everything in the shop. She didn't see Cameron at all, but he called every night, usually around ten.

On Friday morning he phoned around eleven to say he'd have to work most of the next week to make up for missing Saturday.

"Darn," Abby sighed. "I had hoped we'd see each other some time soon."

"I have an idea that you might like," Cameron said. "After we finish the shoot, why don't you and I play hooky for the rest of the day and go boating on the French River? Pete has a twenty-two foot cabin cruiser and he said I could borrow it any time. What do you say?"

"I say—I'll bring the wine. *You* bring the food." Abby laughed and added, "That sounds like a wonderful plan. I'll look forward to it."

"I've got to go now," Cameron told her. "I'm working in the office until two, to catch up on some paperwork." Then he hung up.

Acting on impulse, Abby took an early lunch, went next door to Maggy's and picked up a light lunch for two and several bottles of cold juice, then drove to Cameron's office.

There were only two cars parked outside, and no one was in the office when she walked in the front door. Abby glanced into the hallway, then wandered into the kitchen but there was no one around. With a frown on her face, Abby went back through the hallway to the front door, then stilled as she heard voices upstairs. A male...and a female voice...upstairs.

Abby's heart leaped into her throat, then she forced herself to calm down. There were lots of reasons why Cameron would be upstairs...with Lorraine. She had to stop jumping to conclusions.

"Hello? Anybody home?" Her voice seemed to echo through the house, then after a few seconds, Cameron answered back, "Be right there."

Minutes later, he was rushing down the stairs with a warm smile on his face. *Did he look a little...dishevelled?*

"Abby! What a nice surprise!"

He seems pleased to see me, Abby thought, *but...where the hell is Lorraine?*

"We were just unpacking some of my old files," Cameron explained warily.

He expects me to explode again, she realized. That shamed her. "I thought we might have lunch together," she told him softly. "I brought enough for the both of us."

Just then Lorraine came into view at the top of the stairs, an armload of files against her chest.

"Hello, Lorraine," Abby said, acknowledging the woman's presence.

The other woman nodded cooly, her face remarkably bland as she descended the stairs.

This isn't going to be easy, Abby thought. But it had to be done. Abby took a deep breath, then said, "I apologize for my behaviour the last time we met, Lorraine."

"Apology accepted," Lorraine replied after a slight pause. Then she turned to Cameron and said, "I think I'll take an early lunch."

Cameron waved Lorraine off without a second glance and led Abby into the kitchen.

Lorraine opened a small closet in the hall to get her purse, then glanced toward the kitchen. Her face twisted with fury as she watched Abby melt into Cameron's arms. The air hissed between her clenched teeth; she wanted to bang the wall and howl with rage. When she got to the front door, it was all she could do not to kick the door down with her feet.

"So....how's it going with Lorraine the Lovely?" Abby teased as she finished the last drop of her juice.

Cameron grinned ruefully. "She's dropped the femme fatale act—thank God. She's actually a very good employee."

Abby snorted, but said nothing.

Chapter Eleven

Abby couldn't believe her eyes as she followed Nick's production assistant to the makeup trailer. Champlain Park was packed with people and equipment.

Dozens of people scurried to and fro, like ants preparing for winter. Along the perimeter of the park, a row of trailers contrasted sharply with the newly constructed native village built around the edge of the lake.

Abby gazed at the circular grouping of birchbark wigwams with a sense of awe. *This is how it must have looked four hundred years ago,* she thought, *when Champlain stepped on shore for the first time.* Then a powerboat cut across the lake in front of the village and the image faded abruptly.

"You're in makeup first," Claire the assistant, was saying, "then you go to the fifth trailer down for a wardrobe fitting. Then make your way to the set and Nick will take it from there." Claire turned to Cameron and grinned, "Follow me. You're in makeup in trailer four."

Abby stood at the door, watching as Cameron walked to the next trailer. Then he waved and stepped inside.

She climbed the stairs hesitantly, then peeked through the open door. The trailer was brightly lit with mirrors down one side and a row of chairs in front of a long counter. Each chair, except for one, was filled with native women. Some were getting their hair dressed, others were being plastered with makeup.

"Hi...you must be Abby," said a bright young woman in a blue smock and jeans. With her long brown hair tied back in a ponytail, she looked about sixteen. "I'm Sara. Strip down in the changing room at the back and put on the robe I left out for you. I'll be ready for you in a minute."

Ten minutes later Abby was standing on a chair in the change room dressed only in her panties, while Sara covered her skin with a bronze-coloured body foundation.

"There...that should do it," Sara said as she eyed Abby dispassionately. "Put that robe on carefully, then meet me at the chair and I'll do your face. We still have that bloody gash to put on your head."

Much later, when Abby stepped out of the trailer, she looked like a victim of a vicious attack, but no one paid her the slightest attention. She walked over to the trailer marked 'wardrobe,' then stepped inside.

A half-dozen women in various states of undress were being helped into buckskin clothing covered in blood.

Abby stood awkwardly and waited for someone to tell her where to go. Just then a harried older woman with frizzy orange hair looked up and spotted Abby at the door.

"Are you Abby?" she demanded brusquely.

When Abby nodded, the woman, whose nameplate read Ida, pushed her toward a corner where a beaded buckskin outfit hung from a rack.

"I'll help you get into this," the woman said. "Be careful where you sit."

Abby eyed the top skeptically. It was covered with grime and blood, with a large rent in the front of the top.

The woman made a barking sound that Abby assumed was laughter.

"I know it doesn't look like much," the woman grinned, "but we only have one copy of this outfit—that's why I want you to be careful. With some costumes we make several copies.

"Take off the robe," the woman told her.

Abby glanced around at the other women shyly, then dropped the robe. She felt a little self-conscious standing in front of a total stranger clad only in a pair of panties, but the other woman took no notice.

"Here, put these moccasins on first," Ida told her. "They should fit."

Abby took the soft, light-brown fringed slippers and eased them onto her feet. Abby fingered them, admiring the skill involved in the intricate work.

"That's porcupine quills they're decorated with," Ida explained. "That's what the Nipissing tribe used at the time of Champlain to jazz up their clothing. We're trying to make the costumes as authentic as possible."

"Now, step into this skirt, then I'll help you into the tunic top. Try not to smudge your makeup," Ida reminded her.

Abby did as she was told and stood like a mannequin as Ida adjusted the costume.

Then Ida leaned back and eyed Abby from head to foot. All the while, she made little clucking noises, her forehead furrowed by deep frown lines. "Let's get the tinted contacts in and the wig on and see if that helps."

Abby had a hard time putting in the dark contacts, but finally managed. Then she sat in a chair while Ida fussed with the long black wig that she slid over Abby's head. Lifting a lock of hair Ida quickly braided it to one side.

"That'll keep the hair off your wound for your close-up," Ida explained. "Yes...that's better now. You'll do. Take a look in the mirror."

Though the older woman seemed satisfied, Abby didn't know what to expect. She almost recoiled at what she saw because she simply didn't recognize herself. Abby Fulton was gone. In her place was a native woman with dark eyes, dark hair, and bronze skin covered with blood—a woman who looked close to death. Abby got goosebumps as she checked out the side of her head in the mirror. It looked almost too real. Then she glanced down. Her heavily fringed, sleeveless tunic was ripped down the front and covered with gore. Abby was fascinated, yet repulsed at the same time, by the realistic costume.

After getting directions from Ida, Abby stepped back outside and wandered down to the set. She passed through the village of wigwams and noticed many details that made the scene appear almost surrealistic. The baby cradleboard propped outside a wigwam, the birchbark utensils and dishes by the fire. The spread of pickerel on a wooden rack drying in the sun. The bow and quiver beside a doorway, as if just dropped by a hunter home with fresh deer.

Abby felt a chill run down her spine that owed nothing to the cool morning air. It was as if she'd stepped back in time. As she walked through the empty village, Abby felt the presence of the Indian maiden waiting impatiently for her lover to come home. The lover who had left to guide Samuel de Champlain to the 'Big Water.'

Abby gazed across Lake Nipissing to a point where blue water met blue sky. She thought she heard something then, like whispering voices echoing from the past.

"Abby! Over here!"

Abby shook herself, then turned toward Cameron's voice. She stared at him as if waking from a dream. If he hadn't spoken, she would have walked right past him—he looked so extraordinarily different. This man had deep brown eyes instead of vivid green. His hair was covered by a black wig parted in the middle and braided loosely over each shoulder. Part of an eagle feather perched over the crown of his head. He was dressed in buckskin discoloured by sweat and dirt. He looked tired, as if he'd finally made it home after a long, harrowing journey. His made-up face reflected a weary exhaustion that was so real, it was almost eerie. Abby stared at him in wide-eyed fascination.

As he did her.

"I think they did *too* good a job," Cameron said huskily. "You look like you're going to die any minute now."

"That's the idea," Nick said briskly as he joined them. He eyed Abby dispassionately, then nodded to himself. "Yes, that's the look I wanted."

"Rene," he shouted to a man sitting on a raised camera platform, "is the light ready?"

"Give me five more minutes. Then it's a go," the man replied.

Abby glanced around at the dozens of people hard at work. They all seemed to know exactly what to do. Some were setting out props, others were adjusting sound levels and positioning the microphone boom, several others were working around the large camera platform.

"Watch the cords," Nick cautioned when Abby would have tripped over one of the dozens of wires that covered the ground.

"At least the early natives didn't have to worry about these," Abby laughed as she stepped gingerly over the wires.

Nick grinned, then picked up a clipboard. "Right, let's get to it," he muttered to himself. Then he nodded to his AD and said, "Okay Roche, get the gang together."

The assistant director quickly assembled about two dozen characters, all men. Some were dressed in native garb like Cameron, but most were in leather pants and shirts, with caps on their heads and knee-length moccasins on their feet. Standard dress for the early French voyageurs. One stood out. He was better dressed and seemed to command more attention. Abby knew from Nick's earlier introduction that this was Charles Neveau, the French-Canadian actor playing Samuel de Champlain. He was right into the part, walking with the swagger of a natural leader.

"All right, listen up," Nick said. "We're going to do the landing scene first. Charles, you and your men will take the two canoes out about a quarter of a mile so we can get some footage of the landing, then you edge the canoes right onto land. Then Cameron, you jump out and head toward Abby. We'll try to get all of that in one take, then we'll do the close-up scene after."

"I'm sure damned glad these guys know what they're doing," Charles laughed. "I've been up the creek without a paddle once or twice in my life, but I've never been in a canoe before this morning."

Everyone laughed, then Nick added, "Look busy Charles, but leave the paddling to the experts. These guys from the canoe club know what they're doing. Just make sure you don't fall out of the canoe."

"He doesn't act like a big movie star—does he?" Abby whispered to Cameron.

"No, he doesn't," Cameron agreed. "And he speaks very highly of your ex. Apparently Nick is the hottest new director in Canada. They expect this movie to be a real hit."

"I still find it hard to believe that Nick 'the model' turned into Nick 'the director.' When we were married, it was like pulling teeth to even get him to a movie." She watched Nick at the edge of the beach, talking a mile a minute to his assistant while the two forty-foot canoes pushed off from shore. "I mean…he could barely remember to bring milk home when we were married and now he's coordinating all this!"

"Quite a few models get into acting," Cameron told her. "Maybe Nick could find you a part in his next film. If you're interested."

Abby caught the edge in his voice and smiled at him. "I *don't* think so," she told him sunnily. "I couldn't stand doing this day in and day out—could you?"

Cameron sighed in relief. "Nope. I'd go nuts. But Nick seems to be in his glory."

"Nick's been insane for years," Abby said dryly. "But around this bunch—who'd notice?"

"Come on, Cameron, we need you now," Nick shouted with a touch of impatience. "Get into the second canoe."

"The master calls." Cameron sighed dramatically. "I'll see you later."

Twenty minutes later the canoes were finally in position, the set was cleared, and Nick called, "Action."

They filmed the landing in two takes. The first time Champlain almost fell overboard, so Nick called a halt and they had to try again. The second take was perfect and Nick called, "Cut!" then, "Print it!"

Thirty minutes later, Abby was in position, leaning against a huge boulder, waiting for Nick to give the word. For some inexplicable reason she wasn't nervous, rather she felt strangely in tune with the young maiden's tragedy.

"All right! Torch the village!" Nick cried, his voice crackling with excitement. "Let's do it right the first time! We won't have another chance."

She was dying. Blood from the gaping wound between her breasts dripped relentlessly from her body, seeping into Mother Earth. Each breath was a victory won at great cost. She knew she would be one with The Creator very soon. And yet she hung on…waiting.

"Ah-iii!"

He comes! She heard the painful cry of her beloved and knew he was close at hand. She gasped for breath and held back the darkness that was edging closer. She had to feel his touch one last time.

Then he was holding her broken body in his gentle hands; his eyes, filled with unbelieving sorrow, roamed her pale, bloodstained face. His trembling fingers touched the deep bloody gouge in her forehead where the first Iroquois war club smashed her skull and knocked her to the ground.

He made a keening noise in his throat that was unrecognizable as human—its unearthly cry echoing through the cloudless sky overhead. All the while, he rocked her tenderly in his arms, her blood staining his deerskin shirt. She had made that shirt for him when they wintered near the Big Water.

Black smoke from the burning wigwams drifted under her nostrils, stealing what little air remained in her lungs. She gasped and choked for life, her body convulsing with each passing second. Bright red blood bubbled from the jagged gash in her chest where the second Iroquois warrior had buried his hatchet—after his vicious violation of her body.

Her beloved stroked her dirt-streaked face, his touch calming her pain-wracked body. With her last bit of strength, she lifted her eyes to meet his. "Mii-gwetch," she breathed softly—*'thank you—for loving me,'* she told him—then died.

"Cut! And—that's a print!"

Nick laughed, then rushed forward to hug Abby. "You're a natural, babe. I knew you could do it! You were good too…Cameron."

Then Nick turned away and yelled, "Okay, let's get our dead bodies into position so we can get the carnage sequence filmed before all the smoke is gone."

ABBY'S STORY: BETRAYED BY LOVE

Abby was still caught up in the emotional tension she'd felt while doing her scene. But as she watched the assistants scurrying people into pre-marked chalked positions, reality returned.

"Do you want to stay and watch?" Cameron asked.

"No." Abby shook her head. "I've seen enough blood and guts for one day—thank you very much. Let's get out of here. The smoke is making me choke."

"Wait for me by the truck if you get out of makeup before me," Cameron told her as they headed for the trailers to clean up.

Twenty minutes later, they were in Cameron's truck and on their way to the marina. When they got to the parking lot, Cameron hauled out a cooler, Abby grabbed their canvas bags, and they headed down the wooden dock looking for the right boat slip.

"There it is," Cameron said, pointing to a large grey boat with a bright green canvas top.

Abby frowned. "It's really big, Cameron." She glanced at him, then asked, "Are you sure you know how to drive a boat this size?"

Cameron grinned. "Oh, I think I can manage. Nipissing is a long shallow lake and a storm can come up in no time, so most of the boats on the lake are this size or larger." He put the cooler down on the dock beside the boat, then leaned forward and began unzipping the camper top. In minutes, the sides were open and Cameron hopped inside. He unlocked the cabin and turned on the engine.

"Whoa, it's hot in here," he shouted. Then he leaned over the side, grabbed the cooler, and set it out of the way on the green carpeted floor. Abby handed him their two bags and he threw them into the cabin, then helped her into the boat.

"This is much roomier than I thought it would be," she said as she peeked into the cabin. It had green wraparound seats and matching curtains on the small windows.

"It's about twenty-two feet long," Cameron told her, "with a 205 engine. This baby has lots of power."

Abby laughed. "Why is it that men get excited by anything with an engine in it?"

"I get excited by things without an engine too," Cameron teased.

Abby jumped up into the tall swivel chair opposite the driver's. "Keep that thought," she laughed. "I'll remind you of it later."

Cameron's eyes burned brightly. "Sounds to me like you're in a *playful* mood."

"Could be," Abby grinned cheekily. "Time will tell."

Cameron finished unzipping the two side panels and set them in the cabin. He settled into his chair, then said, "Hold on, Abby. I'm taking this baby out."

They eased their way out of the marina, then made for open water. It was a warm day for the end of August. The sky was clear and the sun sparkled on the water with dazzling brightness.

Abby fumbled in her bag for sunglasses, then pulled off the jade-green jogging top she had slipped over her blue bikini. She leaned back in the pedestal chair, her long brown hair flying behind her as they streaked across the waves. She turned to grin at Cameron and caught him watching her, his face alight with desire.

"I hope you know where you're going," she shouted over the noise of the engine.

Cameron pointed to his right, indicating miles of open blue water. "That way," he laughed. Then, with one hand on the wheel, he unbuttoned his striped shirt and took it off, throwing it into the cabin.

Abby couldn't help it, she stared, fascinated by his naked chest. She'd made love to this man several times, but this was the first time she'd seen him without a shirt. He would put Brad Pitt to shame! His chest and muscular arms rippled as he moved and he looked smooth and golden, like a warrior from the past. Then he kicked off his shoes and, again holding onto the wheel with one hand, he pulled down his navy shorts.

Abby's mouth went dry. In a navy spandex bathing suit splashed with vivid orange, Cameron was all male! His long legs were muscular, covered by a light matting of silky dark hair. His chest hair was more springy, with a thin line edging down into his briefs.

Abby's eyes followed that line and froze. Cameron's manhood was clearly outlined—and clearly aroused.

"See anything you like?" he shouted as the boat skimmed over the light waves.

Abby grinned weakly, then looked away.

They drove across the lake for hours, passing sailboats, fishing craft, and other large pleasure boats as well. They slowed down once to let a small boat pass by and Cameron leaned over to steal a gentle kiss.

By mid-afternoon, Abby was ready for a break. So when Cameron pointed to a small deserted island and raised a brow, she nodded her agreement and he arced the boat toward the small beach.

Cameron slowed the boat down and headed for a small natural cove formed by the outcropping of some rocks. Then he cut the engine, raised the foot on the motor, and let the boat drift into shore.

"We're lucky," he said as he looked around. "We have the place to ourselves today."

"Do you think the owners will mind if we spend some time here?"

"This is crown land. There are small islands like this all over the lake. People use them all the time. We just have to clean up after ourselves and put out our fire before we leave."

Cameron jumped into the water and helped Abby out. Then he pulled the boat onto shore and tied it securely around a tree.

"You stay there and I'll pass you our stuff," Cameron said as he climbed back into the boat. He passed Abby the bags, two lawn chairs, and a blanket. Then hauling the cooler onto the edge of the boat he jumped into the water again, then carried the cooler to the beach.

They worked quickly together, arranging their chairs and blanket on the sandy beach and storing the cooler under a shady tree.

"I don't know about you but I'm ready for a swim," Cameron said as he wiped the sweat off his forehead. He ran into the water and dove in.

Abby dropped her sunglasses on her chair, kicked off her sandals, and eased her jogging pants down her legs. All the while her eyes searched for a sleek dark head in the waves. When she was just taking her first tentative step into the cold water, he surfaced farther out than she expected, then turned and headed back to shore.

"Jump right in or you'll never make it," he warned.

"Oh, it's cold," she complained, her body shivering. When Cameron laughed and disappeared again, Abby splashed through the gentle waves, then lowered herself up to her neck. Once the first shock was over, the water felt refreshingly good. She swam out to meet Cameron, her eyes as bright as the sunlight dancing on the lake.

They splashed and played endlessly, like two children enjoying their first day at the beach. Every once in a while their legs tangled or their bodies slid against each other, but the touching wasn't sexual for once. They were in a world of their own, with only a few seagulls overhead to remind them that their paradise was shared.

"I'm going in to shore," Abby said breathlessly, "before I turn blue."

Cameron nodded and swam beside her, helping her to stand when they reached the sandy bottom. "You're shivering," he said as he reached for a towel. "Here, let me dry you off."

Abby stood passively and let him dry her skin. The towel was warm from the sun and his hands were brisk and firm. He rubbed her hair gently, squeezing the water from the long tresses.

"There, that should do it." His voice was husky as he passed her the towel. Their eyes met and held, his a burning green flame, hers half-shut and heavy-lidded.

"I want you in my arms right now," Cameron said huskily.

"Cameron..." Abby was torn by indecision. She didn't know how to say what she felt without hurting his feelings. She wanted him too—but not yet. There was so much more about him she wanted to know. For now, talking was more important than touching.

Cameron sensed her mood shift. "I know...my timing's off," he laughed ruefully. "How about if we put lovemaking on the back burner for awhile. Instead, we'll have a glass or two of wine, maybe explore the island, or have another swim. Then I'll barbeque some steaks for dinner. How does that sound to you?"

Abby smiled in delight. "It sounds wonderful," she told him softly. "Just perfect."

Cameron knew he was on the right track. "And perhaps later—who knows?" he said with a cheeky grin. Cameron saw the answer he wanted in Abby's luminescent smile. It wasn't easy holding off loving her again, but she was right. They'd slept together—but never had a date. He'd give her a day she'd remember always.

"Did you bring any suntan lotion?" Cameron asked as they dropped onto the blanket.

"I have some in my bag. Do you want me to do your back?"

"Please." Cameron turned over and rested his head on his outstretched arms.

Abby knelt beside him and swallowed hard. She poured some of the creamy liquid into her hands, then leaned forward and began to smooth it into his supple shoulders and broad back. She rotated her thumbs into his tanned neck, lathered his muscular arms, then inched down his spine.

"Will you do my legs too, Abby?" Cameron's voice was hoarse and muffled as he spoke.

Abby breathed deeply. *The man was pushing it!* She stared down at his lightly-haired, muscular legs and almost groaned out loud. *Was he trying to drive her crazy?* Abby paused, then understanding dawned in her eyes. *Well, two could play that game.* She poured some more lotion into her hands, then edged toward his feet. With an impish smile, she started at his toes, massaging between each digit with slow, caressing strokes.

Cameron stifled a groan, but remained unmoving.

Abby moved into the space between his spread legs and worked her way up his well-defined calves. His muscles tensed when she grazed the inside of his thighs and his hands dug into the sand, but other than that he remained motionless as she worked her way up his body. She kneaded his strong thighs with slick, hot fingers and felt his muscles tremble as she moved higher. Then she sat back and bit her bottom lip. *Should she chance it?*

Abby tipped the bottle one last time onto her fingertips, then caressed his inner thighs slowly—one inch at a time—from knee to crotch. By the time she was finished, Cameron was breathing heavily—and so was she.

He lifted his head and looked at her, his dark lashes almost fanning his cheeks. "I'll do you now," he said hoarsely. "Lay down on your stomach."

Abby groaned silently. She knew it was payback time. She eased down onto the warm blanket, then closed her eyes in dreaded anticipation.

Cameron snapped her bra top open, then poured cool lotion down her spine.

"That tickles," she complained softly, then sighed as Cameron started to massage her shoulders. His hands were strong and soothing, draining the tension from her body like magic. He rubbed her relentlessly, much longer than she had him. Abby was in a dream world, drifting off to sleep. Then she felt him kneel between her legs and she snapped back to full consciousness.

He parted her legs a little more, then began to stroke her narrow feet, massaging her instep with such skill, Abby groaned out loud.

He had her now, Cameron knew, as he pressed her firm calves with his slick hands. His eyes sought the juncture of her legs and noticed the slight tensing of her muscles there. He clamped his jaws together, and forced himself to move up her inner thighs with gentle hands. *Easy!* he told himself. *Don't blow it now.*

Then Cameron touched the soft skin on her buttocks left exposed by her bikini bottom, his thumbs stroking her with a maddening gentleness. Her breath caught in her throat as he inched closer to the juncture of her thighs. Then he stopped. When Abby felt him shift to his feet she wanted to howl in protest. He did up her bra strap, then straightened.

Abby turned over and let her eyes travel up to meet his.

Cameron hesitated. She looked so expectant, so poised for more, that he almost said to hell with it and took her in his arms. Then he remembered the words she'd throw at him in anger. Words that he knew were based in truth.

"How about a cold drink or a glass of wine," he asked abruptly as he moved to the cooler.

"No!" Abby's voice was louder than she intended. She saw him watching her, ready to follow her lead. "How about another swim, instead," she muttered. "I need to cool off."

Cameron grinned and raised his brows. "You and me both." Then he picked her up and carried her through the waves, high in his arms.

Knowing what was coming, Abby said something unladylike under her breath just before he threw her in. She was sputtering when she surfaced, but not for long. But she shrieked out loud when something eased through her legs underwater.

Cameron was laughing at the look of outrage on her face when she grabbed his head and forced it underwater. Then the game was on.

Ten minutes later, exhausted but happy, Abby floated while Cameron tread water nearby. Watching the wisps of clouds drift overhead, she felt unusually relaxed and content. Her instincts told her she was seeing the real Cameron at last. At times, he was laughing and charming, with a great capacity for living. But he was also reflective and caring, with a responsible attitude that permeated his actions. She could understand why Leah had loved him so—loved and trusted him completely. Abby loved him too, and was starting to trust him at last. She was surprised to realize how much she *wanted* to trust Cameron. She had never consciously felt that need when she was married to Nick. She'd given up trusting people a long time ago. But since coming to Howard's Bay her attitudes were slowly changing.

Abby swam closer to Cameron's side. The smile he gave her was as warm as the sun on her back, his dancing eyes reflecting the diamonds of light on the water. His black lashes were spiked by drips of water that trickled down his face and pooled in his dimple. His curly, thick hair, streaked with red highlights, was slicked against his skull. In that moment, Abby wanted him desperately. She curled her arms around his neck and twined her body with his.

"Getting hungry?" Cameron asked, his voice tight.

He wasn't talking about food and they both knew it. "I'm starved," she told him, her azure eyes eloquent with need.

Cameron grinned, then kissed her slowly, one hand finding her firm bottom underwater.

Abby sighed and opened her mouth, her arms pulling him closer.

With genuine reluctance Cameron broke the contact, then said, "Come on, you can help me get the steaks ready."

Abby blinked, her mouth dropping open in shock. That was *not* what she had in mind!

Cameron smiled lazily and pulled her along with him into shore.

Abby dried herself off very slowly, watching *him* watch *her* out of the corner of an eye.

In a last-ditched effort to keep his hands to himself Cameron threw Abby her shoes and said abruptly, "Come on. Let's explore the island."

Abby's eyes widened but she managed to slip on her shoes without a word. It was her own damned fault he was being such a gentleman! So she had no choice but to follow his lead and behave.

The island was rocky, with patches of moss and several skimpy pine trees for shade.

"See if you can find any berries," Cameron told her. Several minutes later, Abby spied a small patch of plump blueberries, and they knelt down and fed each other the tiny, sweet fruit.

"Your lips really are blue now," Cameron laughed, his face inches from hers. But the laughter died away when Abby rimmed her mouth with her flicking tongue to clean off any remaining juice.

"If you're trying to drive me crazy, you're succeeding," he growled as he hauled her to her feet. "Let's keep moving, but watch out for poison ivy."

Abby smiled with impish satisfaction as he pulled her along. She'd seen the bulge in his spandex suit and marvelled at his restraint.

Twenty minutes later, they'd covered the island from end to end. The only downside to the day was finding piles of garbage scattered on the far point.

"There's no excuse for this," Cameron said grimly, his hands on his hips.

"I'll start to pick it up," Abby told him as she gingerly stepped over some broken glass. "Do you have a garbage bag in the boat?"

Cameron nodded, and headed back through the brush. In minutes, he returned and they picked up pizza cartons, beer bottles, and empty cans. When the clearing was free of debris at last, they smiled at each other in satisfaction, then walked back to the beach hand in hand. They decided to have one last swim before dinner and Abby challenged Cameron to a race—which he easily won.

Abby headed for shore, staggered to the blanket, and dropped down in relief. She was still gasping for breath when Cameron eased down beside her and offered her a cold diet coke.

She sipped it and put on her sunglasses, content to let the hot sun dry her off.

"Did you picnic a lot with your family?" Cameron asked drowsily at her side.

"Only once," she said abruptly. "It wasn't a pleasant experience."

"Like your childhood…?"

Abby frowned, and kept her eyes closed. "Oh…compared to some, it wasn't too bad," she sighed. "It was just very…"

"Lonely?"

Abby was glad she was wearing her sunglasses. She was embarrassed by the tears filling her eyes.

But one wayward tear slid down her face, and Cameron saw it. He leaned over and licked the salty drop from her cheek, then pulled her into his arms and held her close.

"You have *me* now," he whispered against her neck.

Abby choked, then held onto him for endless moments.

The T-bone steaks were sizzling on the portable barbeque and a mouth-watering mixture of sliced potatoes, onions, and butter was steaming away in a tinfoil pan.

"I'm impressed, Cameron," Abby told him as she watched him take out heavy plastic dishes, cutlery, and napkins from a picnic basket. She sipped lazily on her wine. "I feel very pampered and spoiled. Are you sure there's nothing I can do?"

Cameron grinned at her. "You just sit back and relax. Leave everything to me."

"You certainly seem to know what you're doing."

"Thanks to Pete," he told her as he sliced tomatoes onto a plate. "Whenever my Dad used to take us fishing, we'd pack a few peanut butter sandwiches and take off. But Pete's a man who likes a big shore lunch. I've developed that habit too. Mind you, we should have brought a couple of rods and caught some pickerel—there's nothing better than fresh pickerel for a shore lunch."

"Are you and Pete close friends?" Abby leaned back against the cooler, interested to hear his response.

"We're getting closer," Cameron said slowly. Then he frowned. "I'm kind of a loner, Abby. I'm not one for a lot of friends…but the ones I have, I value."

Abby nodded. "We're alike in that way," she told him. "To me a friend is someone I don't have to mince my words with...someone I can trust...someone who likes me enough to tell me when I'm wrong. Maggy's my friend and so is Libby. And you," she added softly. "I hope you're my friend, too."

Cameron swallowed the lump in his throat. Her eyes were so soft, so trusting. He felt an overwhelming need to hold her close, fuelled by a fierce protectiveness he'd never experienced before.

"Yes, we're friends, Abby," he whispered softly, "but I want us to be so much more." He leaned over and kissed her with a pent-up longing that wouldn't be denied any longer.

The kiss was sweeter than any Abby had ever tasted—even with him. It seemed endless, and too short. All at the same time.

Abby lifted her lips and smiled at him, then laughed teasingly. "Something's burning—and it's not just us."

Cameron groaned, "Oh, God—the steaks!"

"I'm stuffed!" Abby groaned as she leaned back in her chair. "That was absolutely wonderful!"

"More wine?"

"God no! I'd burst."

Cameron nibbled on the last few potatoes on his plate and watched the sun moving toward the horizon. "I hate to say it," he sighed, "but I think we'd better head back. We've been very fortunate that the lake's so calm, but that could change very quickly."

Abby nodded, then began to pick up the remnants of their meal. When Cameron's hand grazed hers, she stilled, then looked into his eyes.

"Today was perfect, Cameron. Thank you."

Cameron smiled. "My pleasure." And he meant it.

It cooled down very quickly on their homeward journey, so Cameron stopped several hours later to attach the plastic side panels and top—to keep out the wind. While the boat was stopped Abby slipped into the cabin and changed back into her jogging suit.

The sun was slipping below a pink horizon, and the wind had picked up. The boat was rocking to and fro so Abby had difficulty balancing herself as she climbed out of the cabin and into her chair. She glanced at Cameron with a worried frown. "Is it going to storm?" she asked.

Cameron finished the last zipper, then smiled at her reassuringly.

"Nope. It's just going to get a little choppy." He started the engine and turned the boat in the opposite direction.

The wind became stronger and white caps topped many waves. Before long the boat was plowing through an endless stretch of black, angry water, the heavy spray making visibility almost nil.

But though Abby was agitated, Cameron was not. He smiled at her often, talked casually of Libby's new house, his calm manner more reassuring than his words.

It was nearly eleven before they eased into the marina and Abby was exhausted from tension. Her legs were rubbery, but she managed to helped Cameron unload the boat. Once in the truck, within minutes she was dozing in her seat, her head limp against the leather.

She was worn out, Cameron realized. She couldn't help it. Being on the lake affected many people that way.

When he pulled into her driveway and saw her dark lashes fanning her cheeks, he knew their date was at an end. A very different ending from the way he had planned.

"Come on sleepyhead," he muttered tenderly, kissing her softly on the lips. "We're home." He turned on the interior light in the truck so she could see where she was going.

Abby half-opened her eyes, then reached out and caressed his cheek. "Will you spend the night with me?" she whispered. Her voice was husky and warm, her smile tremulous in the dim light.

Heat coursed through Cameron's body and his eyes widened in surprise. "Are you sure?" he said. *Now that, he didn't expect!*

"I want you," she whispered softly. "I want to make love to you…then sleep in your arms for the rest of the night."

Cameron almost tripped over his own feet in his haste to get out of the truck.

Chapter Twelve

Abby opened the door, threw her bag on the floor, then turned into his arms. She wasn't tired any longer.

Curling her arms around his neck she leaned against his hard, muscular body, then smiled up into his eyes. "I've been waiting for this all day."

"Was it worth the wait?" His hands smoothed down her back and gripped her bottom, edging her closer to his rigid flesh.

"Yes," she gasped. "Although there were times I thought I was going to explode."

"I came too close for comfort when you were putting suntan lotion between my legs," he chuckled, nibbling her neck.

Abby swayed in his arms and burrowed into his chest. "I'm sticky and I have sand in places I'd rather not. Do you mind…I think I'll have a shower first."

Cameron lifted his head and smiled into her slumberous eyes. "Only if I can join you."

"Will you do my back?"

Cameron grinned wickedly. "And your front. I intend to do a bit of everything!"

Abby lifted her chin and stared at him, her eyes filled with a dark intensity.

Then she stepped back and cooly peeled off her jogging top. She dropped it on the floor, then kicked off her shoes. Without breaking eye contact, she pulled down her pants, then kicked them away too. Her chin tilted higher and there was a touch of challenge in her eyes as she stood before him naked, proud, and unabashedly female.

A small light over the kitchen sink illuminated Abby's skin, making it glow like alabaster.

"My God, Abby! You're so beautiful!" Cameron whispered. His voice was low and reverent, but his eyes were hot and glittery.

"Your turn now."

Cameron read the laughing challenge in her azure eyes, but also noticed a slight tremor in her body. She was not as nonchalant as she was trying to let on. He smiled tenderly, then began to undress. He stripped his shirt over his head, kicked off his shoes, then unzipped his jeans. He paused when her eyes shifted to his bulging fly.

"You do it. I like the feel of your hands on my body."

Abby's eyes widened, but she quickly bent down to comply. She knelt on the floor, then pulled his jeans and white briefs down to his knees. She swallowed hard when his engorged manhood sprang out and grazed her cheek.

"You do the rest," she told him hoarsely. "It'll be faster that way."

Cameron did as he was told.

Abby gasped aloud. *Hot damn! Eat your heart out Lorraine Reilly!*

Unaware of the impact he was having, Cameron pulled her up into his arms, letting their bodies touch at last. He sighed, a smile of satisfaction curling his lips. "Have you any idea how long I've waited to feel you like this? I've had fantasies where all I did was touch your naked skin. You feel like hot silk," he panted. But he held her as gently as he would a newborn.

Abby eased back, then lifted both hands to cup his stubbled jaw. "I've dreamt of you too, Cam. Too many times to count." She leaned up on her toes and slanted her mouth over his, her tongue dipping inside to taste.

Cameron's swollen body hardened painfully. His mouth melted on hers, tasting her inner sweetness with a wild hunger. When her soft thighs pressed against his swollen shaft, he nearly lost it. He tore his mouth away, then lifted her into his arms. "Which way to the shower?" he demanded hoarsely. "If we wait any longer, it'll be over before it starts."

Abby pointed to a room off the kitchen and Cameron carried her across the room like a man on fire. When Abby flipped on the light switch, he let her slide down his body to her feet. He smiled at her, then slid back the shower door, and turned on the water. He stepped inside, then held out his hand to Abby.

"Come on," he grinned. "This water's a lot warmer than the lake."

Abby eased inside at Cameron's back. She was amazed at how natural it felt to be with him like this. With Nick, she'd been conscious of every body flaw, every blemish. Of hips just a tad too full, of breasts just a smidgen too small. But, with Cameron, she felt sleekly beautiful and proudly female.

"I'll do you first," she offered, eager to touch every inch.

Cameron passed her the soap, then stepped into the spray. "Be my guest," he laughed, as he braced both hands on either side of the shower nozzle.

Abby lathered her hands, then soaped his broad back and neck, enjoying the feel of his rippling muscles. She washed down his arms and along his sides, then inched around to palm his chest. His nipples rose to sharp peaks when she rimmed them with her fingers.

"You're bad," he growled in warning. "Don't forget—my turn will come."

"I'm counting on that," she purred, her voice as low as her roving fingers. She lathered up some more, then soaped his rigid abdomen, the tips of her fingers dipping into the springy hair below.

Cameron groaned and stiffened, muscles tensing in his arms and legs.

Emboldened, Abby massaged his firm shanks with tender adoring hands, then—ever so gently—traced the crease in between.

"Dear God, Abby! There's only so much I can take!"

His words freed the hellion in Abby making her even more bold. Spooning her body to his, she reached around and took hold of his penis, holding him gently with both soapy hands. Then slowly, her fingers rimmed him, up and down for long immeasurable seconds.

He groaned, then jerked away, his body racked by powerful shudders. "That was *too* close," he muttered. "Now it's your turn."

Abby eased in front of Cameron and leaned into the spray, her body tense and ripe for pleasure.

Cameron raised Abby's arms against the shower stall, then caressed her exactly as she had done him. When his hands touched her bottom, she, too, shuddered, then moaned. Her body tensed even more, waiting for Cameron to unleash his passion. But this time, his touch wasn't violent, just very gentle. So gentle he had her trembling with need before he even touched her intimately.

He leaned against her back as his soapy hands massaged her firm breasts. As he teased her hard nipples, she started to burn, deep inside.

She rubbed her thighs together in desperation, trying to find some surcease, some relief. By the time his hands inched slowly down her belly to touch the pouting button hidden between her legs, she was almost sobbing.

"Now!" she demanded hoarsely. "No more playing. I want you inside me now!"

"No," he whispered softly. "This time, we do it right. I'm going to love you the way you deserve. The way I should have done that night in Libby's shop."

Abby froze. She glanced back over her shoulder, her eyes searching his.

"No...don't look at me like that, Abby! I never want to see that look in your eyes again." He grabbed the nozzle and quickly washed the soap from both their bodies, then stepped out of the shower and lifted Abby out onto the mat. He towelled her briskly, his mouth no longer laughing, but grim. "I'll make it right," he muttered as much to himself as to her. "Just give me one more chance."

Abby heard an edge of desperation in his voice and knew he meant every word. She took a towel from the bar and dried his shoulders as he bent to do her legs. When he trailed the towel up her thighs and dried her silky brown mound, they both groaned and threw the towels away.

Cameron kissed her moist lips as he carried her into the bedroom. He settled her in the middle of the bed, then eased down beside her.

"Leave the lights off," she told him, her voice like liquid honey in the darkness.

Her sweet breath caressed his cheek as he pulled her under his body.

Abby's legs were trembling when he parted them, her cleft slick with moisture, ready for his possession.

Cameron bent and kissed her slowly, skimming and probing her swollen nether lips with infinite patience.

But Abby had reached the end of her tolerance. She knew she'd asked for this tender loving, but she couldn't take any more! He was driving her slowly round the bend! She reached between their bodies and took him in hand, to guide him home.

"Abby! Not yet!"

"I can't take any more of this Cameron! I want you inside of me—now!"

That was all he needed to hear. Cameron reared up, then eased into her tight sheath. He paused at the entrance, then grasped her hips and drove deep, penetrating her body with one strong thrust. The silence was broken by their sighs of relief.

Abby gripped his buttocks, wrapped her long legs around him, and took all that he had to give. She slid against him, her body sleek with sweat, enjoying the friction of his slow, steady strokes.

Cameron slide all the way in, then withdrew all but the tip, repeating the stroke time and time again, with the same maddening rhythm. It was just about killing him to move so slowly, but he would keep it up all night if that's what it took.

Head thrown back, Abby groaned deep in her throat. His smooth relentless thrusts were sheer torture. "Cameron," she gasped, "do—something! I can't—take much more of this!"

"Yes you can, baby," he crooned. "You can do it. Feel me inside you. Feel the way my body fills every inch inside yours. We're a perfect fit." He groaned as if in mortal pain, then bit out, "I can feel you grabbing me, Abby. I can feel you building. Get ready, baby…this is going to feel so *good*! I'm talking—just to hold it back, Abby. Oh God! I can't take much more either!"

Abby could heard his words but they weren't registering. She was lost in a pleasure so rare…so unbelievable pure, all she could do was move with him and follow where he led. His velvety-hard shaft pushed her higher, compelling her to reach for something just beyond her grasp. Her body surged around his, building in intensity, coiling ever higher—demanding release. Then she shuddered and came, pleasure pulsing through her body so forcefully, a scream of fulfilment ripped from her throat.

Her first tremors triggered his release and Cameron thrust hard into her body, spurting so violently, his world turned black for a moment. When the last tremor stilled, he eased down onto her quivering flesh and held her close, kissing her tenderly time and time again.

Abby gasped for breath and snuggled into his shoulder. She felt so wonderful, yet so deadly exhausted. Words of love trembled on her lips, but were never spoken and in seconds she was fast asleep.

Cameron eased her onto her back and pulled her close. He heard her murmur softly in her sleep, but couldn't catch the words. As he caressed her satiny cheek he whispered, "I love you Abby Fulton." He knew she couldn't hear him, but said the words all the same. For his sake, if not yet for hers. Cam held her close for the rest of the night as he'd dreamt of doing for so long. Then he, too, slept. The best sleep he'd had in years.

Abby was yawning as she entered Maggy's office Monday morning.

"Looks like you had quite an...energetic weekend," Libby teased, with a wink at Maggy.

Abby sipped her coffee and eyed Libby haughtily. "And your point is...?" she drawled.

"Oh...nothing," Libby said airily. "You just look like sleep was on the bottom of your agenda this weekend."

Libby's light blue eyes were wide with innocence, but Abby wasn't fooled. They *knew*. That fact was soon confirmed.

"Was that Cameron's truck parked in front of your place all weekend?" Maggy asked, her eyes dancing with mischief.

"Yes it was—not that it's anybody's business." Abby's tone warned that they were skating on thin ice.

"Well, Ross was afraid it might have broken down. After all, it never moved from Saturday night until this morning." Maggy kept a straight face for ten seconds more and then cracked up. "We were wondering if we should sent over some food—to help you keep up your strength—or a doctor to make sure you were both still alive."

"Oh for pity's sake," Abby groaned.

Libby giggled, then added, "Rayce thought we should go in and hose you guys down. But I held him off."

"You're *too* kind." Abby tilted her chin, then eyed them warily. "I'm not going to get any break from you two, am I?"

"Not until you tell all." Maggy smiled complaisantly, sipped her tea, and waited.

But Libby was more impatient. "Did you do that part in Nick's movie?"

"Oh yes," Abby sighed. "I was covered in blood and gore and I just about roasted to death in my costume. That wig must have weighed a ton. But," she added with a slight smile, "it *was* kind of fun. Cameron looked very realistic."

"Did you two get to ride off into the sunset together?" Libby leaned forward, resting her arms on her jean-clad knees, her eyes alight with genuine interest.

Abby smoothed a fold in her long camel-coloured skirt, then shook her head. "No," she said, a smile curving her lips, "I got to die quite dramatically in his arms. It was really quite romantic."

"Set the tone for the rest of the weekend—from what I see," Maggy said sardonically, her green eyes full of laughter.

"Oh good grief! Give me a break," Abby groused. She gulped her coffee and nearly burnt her tongue. "Now see what you made me do!"

Maggy and Libby burst out laughing at the wounded outrage on Abby's face.

A few seconds later Abby grinned as well. She relented enough to add, "Not that it's any of your business, but yes—I had a wonderful weekend. And yes, Cameron and I spent it together. And no—I won't tell you any more than that!"

"We'll see," Maggy said, with a devilish glint in her eye. "We have our *ways!*"

"That's what's wrong with this world," Abby sighed as she straightened the collar of her silk shirt. "The world's gone gossip crazy."

"You love it too," Libby scoffed. "Except when it's about *you*."

Maggy grinned knowingly, then turned to Libby. "Better start the meeting, Lib. When she gets that thinned-lipped, old-maid look about her—she'll be on her high horse for a while."

Abby listened absently with one ear while Libby brought them up to date on a seminar for new businesses being offered at a local college. She enjoyed their teasing and would normally have told them what they wanted to know. But, not this time. Her weekend with Cameron was too fresh, too special to share, even with her best friends. She thought back to the last twenty-four hours and couldn't suppress the smug grin that lifted her lips.

"Abby! Will you get your mind out of the bedroom and pay attention to business!" Libby snapped, exasperation tingeing her voice. "If your weekend was even half as good as that look on your face suggests—no wonder you're exhausted!"

Abby stared intently at Libby, her hooded expression barely readable. "It was so good," she drawled softly, "I won't be walking properly for a week."

Maggy laughed uproariously at the bawdy comment. "Is that boasting—or complaining?"

"I haven't decided yet," Abby replied with a yawn. "But I feel so damned good—if I could market this feeling, I'd be a millionaire."

Libby sighed and folded her arms across her red sweatshirt. "I thought you weren't going to tell us anything."

Abby grinned. "I couldn't help it. My brain hasn't started to function yet."

"Probably still on pleasure mode." Libby closed the agenda book with a snap. "Meeting adjourned. Maybe by next week Abby will be down from cloud nine."

"I don't know about that…"Abby teased impudently. "Don'y forget, next Monday is Labour Day. Cameron's taking three days off."

"Oh, that reminds me," Libby interjected. "We're having a corn roast next Saturday evening at Tom's cottage. You're all invited. Just bring your own lawn chairs and whatever you want to drink."

"Oh, that's a great idea," Maggy smiled. "I love peaches and cream corn."

"That's what we're having," Libby promised. "Tom ordered ten dozen." Libby turned to Abby and added, "Rayce is going to invite Cameron this morning. They're meeting at his office at ten."

Abby nodded, then stood up. "Sounds like a lot of fun. I haven't been to a corn roast in years."

"Rayce said Tom cooks it with the husks on—in burlap bags over a fire."

Abby wrinkled her nose. "Really…well, maybe I'll bring along a peanut butter sandwich or two. Cameron has quite an appetite."

"There she goes boasting again," Libby sighed.

"That's it! I'm out of here," Abby laughed. She drained her coffee, mumbled a 'good-bye' and sauntered out of the office.

"Well, Abby's mood has certainly improved," Libby said.

"It's about time," Maggy agreed. "Now…fill me in on this corn roast. Anybody interesting going to be there?"

"Just the usual crowd, I think. But you know Rayce. He'll probably invite the whole town."

Abby walked into her shop and smiled at Edith Gavin who was rooting through a remnants bin. "A new shipment of that polished cotton you like should be arriving tomorrow," she told the old woman. When Edith nodded, Abby patted her on the arm, then headed into her cubbyhole of an office.

Once there she sank into an old swivel chair and closed her eyes in relief. She really was exhausted! Perhaps it might have been wiser to take the day off, she mused, rubbing her weary eyes. But it was no wonder she was tired. She and Cameron had spent most of the weekend in bed, making love…dozing…making love again. The only time they'd left her room had been to grab a snack or a shower. She'd spoken the truth a little while ago. She *was* finding it difficult to walk. But she didn't care. It had been an incredible weekend! And he was coming back tonight for more.

Later that night, Abby was curled up on the couch, snuggled in Cameron's arms. The News was blaring on the TV but they were both nearly sound asleep.

Cameron had appeared at Abby's doorstep around nine, his face drawn with fatigue. After wolfing down a plate of Abby's warmed-up stew, he'd barely made it to the couch. And hadn't moved since.

"Did Rayce tell you about the corn roast Saturday?" Abby mumbled.

"Yeah. He invited all the crew. Sounds like fun. Are we going?"

Abby liked the sound of that 'we.' "I told Libby we might," she answered sleepily.

Cameron yawned. "Sounds good. I don't know about you, but I'm beat. Are you ready for bed?"

Abby turned off the television and stood up. "Hours ago," she told him.

Wrapping one arm around her, Cam pulled her toward the bedroom. "Would you mind if we just catch up on some sleep tonight?" he asked, exhaustion draining his voice. "The weekend just about did me in."

"You too? Thank God," Abby groaned. "I thought it was just old age catching up with me. I almost fell asleep at lunch. My face was heading for the soup dish when Maggy saved me."

Cameron laughed and dropped a kiss on her lips. "I'll have to send Maggy flowers," he teased.

Once in the bedroom Abby quickly stripped, then reached for a nightgown on the chair.

Cameron stopped her hand. "Don't bother," he told her huskily.

When Abby hesitated, he kissed her lips with a renewed vigour she hadn't expected. Abby's eyes widened incredulously. "I thought you were too tired."

"I thought so too," Cameron grinned. "Until I looked at you." Then he tossed away the nightie and pulled her into his arms.

Abby groaned half-heartedly. "I don't know if I can do this."

"Let's find out," Cameron suggested as he eased her onto the bed. "We'll probably sleep better—afterwards."

He was absolutely right.

On Saturday morning, Cameron kissed Abby's eyelids and smiled when she protested lightly in her sleep. Then he nudged her until one azure eye blinked open.

"I'm leaving now, honey," he told her. "I'll be back to pick you up for the barbeque around seven tonight."

Abby mumbled something unintelligible, then rolled over, instantly asleep again.

Cameron grinned. Abby was not a morning person. He tucked the blankets around her shoulders, checked to make sure her alarm was set for seven-thirty, then padded out of the room.

He was tired, too, but not overly so. He'd stayed at Abby's every night so far this week, but he'd managed to get enough sleep to survive—but just barely. Each night he swore he was going to do nothing but sleep in Abby's arms, but before long, his craving to love her was more powerful than his need for sleep.

Cameron was grinning lazily while he tied his workboots. Time enough to sleep when he was an old man. He could smell coffee brewing in the kitchen, and, checking his watch, figured he had enough time for one cup and a bite of toast before he headed out to the site. He was standing over the sink, sipping a strong Colombian blend when Abby staggered into the kitchen wrapped in his navy bathrobe.

He grinned, then poured her a cup. He'd learned the hard way that Abby was nearly comatose until the first cup was emptied.

Abby drank deeply, then groaned in pleasure. "God! That's good! Are you on your way?"

"Yes, I'll be out at Rayce's new house."

Abby nodded. "By the way, Maggy asked me yesterday what we were planning for Thanksgiving. She'd like us to go there for dinner."

"Thanksgiving! Today's the last day of August."

"I know," Abby sighed. "But that's Maggy for you. She's already got half of her Christmas shopping done."

"Good Lord!" Cameron laughed then said, "I'll leave it up to you."

"Well...I thought you might like to invite your two brothers to spend Thanksgiving weekend with us."

Cameron's face darkened instantly. "I don't think so," he said cooly. "I couldn't face a whole weekend of indigestion."

"My cooking's not *that* bad," she said indignantly.

Cameron grinned. "No, I was referring to my older brothers. We don't get along very well."

"Oh." Abby was disappointed. She had been hoping that Cameron would want to introduce her to his family.

"How about if we go to Maggy's?"

"I guess," Abby agreed abruptly. But her eyes were clouded with doubt.

Cameron frowned. "Abby, it has nothing to do with you. My brothers and I have fought all our lives. We're not very close."

Abby nodded, then kissed his cheek. "I'd better get in the shower," she told him quietly. "I've got to get to work. See you tonight." Then she left the room.

Cameron hesitated, worried that he might have hurt her feelings. Then he sighed and headed out the door. He was late as it was.

It was nearly seven-thirty by the time Abby and Cameron turned into the narrow laneway that led to Tom's cottage. Abby sat close to Cameron, one hand resting on his firm thigh.

"I think there's going to be quite a crowd," he told her. "Tom said Rayce invited everyone he knew."

Abby grinned. "Sounds like he's in the mood for a party."

"How about you?" Cameron teased. "You ready for a party—later?"

"Time will tell." Then her eyes widened in surprise. "My God, look at the cars!" she said as she spotted a long line of vehicles edging the road.

Cameron frowned. "I'd better park here and we'll walk the rest of the way." He pulled in behind a small Toyota, turned off the engine, then said, "If you'll bring our jackets, I'll carry the cooler and lawn chairs."

Abby opened her door and laughed. "They sure are a rowdy bunch. I can hear them from here."

"I hope Rayce invited the neighbours. I don't think they'll be getting any sleep tonight."

Abby and Cameron walked down a winding dirt road to a small cottage on the edge of the lake. People of all ages milled about, many lounging in lawn chairs around an enormous fire. "Maggy and Libby must be here already," Abby said. "I can see Sasha and Kyra on the beach."

Cameron nodded. "There's Rayce near the fire talking to Harley. Looks like a good crowd."

Abby scanned the area, then frowned. "I see Lorraine the Lovely was invited," she said dismissively. In tailored jeans and a coral silk shirt Lorraine looked slightly overdressed—and very bored.

"Yeah." Cameron sighed, as he returned Lorraine's wave with a nod of his own. "Rayce invited the whole office. But I didn't think she'd bother to show up."

Abby gripped his hand, then pasted a smile on her face. There was no way she was going to let that woman spoil her evening.

And she didn't. For the next few hours, with Cameron close by her side, she talked with her friends, sipped a glass of wine, and relaxed around the fire. Every once in a while she caught Lorraine staring their way, but Abby ignored her as she did a mosquito that circled her head.

"Excuse me, people…can I have your attention please?"

The crowd slowly quieted and all eyes stared curiously at Rayce. His face was alight with excitement as he hugged Libby close to his side.

"She looks a little flustered," Abby whispered to Cameron. "I wonder what's up."

Rayce kissed Libby tenderly on the lips, then smiled at the waiting crowd. "This seemed like a good time to share our good news. We wanted all of you to know that Libby and I are expecting our first child in February."

A gasp flashed through the crowd, then everyone started to cheer and clap.

Abby was quiet for a moment, then said softly, "Isn't that wonderful news?"

Cameron nodded, but a muscle clenched in his jaw.

Abby felt his tension. Panic gripped her as her mind swirled with an old pain. "Do *you* want children, Cameron?"

He hesitated for a moment, twirling a beer bottle back and forth between his hands. Then he met her eyes and said quietly, "I'd like one or two. If possible." He stared at her intently, then murmured, "How about you?"

"Oh…I'd love to have a child of my own." Her voice was weary as she added, "But it probably won't happen, I'm afraid."

"You could always adopt a child. With the right man at your side."

Abby's eyes widened, then a luminous smile lifted her lips. "Yes, I suppose I could," she agreed softly. "With the right man at my side."

Cameron nodded, then pulled her to her feet. "Let's go offer our congratulations."

As they made their way through the crowd of well-wishers surrounding Libby and Rayce, Abby was almost bursting with joy. She replayed Cameron's words over and over again in her mind. There was no doubt about it. He'd talked about adopting…talked about the right man at her side. Smiled at her as he'd said it. Could that mean he wanted a future with her? God, she hoped so!

When Abby finally reached Libby, she threw her arms around her friend and hugged her tight. "I'm so happy for you, Libby," Abby smiled. Then she skimmed Libby's still slender body and teased, "Are you sure you're four months pregnant?"

"Positive!" Libby's light blue eyes danced with happiness. "It's been a real pain keeping the news to myself, but Rayce wanted to tell everyone tonight."

"You'll make a great mother, kid," Abby said, her voice cracking a little.

Libby hugged her friend, then whispered so only she could hear, "Your day will come, Abby. I know it."

Abby met Cameron's glittering eyes over Libby's head. "Perhaps it might at that," she agreed, a ghost of a smile lifting her lips.

Several hours earlier, Tom and Rayce had punctured a huge old tub with multiple holes on the side. They set the tub on a grate in a firepit, then filled the tub with four inches of sand. They saturated two burlap bags filled with corn by dumping the bags in the lake, then placed the bags in the centre of the tub, away from the sides. After filling the tub with sand, they poured buckets of water overtop, let the excess drain, then started a large fire under the grate.

When the smell of steaming corn had every mouth watering, Tom and Rayce lifted the large tub off the grate and set it in the sand. When the last trickle of water drained from the holes, they used shovels to gingerly lift the burlap bags of corn and carry them to a nearby table. There, a group of men carefully shucked the corn and filled large roasting pans with the steaming cobs.

Meanwhile, at another table away from the fire, Polly McMaster and Wendy Hughes were pouring boiled water into several gallon pickles jars. Then Maggy carefully added melted butter on top of the boiled water while Libby placed paper plates, salt, and napkins in the centre of the table.

Rayce carried a roast pan full of the sweet-smelling corn to his wife. "Here it is ladies...and there's lots more on the way."

With long tongs, Maggy dipped a corncob into the jar of melted butter then placed the corn on the paper plate Libby offered. In less than a minute, the table was covered with mouth-watering cobs.

"Corn's ready," Rayce yelled to a nearby group. "Help yourself."

At the other end of the table Abby started to dip corn into the other jar. Soon she was passing it to people so fast the pan was almost empty. Just in time, Cameron was by her side with a fresh batch. He dropped a kiss on her lips and whispered, "Having fun?"

"You bet," she told him, and meant it.

Fifteen minutes later, only the odd murmur could be heard as everyone munched contentedly on one cob after another. Abby had just handed Harley his third, when she smelled a strong, overpowering perfume.

She glanced over her shoulder and saw Lorraine watching her intently, a condescending smirk on her face.

"You look right at home—slopping corn," Lorraine quipped.

"Do you want one, Lorraine?" Abby asked dryly.

Lorraine bristled at the disdain on Abby's face. "I think not," she drawled. "Butter dripping down my chin is not my idea of a good time."

Abby bit back a sharp retort. "Suit yourself," she sighed, then turned back to dip an ear of corn for herself.

"Look at that," Lorraine said, her finger almost under Abby's nose. "Cameron is having a ball. He certainly seems to like children."

Abby didn't see him at first, then spotted Cameron on the beach. He was sitting beside Sasha, holding her corn while she nibbled away. Abby smiled when she heard his husky laugh. "Yes," she whispered softly, "he loves kids."

"I'm sure he wants some of his own," Lorraine added, with an edge in her voice that had Abby swivelling around.

Abby's eyes narrowed at the open malice on the other woman's face. "He'd like one or two," Abby said deliberately, crossing her arms over her chest.

"Really...how sad." Lorraine looked anything but.

"Sad?"

"Yes, it's sad. That you can't give him any," Lorraine added pointedly.

Abby froze, as the shaft hit home.

When she saw the pain in Abby's eyes, Lorraine curled her lips in triumphant then walked away.

Abby was shaking with rage. She wanted to race after the bitch and tear her limb from limb, but just then Maggy took her arm and turned her in the opposite direction.

"Breathe deeply, and swear if you must—but quietly please," Maggy cautioned. "There are little ears in close range."

"I won't swear," Abby seethed. "But I may need a lawyer in the morning." Abby winced, then asked quietly, "How did she find out, Maggy?"

"Who knows," Maggy sighed. "Who cares? Ignore the b...witch."

"Easier said than done."

"Abby! Hey...wait up!"

Abby turned and saw Cameron racing down the beach toward her. When he reached her side, he paused, then glanced at Maggy and asked, "What's up? Something I should know about?"

Abby hesitated, then shook her head. "Maggy and I were just talking...about Libby. Nothing's wrong."

"Are you ready to go home?" he asked.

"What! Already?" Maggy asked.

"We...have another party to go to," Cameron answered with a slight wink at Abby.

Maggy smiled in understanding. "Sounds like my kind of party," she laughed. "Have a good time."

Abby and Cameron headed back to the fire to say 'good-night' and took a lot of good-hearted ribbing about their early departure. Abby grinned at Cameron, then picked up their jackets and followed him down the beach. Abby couldn't help noticing Lorraine leaning against an old oak tree, looking sullen and bored. Harley and his wife Bessie sat nearby. As Abby and Cameron passed by them, Harley shouted out, "You go straight home to bed now."

Staring directly at Lorraine, Abby said deliberately, "That's exactly what I plan to do, Harley."

When Lorraine flinched, then looked away, Abby smiled in satisfaction, knowing her message had been received, loud and clear. In that moment, revenge tasted as sweet as the peaches and cream corn.

"You're very quiet," Cameron said when they were almost home. "Tired?"

"No, not really. I was just thinking."

"Did you enjoy yourself?"

Abby laid her hand on his thigh and squeezed gently. "I always enjoy myself when I'm with you."

Cameron sighed in relief. He was starting to believe he was getting somewhere with her. She'd handled his comment about adoption quite well, he thought. That had to be a good sign. Now if he could just get her talking about marriage, he'd be home free. He would just have to be patient a little longer.

In Abby's bedroom, the lights were dim, the sheets were cool and turned down in invitation. Abby had showered while Cameron rinsed out the cooler. She waited in her bed for him to join her, her eyes fluttering with exhaustion.

When Cameron padded naked into the room, he found her reclining on top of the covers, sound asleep. He smiled ruefully and looked down at his burgeoning body. "Sorry fellah," he whispered to himself. "Looks like you're out of luck tonight. The lady needs her sleep more than she needs you."

Cameron lifted Abby's long, slim legs, tucked them under the covers, then slid into bed at her side. He nestled her in his arms, and was soon fast asleep himself.

Chapter Thirteen

Before Abby knew it, September had given way to October. With Cameron virtually living with her now, life was very different, but very good—though some days they seldom saw each other. Once in awhile, he'd wake her at five to share his bacon and eggs breakfast. At other times, he'd pop over at lunchtime and grab a sandwich with her at Maggy's tea room. But many times, she only saw him late at night when he woke her with loving kisses and demanding hands. Those were the times Abby liked best.

The Monday before Thanksgiving Cameron was on his way out of the office when Lorraine called him back.

"Call for you on line two," she told him.

Cameron walked into his office and shut the door. Minutes later, he was back in the main room, bristling with excitement. Just then Pete came through the front door. "I'm glad you're here, Pete," Cameron said as his partner sauntered in. "Wait till you hear the news. That was Johnson at the ministry. He wants to meet with me in Toronto this Friday to go over our bid for those two seniors complexes in North Bay. If we can come down five percent, we have a good chance to get the contract. That's a year of guaranteed work," he added, his green eyes brimming with enthusiasm.

"Oh Cameron, that's great!" Lorraine smiled.

"We should be able to reduce the bid," Pete said slowly. "We added an extra seven per cent to cover fluctuating lumber prices. That should give us some leeway."

"Pull the file, Lorraine," Cameron said brusquely. "I'll have to get at it this afternoon."

"How long will you be in Toronto?" Pete asked as he poured himself a coffee.

"At least till Monday night. Johnson offered to meet with me all weekend if necessary. The project is way behind schedule, and with an election coming up, the premier wants to announce a series of projects in the next few weeks. Johnson was not too pleased about having to give up his Thanksgiving break, let me tell you."

Cameron grinned at Pete, them took the file Lorraine passed him and turned to go to his office.

"Cameron, how are you getting to Toronto? Are you driving down?" Lorraine asked as she played with the fuchsia silk scarf around her neck.

Cameron turned back and frowned. "I suppose. Though, I really don't want to take the truck." He thought for a minute, then asked, "Pete, could we trade vehicles this weekend? I'd prefer to take the Suburban to Toronto—if you don't mind."

"Not at all," Pete said. "As long as I have one of the company vehicles, I don't care which one I drive. While you're gone, I'll get the crew to finish up the drywall at Rayce's place on Friday, then I'm taking the weekend off. We've been putting in such long hours, my wife's starting to think I left town."

After listening intently, Lorraine interrupted. "Cameron, do you think I could catch a ride to Toronto with you? A friend of mine has invited me for Thanksgiving."

"You never mentioned that before," Pete said, a scowl darkening his face. "Mom's expecting all of us for dinner at her house."

"I can't make it," Lorraine snapped. She threw her brother a withering look. "I'm going to Toronto." She glanced at Cameron and asked bluntly, "Well, can I hitch a ride with you?"

Cameron hesitated. He didn't relish the idea of travelling with Lorraine, but couldn't refuse without good reason. "I suppose you could come along," he muttered.

Lorraine noticed his lack of enthusiasm but ignored it. "I really appreciate it Cameron," she said, then left the room.

"I guess this means you won't be having Thanksgiving with Abby," Pete reminded his partner.

Cameron frowned. "You're right. And Abby's not going to like that one bit. Oh well, it can't be helped. She'll have to go to Maggy's alone."

"Women don't like that," Pete said. He grinned broadly and wagged a finger at Cameron. "You're going to be in the doghouse for awhile."

Cameron shrugged. "I don't think so. Abby's a business woman herself, so she's very reasonable when it comes to my work." He paused, then glanced back at Pete, a hesitant look on his face. "Mind you, there is something she won't be very reasonable about."

Pete raised his dark bushy brows. "I bet it has something to do with my sister, Lorraine. Right, bud?"

"You got it," Cameron agreed. "I don't mind giving Lorraine a lift," he said, "but if Abby finds out about it she'll make my life…"

"A living hell?"

Cameron grinned ruefully. "Well, not quite…but close."

"So…?"

"So…could you keep it to yourself that I'm driving Lorraine to Toronto?"

Pete shook his head. "I think you're making a mistake, Cam. Take it from an old married man. Abby will find out. Women have a way of finding out these things. It might be smarter just to tell her yourself."

Cameron's eyes narrowed and he thought about it for a moment, then shook his head. "No, I don't think so. Abby's the jealous type. There's no point in getting her all riled up for nothing."

"Well, it's your call," Pete said. "But, don't worry. I won't say anything."

"Thanks." Cameron sighed. "Well, I'd better get at that bid."

That afternoon Abby was serving a customer when Cameron came into the shop. He grinned at her, then mimed that he'd wait in her office. Abby nodded, then finished cutting the length of cotton in her hand.

When the customer left, Abby walked into her office and found Cameron at her desk, on the phone.

"Yah…okay, Lorraine. Any more calls?"

Abby saw Cameron frown darkly, then pick up a pen on her desk. As he listened, he began to rap the pen against her desk with increasing force. Then he muttered, "All right. I should be back in the office by five." Then he hung up.

"You look all out of sorts," Abby teased as she put an arm around his shoulder and kissed his lips.

Cameron grunted, then hauled her into his lap.

Abby gave a shout of surprise and giggled. "Cameron! I could have a customer coming through the door at any minute."

"Then they'll have to wait their turn."

When he kissed her gently, Abby sighed and melted into his arms. She lifted her head and noticed a shadow in his eyes. "What's wrong?" she asked. "And don't tell me 'nothing' because I won't believe you."

Cameron smiled grimly. "Lorraine said my oldest brother, Gerald, called. He wants me to call him back."

"So…what's the problem?"

"Whenever my brother calls, it means trouble follows."

Abby arched her brows. "That bad?"

Cameron sighed, looking like a little boy confessing a crime. "I haven't spoken to either of my brothers in years. And frankly, I don't care if I ever do again. When Leah was in the hospital, they only came to see her once, and never bothered to make it to the funeral. Gerald's wife, Heather, is a real pain. Her father owned the car dealership before Gerald took over, and she never lets anyone forget it. Heather didn't like Leah, so we never visited much."

"She didn't like Leah?" Abby said incredulously. "How could anyone *not* like Leah?"

Cameron smiled warmly at Abby's defense of his late wife. "I don't know," he answered softly. "But she made Leah feel very unwelcome. So, Gerald and I drifted apart."

"What about your other brother? Are you close to him?"

"Hal? No…not really. Hal and Gerald get along all right—they're only two years apart in age. And have the same temperament. Hal works for Gerald, managing one of his dealerships. But I'm not close to either one of them."

"Maybe that could change," Abby said slowly, "if you ask them up for a visit."

Cameron shook his head. "I don't think so, but I'll call Gerald tonight and see what he wants."

Abby snuggled closer to Cameron. "I can't wait for the weekend," she told him. "We'll finally have three whole days together."

Cameron stiffened, sat up straighter, then said, "I'm afraid not, honey."

Abby lifted her head off his shoulder and stared at him. "What does that mean?" she said, her voice tight.

"It means I have to go to Toronto on Friday and I'll be there all weekend. We got a call today on the seniors complex project. I have to meet with ministry officials all weekend."

"On Thanksgiving!" Abby scoffed. "Since when do politicians work holidays?"

"The ones I'm dealing with will. They're on a deadline." Cameron answered with more abruptness than he intended.

Abby pushed off his lap, and straightened her grey wool slacks. "So, I guess that means dinner at Maggy's is out?"

"I'm afraid so."

Abby's mind was working furiously. "How about if I come with you?"

Cameron shook his head. "There'd be no point, Abby. I'm going to be so busy, I wouldn't have any time to spend with you. At least here, you can have dinner at Maggy's."

"Alone."

"I'm sorry, Abby. But there's nothing I can do. We really need this contract. Do you understand?"

Abby looked away. That was the hard part. On one level she understood how important this contract was to his company's future. But she had been really looking forward to three uninterrupted days alone with him. "You're going to owe me—big time—when you get home, Cameron Wallace," she told him with a sigh.

Cameron grinned, relief in his eyes. "I'll clear a weekend very soon," he promised. "And we'll lock the doors and spend it in bed."

"Yes, we will!" Abby kissed him fiercely. "Now...get out of here," she said, pushing him toward the door. "You're not the only person with a business to run."

Cameron searched her face and was reassured by her sunny smile. He kissed her lightly, then left.

On Saturday morning, Abby had a hard time hauling herself out of bed. She was supposed to be over at Maggy's giving her a hand making salads for tomorrow's Thanksgiving dinner, but she could barely lift her head off the pillow. It didn't help that Cameron was in Toronto and she was alone. She felt sluggish and grouchy, her breasts were sore and her stomach was queasy.

"Just what I need—to get the flu on my first weekend off in months," she growled as she slid back the shower door. However, by the time she was dressed in cranberry woollen slacks and a matching heavy pullover, she felt a lot better.

The air was crisp and cool when she stepped onto her porch. Everywhere she looked the ground was covered with colourful leaves. They drifted from trees all over the street, littering yards with their autumn splendour. Sasha and Kyra were scooping up piles of the dried and crackling leaves, then tossing them in the air.

Abby walked across the lawn, then paused before opening Maggy's patio door. She grinned in delight as Kyra's puppy chased the two giggling girls around the corner, barking furiously all the while.

Abby was still smiling when she stepped into the house. Instantly the aroma of pumpkin pie filled her nostrils and Abby paled, knowing she was going to be sick. She raced through the family room with her hand over her mouth, ignoring Maggy's startled cry of alarm. She barely made it into the downstairs bathroom before vomiting the coffee and toast she'd had for breakfast. Then she was sick again. And again.

As she leaned over the toilet, Abby was shaking severely. When Maggy placed a cold cloth in her hand, she took it gratefully and wiped her mouth, pushing a curtain of silky hair away from her face.

"I don't know what happened," Abby gasped. "I must be getting the flu. I've been feeling rotten for a few days now."

Maggy took her by the arm and sat her on the edge of the tub. "Rest for a minute, Abby. You look like you're going to pass out."

Maggy took the cloth from Abby's hand, rinsed it out, then handed it to her again. "It wasn't that long ago I was the one upchucking all over the place," Maggy teased gently. But her eyes watched Abby with the intensity of a hawk.

Abby looked confused for a moment. "Oh…you mean…when you were pregnant with the twins?"

"Yes…that's exactly what I mean."

"Well, this is a little different, Maggy. I've got the flu. I'm certainly not pregnant," Abby snorted.

"Is that…totally out of the question?" Maggy probed quietly.

"The likelihood of my being pregnant is extremely remote," Abby said sharply, "so get that look off your face."

"Have you had any other symptoms?"

"Symptoms? What do you mean?" Abby's eyes widened in shock. "Maggy, don't be ridiculous! I am not pregnant! Get that out of your head. I have the flu—that's all!"

"When was your last period?"

Abby sighed and hung her throbbing head. "I'm not regular—haven't been for years."

"When?"

"Oh…the beginning of…July, I suppose," Abby answered with a weary sigh.

"Any achy breasts?"

"God yes!" Abby muttered. "They're so tender, I could hardly sleep on my side last night." Then she stilled as Maggy's smile widened.

"It's impossible," Abby gasped.

"Impossible—or improbable?" Maggy demanded. "Which one did the doctors say?"

Abby's mouth was open, but no words would come out; her eyes were a startling blue in her pale face. She shook her head from side to side as if to negate something that was too unbelievable to comprehend.

"I can't be," she mumbled over and over. Then Abby's eyes brimmed with tears. "He said…improbable," she whispered softly. "Oh Maggy!" she choked. "What if I am?"

"How would you feel about that?" Maggy asked, her eyes warm and gentle.

"Like I'd been given the world," Abby replied breathlessly. "Oh Maggy…I'm afraid to hope."

Maggy stood up and tossed the face cloth in a hamper. "If you'll watch the girls, I'll drive into North Bay and pick up a pregnancy test for you. I have a feeling you're going to be a basket case until you find out."

"Oh—would you?"

Maggy grinned. "Of course I will. I'll call Libby to come over and keep you company till I get back."

"I'm all right," Abby insisted as she stood up.

"You're shaking like a leaf. Now…go lie down on the couch and I'll bring you some crackers. We'll see if that helps."

Abby lay down on the couch in the empty family room. Her head whirled alarmingly as she tried to accept the idea that she might be pregnant. She'd wanted a baby for so many years, given up hope for so many more.

"Here. Try these," Maggy said as she offered Abby a plate of dry crackers.

Abby took one and nibbled on it absently for a few moments. "That does seem to help," she said with a sigh.

"Good. Libby's on her way over."

"Did you...tell her where you're going...and why?" Abby's eyes were shy as she spoke, making her look years younger than she was.

"Of course," Maggy grinned. "Libby wormed it out of me."

Abby snorted in derision. "Yah...right."

After tying her hair back with a scarf, Maggy said, "I won't be long. You rest until I get back." Then she grabbed her purse and headed down the hall and out the front door.

A few minutes later Sasha and Kyra came into the room and stood hesitantly beside the couch. "Mom said to keep an eye on you, Abby," Kyra said, her eyes alight with curiosity. "Are you sick?"

"No...not really. I think I've got a touch of the flu."

"When I had the flu I threw up all over my bed," Sasha said. "It made a real mess," she added with a tinge of pride.

Abby gulped, feeling very nauseous again. "Thanks for telling me," she croaked. She closed her eyes hoping her stomach would settle.

As she listened with one ear to the little girls playing with their Barbies, reality set in. *Could it really be true? Could she be carrying Cameron's child? Would it have Cameron's dimple? Would it have blue eyes—or green?* Abby's eyes burned with unshed tears. It was too much to take in all at once. It just couldn't be true.

The front door slammed and Abby heard the clip-clop of shoes down the hall.

"Abby...are you all right?" Libby demanded as she rushed into the room. "I thought Maggy was pulling my leg. How do you feel?"

Abby slowly sat up, then glanced at the two little girls listening avidly to every word.

"Thanks for looking after me, kids," she told them. "You can go out and play now."

"We always have to leave when grown-ups talk about good stuff," Kyra sighed. But she and Sasha took their dolls and went out the patio door.

"I think Maggy's nuts," Abby said caustically. "She's got it in her head that I'm pregnant, but I think I've got the flu."

"Ohhh." Libby's face fell, then she put her hand on Abby's shoulder. "I'm sorry Abby. I know how much you want a child." She frowned, then sat down on the couch. "I don't understand," she murmured. "Why did Maggy tell me you might be pregnant?"

Abby sighed, then filled her in.

As Abby spoke, a slow smile curved Libby's full lips. "That's exactly how I felt when I was first pregnant. It's not so bad any more."

Abby's mouth dropped and her face flamed. She was trembling so much, she had to lay down again. "This is too much," she mumbled. "Where in the hell is Maggy?"

At seven on Sunday morning, Abby wandered out of her bathroom, dressed in a pink flannel nightshirt that reached her ankles. She sat down on the couch and eyed her two friends. Maggy wore a green satin robe and matching slippers and Libby was dressed in a blue jogging suit, but her hair was all tangled as if she'd just got out of bed.

"Well?" they demanded in unison.

"Looks like I won the lottery after all," Abby said, her azure eyes glowing with wonder. "I'm going to have a baby. I still can't believe it."

"Can I assume we'll be planning another wedding soon?" Maggy asked dryly as she stood and headed for the kitchen.

With an arch of one fine eyebrow, Abby said, "That had better be the plan!"

Libby sat down in an armchair and tucked her bare feet underneath her legs. "Are you going to call Cameron in Toronto and tell him the news?"

"No. I want to see the look on his face when I tell him," Abby replied. Her lips curved as if recalling something very special. "I have a feeling he'll be quite pleased."

"When's he coming home?" Maggy called over her shoulder. She filled a kettle full of water and plugged it in.

"When he called last night, he said he'd been home sometime Monday night. But it might be very late. The presentation Saturday went well, but he has several more meetings today and tomorrow." Abby stretched out on the couch, grinning from ear to ear. "I still can't believe it," she whispered, more to herself than to anyone else.

"Believe it," Maggy teased. "And get as much sleep as you can. Before long your nights will be filled with feedings—not sex."

"Our babies will be almost the same age," Libby laughed. "They'll grow up together…be in the same classes at school…maybe be friends for life."

"Or they'll fight like cats and dogs," Abby teased wryly.

"Or marry each other," Maggy added as she walked back into the room.

Abby's eyes widened, then she burst out laughing. She laughed so hard her sides hurt; she couldn't remember ever feeling so happy.

Cameron walked into his hotel room around two on Sunday afternoon and wished he were home. He threw his room key onto the top of the television set, kicked off his black loafers, and sighed wearily. He took off his grey suit coat and hung it carefully over the back of a chair. He had more meetings in the morning and couldn't wear a wrinkled suit.

When the pants were off and folded over a hanger, Cameron dropped onto the bed and closed his tired eyes. His first impulse was to phone Abby, but he knew she'd be at Maggy's helping to get dinner ready and wouldn't have time to talk. Besides, if he heard her voice, he'd only feel worse.

Johnson's behaviour today had been erratic to say the least. He'd barely glanced at their revised bid, mumbled something about 'other bids to consider,' then had ended the meeting abruptly, pleading a bad toothache! *What a godawful waste of time!* He should have stayed at home and spent Thanksgiving with Abby.

Cameron sighed, then lifted the phone. He turned on his side, checked a piece of paper he'd left on the night table, then dialed the number Gerald had left with Lorraine. Much to his surprise his brother answered on the second ring.

"Gerald…hi. It's me…Cameron."

"Cameron! Thanks for calling back. It's…uh…good to hear from you."

Cameron raised his brows at the hesitation in Gerald's voice. He knew right then something was wrong. Gerald was a born salesman—always up, always hearty. Yet now, he sounded low, defeated somehow.

"What's wrong, Gerald?"

"Well, it's hard to talk about it over the phone," Gerald sighed.

"Where are you? I didn't recognize this number you left."

"I'm staying at a friend's condo in Toronto. I'm right downtown actually."

"I'm here too—on business," Cameron told him. "I'm at the Delta Chelsea on Yonge. Give me your address and I'll be there as soon as possible."

"You're here…in Toronto? Thank God! We need to talk."

Forty minutes later, Cameron paid the cab driver, slipped his change into his jean pocket, then ran up the front steps of the luxury condo. *Trust Gerald to make sure he suffered in comfort,* Cameron thought as he walked across the opulent lobby to the desk. He drummed his fingers impatiently on the oak counter while the security guard verified that he was expected.

Minutes later, he was in the elevator heading for the fifteenth floor. The hall was quiet when he stepped out. He turned left and started for the far end, checking door numbers along the way.

"I'm down here," Gerald called from the end of the corridor.

Cameron nodded and quickened his step. Gerald was still in his bathrobe, even though it was after three in the afternoon. That wasn't a good sign. He hadn't shaved and his grey thinning hair looked oily and unkept. Now Cameron was really concerned. Gerald was a vain man who always took great pride in his appearance. For him to let himself go like this, something was very wrong indeed.

"Come on in and have a drink," Gerald said, his voice booming in the empty hallway.

"Isn't it a little early?" Cameron said brusquely as he followed Gerald into the large main room. Furnished in black leather, brass, and steel, the room had a cold, futuristic look. Certainly not to Cameron's taste.

"Quite a spread—eh?" Gerald said, as he walked to a black lacquer bar and refilled his glass to the brim. "What'll you have?"

"Nothing, thanks." Cameron sat down on an extremely low couch, crossed his legs, and eyed his brother warily.

Gerald was a tall man who carried a lot of weight. Too much so, from what Cameron could tell. His skin was ruddy, flushed across the cheekbones, and his eyes were red-rimmed as if from lack of sleep. Most likely from the booze, Cameron surmised with a frown.

"Okay Gerald...let's have it? What's going on?"

"Heather left me," Gerald said baldly, then he sank into a chair as if all his bones had suddenly turned to mush. His voice was low and barely audible. "I went to an auto convention in Detroit, and when I came back, the locks had been changed on the doors and she wouldn't let me in. She opened a window upstairs and threw all my clothes on the lawn. She said she was in love with someone else...and wanted a divorce. And she wants her daddy's company back, she says. Fat chance of that," he growled, his eyes darkening with anger for the first time. "She can have the house—and the kids for that matter—but

I'm keeping my company. Her old man was on the edge of bankruptcy when I took over, and I built it up to what it is today. Nobody's going to take it away from me!"

Cameron sighed. "What about the kids—how are they handling the breakup?"

"Oh…those brats stick up for their mother. As long as she keeps giving them cars and an allowance—they'll dance to her tune. Carol's flunked out of two universities so far and Adam dropped out of high school when he was sixteen. I gave him a job on one of my lots, but that kid couldn't sell a car if his life depended on it."

"The kids are that old?" Cameron shook his head. "Funny, in my mind they're about twelve or thirteen."

"You haven't seen them in years, Cameron," Gerald said.

"I know. We're not exactly the Walton family—are we?"

Gerald closed his eyes and leaned back against the chair, his drink resting on his ample belly. "Remember when we were kids, Cameron, and the old man used to come home and beat the hell out of us? I always swore I would do better with my own. But I sure as hell didn't. I never touched them—mind you. But, I was always so busy at work, I never spent much time with them. 'Quality time'—isn't that what they call it on TV? No, they don't care if they ever see me again. And that's a direct quote from my son." Gerald laughed harshly and downed half the contents of his glass.

"Do you know who the other guy is? Maybe it's not serious."

Gerald groaned, then finished the rest of his drink. He stood up, weaving a little as he made his way to the bar. "That's where it gets a little…interesting," he muttered, his back to Cameron. "I *do* know who Heather's living with." Gerald splashed more liquor into his glass, then turned around, his eyes glittering angrily. In a voice cracking with emotion, Gerald said, "She left me for her bridge partner…Madeleine Bromwell."

Cameron's eyes widened and his jaw dropped. "She left you for a *woman*?"

"That's it in a nutshell." Gerald's mouth thinned. "Our sex life was the pits right from the start, but I figured Heather was frigid. Now I find out she's turned on by a thirty-five year old lesbian who sells art for a living. Can you believe it? And…what sticks in my craw…they're living in *my* house!"

Cameron had no idea what to say. It was clear that Gerald's pride was hurt—but not much else. "I'm sorry, Gerald," Cameron said quietly, "I'm sure this must be very hard for you."

Gerald sighed. "That's decent of you, Cameron, considering what a bastard I was when Leah died. I should have ignored Heather and gone to the funeral by myself. But I didn't...and I'm sorry."

Cameron nodded. In that moment he felt no anger toward his brother, only a deep sorrow that he really didn't know the man.

Gerald sat down again. "How are you doing, anyway?" he asked. He was leaning forward, as if he genuinely wanted to know.

"I'm fine," Cameron smiled. "Actually, I'm thinking of getting married again."

Gerald's bushy brows rose, then a wide smile curved his thin mouth. "That's great, Cam. I really mean it. You deserve to be happy—after all you've been through."

Cameron grinned. "Thanks," he said huskily. "Abby's a terrific person. I'm lucky to have her in my life."

"Did you just meet her?"

"No...she was a friend of Leah's and mine."

"I always envied how close you and Leah were, Cameron. That kind of love is very special."

"Yes it is," Cameron sighed. "When Leah died, I thought I'd never love that way again. But life is so strange. And now I have Abby. I love her...it's just...different from what I had with Leah."

"Oh...well...even if you can't love Abby as much as you loved Leah, you can still have a good life together."

"I love Abby more," Cameron admitted softly. "It threw me at first when I realized what was happening. I feel like Abby's a part of me...like I'm only half alive when I'm not with her. I survived Leah's death," Cameron murmured quietly. "It was tough, but I dealt with it in time. But, if anything happened to Abby, I'm not sure I'd want to go on living."

Gerald frowned as he stared at Cameron. "I've never felt like that for anyone," he said morosely.

Cameron stood up, then paced the room. "Look...there's no point in our hanging around here. Why don't you get dressed and we'll go out and have dinner somewhere?"

"Actually, I called Hal to tell him you were in Toronto and he invited us to come out to his house for Thanksgiving dinner."

Cameron grimaced. "Has Pat learned how to cook yet?"

"No," Gerald grinned, "but Hal has smartened up. They hired a cook and she's incredible."

"All right then! Go get cleaned up. I'm starved!"

When Cameron got back to his hotel room just before midnight, he felt tired—but a good tired. He glanced at the clock, then decided it was too late to call Abby; he'd call her in the morning instead.

As Gerald had predicted, dinner was wonderful. Whatever Hal paid his cook, it wasn't enough. At first, the conversation had been strained and stilted. Both Hal and his wife had apologized—somewhat awkwardly—for missing Leah's funeral. But Cameron had waved it off. It just didn't seem worth arguing about. When Lorie and Susan, Cameron's young nieces, came in from visiting their friends, Cameron hadn't recognized them. They'd grown up so much. He couldn't believe Lorie was almost finished high school. They were nice kids. That surprised him. They seemed genuinely pleased to see their uncles and had hung around the dinner table after the meal, sprinkling the conversation with their ready wit. For all his faults, Cameron thought, as he stripped and climbed into bed, Hal was a terrific father.

Cameron switched on the TV, more for company than interest, and wondered what kind of father he would be if he ever got the chance. He worried about that more than he liked to admit. His own father had been a first-class bastard...a mean-spirited drunk who used his fists on his wife and kids to work out his own fear and anger. Michael Wallace had been a carpenter by trade, but not a very good one. Half of the time he'd been out of work, and they'd had to scrounge for food. Yet, there'd always been a case of beer in the house.

His mother, Lily, had been pretty at one time, but was a very old forty-five when she died of heart failure. Why she stayed with the man who abused her, Cameron never could understand. Too many times when he was young, he'd woken up to his mother's shouts of pain and his father's drunken rants. The screaming seemed to go on forever, but what followed was much worse. It was only later, when he entered his teens, that Cameron came to comprehend what the banging bedsprings meant. At the time, all he knew was that his father was hurting his mother terribly— and he was too young to help her.

Cameron was sixteen when she died. After her funeral, he had walked the streets for hours, torn up inside over his mother's death. When he finally got home, his father was at the kitchen table, mean-eyed drunk, and eager for a fight. He got it and a lot more. By the time Cameron had finished with him, Michael Wallace was on the floor, sprawled in his own blood. Cameron had stepped over him, walked out the door, and never looked back. When the old man died five years later, Cameron had stayed away from the funeral. What was the point in going? What little feeling he'd had for his father had been beaten out of him long ago.

At sixteen, Cameron had been a big, strong kid and looked older than his years, so he'd had little difficulty finding a job as a labourer on a construction site. He'd worked with the same contractor for years, slowly learning his trade, building houses by day, and taking high school courses by night. He'd been bound and determined to get his diploma, then take a trade course.

He'd met Leah at a time when he was very lonely, desperately in need of someone to love. With her gentle, undemanding nature and trusting soul, Leah had been just what he needed. She had loved him dearly. He would always be grateful for that love and treasure her memory.

But, as he drifted off to sleep, it was Abby's face who filled his dreams. Abby with her flashing eyes and full red lips. *Would she marry him?* he wondered. God, he hoped so! Perhaps when he got home, it was time to find out.

The next day was one of the longest in Cameron's life. He'd phoned Abby at six-thirty, but she was barely coherent, so he'd hung up and gone out for breakfast.

Johnson had arrived at their meeting an hour late, with a surly attitude and an obvious hangover. At one point, about an hour into their meeting, Cameron had snapped shut his briefcase and stormed out of the room in disgust. But Johnson had come running after him, apologizing left and right. After that, discussions had begun in earnest.

By eight o'clock on Monday night, the agreement was signed, and by nine, Cameron was back at his hotel, changed, packed, and ready to head home. All he had to do was pick up Lorraine, then he could be on his way.

Just as he closed his suitcase, he heard a soft knock. Cameron zipped his case, then walked over and opened the door.

"Lorraine! What are you doing here? I was just on my way to pick you up."

"I called the hotel an hour ago and they told me you were checking out soon, so I took a cab over to save some time."

Cameron frowned, then stepped aside. "Well, come on in," he said abruptly. "I'll just be a few minutes."

Lorraine sat on the edge of the bed and crossed her legs. She was dressed to kill as usual in a dark leather coat, a lilac cashmere pullover, and tailored lilac pants. She watched Cameron gather up toiletries from the bathroom and stuff them haphazardly in a carryall bag. Her cool eyes followed his every move, appreciating the way his tight jeans outlined his muscular thighs and buttocks.

Cameron was pissed off. He knew what Lorraine was up to. He saw the blatant invitation in her eyes. She had no business here and she knew it. Just like she knew there wasn't much he could do about it now. He'd put up with her snide remarks and gossipy innuendoes on the trip down, but he didn't know if he could tolerate any more on the trip home. Luckily, so far she was quiet...almost too quiet. As he packed his carryall, Cameron glanced at her out of the corner of his eye and caught her staring at him. It made him vaguely uneasy.

"I'll be ready in a few minutes," he said from the bathroom door. "Then we'll hit the road."

As Cameron slammed the door behind him, Lorraine smiled cooly, her heavy-lidded eyes filled with malicious amusement. He was uncomfortable with her in his hotel room. She'd figured he would be...that was why she'd come.

When the phone rang, Lorraine glanced at the bathroom door, but the water was running—so perhaps Cameron didn't hear. She picked up the phone, then almost groaned in delight when she heard Abby's soft, "Hello?"

"Abby," Lorraine said, "Hello. How are you?"

"Lorraine!"

Lorraine heard Abby's gasp of disbelief and wanted to laugh out loud. "Yes, Abby. What do you want?"

"Could...I speak to Cameron, please?"

"No, actually you can't," Lorraine said cooly, her eyes alight with triumphant relish. "He's taking a shower. We're a little behind schedule. It's been...quite a weekend."

"I didn't know you were with him in Toronto."

A malevolent smile curled Lorraine's lips. "Didn't he tell you? I drove down with him on Friday." She let that sink in then said, "Was there a message you wanted me to pass on?"

"No. I'll talk to him tomorrow," Abby replied, then she hung up.

Just as Lorraine was replacing the receiver, Cameron opened the bathroom door. "I thought I heard the phone," he said, a frown creasing his forehead. "Why didn't you call me?" His tone was brusque, demanding an explanation.

"It was just a wrong number," Lorraine replied, without blinking an eye at the lie. "They wanted 514, not 415."

Cameron's eyes narrowed for an instant, then he shrugged. "Come on," he said, "let's get out of here. It'll be after midnight as it is before we get home."

In actuality, it was nearly three. By the time they passed Gravenhurst, they hit an intense rainstorm and Cameron was forced to reduce his speed to a crawl. To make matters worse, when they finally turned off the highway into Howard's Bay, the side road where Lorraine lived was totally blocked by a fallen tree.

When Lorraine asked if she could spend the rest of the night at his house, Cameron was too tired to argue. At three o'clock in the morning, he couldn't leave her at the side of the road. No matter how much he wanted to.

Chapter Fourteen

Abby was exhausted from lack of sleep. She'd been up most of the night, pacing the floor, her mind whirling with licentious images of Lorraine with Cameron.

At six-thirty she dressed in a warm pair of red wool slacks and slipped on a red and black pullover. Then she put the coffee on to brew while she washed and made up her pale face. Abby applied her blush, looked at herself in the mirror and grimaced. The mascara accented the dark circles under her eyes and the blush she wore made her pallor all the more pronounced. She looked like a ghoulish extra in a Halloween movie. Abby grabbed a face cloth and scrubbed her skin clean. At least now, when she looked in the mirror, she saw someone she recognized.

Hoping she hadn't forgotten to set the timer on the coffee machine, Abby headed for the kitchen. She would need at least three cups, she figured, before she faced Cameron. She padded into the room in her stocking feet, caught a whiff of coffee, and started heaving. She made it to the bathroom just in time. She washed her face again and rinsed out her trembling mouth, then put a hand protectively over her belly. "So coffee's out for the duration—is that what you're trying to tell me? You're going to be one demanding kid! Must take after your old man."

She returned to the kitchen, pinched her nose, and poured the contents of the coffee pot into the sink. Only when the grounds were outside in the garbage did her protesting stomach finally settle down. Abby poured herself a glass of milk, made herself a piece of dry toast, then sat at the kitchen table, munching slowly, waiting until the clock said seven.

At the start of the new hour, her face grim with determination, she slipped on her shoes, grabbed her purse, and headed out the door. One way or another, she'd get some answers—or know the reason why.

Abby pulled into Cameron's driveway and noticed one vehicle, the company Suburban, in the yard. *At least he's alone,* she thought as she walked toward the door. It was locked. She hesitated for a moment, then pulled out the key he had given her, and inserted it in the lock. She stepped inside and listened, then shut the door behind her. She thought she could hear Cameron moving around in the kitchen, so she walked down the hall and stopped at the doorway. His back was turned to her. He was busy at the sink pouring himself a coffee, while waiting for his toast to pop up. At the smell of the coffee Abby was hit by another bout of nausea and, in a panic, glanced around for the garbage pail. Then froze when she spotted a red leather suitcase by the hallway door. And a matching red makeup case.

Tears threatened to spill and her stomach started to heave, so Abby took a deep breath, then several more. *Don't panic,* she told herself. *Give him a chance to explain.* More than anything in the world she wanted to believe that her trust in Cameron wasn't misplaced. There could be any number of reasons while Lorraine had been in his hotel room. Any number of reasons why her suitcase stood in his kitchen.

Her emotions under tenuous control, Abby watched him avidly, noticing how the muscles in his back and arms strained the seams of his navy work shirt. Even in his work clothes, he looked incredibly sexy.

Then he turned around, saw her at the door and froze, his eyes dilating instantly. The coffee sloshed a little over the rim of the cup, spilling onto his thumb, but he didn't seem to notice.

"Abby! What are you doing here?" Cameron stammered.

Dread filled Abby's heart at the look on his face. She *knew* then, what she'd come to find out.

"What...not pleased to see me, Cameron?" Abby drawled with an insouciance she didn't feel.

Cameron recovered quickly. "Of course I am, Abby." But his tone was wrong, his voice just a little too loud and forced.

"I thought—since you've been gone for four days—I'd surprise you by cooking some breakfast."

He was blinking rapidly now and Abby could see a pulse working overtime in his throat.

"Uh...I'm not really hungry this morning, Abby."

I'll just bet you aren't, she fumed. Abby nodded slowly to give herself time to think. She walked over to the table and asked, "Mind if I sit down?"

A film of sweat was breaking out on Cameron's forehead. He frowned, then muttered, "Actually, Abby, I have to leave right now. I'm due at the job site any minute."

Abby's eyes narrowed and her nostrils flared. "Damn it all, Cameron, stop lying to me," she snapped. "You were making yourself a coffee and toast when I walked in the room."

Cameron sighed, then ran his hands through his hair. "Abby, if you would just listen for a moment, I can explain..."

"Explain what, Cameron? Explain why Lorraine was in your hotel room when I called last night?"

Cameron's eyes widened with enlightenment. "That was *you* on the phone last night?"

When Abby nodded tersely, he frowned, his mouth thinning ominously. "Then why...?"

"I'm sorry...am I interrupting a private conversation?" Lorraine asked from the doorway. Dressed in one of Cameron's shirts that exposed long shapely legs and jutting breasts, she looked like she had just rolled out of bed after a long, strenuous night. A slight, mirthless smile tilted her lips, and her dark eyes were burning with excitement.

"What the hell!" Cameron's roar of outrage filled the room.

"Oh Cameron...stop it," Lorraine laughed, as if genuinely amused by his behaviour. "You promised me this weekend you'd tell her the truth."

"What in hell are you talking about?" he demanded, his face black with fury.

"Cameron, I warned you two weeks ago this might happen," Lorraine said cooly as she flipped a strand of hair off her shoulders. "It was only a matter of time before she found out about us. You said in Toronto that you would end it with her. Now do it. Tell her you want to marry me—not her. Tell her you want a wife who can give you children of your own."

"She's lying, Abby," he said hoarsely, his eyes pleading as he searched Abby's white face.

"Was she with in your hotel room in Toronto?" Abby's voice was lifeless, her eyes empty and bleak.

"Yes...but..."

"And she's here now—dressed in your shirt," Abby said coldly, her anger building. She flicked her hand contemptuously at Lorraine. "Did she spend the night?"

"It's not the way it looks, Abby. Give me a chance..."

"No!" The word cracked through the room. Then Abby swivelled to stare at Lorraine. "He's all yours, Lorraine. But let me give you a piece of advice I learned the hard way. Don't trust him. He cheated on Leah. He cheated on me. He'll do the same to you."

Abby turned and headed for the door, shoving Cameron out of the way. Then she glanced over her shoulder and added bitterly, "You're a good pair. You two deserve each other." She rushed down the hall as if all the hosts of hell were snapping at her heels.

Cameron was in a state of disbelief. He was still reeling when the slamming of the front door shocked him back to awareness.

His eyes narrowed as he stared at Lorraine. With one bare foot crossed over the other, she leaned casually against the door frame as if she hadn't a care in the world. Her eyes danced with such apparent amusement, he had an overwhelming urge to choke the life out of her.

"Was it worth it?" he asked softly, his hands balled into white fists at his side.

"To see you squirm...to see her suffer...yes. It was worth it," Lorraine smirked. "It was the most fun I've had in years."

"You know, of course, that you're fired," he snapped, his voice shaking with rage.

"Try it!" she warned, "and I'll sue you for sexual harassment."

"It'll never hold up in court!"

"Maybe not," she admitted, as she peeped at him from below her lashes. Then she tilted her chin defiantly. "But in the meantime, your precious reputation will be ruined and your business will go down the tubes."

"If my reputation is ruined, so is Pete's. You'd do that to your own brother?" Cameron stared at her as if scrutinizing a strange species from outer space.

Lorraine scoffed contemptuously. "Pete can handle himself. He doesn't need you. He did all right when you took off and left him to pick up the pieces of the business."

The business had been on the edge of bankruptcy by the time Cameron had returned. But there was no point in arguing with the bitch. It was time to play hardball and finish it.

"I meant what I said, Lorraine. You're fired. Pack up your things and get out of here. I'll see that Pete gives you whatever money we owe you."

"You fool!" she spat. "If you think I won't lay harassment charges…"

"No you won't," Cameron interrupted sharply, "or I'll be forced to lay some of my own."

Lorraine froze, confusion narrowed her dark eyes. "What…what are you talking about?" she demanded.

"Theft, Lorraine. *Your* theft of *our* interim working funds. And I've got the records to prove it. There should have been five thousand dollars in that account, but there's only two. The bank statement was in the mail I just opened. They included a copy of a cheque that I didn't sign, though my name's on it. *You* forged my name, Lorraine. I recognized your handwriting."

"I was going to put it back," Lorraine whined. "I just needed a temporary advance."

"Tell it to the judge!" Cameron snapped contemptuously. "Or leave now. If you make any trouble, I'll call the police so fast you won't have time to spit."

Cameron could almost see the cogs in her mind turning. He knew he'd won when she sneered at him, then stomped out of the room. He sagged against the counter, and fought to still his raging pulse. He felt sick, wanted to throw up. He'd known Lorraine was calculating, but he'd never guessed how enormously vindictive she could be. He shook his head, trying to make sense out of what had just happened.

How could Abby have believed Lorraine and not him? That's what hurt the most. He had begun to believe that Abby trusted him. God! He'd been planning to ask her to marry him! And now this. Cameron swore under his breath, then rammed his palms into his eye sockets, grinding them back and forth, as if in doing so, he could erase the last few minutes from his memory.

He didn't want to think about the look on Abby's face—but couldn't drive it from his mind. She'd looked so lost…so empty…so unforgiving. Cameron swore again. *Well,* he thought grimly, *he was going to pay her a little visit after work. And, she was going to listen—if it took all night.*

The sound of heels clicking down the stairs pulled Cameron back to reality.

When Lorraine sauntered into the kitchen, he was ready for her, at the door, her suitcase already on the step.

"Good-bye, Cameron," Lorraine said saucily. "You made a big mistake, you know. We could have had a great time together."

Cameron's eyes blazed with fury. He clenched his jaw and held open the door. "Get out, Lorraine. Now!"

"Ooooh. You look almost dangerous," Lorraine purred. She stepped closer and touched his chest with a long, red-tipped finger. "I like that. If you change your mind, just give me a call." Cameron marvelled at her gall. He stared at her appraisingly then said in a silky voice, "Lorraine, you have a perfect figure, perfect teeth, perfect hair, perfect skin. Too bad you're also a perfect bitch." He heard her gasp of outrage just as he took her finger and thrust it away. "You leave me perfectly cold." He smiled mirthlessly. "But then, you always did."

That wiped the smile off her face. She lifted a hand to slap him, then thought better of it, heeding the warning in his narrowed eyes.

When her hand dropped, he smiled cooly and shoved her out the door. "Smart move, Lorraine," he drawled mockingly. "You wouldn't have done it twice."

At suppertime, Abby chewed the last piece of turkey, then placed her knife and fork on top of her plate and leaned back in her chair. She had made her favourite dinner that night: rice, turkey, and salad, but it might as well have been sawdust for all the interest she gave it. But she ate it anyway, down to the last grain of rice. For the baby's sake she had to keep physically fit—although her mental well-being was another matter entirely.

With grim efficiency Abby cleaned the table, changed into a flowered silk caftan, and settled on the couch to rest. For the first time in her life she could understand the allure of 'naps.' She needed them frequently now, just to get through each day.

Since leaving Cameron's house that morning, she'd been on autopilot. She'd stayed in the shop all day; didn't bother to go to Maggy's for lunch. She hadn't wanted to see anyone, but especially not Maggy or Libby. She had to get her head together first, figure out how she was going to cope, before she could deal with anyone else.

Her biggest concern now was for the baby. Should she tell Cameron—or not? Abby wasn't sure what to do at the moment. Her instincts told her he had a right to know, but she was so devastated by his betrayal, all she wanted to do was hide.

When the room started to fill with shadows, Abby left the lights off and dozed restlessly on the couch. Later on in the evening, when a knock came at her door, she started fitfully but remained asleep.

Cameron knocked again and waited. When Abby didn't answer he tried the handle, found it open and stepped inside. The room was in darkness except for a small light in the kitchen. When his eyes adjusted, he noticed Abby curled up on the couch. He walked closer and stood beside the couch. She was sleeping so peacefully, he was tempted to leave and go home. Then his heart hardened and he bent down and shook her shoulder. She muttered softly, but didn't wake up, so he shook her again, then turned on a light over her head.

"What the...?" Abby slowly opened her eyes and gazed about her in bewilderment. She was still groggy with sleep and couldn't understand what she was doing in the living room. Then she spotted Cameron sitting in the chair opposite the couch. He looked relaxed, with one leg drawn up over the other knee, but his eyes were cold. Abby frowned. *Why was Cameron looking at her like that?* She sat up and rubbed her eyes.

Then memory surged and Abby sat up straight. She stared at Cameron intently, her eyes never wavering from his face. Striving for aloofness she asked, "Why are you here? We said all there was to say this morning."

"You didn't give me a chance to say *anything* this morning," Cameron snapped abruptly. "When I've said my piece, I'll leave."

Abby's nostrils flared and her chin went up defensively. She wasn't going to like what he had to say, but she didn't give a damn.

"Say what you have to say, then get out."

A pulse jumped in Cameron's cheek. "Lorraine lied. I gave her a lift to Toronto, dropped her off, and never saw her again for the rest of the weekend—until she showed up at my hotel to get a ride home. I never touched her...or slept with her...or had any type of relationship with her—outside of the office. She lied about everything," he reiterated coldly, "and you fell for it hook, line, and sinker."

"Why didn't you tell me you were giving her a lift to Toronto? That in itself is a lie by omission." Abby's heart was beating so fast she found it hard to breathe; a hammer was pounding insistently inside her skull. She wanted more than anything to lay down, but refused to show any sign of weakness in front of Cameron. Her face was calm...perhaps a little pale, and the vein on the side of her forehead was quite pronounced; but, other than that, she gave no outward clue how close she was to breaking down completely.

"I didn't tell you," Cameron stated grimly, "because I knew exactly how you would react—or should I say *overreact*."

Abby bristled, but held onto her temper. "Cameron, is there a point to all of this?"

At the look of indifference in her eyes, Cameron started to burn. All day long he'd assumed she would be ready to apologize the moment he walked in the door. He knew Abby was stubborn, but not unfair. He needed to hear her say, 'I'm sorry for not trusting you, Cameron.' *Why in hell wouldn't she say the words?*

Cameron reined in his anger, his mouth a tight, grim line. "Oh, there's a *point* all right, Abby! It all boils down to trust. Instead of listening to Lorraine, why didn't you believe *me*?"

Abby stared at him incredulously. "She was in *your* room in Toronto...she came down from *your* bedroom...dressed in *your* shirt...what in hell was I supposed to believe?" Abby demanded cuttingly.

"You were supposed to believe *me*," Cameron said bitterly. "Instead of believing that bitch, you should have given me a chance to explain."

Abby's eyes were wild with confusion. Cameron seemed so angry, so outraged. *Had she been too hasty? Could he be telling the truth?*

Abby frowned, then looked away, her mind unwilling to admit that she might have made a grievous error. If she were wrong, then he had every right to be furious, she realized suddenly. Abby lifted her eyes and stared at him. "All right," she said grudgingly, "tell me what happened."

Cameron heard the tone in her voice and snapped. "Right! Now you're willing to listen," he said, as acid surged up his throat. "Well, it's too little—too late. We're through, Abby. Finished. The irony is...I was going to ask you to marry me," he said. His eyes were dark-green pools of bitter pain.

Abby shuddered, her face stark with misery. She realized then the full enormity of what she had done. For an instant she was tempted to tell him about the baby, but bit back the impulse. If he knew, he would want the baby. She couldn't take the chance of losing her child—it was bad enough she'd lost him.

Pride stiffened her back, forced up her chin, quelled the fear in her heart. "If that's the way you feel, Cameron," she said coldly, "then leave."

Cameron seethed with anger, an anger tinged with pain. *She was taking their breakup so calmly...so cooly, as if nothing could touch her ice-princess heart.* Pain ripped through him, as well as resignation. When he walked out the door, she wouldn't try to stop him. She didn't care enough.

Cameron stood and glared down at her, his eyes burning with sorrow. "I don't know you, Abby. I suppose I never did. I thought we had something very special, but I guess I was wrong."

He waited for what seemed like forever, hoping she would say something—*anything*—to end their stalemate. But Abby just stared at him, her face as empty as her heart.

Cameron shuddered, his eyes wild with emotion, gripped by a overwhelming sense of loss. "I could never live with a woman who didn't trust me. I thought I could—but I can't."

"Go away, Cameron," Abby sighed wearily. "Let's end this with a little dignity." She closed her eyes and rubbed her forehead with a shaking hand.

Cameron stared at her. She looked so defeated, so exhausted—almost ill. *Was he wrong to leave it like this...to give up without a fight?*

Abby looked up then and smiled listlessly, a humourless attempt at keeping face. "You're right to end our affair, Cameron. We came together for all the wrong reasons. Reasons I tried to ignore at the time. It's better if we don't see each other any more. Who knows, perhaps in time, we might be able to be friends again."

"That won't happen, Abby," Cameron snarled. "It was never friendship I wanted from you."

"Oh...I know that," she told him bleakly. "I knew that right from the start." She combed trembling fingers through her long hair. "Get out of my house, Cameron," she said, her voice frozen and remote. "And don't come back. You're no longer welcome here."

Cameron towered over her. "I *won't* be back, Abby!" he snarled, the muscles in his jaw working furiously. "I'm going to get on with my life and forget you ever existed!" He turned on his heel, and left, slamming the door violently behind him.

Abby shuddered as the sound echoed through the room. She stood up, padded across the room, and locked the door. Then went to bed. She didn't cry...didn't toss and turn...didn't give in to her grief. She lay in the middle of the bed like a corpse, with her hands crossed protectively over her belly. She had her baby to think of now, and she couldn't allow herself the luxury of tears.

But later, when she finally slept, the tears came anyway, releasing the anguish she'd held in for too long.

ABBY'S STORY: BETRAYED BY LOVE

For the rest of the week, Abby moved with the precision of a mechanized robot. She ate three tasteless meals each day, forced glasses of milk down her throat, took long, tiring walks each night after supper. But always alone. She brushed off Maggy and Libby during the day with vague excuses, took her phone off the hook at night, and locked up as soon as she got home. When Maggy and Libby stopped by several times, she hid in the bedroom and refused to answer the door.

Early Saturday morning, Maggy was in her office, breakfast on a tray, waiting impatiently for Libby to show up.

When Libby dashed into the room, out of breath, her blond curls flying every which way, Maggy brushed off her explanation and plunked her into a chair.

"Drink your juice," Maggy said brusquely, "and eat that bran muffin, while we figure out what's wrong with Abby."

"I already know what's wrong," Libby said grimly. She took a long pull of her juice then added, "Rayce told me last night that Cameron broke up with Abby."

"What? Are you sure?" Maggy's light green eyes widened in alarm. "Does Rayce know what happened?"

"Not really, but there's more. Cameron fired Lorraine last Tuesday."

"That's when Abby started acting so weird," Maggy said slowly.

"That's not all," Libby continued, "Lorraine was with Cameron in Toronto."

"Oh my God! That's got to be it!" Maggy groaned. "Abby must have caught Cameron with Lorraine. That stupid ass! I thought Cam had more sense." Then Maggy frowned. "But...if Cameron was having an affair with Lorraine, why did he fire her?"

"That's where it gets really strange. Pete told Rayce that Lorraine deserved to be fired, but he wouldn't explain why. Said it was Cameron's business—not his."

"Has Rayce talked to Cameron about it?" Maggy asked pensively.

"Rayce tried, but Cameron bit his head off and told Rayce to mind his own business. Rayce said Cameron is very bitter and angry. He won't talk to anyone."

"Well," Maggy sighed, "we're not going to get anywhere until we corner

Abby and find out from her what happened."

"But how are we going to do that? She won't even answer her door."

"I know. But she does go to work every day. We'll give her the weekend to rest and tackle her at our meeting on Monday morning."

"What if she doesn't show up?" Libby said, her blue eyes wide with worry.

"Then we'll corner her at the shop."

Libby sighed, "I don't know, Maggy. She's pretty fragile now. We don't want to do anything to upset her or the baby."

"It's precisely because of the baby we have to get to the bottom of this mess. If she and Cameron are really finished, she'll need her friends more than ever."

"I wonder if Cameron knows about the baby," Libby mused. Then she froze and a look of horror filled her eyes. "You don't think *that's* why he broke up with her—because of the baby, I mean?"

Maggy frowned, then said quietly, "I'd bet my bottom dollar he doesn't even know that Abby's pregnant. Knowing Cameron and the way he loves kids, I can't see him abandoning Abby when she's carrying his child."

"What a mess!" Libby sighed.

"I know," Maggy said. "But when Ross and I were separated, Abby stood by me and helped me through the worse time of my life; that's why I know she needs us now more than ever. Even if she won't admit it."

"So, if nothing happens before Monday, we corner her at work—agreed?"

"Agreed," Maggy said softly. "Let's hope she's ready to talk by then."

Cameron worked all through the weekend at Libby and Rayce's nearly completed home. The painters had finished the final topcoat of paint, the birch cupboards had been installed, and the hardwood floors had received their last coat of sealant.

On Sunday, Cameron worked from dawn to dusk, cutting and fitting the birch trim, room by room. It was tedious, painstaking work, but it kept his mind busy, and off of Abby.

At ten o'clock at night, he dropped to the floor and settled against the new walk-around fireplace that divided the living and dining space. He poured himself a cup of lukewarm coffee from his flask and opened the sandwich he'd made for himself that morning. His first food of the day. The ham looked unappealing, but he bit into it anyway. He'd dropped enough weight as it was.

ABBY'S STORY: BETRAYED BY LOVE

He ate slowly, not really tasting his food, though the bitter coffee made him shudder in disgust. But he drank it anyway. And brooded. He hadn't seen her in five days. Five long, empty days—and nights. The nights were the worst. He could work like a bull during the day, but at night, when his body shut down at last, he was tormented by images of her. In his bed. Writhing in his arms.

Cameron groaned out loud in the empty room, his eyes bitter and filled with grief. "How long?" he asked the silence. "How long before this pain goes away?" Then he crawled to his feet, his body weary beyond his years, and packed up to go home.

Maggy and Libby waited patiently for Abby to show up for their regular weekly meeting, but weren't surprised when she gave it a miss.

"That's it," Libby said determinedly. "This has gone on long enough. When do we do it?"

"Tonight...at five. Before we go home," Maggy replied, her eyes filled with resolution.

"I'll meet you here and we'll go together."

Maggy nodded. "We'll have to be firm with her. This can't go on—or she'll make herself ill."

The meeting broke up quickly. Without Abby, it was an exercise in futility.

At five o'clock on the dot, Maggy and Libby entered Abby's shop, but she wasn't there. Delia was working behind the counter and looked up when they walked into the room. Right away she read the grim determination on their faces. "It's about time somebody took her in hand," Delia whispered. "She's on the edge of collapse." Then Delia pointed toward the back. "She's in her office," she added. "Been there most of the day."

Maggy and Libby nodded, then headed to the small cubbyhole office.

When they rounded the corner and peeked inside, both gasped in fright. Abby's head was on her desk, her face pale and bloodless.

"Abby!" Maggy and Libby said in unison. Maggy rushed in, put her arms on Abby's slender shoulders, and shook her gently.

"She's asleep, I think," Libby said tightly.

Just then Abby stirred and her heavy lids slowly opened. "What are you two doing here?" she asked softly, her voice husky and tired.

"Checking up on you," Maggy told her. She tried to keep her voice light, but tears threatened to spill from her eyes. Abby looked so lost...so alone.

"I'm all right," Abby mumbled. Then she sat up and attempted to straighten her hair.

Libby and Maggy glanced at each other as they noticed how Abby's hands trembled as she retied her long brown mane into its fastener.

Maggy pulled up a chair for Libby, then kneeled down at Abby's feet. "Abby," she began resolutely, "this has got to end. Libby and I are your friends. We know you're hurting. Talk to us so we can help."

Abby saw the worry in Maggy's eyes and sighed. "I'm all right," she muttered wearily.

"No you're not!" Libby snapped. When Maggy glared at her, Libby shook her head and said defiantly, "We're not getting through to her with this 'kid-glove', 'hands-off' approach, Maggy! So it's time to get down to brass tacks."

Libby stared at Abby, her eyes stern and unwavering. "You're one of my best friends, Abby Fulton, so that gives me the right to tell you a few home truths!"

"Libby!" Maggy warned.

Libby shook her head impatiently and added, "No, damn it all! We've pussyfooted around her too long. Now look, Abby....we know you and Cameron broke up. And we know you're hiding away—even from us. Don't do that," she begged. "Talk to us. Let us help you."

Abby's eyes softened—just a little. "Settle down, Libby," she said quietly. "It's not good for your baby if you get yourself upset."

"Will you listen to yourself?" Libby fumed. "You're pregnant too!"

"Oh, I'm quite well aware of that fact," Abby drawled, a hint of laughter lighting her eyes.

Maggy saw the humour and held her breath. *Maybe Libby was on the right track!*

"Well, if you're aware of that fact, why do you look like a walking skeleton?" Maggy demanded.

Abby's fine brows rose, and her chin tilted defiantly. "I'll have you know I have not lost one pound! I'm eating properly and taking care of myself—so back off!"

"We will not back off!" Maggy barked, her eyes snapping dangerously. "You're too damned stubborn to see how close you are to the edge, Abby!"

Abby broke then, her eyes glittering with unshed tears. "Don't you understand," she whispered, "I can't talk about it. It hurts too much!"

"That's precisely *why* you have to let it all out," Libby answered, as a lone tear trailed down her cheek.

Abby's face twisted with pain, her hands balled at her side. "You don't know...," she said hoarsely. "It's all my fault and I have no one to blame but myself."

"Tell us," Maggy commanded. "What happened?"

Tears flooded Abby's eyes. The tears she swore each night she would not shed. One fell and then another, until at last they rained down her face like spring water overflowing a dam. Abby sobbed and gasped for breath, rocking back and forth. Wracked by a terrible pain too awesome to bear, Abby hunched protectively over her stomach and cried as if her heart were breaking. As indeed it was.

Maggy leaned forward, followed by Libby. They held her in the circle of their arms, rubbing her back soothingly, while she howled in anguish.

After that, Abby began to talk.

A long time later, Maggy leaned back and looked at Libby. Libby raised her brows, but shook her head slowly, her eyes shadowed by bewilderment.

"Don't signal to each other over my head," Abby snapped. "I know damned well this is my own fault."

"Good," Maggy said quietly. "Now, what are you going to do about it?"

"Absolutely nothing." Abby wiped a last tear from her cheek and glared defiantly at her friends.

"It seems to me, you have two choices," Libby said slowly.

Abby raised her brows, folded her arms, and waited. When Libby said nothing, Abby sighed, "All right! What are my choices?"

"You can apologize and beg his forgiveness..."

"Or?" Abby crossed her arms defensively.

Libby smiled gently. "Or...apologize...and beg his forgiveness."

"That's no choice at all!"

"I know," Libby replied cooly. "But if you love Cameron, that's what it's going to take."

Maggy's eyes narrowed. She had been watching Abby's face while she sparred with Libby and was pleased to see colour returning to her cheeks. But she was troubled by Abby's stubborn defiance. She knew Abby found it hard to admit she was wrong. But her behaviour went far beyond mere stubbornness.

"Do you love Cameron?" Maggy demanded abruptly.

Abby stared at Maggy. "Yes, I love him," she admitted finally. "That's not the problem. I don't trust him. I've tried to…but something in me holds back." She sighed and shook her head. "Do you know what I felt when he told me it was over?"

Abby paused, then stared off into space. "I felt…relieved. I guess in my heart I knew we didn't have a chance…that it could end at any time…that he'd wake up one morning and decide he'd had his fill."

"Abby!" Maggy said, her voice filled with exasperation, "for an intelligent woman, you sure spout a lot of garbage!"

"Damn right!" Libby agreed. "I think you used this *Lorraine* business as an excuse to end things with Cameron because you're afraid to love again."

"Don't be ridiculous!" Abby glared at Libby. "Are you telling me that if you came home and found another woman coming downstairs dressed in your husband's shirt, you wouldn't flip out?"

"Sure I'd flip out," Libby said with a grin. "But when I finally calmed down, I'd demand an explanation. And I wouldn't leave until we got it settled."

Maggy touched Abby's arm to get her attention. "Do you think it was easy for me to let Ross come home when he thought my baby wasn't his? It was damn hard. But I had to decide if I wanted to spend the rest of my life with him, or without him. So I swallowed my pride, and hoped for the best." She frowned at Abby. "You're such a black and white person. Everything's either wrong—or right with you. Well, this time—you're wrong."

When Abby opened her mouth to argue, Maggy held up her hand. "No! Let me finish, Abby. I can see why you're upset with Cameron. He should have told you about taking Lorraine to Toronto. But when he came over that night and explained, why didn't you apologize for the way you overreacted? Don't you think he might have been waiting for an apology?"

"No. I don't," Abby said adamantly. "I think he was just looking for an excuse to breakup with me. And I think he said that bit about marriage—just to rub salt in the wound."

"Marriage!" Libby stared at Abby in shock. "What are you talking about?"

Abby's mouth tightened. "That night…Cameron said he was going to ask me to marry him."

Maggy tsked in exasperation. "See! That just proves my point."

"This is a total waste of time," Abby sighed. "Listen to me. Don't harp on this any more. Accept what I'm telling you—please! Cameron and I are finished. I'm going to raise my child by myself and run my business, and my own life. I don't need him or any man," she added tiredly. "But I do need my friends—more than ever."

"Are you going to tell him about the baby?" Maggy's eyes were brooding, her mouth tight with repressed anger.

"I'm not sure," Abby answered. "Maybe."

Maggy sighed in defeat. "All right, Abby. We'll play it your way." She stood and stared down at her friend. "But...I'm ashamed of you, Abby. I never thought you were a coward."

Abby choked at the lump in her throat; her eyes filled with tears.

Maggy bent down and dropped a kiss on Abby's forehead. "I'll see you tomorrow," Maggy whispered, then walked out.

Libby hung back, appalled by how badly the visit had gone. "Are you all right?"

Abby nodded, but her chin trembled.

"She didn't mean to hurt you," Libby said, stroking Abby's hair.

Again Abby nodded, but said nothing.

"But Maggy's right, Abby. And I think you know it." Libby stared into her friend's eyes, washed by large spilling tears. "I know you're afraid to face Cameron. But is pride worth losing him altogether?"

Libby pressed Abby's shoulder as she walked by, then left.

Abby was still sitting at her desk, lost in a world of her own, when Delia stuck in her head in to say 'good-night.' Abby waved her off without a word. *They were right and she knew it. And she was wrong. Wrong about Lorraine...wrong to accuse Cameron without reason...wrong to let him walk away without trying to set things right. But it was too late now. Too much had gone wrong between them. He'd had enough of her—and she didn't blame him. Now, she had to pick up the pieces of her life and go on.* Then a thought hit. *Could she do that—and remain in Howard's Bay? Could she face seeing him around town...perhaps with another woman? No. That would be more than she could bear. Perhaps it was it time to move on—and start over. Some place else. Any place away from him.*

Chapter Fifteen

Abby stepped out of the medical building and shivered. She zipped up her long green winter coat and raised the fur-trimmed hood, glad that the covered entrance of the building provided some protection from the wind.

A minute later Libby came out of the building too. She buttoned up her Hudson's Bay car coat and joined Abby. "Can you believe how cold it is today?" Libby said as she slipped on leather gloves. "And it's only the middle of December."

"How was your checkup?" Abby asked.

"Dr. Jacobs said the baby and I are doing fine. I'm at the beginning of my last trimester, and he wants me to enroll in a six-week prenatal program. Do you want to go too?"

"Sure. Sounds like a good idea."

Libby shivered as a gust of wind hit her in the face. "God, I'm cold. I hope Rayce gets here soon. I'm freezing. By the way...how did *your* checkup go?"

"Oh, everything's fine, I guess."

Libby frowned and stared at her friend. "What does that mean, Abby? Is there a problem with you or the baby?"

Abby sighed wearily, then admitted, "I don't really care for Dr. Samuels. Oh...he's competent enough. But he's always after me about my weight. I've only gained eight pounds and he thinks I'm deliberately trying to keep my weight down so he harps on it constantly. Today, he asked me bluntly if I plan to keep the baby—or give it up for adoption."

Libby gasped. "Are you serious? Where does he get off asking you something like that!"

"He's got a 'thing' about unwed mothers. He kept going on and on about how difficult it is to raise a child alone—as if I don't know that." Abby's eyes were enormous in her pale face. "If it weren't for the fact that it's almost impossible to get an obstetrician these days, I'd find another doctor to deliver my baby."

Libby touched Abby on the arm. "Would you like me to call Dr. Jacobs and see if he'll take you on as a patient?"

Abby's eyes brightened and she nodded eagerly. "Oh, would you? I really don't like this guy."

"Libby—is that you?"

Both women turned and glanced down at the man standing at the base of the stairs. Abby gasped, then inched behind Libby as she stared at Cameron for the first time in weeks.

"Hello, Cameron," Libby said brightly. "What brings you into town today?"

"The lights for the tourist camp arrived, so I came into town to pick them up. Do you...two...need a ride home?" All the while he spoke, Cameron never even glanced in Abby's direction.

"No thanks. Rayce is coming to pick us up."

Abby noticed how carefully Cameron avoided her eyes, as he had each time they met. Since they'd broken up he'd ignored her completely. It hurt, more than she cared to admit.

Just then Cameron noticed the medical sign on the building and his eyes narrowed. "Are you sick, Abby?" he asked baldly.

Abby was so startled by his question, she had to clear her throat before speaking. "No," she stammered. "I'm just here with Libby because Rayce had a meeting."

He nodded curtly. "Are you sure I can't give you both a lift? It's cold out today."

Libby was tempted to say 'yes,' but knew it would drive Abby into a panic and Abby was too fragile as it was. "Thanks anyway, Cameron, but Rayce said he'd be here around two."

Cameron glanced down at his watch. "It's five to two now," he muttered.

"Well...I'd better get going."

"Thanks for the offer, Cameron," Libby said with a smile.

Cameron nodded, then turned abruptly and left.

Abby let out the breath she'd been holding. Her eyes drank in his tall body as he crossed the street and walked away.

"Are you all right?" Libby put a hand on Abby's arm and stared at her friend in alarm. Abby looked like she was ready to pass out.

Abby sighed wearily and stiffened her spine. She'd seem him twice before in the last two months, and it wasn't getting any easier.

"He seemed concerned about you," Libby said quietly.

"You're imagining things, Libby. Cameron was being polite. Nothing more."

"Abby! At least this time he spoke to you! You never even said 'hello' to him."

"What's the point?" Abby said. "Look, can we drop it, please? I really don't want to talk about Cameron Wallace any more."

Libby tightened her mouth but said nothing else. Snow was falling gently from the sky and the pale sun made the day seem later than it was. Minutes later her face brightened. "There's Rayce now."

"Watch your step," Abby warned as they picked their way down the icy steps.

Once in the back seat of Rayce's new white van, Abby rubbed her hands together and tried to warm up. But, while the heater could warm her body, nothing could defrost her frozen heart. She listened with half an ear as Libby laughed with Rayce, telling him all the myriad details about their new baby. Abby envied Libby in that moment, envied the loving glances Rayce sent her way as she talked.

Abby had no one other than Libby and Maggy to talk with about her own pregnancy. When she'd felt life for the first time, she'd been alone, with no one to share her joy. She wasn't sure if Ross and Rayce knew about her pregnancy. If they did, they said nothing to her. So far, no one had guessed, probably because she could still wear her own clothes. She had always favoured loose, tailored outfits; so, by leaving her blouses out rather than in, Abby was able to hide her secret from the world. But not for much longer.

"My car is parked at the mall, Rayce. Would you let me out there, please?" Abby asked.

"Sure thing," Rayce replied, signalling a left turn.

A few minutes later, Abby was standing at the mall entrance, feeling more lonely than ever. She headed indoors and unbuttoned her coat. These days, she was either frozen or boiling hot, her hormones working overtime, the doctor said. Abby stopped at the food centre and forced herself to eat a bowl of soup and a sandwich. After the light lunch, she felt more energetic and decided it was time to look for a couple of maternity outfits and perhaps a few things for the baby.

Stepping inside a shop called 'A New You,' Abby glanced around cautiously, an alien in a new world. Then a soft white bunting bag caught her eye and she felt an overwhelming compulsion to touch it and did so almost reverently.

"It's beautiful, isn't it?" A young woman stood at Abby's side, a smile of understanding hovering around her lips. "Can I help you?"

"Yes, perhaps you can," Abby said. She blinked several times, then smiled. "I'll take this please," she said, indicating the bag. "Then I'd like to see what you have in the way of maternity clothes."

"This little bunting bag will be perfect for a winter baby," the woman cooed. "Is that when your baby is due?"

Abby hesitated. Up until now, she hadn't discussed her baby with anyone but Libby or Maggy—and even with them, she'd said very little. But, something about the young woman, or the ambiance in the store, freed Abby from her reticence. "My baby's due in April. But the bunting bag's for my friend. Her baby's due in February."

The young woman smiled, then led Abby toward the back of the store. Before Abby knew it, she'd purchased a champagne-coloured silk tunic with a mandarin collar and full sleeves, as well as three more silk tops in red, peacock, and winter white. She tried a pair of tailored slacks with a waistband that could be adjusted as needed. Abby was so pleased by the elegant slacks that she bought three pairs in black, taupe, and grey. Her last purchase was a blue wool dress, in a shade that matched her eyes. It's high-waisted style and loose pleating gave the dress a deceptive elegance. No one would suspect it was a maternity dress, the woman assured her.

"Did you want to see our baby line?"

Abby paused, then couldn't help herself. With a hesitant nod, she followed the woman from one display to the next, her eyes wide with pleasure. She bought several newborn sleepers, a few unbelievably tiny undershirts, and two receiving blankets.

"I'll come back in a few weeks for some more things," Abby said, as she fingered a soft aqua sleeper. I think I have enough to carry as it is."

While the woman rang up her purchases, Abby glanced around at various displays, her mind making a mental note of several more items she'd need to purchase shortly. Buying the baby its first few bits of clothing had pleased her enormously and, for the first time in months, she felt a pang of happiness.

Fighting a blinding headache, Cameron drove back to Howard's Bay. He'd been getting them quite often in the last few months and had gone to a doctor the week before. Only to be told it was probably 'stress.'

Cameron had been relieved—but not surprised. He knew he was stressed out. Had been for months—since the breakup with Abby. He couldn't sleep for more than two or three hours at a stretch, his appetite was gone, and he was often short-tempered.

But he just didn't know what to do about it. At first, he'd been so sure she'd call him. He'd even planned how he would handle it. He'd be cool…aloof, at least until she apologized. Then they'd talk it out. Settle their differences. Get back together again.

But three months had gone by, and Cameron had long since faced reality. Abby was never going to call him. She had taken him at his word and kept her distance. He'd seen her half a dozen times, but only been close to her twice before today. Both times, she'd been reserved and quiet. Not once had she even bothered to say 'hello.'

This afternoon, when he saw Abby and Libby standing on the top step of the medical centre, he knew he should walk away. But he was so hungry to see her face, to hear her voice, to catch a whiff of the soft perfume she wore. He'd been shocked by how pale and thin Abby was and hurt by the way she avoided his eyes.

Cameron frowned as a thought struck. *If she didn't give a damn, why did she find it so difficult to talk to him, or even look at him?* As that thought took hold, Cameron's headache seemed to fade. He started to smile and his eyes brightened with a dawning hope. He knew that Abby wasn't dating anyone else. Surely that was a good sign. With Christmas coming, they'd be at the same gatherings, the same parties. Maybe it wasn't too late to talk…to explain. This time, he wouldn't make the mistake of letting his anger overrule his common sense. *Would she be willing to talk to him now?* he wondered. *Was he ready to risk being hurt all over again?*

Cameron was still very hurt by Abby's lack of faith, but in hindsight, he could understand how it must have looked to her. But he'd also come to realize that Lorraine wasn't the reason behind their breakup—she was only the catalyst. If he and Abby had been able to communicate their feelings, nothing Lorraine said or did would have mattered.

If I can get her to talk to me again, maybe I can convince her to give us another chance.

The last few months had confirmed something Cameron already knew. He was lost without her, like a ship with a broken rudder, going nowhere—fast.

On Christmas Eve, Abby walked into Maggy's office and poured herself a cup of herbal tea from the tray on Maggy's desk. "I'm going to close up shop at four today," she sighed, sinking gratefully into a chair.

"I am too," Maggy said, "but I think Libby's going to stay open until five-thirty."

"She must get a lot of the 'last minute guilt' business," Abby laughed, "especially from husbands."

Maggy grinned and poured herself a refill. "She told me that Christmas Eve is one of her busiest days of the year. She sold out her poinsettia order last week and had to order more."

Abby bent down and slipped off one shoe. "God, my feet are killing me," she groaned. "I'm so tired, I'm tempted to stay home from church tonight."

"Oh Abby—don't! You know how much you enjoy the candlelight service. And besides, you promised to come over to our house afterward. Libby and Rayce are coming too."

"I know…I know. Don't worry. I'll probably show up." Abby pulled her hair straight back off her forehead. "I don't know what's wrong with me," she sighed. "I feel grouchy and out of sorts. Even my hair is driving me crazy. I'm tempted to get it all shaved off. I'll start a new trend—the bald-madonna look."

Maggy gave Abby a pointed stare, then sipped her tea.

"What was that *look* for?"

"I know what's wrong with you. But if I tell you—you'll just bite my head off," Maggy drawled.

Abby rolled her eyes, then curled her upper lip. "All right, let's hear it."

"You're horny."

"What!"

"You heard me. You need a long night in bed with a good man." Maggy's eyes twinkled and her lips twitched, but other than that, she looked totally serious.

Abby gulped her tea and sent her friend a look that would have withered anyone else.

But Maggy took it in stride and shrugged her shoulders. "Don't believe me if that makes you feel better," Maggy said, her tone offhand and calm. "But that *is* what's wrong with you—I recognize the symptoms. I felt the same way when Ross and I were separated."

Abby scowled. "Sex doesn't solve all the world's problems."

"No...you're right." Maggy grinned. "But after *good* sex, it's amazing how clear things appear. I bet most scientists come up with their latest discoveries after a night of great sex."

Abby sighed. "I've had good sex, Maggy. But it wasn't enough."

Maggy decided to change tactics. "I hear you saw Cameron the other day. How was he?"

"How should I know?" Abby plucked at the sleeve of her red silk top. "A little thinner...I guess."

"Rayce said he worked like a fool to finish their house. I don't think he's any happier about this breakup than you are."

"It was *his* idea," Abby snapped.

"Did you leave him any choice?"

Abby opened her mouth to protest, then stopped, her eyes shadowed with pain. "Probably not," she admitted raggedly. "But what good does it do to go over the same ground again and again?"

"A few months ago you were too angry to listen to anyone—especially Cameron. He's not dating anyone else, Abby. Maybe it's not too late to try to talk to him."

Abby raised her brows and stared at the wall. "I do want to apologize," she admitted softly. "I should have done it long ago." She stared back at Maggy with a brooding expression on her pale face. "He was right, you know. I should have given him the benefit of the doubt and listened to *him*, not Lorraine."

"Oh good grief!" Maggy giggled. "I forgot to tell you the latest. You'll never guess what happened to Lorraine."

Abby sniffed. "I could care less about that bimbo."

"She got arrested last Friday!"

Abby's eyes nearly popped out of her head. "What on earth for?"

"They raided an escort service and she got hauled off to jail, till her family bailed her out. Apparently, she was just the receptionist—or at least that's what she told her family. But her picture was in one of those nasty tabloids, and she's just livid. Pete told Ross all about it."

Abby tried to keep a straight face, but when Maggy grinned at her, Abby exploded with laughter. "Oh...I can just see her face! Lorraine...behind bars with a bunch of hookers. It's too good to be true!"

"Oh, it's true all right." Maggy snorted. "She's threatening to fight her case all the way to the Supreme Court."

Abby roared all the more. Before long, tears streamed down her face and she was soon gasping for breath. "Oh, I needed that," she panted.

Maggy grinned, delighted to see Abby laughing again. When the laughter finally drifted away, Maggy asked, "So, are we on for tonight? You could ride to church with us."

"Yes, I'm going," Abby told her. "Suddenly I feel a whole lot better."

Abby dressed warmly in her new black pants and red silk tunic top. Her regular pants were a little too snug for comfort now. She pulled her hair back off her face with two combs and used more makeup than usual to hide the pallor in her cheeks. She still looked tired and wan, she realized, but it couldn't be helped. Grabbing a black car coat she headed out the door.

The sight of twinkling strings of lights surrounding Maggy's house made Abby feel ashamed that she hadn't done more to decorate her own home. She'd put up a small artificial tree on a coffee table, but that had been all she'd been in the mood to do. This year, it seemed kind of pointless and a lot of bother.

Ross had the car running and Kyra and Kyle were flinging snowballs at each other when Abby rounded the corner. One snowball whizzed passed her nose and she ducked in a hurry.

"Hey guys, cool it!" Ross warned as he hurried across the path. "Are you okay, Abby?"

Abby laughed, her eyes twinkling with good humour. "I'm fine. I'd take them on, but they're both better shots than I am."

"You're right. They nearly buried me in snow this afternoon." Ross grinned, then held the back door open for Abby. Once she was settled, he climbed in behind the wheel.

"You didn't work today?" she asked.

"No, we closed at noon. There was an office party for the staff, but I decided to come home instead."

"I'll just be a minute," Maggy shouted from the front step, then she disappeared back inside the house.

"Jonathan knows we're going out tonight. He's giving Ardith a hard time about going to bed," Ross explained.

Soon, that'll be me...worrying about babysitters...always rushing to go anywhere. Then she smiled and rested her hand over the small bulge below her waist.

"That son of yours is something else," Maggy fumed as she jumped into the car and glared at Ross.

Ross arched his brow and smiled at Abby. "They're always *my* children when they're acting up."

Maggy made another face at Ross. "Let's go," she commanded. "I hate being late."

The parking lot was nearly full when they pulled up to the church. Abby stepped out of the car and took a deep breath of the fresh, cold air. The sky was dark, sprinkled with twinkling stars. Abby looked up, searching for that one special star that shone more radiantly than the rest. From the time she was a little girl, she'd performed the same ritual every Christmas Eve. And tonight—as always—she spotted one star that stood out. Abby smiled contentedly, then followed Maggy inside.

The church was decorated with fresh pine branches, plaid bows, and many flickering candles. A tall spectacular pine, decorated with strands of gold beads, plaid bows, and tiny white lights towered over the room, filling it with a warm glow.

Maggy led the way to the Howard family pew where generations of Howards had sat from the time the church was built at the end of the last century.

Abby stood back, waiting until all the family were seated together, then she sat down at the end. She undid her coat and looked around, smiling at friends and customers. Just then someone tapped her arm and Abby glanced up.

"Hi," Libby whispered, "are you going to Maggy's afterwards?"

When Abby nodded, Libby smiled her approval. "I'll see you there," she added, then sat down several pews ahead, beside Sasha and Rayce.

The service was poignant and moving, filled with joyous Christmas carols led by an exuberant choir dressed in wine-coloured robes. People from the congregation took turns reading the bible, retelling the story of Christ's birth. At one point, Abby felt a nudge on her leg and Kyle excused himself quietly and slipped out of the pew. He walked carefully up the steps to the pulpit, opened the bible he carried, and said in a loud quivering voice, "And there were shepherds abiding in the field…"

A shimmer of tears slipped from Maggy's eyes as she gazed proudly at her son.

Abby listened intently, enjoying the old familiar words that seemed new and exciting each time she heard them.

Kyle's voice echoed through the room, bringing to life the miracle of Christ's birth with a passionate intensity that moved many to tears. Once finished, Kyle stepped down from the pulpit, a sheepish smile on his face. As he edged past Abby to rejoin his family, she squeezed his hand and whispered, "I'm so proud of you."

He grinned awkwardly at her words, his face flushed and warm, but his eyes were shining with pride. When he sat down, Maggy took Kyle's hand in hers, and smiled warmly into his eyes.

At the end of the service, Abby made her way slowly through the crowd until it was her turn to wish the minister a 'Merry Christmas.' She shook hands with him, then headed outside, feeling stifled by the heat and pressing people. She descended the stairs carefully, watching for patches of ice, then moved to one side to wait for her ride home.

It was colder now, and she shivered a little despite her warm coat. She stamped her feet and glanced around, wondering what was keeping Maggy. Then her eyes collided with Cameron's. He was standing on the other side of the stairs, closer to the road, watching her intently. He was alone, like herself, his stare brooding and intense. No smile lit his eyes or curved his lips.

Abby was helpless to look away. His eyes were so compelling, so mesmerizing, drawing her in like a magnet. Then a touch on her shoulder startled Abby back to awareness.

Maggy had a puzzled look in her eyes. "Are you all right, Abby? You look a little strange."

"No…no…I'm fine. Just a little cold."

"Are you ready to go home?"

"Yes…whenever you are," Abby replied huskily. Then she looked back to where Cameron had been and saw that he was gone.

"The car's over here," Ross called from across the road. He had parked on the edge of the street, under a bright street light. "Get in before you freeze."

Abby ran across the road and was just about to get into the vehicle when she heard Cameron's voice.

"Hold it a minute everyone. I want to wish you all a Merry Christmas,"

Cameron said, his voice as crisp as the night air.

Abby's head swivelled and she froze. He was only inches from her, staring directly into her eyes! Her breath caught in her throat and her eyes dilated as she read the dark misery on his face.

"Merry Christmas to you, Cameron," Maggy smiled, with a slight nudge in Abby's side.

"M-M-Merry Christmas, Cameron," Abby managed to stutter, then she dropped her eyes, hoping he wouldn't notice the red stain she could feel heating her pale cheeks.

"If you're going to be around during the holidays, drop in," Ross offered.

"Thanks...I just might do that."

He seems edgy, Abby thought, as she peeked up at him from under her lashes.

"Are you going somewhere special for Christmas dinner?"

Abby cringed inwardly at Maggy's probing question.

It seemed to startle Cameron as well. "No...actually I'm having company for the holidays."

A look of dismay darkened Abby's eyes. A look that Cameron caught just before she lowered her lashes again.

With his heart pounding in his chest, Cameron swiftly added, "My brother, Gerald, is coming tomorrow to stay with me for a few days."

Abby had a hard time holding back a sigh of relief. *His brother! Thank God it's not a woman!*

Cameron's eyes roamed her face. He thought he'd caught a fleeting look of dismay on her face when he'd mentioned he had company coming. She said nothing, gave no hint of how she felt, but once again she peeked up at him from underneath her lashes, then glanced away quickly when she caught him watching her.

Hope burst to life in Cameron's heart. *She wasn't indifferent to him—he'd bet his life on it!*

"I didn't know you had a brother," Ross commented.

"Yes, I have two, actually. We've not been very close in the past, but just lately, we've been trying to remedy that."

"Christmas can be very lonely without family or friends," Maggy said softly.

A muscle was working overtime in Cameron's jaw, and his mouth was tight. "Well, I won't keep you," he muttered quietly. "Good night." He turned to walk away, the overhead street light picking up the loneliness in his eyes.

Maggy stared after him, then bit her lip. "Forgive me Abby," she whispered abruptly to her friend, then Maggy took a step forward and called, "Wait Cameron!"

Cameron turned hesitantly, and, even before the words were out of Maggy's mouth, Abby knew what she was going to say.

"A few people are coming to our house for some eggnog," Maggy said brightly. "Why don't you come along?"

When Cameron hesitated, Abby held her breath, not sure what she wanted him to do.

"All right," Cameron nodded. "I'd like that very much." His eyes drifted to Abby's white face, then he turned and walked away into the darkness.

"Don't say one word," Maggy warned. "He looked so lonely. I just couldn't see him alone on Christmas Eve. He's my friend too, and surely to goodness you can be polite to each other for a few hours!"

"Did I say anything?" Abby drawled, as she climbed into the car and huddled in her coat for warmth. The mood Maggy was in, it wasn't safe to argue.

"You didn't have to say anything," Maggy snapped as she slammed the door behind her. "Your eyes say it all."

"Look—don't worry about it. I'm sure Cameron has no more intention of spoiling your party than I do. I'll behave, I promise."

Maggy mumbled something under her breath, that sounded suspiciously like 'that'll be the day,' then asked Ross to turn the heat on high.

All the way back to Maggy's, Abby alternated between anticipation and worry. *What if he ignored her completely? What if he didn't—should she talk to him?* Part of her hoped that he would seek her out. Then maybe she could find the right time to apologize for her behaviour.

More than anything, she wanted to be friends again with Cameron. She missed him dreadfully, missed his laugh...missed his smile. She shied away from memories of his touch, that road was too painful to walk.

It was time to make amends, to settle the rift between them, if Cameron was willing.

Perhaps then, in time, she could tell him about their child.

After washing another tray of glasses, Abby came out of the kitchen and stepped into the family room. It was crowded with friends and neighbours who stopped her every few feet to offer Christmas hugs and kisses.

Cameron was by the fireplace talking to Rayce, his back to her as it had been from the moment he entered the room. She was so disappointed. Like a fool, she'd imagined he'd walk in the house and head straight for her side. Instead, he'd stayed in the opposite corner, and hadn't looked at her once. Abby made her way to the grey couch by the tall scotch pine in the corner and sat down. She stared absently at the tree and touched a paper angel with her finger. The tree was beautiful, filled with red velvet bows and handmade ornaments that Maggy and the kids had made. She smelled its fragrance and sighed, wishing she could take more pleasure in her surroundings.

"You seem very pensive," Cameron said quietly. He stared at her for a moment, then sat close beside her on the couch.

Abby jumped a little, startled by his nearness. "I was…uh…just looking at the angel Kyra made at school," Abby stammered. A flush of warmth swept up her neck as she breathed in his scent. Instantly, she was aroused—for the first time in months. She twisted slightly in her seat and prayed he wouldn't notice.

"How are you, Abby?"

"I'm fine," she said huskily, playing with a button on her silk tunic.

His eyes were a brilliant green as he watched her every move. He could see a small pulse throbbing in her neck and wanted to taste it with his tongue. Usually that maddening little pulse had been a sign that she was aroused. But, perhaps tonight, it just indicated nervousness. She was quite agitated by his presence and he didn't know if that was bad or good.

Abby's mind raced as she tried to think of something innocuous to say…anything to keep him talking. "Maggy's got quite a crowd here tonight," she murmured desperately.

Cameron nodded and looked around, his white-knuckled hands gripping his knees. He cleared his throat then asked, "Have you been out to Libby and Rayce's new house?"

"Not yet," Abby said softly, "but I'm going to their New Year's Eve party."

"Me too," he nodded, his eyes colliding with hers.

She was lost in his gaze, her eyes wide and filled with longing. "Libby said the house is beautiful," she told him. Her lips were dry and parched and she licked them unconsciously.

Cameron swallowed visibly, his eyes fastened on her mouth. He was hard, had been from the moment he'd sat down beside her. He'd felt this same kind of intense longing, tinged with desperation, the night she'd come to him at Libby's shop.

"I'm pleased with the way it turned out—the house I mean." His tone was more abrupt than he'd meant, but it was agony to be so close to her and not be able to touch.

Abby heard the clipped tone in his voice and her eyes turned bleak. He'd leave any moment now, she figured. He'd done the polite thing, and now was impatient to get away.

"What are you doing for Christmas?"

Abby lifted her eyes again to his. "I'm having it here…with Maggy's family."

He nodded, a brooding look on his face. "I'm cooking a turkey—for me and Gerald. He should be at my place around noon."

Abby felt like she was in the middle of a maze, following this turn and that without a clear idea of where she was going. "I was quite surprised when you told Maggy your brother was coming for Christmas. I thought you weren't very close."

"We aren't. But I decided to go and see him. His marriage just broke up and he's finding it a little rough. Oddly enough, now that he's away from Heather, he's quite pleasant company. He even apologized for treating Leah so badly."

"That meant a lot to you—that he apologized?"

Cameron stiffened, then nodded slowly. "Yes…it did. It told me he cared enough to make the effort."

Abby knew right then, they were no longer talking about his brother. She sighed raggedly, then stared into his eyes.

"I'm sorry too, Cameron," she whispered softly. With a trembling hesitation, she lifted her hand and placed it over his. "I was wrong to believe Lorraine. I should have given you a chance to explain. And…I should have said I'm sorry, long before now."

Cameron read the honesty in her eyes and shuddered. He had waited so long to hear her say those words, and yet now that she had, it didn't seem to matter any more. All that mattered was that she was talking to him at last.

"After I calmed down, I realized how bad it must have looked to you," he admitted gruffly.

"It seemed like a repeat of the scene with Nick—when I caught him in bed with Celine."

Cameron nodded slowly, his mouth grim and tight. "Yeah…I can see that…now." He took her hand in his and stroked it absently, then lifted his eyes to hers. "I miss you."

His quiet words seemed to reverberate through the room. Abby's eyes swam with tears and she dropped her chin to hide them from him. "I miss you too," she whispered brokenly.

"Do you think we can ever be friends again, Abby?"

Abby gripped his hand painfully, then let him see her tears. "I hope so," she said. "I want that more than I can say."

A muscle jumped in Cameron's cheek and he swallowed the lump in his throat. *He'd waited so damned long for this chance! He wasn't going to blow it—not this time!*

Cameron leaned forward and very gently kissed Abby's pale cheek. "Merry Christmas, Abby," he muttered hoarsely.

Her heart was in her eyes as she whispered back, "It is now, Cameron."

They remained like that for a long time, hand in hand, content just to be at each other's side.

At the other end of the room, Libby and Maggy watched with bated breath the tableau taking place on the couch. When Cameron leaned over and kissed Abby's cheek, they gasped in unison, then tears ran down both their cheeks.

Ross grinned at Rayce, then poured him another drink. "If they get Cameron and Abby back together," Rayce said, "we'll never hear the end of it."

Ross smiled, then glanced at the couple in the corner. "Better buy some earplugs," he said, "because I think their plan just might do the trick."

Chapter Sixteen

Abby didn't wake up until nine on Christmas day. She showered and slipped on a green jogging suit that was a little snug, but still fit, then headed into the kitchen where she made herself a bacon and mushroom omelette, a fresh fruit salad, and a pot of herbal tea. For some reason, she was starving!

With her tray of food on the coffee table, she settled on the couch, flicked on the TV, and channel surfed until she found the original 'Miracle on 34th Street.' She'd watched the same movie each Christmas for as long as she could remember, and never tired of it. When the little Dutch girl sat on Kris Kringle's knee and he sang to her in Dutch, Abby started to sniffle—along with the TV mother—as she always did.

When the movie was over, Abby took her tray into the kitchen, then wandered over to her small Christmas tree. She picked up a small foil-wrapped package from Kyra and Kyle and decided to open it first. She laughed out loud as she held up a pair of gaudy silver earrings made from fake coins. They really needed someone wearing a fluorescent-orange mohawk haircut to do them justice, but Abby put them on anyway. She walked over to a mirror and turned her head from side to side, grinning at the picture she made. "Your mama's turning into a punk rocker," she giggled as she patted her belly.

One by one, she opened the rest of the small pile of gifts and smiled fondly at the carefully chosen items: a silk scarf from Libby and Rayce, a box of lotions and bath oils from Delia and her daughter, and a beautiful hand-knit sweater from Maggy and Ross.

A knock on the door caught her unawares. She hesitated, then went to open it.

Maggy stood there with a large gift-wrapped box in both hands. "I can only stay a minute," she said breathlessly as she hurried inside out of the cold. "I think this is yours," she grinned. "Santa made a mistake and dropped it off at my place." Then Maggy noticed Abby's earrings and her eyes widened. "Oh my!"

Abby rolled her eyes. "Your children have exquisite taste."

Maggy grinned. "Don't they just. Wait till you see the necklace they bought me. I think they picked it up at a second-hand store owned by a retired belly dancer."

Abby smiled and took the large box from Maggy's hand. "If this is an outfit to go with my earrings, I hope you remembered that harem pants are out."

"Open it," Maggy commanded.

"Who's it from?" Abby asked. She sat on the couch and started to rip. "There's no card."

"Only one way to find out." Maggy's eyes glowed like the small emeralds in her ears.

"Nice earrings," Libby commented.

"This morning's gift from Ross. Thank God the kids didn't help to pick them out."

"He has good taste."

"That's what I told him," Maggy said with a laugh.

Abby bit her lip as she tried to rip off the heavy tape that held the large box together. "Whoever wrapped this thing should work for the Post Office," she griped as she finally managed to open the box. Then her mouth dropped and her eyes misted. "Oh Maggy...it's so beautiful." Abby's voice broke as she lifted out a hand-crocheted christening blanket in soft white wool.

"I thought the baby should have a present too," Maggy said softly.

Abby lifted the pure-white fringed blanket to her face and rubbed it against her cheek. "Oh, Maggy, I can't thank you enough. You just made my day."

Maggy cleared her throat. "I have to get back home. Why don't you come over soon and spend the day?"

Abby smiled gently. "Don't worry about me. I'll be fine. I'm going to watch some old movies this afternoon and have a little sleep. Then I'll pop over around four to give you a hand."

Maggy frowned at the fragility in Abby's eyes. "I don't like to think of you here all alone."

"I'm not alone." Abby patted her stomach and grinned. "Baby and I need a little quiet after being out so late last night."

"Are you mad at me, for inviting Cameron over?"

Abby's eyes widened and she reached out to take Maggy's hand. "Not at all, Maggy. Believe me. As a matter of fact, Cameron and I talked and I finally got the chance to apologize for my behaviour. I think, in time, we might even be friends again."

"Friends? Is that…enough for you?"

A shadow flickered in Abby's blue eyes. "It's better than nothing. And more than I thought possible." She gathered up the ripped paper. "Now, go home Maggy and cook your heart out. I'm in the mood for one of your outrageously fattening meals."

"Sounds like your appetite is back."

"In a big way. I ate enough for three this morning."

Maggy grinned in relief, then stood and walked to the door. "If you need anything——call."

Abby nodded as she opened the door. "I'll see you later," she promised.

Maggy kissed her cheek, then zipped her coat, and left.

It was a cold sunny day, but slightly windy. Snow whirls chased around Abby's calves as she watched Maggy run into her own backyard. When she started to shiver, Abby hastily closed the door and went back to the couch. She spent a very enjoyable, but lazy afternoon, watching old classics, reading a bit, and dozing.

"Turkey's on," Cameron called to Gerald from the kitchen. The TV clicked off and Gerald ambled into the room with a glass of scotch in one hand.

"Wow…I *am* impressed." Gerald whistled as he took in the table.

It was set for two, with a Christmas tablecloth and matching napkins to dress it up. A small golden turkey took centre stage, surrounded by mashed potatoes, baby carrots, tossed salad, and fresh pumpkin pie.

"I can't take credit for the pie," Cameron smiled. "Libby brought it over while you were in the shower."

"It looks terrific." He smiled at his brother. "You've gone to a lot of trouble, Cam. I really appreciate it."

Cameron was slightly embarrassed so he grinned awkwardly and pulled out a chair. "Let's eat," he muttered. "I don't know about you, but I'm starved!"

Twenty minutes later the bowls were half-empty, the turkey was missing a breast and legs, but the pie was untouched.

"Let's leave that for later," Cameron suggested. "I don't think I'll be able to eat for days."

"If my memory serves, you'll probably raid the fridge at midnight for a turkey sandwich," Gerald teased, then leaned back in his chair and belched.

Cameron chuckled heartily. "If *my* memory is correct, every time I came down to make a turkey sandwich, you were already on your second!"

Gerald cocked his head, grinning at Cameron's teasing. "You're probably right. I was always partial to leftovers."

"Still are, I think," Cameron said pointedly.

"I know…I know. I'm joining a health club as soon as I go back home." Gerald sighed. "I've got to get back into shape—or I won't have much luck with the ladies."

Cameron's eyes darkened and he dropped his eyes. He absently traced the wreath on the tablecloth pattern, a brooding intensity hardening his face.

"You're thinking about—*her*—aren't you?" Gerald's eyes were sympathetic as he reached out and touched his brother's arm.

Cameron glanced up, startled out of his reverie by Gerald's comment. "Am I that obvious?"

"To one who's been there." Gerald frowned. "I can't change my situation—even if I wanted to, but *you* can, Cameron. If you want this woman, don't let her slip away."

"We talked last night after church, at Maggy's house. She…ah…apologized for believing Lorraine and not me."

"Well *there*!" Gerald said with a broad smile. "That should tell you something."

"She also said she wants to be friends again."

"I see. Is that good or bad?"

"That's the problem," Cameron said quietly. "I really don't know."

Several hours later, when Cameron was sound asleep on the couch in front of the television set, Gerald rummaged through the address book by the phone, then smiled when he found the right name. After writing down the information he wanted, he slipped on his coat, grabbed his car keys, and tiptoed quietly out of his brother's house.

He stopped at a gas station for directions and, without much difficulty, found the house he was looking for. Lights were on inside the small bungalow, so he turned off the car and stepped out into the cold, frosty night.

"That turkey smells absolutely heavenly," Abby sighed as she placed a relish dish on each of the three tables set up for dinner. "I love these Christmas tablecloths, Maggy. Did you have them made?"

"No, I ordered them from Sears." Maggy glanced down the three connecting tables. "I think they add such a festive touch."

"It was a great idea to set up the tables here in the family room," Abby said as she straightened a knife. "That way everyone can eat together."

Maggy smiled, perusing the table with a sharp eye. "I like to have everyone together. When I was growing up, we always went to Grandma's for Christmas dinner. The men ate first, then the children, and the women last. After dinner, the men would sit in the front room talking while the women spent the rest of the night doing a mountain of dishes. I always used to think it wasn't fair that the women had all the dishes to do while the men got to sit around and talk, but, surprisingly enough, the women had as much fun as the men. Everybody helped and the job went fast. "There," Maggy added, with an approving glance at the pristine tables. "I think we're all set."

Just then the doorbell rang and Ross answered it. Two of Maggy's sisters and their families, all loaded down with presents, pushed through the door, stomping the snow from their feet.

Right behind came Esther and Edith Gavin, two elderly quilters who lived just down the street. At the last quilting session before the holidays, Esther had casually mentioned that they'd be all alone for Christmas. Impulsively, Maggy had extended an offhand invitation to come to dinner. The sisters had accepted with such enthusiasm, Maggy had felt ashamed that she hadn't thought of it before.

Over glasses of white wine and spicy eggnog, everyone settled in for a cozy visit until Maggy announced that dinner was ready.

"You've outdone yourself," Esther Gavin commented as she eyed her dinner with true appreciation.

The table groaned with a thirty-pound succulent turkey, flaky meat pies, steaming vegetable dishes, homemade preserves from Esther's garden, and the deep-dish pumpkin pies that were Edith's specialty. Ross said grace, then everyone dug in with unconcealed relish.

After dinner, the kids showed off their presents, then took off upstairs to play with the new computer games Abby had given them.

"The twins got a bigger charge out of the boxes than the teddy bears you got them, Abby," Maggy laughed as she brought a tray of tea and coffee into the tidied up family room.

"That's usually the way," Abby sighed. "I remember I got a new desk for Christmas one year but I had more fun turning the box into a castle. I played with it for a week and ignored the desk completely. My mother was not impressed."

"I think part of what makes Christmas so special is the memories it brings of years gone past," Maggy said, as she poured Edith a coffee.

"On this day I always remember our parents." Esther voice was filled with a bitter-sweet reflection. "They were stern people, but good. They did their best for us…even through the hardest times."

"Mother got me some piano music one Christmas. It came all the way from Toronto," Edith said. A dreamy expression lightened her eyes, a smile of reminiscence softening the harsh lines of her withered face.

Abby looked at Edith in surprise. "I didn't know you played the piano."

The old woman smiled solemnly. "I don't," she admitted with a sigh. "But it was my dream to learn. When I snipped the butcher's twine around my package, and saw what was inside, I threw my arms around Mama and wept. Papa thought it was foolish because nobody in Howard's Bay had a piano at the time, but Mama knew me well. She gave me what I needed— the gift of hope. That's more precious than anything else. I still have those three sheets of music. I've never used them, but you never know, I might in the future."

Abby marvelled at how little she knew about Edith Gavin. On the surface she was a taciturn, sour-faced woman who often seemed bitter and morose. But, just now, a glimpse of the past revealed a dreamer beneath the wrinkled facade.

As if sensing her thoughts, Edith got up and walked stiffly to sit on the couch by Abby's side.

"Surprises you, doesn't it?" the old woman said. "I know what people think of me, Abby. Just a bitter old woman—and they're right."

Abby made a sound of protest but Edith waved it away. "I made my own bed and my own mistakes. Just like you."

Abby's eyes narrowed and her lips thinned.

Edith cackled slyly. "Don't go all prim on me girl—we're too much alike.

ABBY'S STORY: BETRAYED BY LOVE

Once, I had a good man—but I let him slip away. I suspect you're making the same mistake, Abby, my girl."

The old rheumy eyes softened and Edith laid her wrinkled, bony hand on Abby's cheek. "You're a good girl, Abby Fulton. But you're a damned stubborn fool! If you love Cameron Wallace, go after him. If it doesn't work out, at least when you're old, you won't be eaten up by regrets."

Abby blinked back tears and stared at Edith. She knew how much it cost this proud old woman to speak so plainly.

Edith nodded several times, then sighed. She pulled herself up, then glanced at Esther. "Time to go home, sister. I'm ready for my bed."

Abby decided to leave too. It had been a long day and she had much to think about when she got home.

But she'd barely gotten in the door and slipped off her boots and coat, when the doorbell rang.

Abby didn't recognize the burly man standing on her step, but something about him looked vaguely familiar.

"I'm Gerald Wallace," he told her, his husky voice so like his brother's. "I'm Cameron's older brother. If you're Abby Fulton, could I speak to you for a moment?"

Abby hesitated, then opened the door wider. "Yes, I'm Abby Fulton. Come in."

When he'd undressed and seated himself on a chair in her living room, she sat on the couch and waited expectantly, her heart racing in her chest.

"I'm butting in where I have no business," Gerald said with a rueful smile, "but I'm going to do it anyway." He sighed softly, his forehead furrowed by deep lines, then stared pensively at her. "Do you love my brother?"

Abby reacted as if she'd been shot! Her head snapped back and her eyes widened in shock.

Gerald laughed. "How's that for being blunt?"

Abby didn't know how to answer him. "You're more like your brother than I thought."

"And you didn't answer my question. Do you love him?"

Abby stared cooly into his eyes. "Very much."

Gerald nodded. "Good. That's very good," he muttered.

Abby raised her brows, then demanded, "Why is that good?"

Gerald grinned. "Because I'm pretty sure he's in love with you, too. He's been totally miserable since you broke up."

Abby gasped, her heart accelerating incredibly. "Are you sure?"

"As sure as I am that if you don't go over there tonight, it'll take him months to work up the nerve to let you know himself."

Abby's eyes filled with joyous tears. "I can't thank you enough for *butting in*, Gerald. I just hope you're right."

"He needs a family of his own," Gerald said gruffly. "He's a good man—but terribly lonely."

Abby half-laughed, half-cried. "Well, he's going to have more family than he knows what to do with—before much longer."

Gerald raised his brows at her cryptic words.

"I'm pregnant," she told him softly, then grinned widely at his loud whoop of delight.

"I'd love to be a fly on the wall when you tell him," Gerald told her, "but I think you're going to need some privacy. Could I stay here and watch a movie—or two?"

"Make yourself at home," Abby answered, her smile radiant as she stood and headed for the door. "If I'm a little late, there are pillows and blankets in the hall closet," she added while slipping on her boots. She hesitated for a moment, then ran across the room and threw herself into Gerald's arms. "Thank you," she whispered huskily.

"Get going," Gerald commanded, in a gruff voice that fooled no one. "And tell Cameron he owes me one."

"We both do." Abby's smile wobbled as she wiped tears from her eyes, then she kissed him again before racing out the door.

Gerald smiled and rocked back and forth on his heels, feeling better than he had in years.

Only when Abby was finally at Cameron's door did her nerve give out. She lifted a hand to push the doorbell, then paused. *What if Gerald was wrong? What if Cameron didn't love her after all and only wanted to be friends.*

There was only one way to find out. Abby pressed the doorbell several times and stepped back. Her face was pale in the glare from the overhead light and her body shook, but not from the cold. It seemed ages before she heard the sound of footsteps on the other side of the door, but finally the door opened, and Cameron stood there. His feet were bare, and his blue plaid shirt was half out of his jeans. His eyes looked bleary and tired and there was more than a hint of stubble on his square jaw. Abby thought he'd never looked more appealing.

"Abby? Is something wrong? I mean...ah...come in." Cameron stood back to let her pass, then took her coat.

Abby slipped off her boots. "I'd like to talk to you—if I may."

"Sure. Come on in out of the cold." As he led her down the hallway he told her, "My brother's around here somewhere. I'd like you to meet him."

"I already have," Abby replied. "He's at my house right now, watching television." She followed him into the TV room and sat down on the couch.

Cameron stared at her, his brows raised in astonishment. "What on earth is he doing there?"

"Giving me a chance to talk to you alone," Abby said, as she played with the folds of her blue wool dress.

Cameron frowned, then sat down by her side. "I don't understand. Is something wrong?"

"Yes." Abby sighed. "Everything's wrong." She stared at him intently, her blue eyes shadowed with pain. "When we broke up, Cameron, I told myself it was for the best, but I'm miserable without you." Her face flamed but she forced herself to continue. "I miss seeing you...hearing your voice...feeling your touch."

Cameron was frozen, like an ancient statue, his eyes never leaving her face.

"Gerald thinks...you still...care for me, Cameron," she said huskily. "That's what he told me tonight. Is he...right?"

Cameron's face was rigid, his body tense. "Yes...he told you the truth." He hesitated, then added hoarsely, "I love you, Abby. I always have."

Abby gasped and lifted a trembling hand to cover her mouth. Tears of joy welled up in her vivid blue eyes as she stared at him in relief. "Oh, thank God!" she whispered brokenly. "I love you too."

His eyes were shimmery pools of raw emotion. Cameron held her face and stared at her, then kissed her tenderly—oh so tenderly—as if she were made of fragile glass.

Abby returned his kiss with a hunger that more than matched his.

They strained against each other, their need to be close...to assure themselves of the other's presence...more emotional, than physical.

Cameron lifted his mouth, then traced her face with trembling fingers. "I'll never let you go again, Abby. I lost you once because of my stupid pride, but that won't happen a second time. I love you so much," he murmured as he feathered gentle kisses all over her face. "I want to sleep beside you at night and kiss you awake every morning." He stared into her eyes and whispered, "I want to marry you, Abby. I need to know that we belong to each other."

Abby's azure eyes radiated love; her mouth trembled as she traced the sharp angle of his jaw. "I want that too, Cameron," she whispered. "It's what I've always wanted."

He hesitated for a moment, then said cautiously, "Later on, perhaps we could adopt a child together."

Abby froze in amazement, her hands dropping lifelessly into her lap.

When he saw her reaction, Cameron's jaw clenched. "Look...forget I even mentioned it. If that's not what you want, Abby, just say so. As long as I have you, nothing else matters."

Abby's heart melted as she read the pain in his eyes. She knew how much he wanted children. Knowing that he would give up that dream—for her—made her feel terribly humble.

"Oh Cameron," she laughed softly, "I'd love to adopt a child with you."

A smile of relief flashed across his face. "You don't know what it means to me to hear you say that, my love."

"There's just one thing though," she said with an impish grin. "Could we wait to adopt until our own baby is at least three?"

Cameron's jaw literally dropped. Then he took her face in his hands and said hoarsely, "Are you saying—what I think you're saying?"

Abby took one of his hands and laid it over her stomach, a smile of radiant joy lighting her eyes.

Cameron's eyes widened with disbelief. "You're...pregnant!"

"Over five months," she admitted shyly.

"God," he groaned as he drew her into his arms. "We came so close to losing it all."

Abby stroked his back soothingly. "I *would* have told you about the baby, Cameron," she assured him.

"I would have carried you off to a minister the minute I knew."

"That's why I didn't tell you," she replied softly. "I wanted you to want *me* as well as the baby."

"Want you! There's never been a time I *haven't* wanted you!" he growled.

Abby nuzzled his neck, her fingers stroking his thick hair. "I love you," she murmured, sensing his need for reassurance.

He tightened his grip on her body. "You're mine now, Abby. For always.

I'll never let you go again."

For long, endless moments he kissed her desperately, then slowly lifted his mouth and stared down into her eyes. "I ache for you, my love."

"I want you too...so much."

Cameron sighed and shook his head. "But I think the next time we make love should be on our wedding night. Does that make any kind of sense?"

Abby smiled and touched the corner of his mouth with a feather-like kiss. "Perfect sense," she whispered softly.

A week later, on a clear, crisp New Year's Eve, Abby and Cameron walked hand in hand up the steps of Libby and Rayce's new home. Cameron straightened the green silk tie at his neck, unbuttoned his new black suit jacket, then rang the bell.

"You did a wonderful job on the house, Cam. It's really beautiful," Abby told him as she admired the interlocking walkway and circular steps. "I love the way you angled the siding."

Cameron glanced up at the tri-level cedar home, his eyes filled with pride. "Yes, it turned out well, but wait till you see the house I'm going to build for us."

Abby snuggled against him, her heart overflowing with love.

"Abby—and Cameron!" Libby gasped, as she opened the door. Her blue eyes rounded with delight. "I'm so glad to see you here—*together*."

Abby grinned mischievously at Cameron. They hadn't told anyone about their reconciliation, wanting it to come as a complete surprise. They'd spent the last week alone, reaffirming their love and planning their future, and now they were ready to be with their friends.

"I hope you don't mind," Cameron said casually. "I asked my brother to meet me here tonight. He'll be along shortly—if that's all right with you?"

Libby beamed, then put her arm through Cameron's. "The more the merrier," she laughed. "Abby, you look positively radiant tonight," Libby said as she led them down a wide hall. Taking Abby's coat, she said, "Oh, I love your dress! That shade of winter white is very becoming."

Abby glanced down at the flowing chiffon gown. She'd been very pleased to find a style that hid her expanding waist, yet was formal enough for Libby's party. The dress looked like something a medieval princess might wear, with a high waistline, several layers of soft floating skirts, long sleeves, and a wide cowl neckline. When Abby had tried it on, she'd felt like a princess, or even a bride.

"You look pretty terrific yourself, Libby," Abby said. Libby was a madonna in cornflower blue. The maternity top she wore was edged in navy sequins to match the silk evening pants that completed her outfit.

Just then Rayce walked down the hall toward them. "Well...." he drawled lazily, "looks like it's going to be a happy new year after all. Come on into the living room. The rest of the gang are already here."

When they reached the entrance to the sunken living room, Libby announced gaily, "Look everyone...Cameron and Abby are here!"

Abby's mouth twitched and Cameron's dimple grew even more pronounced. "I think she's glad we're back together," Abby whispered out of the side of her mouth.

Cameron chuckled. "How did you guess?"

"Abby!" Maggy was running toward them, the shimmering folds of her celery-green evening gown flying behind her. "Are you—together again?" she demanded, her eyes racing back and forth between them.

Abby nodded, then grinned as Cameron put an arm around her shoulders.

"Well...thank God for small miracles," Maggy laughed. "It's about time you two smartened up." Then a saucy light flashed in her bold green eyes. "Does that mean there's going to be another wedding in Howard's Bay?"

"Perhaps sooner than you think," Cameron said cryptically, his eyes dancing as he winked at Abby.

Ross walked over to the group and shook his head. "I hope you realize what you've done to us, Cameron. Rayce and I will never hear the end of it."

Cameron shot the men a puzzled look. "What are you talking about?"

"Our wives will take full credit for getting the two of you back together." Ross sighed, arching his brows theatrically.

"He's right," Rayce nodded. "We'll never hear the end of it. They'll be setting up every poor bachelor in sight."

Maggy elbowed Ross. "Wait till I get you home!" she said, her eyes promising more than revenge.

Ross bent down to kiss her pouting lips. "I'll hold you to that."

Just then the doorbell rang and Rayce left the group.

Abby glanced around the high-ceilinged room, her eyes flitting from one group of chatting people to another. She noticed Harley and Bessie seated in front of the fireplace talking to Wendy Hughes and her husband. "I love the way you grouped the couch set around the fireplace, Libby. It looks so cozy."

"That was Rayce's idea," Libby told her. "We can cuddle before the fire or watch the lake, without moving off the couch." Libby smiled at Cameron, then added with fervent sincerity, "I know I've said it before, Cameron, but I really love my house."

Cameron leaned down to drop a kiss on her cheek. "I'm glad," he said quietly. "That's what I like to hear." At the sound of footsteps coming down the hall, he glanced up, then smiled in relief. "Good. Gerald's here at last." He bent down and whispered to Abby, "Time to get the show on the road."

Libby looked up and saw two men standing at the entrance to the room. A tinge of red ran up her neck. "Reverent Smylie! "I'm...so glad you could make it to our party."

The minister grinned disarmingly. "I was invited—I assure you, Libby."

"I asked Reverend Smylie to join us," Cameron interjected. "If you'll give me a minute, I'll explain." He dropped a kiss on Abby's lips, then stepped up to the entrance of the room. In a loud, commanding voice he shouted, **"May I have your attention, please!"**

When the noise from the crowd slowly faded away, Cameron smiled tenderly at Abby, then held out his hand to her.

She climbed the steps and edged into the crook of his shoulder.

"Abby and I have a favour to ask," he told the crowd, his dimple out in full force. "We would like all of you to witness our marriage tonight—if Libby and Rayce will allow us to disrupt their party for a bit."

Wild cheers followed his announcement and Cameron grinned down at Abby.

"That sounds like a 'yes' to me," she laughed.

At that moment Libby threw herself into Abby's arms, squealing with delight. "I love it!" she cried. "I just love it!"

"That's a 'yes' all right," Cameron drawled sardonically.

Maggy and Ross stepped up to the happy couple. "We'd be honoured to stand up for you," Ross said as he clapped Cameron on the back.

"That was the plan," Cameron answered. Then he smiled tenderly into Abby's eyes. "Well Abby...are you ready to marry me?"

Abby smiled sweetly and held out her hand. "Ready, Mr. Wallace, and oh so willing."

The short ceremony was poignantly moving. In a matter of minutes Abby and Cameron were married and accepting the best wishes of their friends. They danced all night long, wrapped in a world of their own.

Libby, Maggy, and Ross stood to one side watching the newlyweds.

"Well, we did it," Libby said misty-eyed, smearing her makeup all over again.

Maggy sighed, her eyes lit with a dreamy fire. "I'm so happy for them." She glanced at Ross, then stilled, returning his intent stare. "Uh…Libby…I hope you don't mind if we don't stay too late," she muttered as she moved toward Ross.

Libby grinned with understanding. "If this weren't my party—I'd do the same," she laughed. The laughter caught in her throat when she noticed Rayce heading her way, a look in his eyes she knew all too well. Libby's mouth curved enticingly as she stepped into his path. "Looking for me?" she teased.

Rayce grinned, a knowing look in his eyes, then he bent down to whisper in his wife's ear.

Libby's eyes brightened as she took his hand. No one noticed when they left the party and slipped up the stairs.

By one o'clock, Cameron and Abby were in bed, clasped in each other's arms.

"Did I tell you how beautiful you looked tonight, Mrs. Wallace?"

Abby purred and nibbled his chin. "Yes," she laughed, "at least ten or twelve times."

"I will always love you, Abby," he added solemnly.

"And I, you," she whispered.

"I want to be inside you, my love. It's been way too long."

Abby moaned and arched against him, grinding against his hard manhood.

"Slow down, my love," he crooned. "Tonight we're going to take it…so slow."

And they did…all night long…time and time again.

Chapter Seventeen

"Abby! For God's sake woman—it's ten o'clock at night!"

"I know," Abby grinned. "But I have the worst craving for a Big Mac."

"You never eat hamburgers!"

"I know that," she said reasonably, as if explaining a force of nature to a three-year old. "But I want one now."

"You'd try the patience of a saint," Cameron grumbled as he climbed out of bed and pulled on his jeans. "Well, get dressed," he sighed over his shoulder. "One Big Mac coming up."

The McDonald's in North Bay was virtually empty when they arrived. Several weary employees were hard at it, sweeping floors, and cleaning grills.

"Any chance we could get a Big Mac?" Cameron asked tiredly.

"And a chocolate sundae," Abby added insistently.

"And...two chocolate sundaes," Cameron sighed.

The fresh-faced teenager at the counter grinned and nodded her ponytailed head. "Coming right up."

Cameron yawned and tucked in his shirt. "I'll be glad when this baby is born, Abby. Your cravings are getting stranger all the time."

Just then the cashier brought their tray and gave him the total.

Cameron put his hand in his back pocket and frowned. "Damn...I forgot my wallet," he muttered. "Abby, did you bring your purse?"

"Yes, but I only have a few dollars."

"Get it out and I'll see how much change I have." He dipped into his front pocket and pulled out a handful of coins. "I can't believe I walked out of the house without my wallet," he said, shaking his head.

Abby grinned mirthfully at the disgusted look on Cameron's face. She passed him what little change she had and watched while he counted up the money.

He glanced apologetically at the young cashier. "Make that just one sundae," he told her ruefully. "I'm fifty cents short."

Sympathy shone in the young girl's eyes. "That's okay, sir," she whispered with a conspiratorial smile. "I'll pay the difference for you." Then she pushed the tray toward Cameron, smiled very gently, and walked away.

Cameron picked up the tray and strode grimly to a seat. "Don't say one word," he warned Abby.

"Oh....if you could see your face," she teased. "You're as red as a beet."

"Eat the damn Big Mac," he growled.

Abby munched away contentedly. Cameron mashed his sundae, then grinned. "That's a pretty neat kid," he said quietly. "Very understanding."

Abby froze and a queer expression flitted across her face. "That poor girl. I hope she's very understanding," Abby croaked.

Cameron glanced quizzically at his wife. "Why?"

"Because...my water just broke." Abby groaned. "I'm afraid she's going to have quite a mess to clean—after we leave."

Cameron jumped up and pulled Abby after him. "Thanks for the ice cream!" he shouted to the startled clerks. "Sorry about the mess—but we've got to go! My baby's ready to have a wife!"

Twelve hours later Aaron McDonald Wallace cried himself to sleep in his mother's arms, while his father cradled them both.

Chapter Eighteen

Epilogue

Six months later...

"This is so exciting!" Libby grinned. "I've never been to a premiere before."

"The screen at the Arts Centre is enormous," Rayce added. "It'll be like seeing yourself under a microscope, Abby."

"With my luck," Abby answered dryly, "my nose will look huge and I'll have a zit on my forehead."

"From what I remember," Cameron drawled, "you were covered in fake blood from head to foot."

"Trust you to remember that," Abby sighed, then she glanced over his shoulder. "Oh, there's Maggy and Ross. They made it."

"Hi everyone," Maggy said breezily as she walked toward the waiting group. "I didn't think we were going to make it on time. Did Emily cut that tooth yet, Libby?"

Rayce nodded. "Yes, last night. But she's still a little feverish, so we're heading straight home after the movie."

"Aaron's a little cranky tonight too," Cameron said with a slight frown. "I'm not too happy about leaving him."

"Listen to them," Maggy laughed. "This is our first night out together in a long time guys—let's try to enjoy it."

"And who just phoned home to check up on the kids?" Ross teased.

Maggy's grin was unrepentant. "And you'll do the same during intermission," she said archly, as she slipped her arm through her husband's.

"Let's grab a glass of wine," Cameron suggested. "The lineup's three deep already."

As the men headed off toward the bar, Abby looked around the packed lobby of the Arts Centre until her eye caught a familiar face. "Oh my God! Don't look now," she gasped, "but isn't that…you know…that actress from the law show on TV?"

Maggy and Libby surreptitiously glanced over their shoulders. "You're right," Maggy whispered. "Oh…she's gorgeous. And so tiny!"

"I thought Nick would have wanted his premiere in Toronto or Montreal," Libby commented. "But I'm glad he decided to have it here in North Bay."

"Nick thought it would be good PR to have the opening here, and it looks like he was right. This place is packed with movie people—and politicians. I hear the premier is supposed to be here tonight." Just then Abby heard the sound of enthusiastic clapping. "Maybe that's Nick at last," she told her friends. "He always did love a grand entrance."

Cameron edged in beside Abby and offered her a glass of wine. "Umm," she sighed blissfully. "My first taste in months."

"You did insist on breast-feeding Aaron," Cameron reminded her.

"Yes I did," Abby agreed, "and I loved doing it. But I've had the worst craving for a glass of wine."

"Craving! Did you say craving?" Cameron demanded, his brows raised in disbelief.

Abby grinned. "Relax Cam. I'm not pregnant—at least not yet."

Cameron sent Abby a sharp, appraising look, then drawled, "Is that your roundabout way of letting me know you want to try for number two?"

Just then a sea of bodies parted to allow Nick and his group to enter the lobby.

"Abby!" Nick shouted with a flourish.

Cameras rolled and microphones lowered as Nick rushed to Abby and kissed her resoundingly. "Ready for the big night?" he boomed.

"Can't wait," Abby drawled.

"Your death scene steals the show," Nick assured her. Then he paused and finally threw Cameron a glance. "I hear you two got married...and have a little boy," he said. He put out his hand to Cameron. "Congratulations," he said cooly. "I've never seen Abby look so radiant. So you must be doing something right."

Cameron raised one eyebrow. "I try," he said, with a straight face.

"How's Celine?" Abby interjected quickly.

"Oh...she's threatening divorce...again."Nick shrugged. "I'll worry about that tomorrow. By the way, there's a cast party backstage after the show—you're welcome to join us. See how the other half lives," he added with a rakish laugh. "Well, I'd better get moving. Got to go do the fame thing." His eyes alight with excitement, Nick gave them a wave that would have done a royal proud, then pressed on through the crowd, his entourage in tow.

"How long did you say you were married to that guy?" Cameron scoffed.

"Too long," she sighed.

"Let's find our seats," Maggy suggested dryly. "If the movie's half as good as the pre-show warm-up, we're in for a good time."

Abby leaned closer to Cameron, totally fascinated by the epic drama unfolding on the giant screen. "It's very good—don't you think?" she whispered in Cameron's ear.

"Incredible," he agreed in amazement. "Old Nick really pulled it off."

The hours flew by, the storyline weaving its own magic spell over the entranced audience. When Cameron showed up on the screen at last, Abby gasped audibly, then leaned forward. He looked so wickedly handsome, his eyes so alive and compelling, he took her breath away.

Then Abby saw a familiar setting and her heart began to pound. In the next instant, when the young warrior took the dying maiden in his arms, tears of awe filled Abby's eyes.

On the screen, unbelievable agony wracked the young man's face as he held his dying love. Abby choked up, forcing back a sob in her throat as the end came nearer. When the maiden breathed no more, like the young warrior, Abby was overwhelmed by sorrow. Tears rained down her face and her throat closed.

When he saw Abby up on the screen, so lifeless and pale, Cameron was hard-pressed to swallow the lump in his throat. The scene was so profoundly realistic, it shook him—more than he'd expected. Instinctively, he turned to Abby, needing to reassure himself that she was still warm and breathing. When he pulled her close against his side, he felt her quiver...ever so slightly.

"That was eerie," she whispered.

Cameron nodded in agreement. "Almost *too* real," he said, as he nuzzled her brow.

Later, when the lights came on, he pulled her up and into his arms. "Watching you *die* up there on that screen bothered me more than I thought it would. Let's go home," he said abruptly. "I've had enough."

Abby saw the disquiet in his eyes and inched closer. "We can talk about it when we get home."

"What I have in mind doesn't involve much talking," he growled.

Abby's eyes widened. Then she sent him a smoldering smile. "We won the lottery once, Cameron Wallace," she purred. "How about if we try again? I feel kind of lucky tonight."

Cameron grinned wickedly, his dimple creasing his cheek. "We're both going to get *lucky* tonight," he told her. "Just as soon as I get you home."

"I knew there was a reason I fell in love with you." Abby sighed serenely, took his hand, and followed him up the aisle.

Cameron raised her hand to his lips and kissed it tenderly. "The same reason I fell in love with you," he murmured. "Let's go home, Abby, my love. I want you all to myself."

When they caught up to the other couples, Ross asked, "Do you want to go backstage to the party?"

"Nope," Cameron said. He grinned and added, "We're going home to play the lottery." On that cryptic note, he turned and pulled Abby through the crowd.

Maggy frowned, then understanding dawned. "Good luck," she shouted after them before they disappeared from sight.

"Why on earth would they want to play the lottery at this time of night?" Ross asked, as he wrapped his arm around Maggy and followed Libby and Rayce outside.

"Let's go straight home," Maggy told him, her voice deliberately seductive. "And if you're very lucky, and the twins are still asleep, you just might find out."